A Change of View

NORTHERN LIGHTS COLLECTION

FREYA BARKER

A Change Of View
a novel

Copyright © 2017 Freya Barker
All rights reserved.

*This book is a work of fiction and any resemblance to any
person or persons, living or dead, any event, occurrence,
or incident is purely coincidental. The characters and
story lines are created and thought up from the author's
imagination or are used fictitiously.*

ISBN: 9781988733067

Cover Design:
RE&D - Margreet Asselbergs
Editing:
Karen Hrdlicka

DEDICATION

I am dedicating this book to two people…because I can.

Petra, your colourful personality, your infectious smile, your love for family and friends, and your positive stance in life, have all been inspirational in creating my heroine for this story: Leelo.

You said it yourself so eloquently:
"Someone you feel like you've known and loved forever"
You are that someone to me too.
Love you hard, lady.

Papa, it's the little things that live on in my memories.

The armfuls of peonies you used to bring me every spring are now inked on my skin, to carry with me always.
The easy smile I see around the perpetual pipe in your mouth, when I smell your favourite tobacco.
The special bond we shared ensures I will always wear a smile when I remember you.

Love you, Papa, and rest in peace.
You've had a good run

TABLE OF CONTENTS

ONE

A new season comes both in warning and promise.

Leelo

I recognize the place from the file the lawyer showed me.

A beautiful twenty-acre piece of property, just off Highway 101 east of Wawa; prime land along the shores of Whitefish Lake, which included a quaint little motel, as depicted on the photographs.

Okay, I'm lying; what I'm looking at is nothing like the goddamn pictures from the file.

More like a post-apocalyptic scene from the *Walking Dead.* Dilapidated buildings that look like no one's even been through here in decades, and yet I know for a fact, Uncle Sam was running it just five years ago, until his health started slipping and he ended up in a home.

There's a hole, the size of the Vesuvius crater, smack in the middle of the parking lot. It's going to need a mountain of gravel to fill, before someone gets swallowed up. It's like a damn sinkhole, it's so big. Guess that's the 'minor pothole' Henry Kline of Kline, Kline & McTavish warned me about.

Okay, so it's not exactly Club Med, but I can do something with this.

11

Open eyes, open mind, and open heart, I promised myself. Giving myself pep talks is a skill I'm still developing, after a lifetime of very successful toxic inner dialogue.

Just like I'm doing for myself, I can give this old rattle of a motel a second chance at life as well, with some elbow grease and a lick of paint.

I look around as I open the door of my old, beat-up Jeep Cherokee and stick a tentative leg out. I'm immediately attacked by swarms of black flies, which probably haven't seen a meal in a while, and here I am presenting them with a smorgasbord. The nasty little fuckers reign supreme here in the north from mid-May through to July.

I dive back into the Jeep and pull out my tote, which holds two brand new cans of bug spray, fortified with Deet, the only thing that might slow down these bloodthirsty mini vampires. I spray myself liberally, almost choking in the process. I hate the smell of bug spray, it makes me gag, but it's part and parcel of living in the Great North, so I'd better get used to it.

Zipping up my hoodie, like that would keep them out, I turn back to what's supposed to be my new lease on the future. The small, eight-room motel and bar that belonged to my uncle, up until he died six months ago. Now it belongs to me.

I've never seen the place before, even though Uncle Sam had it for damn near twenty years. I'd always meant to come up here, bring the kids, but life always got in the way. Instead, Uncle Sam would drive down to the city to spend the holidays with us every year, and every time when saying goodbye again, I would tell him we might drive up that summer. We never did.

The main building is set back a ways off the road, shadowed by large trees. A long, one-story structure with eight units; except on the left side of the main building, where a second story juts up above what I presume to be the bar. The large picture windows, I'm surprised are still intact, on either side of the door and the burned-out neon advertising for Molson Canadian hangs lopsided behind the glass.

On the opposite side of the motel units is a separate small building that is supposed to house a laundry facility, a large generator, and storage space.

The house is supposed to be built behind the bar, invisible from the road, and facing toward the lake.

The gravel crunching under my feet is the only sound I hear as I make my way around the bar to find my new home.

-

"Excuse me…"

The same guy who looked me up and down before giving me the stink-eye when I walked into the Home Hardware in town, does a fine job of ignoring me now.

"Sir, I could use a hand," I try again with barely subdued irritation.

The older lady behind me in line at the paint counter clears her throat and that gets his attention.

"Can I help you, Mrs. Stephens?" he says, with a bright yellowish smile for the woman, who steps up beside me. He doesn't even spare me a glance and I'm sure steam is flowing from my flared nostrils.

"Yes, you can, in fact," the woman replies, and I'm about to turn and walk out of the store before I resort to violence.

It's a two and a half hour drive to Sault Ste. Marie to find another half-decent building supply store, but I'll be damned if I let myself be treated like this. I'll just have to go back to the motel and make a complete list of stuff I'll need in the near future, because I won't be making that trip daily. I have a motel to renovate, and even though aside from painting, I don't have the foggiest idea what I'm doing, I'm determined to have at least two or three of the rooms ready to go by the end of June.

"You can start by serving this young lady," she says pointedly, nodding in my direction.

The man audibly scoffs, I presume at the use of both *young* and *lady,* neither of which are what I would call an apt description of reality. I'm going on forty-six and show it, and with my ringed nose, blue-tipped hair, and visible tattoos, I'm hardly *lady*-material. I got away with my appearance closer to the big city, but here in the sparse North, I stand out like a sore thumb.

It doesn't seem to faze the grey-haired woman, who actually looks like a lady, with her carefully coiffed hair, wrinkled but manicured hands, and chaste pearls at her thin neck. Her eyes are bright and fierce on the man across the counter.

"Don't you start with me, Travis McGee. I've known you since your scrawny little tush was still wrapped in diapers, and I know for a fact your mother would turn in her grave if she could see you behave like this."

I watch in amusement as the grown man, at least my age, if not older, blushes and lowers his eyes.

"But, Mrs. Stephens…"

"None of that, Travis. That's no way to welcome a new neighbour now, is it? Last time I saw the old Whitefish Motel, it looked like it would need quite a bit of work. Doesn't seem too smart for the one store in town, that carries the supplies to get the work done, to be turning away good business now, does it?"

I'm actually dumbfounded. I can't remember the last time a complete stranger volunteered to fight my battles for me. She turns to me with a smile on her face, only highlighting the plentiful wrinkles around her eyes. But the eyes are a clear blue and sharp as a blade.

"Let's get introductions out of the way, shall we?" She reaches out a hand to me and I automatically place my work-roughened palm against her soft one. "Charlotte Stephens. If no one has yet, let me be the first one to welcome you to the neighbourhood, so to speak."

Neighbourhood is a bit of a stretch, given that my place is a good fifteen minutes out of town, but in these regions, anyone close enough to visit within an hour's travel is considered a neighbour. To some at least.

"Pleased to meet you," I respond when I finally find my voice. "I'm Lilith Talbot, but my friends call me Leelo."

"Happy to meet you, Leelo. One day you'll have to tell me over a cup of coffee, how you came by that interesting name, but first why don't you let Travis get you what you need?"

I turn to the man who still eyes me with distaste, even though he clearly tries to hide it. I proceed to hand him the paint chips I've chosen for the much-needed fresh coat the motel rooms are crying out for.

Forty-five minutes later, I finish loading the cans of paint, the bucket of drywall compound, putty knives, repair kits, and an assortment of tape, rollers, and brushes. It barely fits. I had to fold down the back seats to stack twenty-two boxes of end of the line, laminate flooring they had on sale, as well as a few boxes of shingles, and my old Jeep is loaded down heavily.

I almost jump when a hand falls on my shoulder.

"Didn't mean to startle you, luv," Charlotte Stephens says apologetically. "I was hoping to catch you before you took off and give you my number." She hands me a folded sheet of paper with a phone number. "I know how daunting it can be to move to a new place, especially when you're a woman alone. I did the same thing, almost fifty years ago, when I moved up here for a teaching position. If not for Elizabeth McGee, Travis' mother, I might've turned tail and ran right back. She took me in as a friend and helped me ride out some bumps. I'd like to offer the same to you. I may not be worth much when it comes to hands-on help needed at the motel, but I assure you, I have a willing ear, I bake a mean pecan pie, brew a good strong cup of coffee, and I have time. More time than I know what to do with most days. You want that ear? Or perhaps just the company? Give me a call anytime."

"Thank you," is all I can manage, taking the paper from her hand, before she nods and turns on her heels.

The unexpected kindness goes a long way to soothing the dark lonely hole in my chest.

16

Roar

"Doyle!"

I close the gate of the truck before I turn to see Kyle Thompson heading toward me with determined strides, as much as his shiny loafers will allow. My least favourite person in this town, and that's saying something since there aren't many people I like to begin with. Kyle is a local realtor and self-proclaimed developer, with questionable morals. I've never liked the guy. Too fucking fancy, if you ask me, and so damn slimy, mud wouldn't stick.

I cross my arms over my chest and grunt in response when he's close enough. I don't like wasting words and certainly not on our local wheeler and dealer.

"How've you been, my friend?" he starts, his recently capped teeth on full display.

I raise an eyebrow at his misplaced familiarity, given that we've never seen eye to eye on anything.

"Busy season coming up?" he continues undeterred, tipping his head in the direction of the load of supplies weighing down my truck.

"Cut to the chase, Kyle. Got shit to do."

The fake jovial demeanour he's trying for quickly slides off his face, leaving a distasteful scowl.

"What do you know about your new neighbour?" he asks, his tone barely civil now.

"Neighbour?" I feign ignorance, even though I know damn well he's talking about Sam's old place, where for the last week or so I've seen an old, navy blue Jeep parked the couple of times I've passed it. Neighbour is a bit of a stretch anyway, since my place is five kilometres up from the turn off, just past the motel, but it's the closest I have to one.

"The Whitefish," he says by way of explanation. "I hear some woman moved in?"

I heard that, too. Travis over at the hardware store just filled me in, actually. Didn't have much good to say, only that some hippy chick, with a nasty attitude, was in to buy supplies earlier. Not that I put much stock in Travis' opinion, he's a piece of work in his own right.

"So I hear," I confirm, shrugging my shoulders. "Here's a suggestion, though; you wanna know something, try talking to her yourself. I'm not one for socializing."

With that I turn on my heels and get in the truck, not waiting for a response. As I drive off, I see his angry scowl in my rearview mirror. Stupid motherfucker should know better than to try and get any kind of help from me. That ship sailed a long fucking time ago.

I have guests coming in tomorrow and want to get these supplies sorted away. I still have to get their cabin and boat ready. The damn engine is still in pieces on my front porch, waiting for the new propeller and fuel line in the back of my truck. Every winter I service the outboard engines of the fishing boats that I rent out, along with the six cabins. Once fishing season starts, my lodge is booked solid and I don't have time to dick around with equipment breaking down. So I make sure everything is serviced.

Except, I'm running behind. We've had one of the harshest winters on record, and I've had my hands full digging out from under the damn snow every day. When the final melt off finally came, three of my six cabins had sustained damage to the roofs and I had busted water pipes at the main lodge.

Up ahead, I can see the sign for the motel. There's an opening in the dense tree line on the north side of the road that cuts back toward one of the many inlets of Whitefish Lake. The motel is set back, about halfway between the road and the water. Weeds have overtaken most of the gravel driveway and parking lot, and the general lack of maintenance, these past few years, has taken its toll on the motel itself as well. The old Jeep is parked in front, and I just catch a glimpse of blue hair ducking into the building.

Who has blue fucking hair?

-

"Roar, your guests are here!" Patti ducks her head into my office, a big smile on her face. "We're in business," she announces, and I can't help but smile at her excitement.

Patti's worked for me since I bought the property, a little over ten years ago, but we've known each other since elementary school. We were part of the same group of friends, growing up in Wawa. She's about the only person I can tolerate for longer than five minutes at a time.

I don't have work for her during the long winter months, and to be honest, she doesn't really need it anymore, having built up a lucrative cleaning business in town. Each spring she's back here, though, getting the cabins ready for the guests. The one time I suggested I find someone else for the couple of days a week I needed a hand, because she seemed busy, I thought she'd deck me, so I never mentioned it again.

I stand up and move around the desk, when Patti blocks my path.

19

"Cabin three is ready for them," she says, putting a hand on my chest as she hands me the keys. "I've put Ace in his pen so he doesn't scare off the guests."

With my hands on her upper arms, I gently move her aside, but not before bending down and pressing a kiss to her forehead.

"I'll introduce him," I reassure her.

My dog looks fierce, with his light blue eyes and massive head, and he can make a lot of noise, but he generally loves people. They just don't always love him, which is why I make it a point to introduce him to every one of my guests myself.

"Ace. Come." I hold open the gate to his fenced-in pen on the side of the small office building. "Heel," I tell him before he lopes off to greet the newcomers.

As it is, I see the two guys hesitate to get out of their car. A nice car it is, too. Not often you see a Lexus coupe in these parts. Not much use for them, especially in the winter. These two are clearly city dwellers, coming up to the Great North to remind them they're still men. A lot of them do. Folks who spend most of their time behind desks and in boardrooms, who forget how to still their minds. Who have lost touch with the universe around them in the pursuit of the holy dollar.

Some come here to get in touch with their humanity, by leaving civilization behind, and some come simply so they can brag later about their prize catch or harrowing adventures. Not sure where to place these two. One guy is older, perhaps in his fifties, and the one behind the wheel looks like a younger version. A father-son combo, by the looks of it.

Finally, the older man in the passenger seat opens his door and gets out. I can sense Ace's excitement, but he keeps his nose right by my hip. I rest my hand on top of his head as I nod at the older man.

"Welcome to Jackson's Point. I'm Doyle, and this here is Ace." I pat his head again. "He's friendly."

TWO

In the blue of endless skies in her eyes, I see a raging storm.

Leelo

"Sorry, Mom, I don't think I can make it up there until the end of June, at the earliest. It's crazy busy; we've got back-to-back jobs lined up here, and you know I spend the weekends at Jess and Dad's new house, finishing that up."

I wince at the reference to my ex and his new wife, and the easy future they seem to be building. I bite my tongue to not to let some snide remark slip out. I've done too much of that already, and it has done irreparable damage to my relationship with my kids.

I'm not sure what I'd been thinking when I called Matt that morning, but the sight of yet another massive leak, in the ceiling of room seven this time, had spooked me. Suddenly not so sure about my plans to do some patch work myself, with YouTube as my instructional guide, I caved and called.

Logically I know they're busy in the spring, I know it would take him a full day of driving to get up here, and I know he doesn't agree to my moving up here, in the first place. I believe his exact words had been; "You've gone fucking mental, Mom!" Yet, as always, there is that small part of me that secretly hopes he'll surprise me and come to my rescue.

That had been my mistake early on. I'd looked at my kids for support when their father first left, putting unattainable pressure on them when the situation had already been difficult enough. A father who'd lied, not only to me, but to them as well, for the better part of a year before walking out, and a mother who could barely get herself dressed in the morning, let alone look after her kids. It had been ugly and I had been rocked to the absolute essence of me. A new reality I could not recognize, couldn't handle. I'd felt so safe, so secure, in my place in the world, as a wife and mother. When the house of cards came down, I didn't even know myself anymore.

That first year had been brutal. I did and said so many things I now wish I could take back, but the damage was done. At the end of it, Gwen, who'd been in her third year in university at the time, had withdrawn altogether, not speaking to either me or David, and Matt started avoiding me. He'd still been in high school and chose to stay with his father.

When Gwen sent me an email, asking me not to disrupt her convocation with my presence, it was an excruciating wake-up call. And when Matt didn't ask me to come to his graduation the year after, I wasn't really surprised. Hurt, yes, but not surprised.

I knew I had to find a new way to define myself. Learn how to choose for me, how to take care of me. It's not been easy.

When Uncle Sam died and left me this place, it seemed like such an amazing opportunity. A chance to start new, to fully stand on my own two feet.

Yet here I am, biting my tongue and fighting tears because my son is too busy to come running to my rescue.

"Of course, honey," I reassure him with fake cheerfulness. "No worries. It's not a big deal; I'll get it done. Your mother's got some tricks up her sleeve, you know?"

I immediately cringe at my awkward assurances. He's not stupid, and no matter what I say, it's like shoving my foot even further down my throat.

"Don't do anything stupid, Mom," Matt cautions me. "Don't go climbing on a roof without someone spotting you. Actually, don't go climbing at all. Call in a professional." My twenty-year-old son is telling me what to do. How's that for lack of faith?

I force myself to shrug it off.

"Gotta go, Mom."

"Sure thing, Bud. Call me when you have a chance, okay?"

I end the call, drop the phone on the counter, and top up my travel mug with fresh coffee from the pot.

I have a choice. I can feel sorry for myself, which won't get the roof fixed. I can find a local contractor and get charged through the nose, which I don't have the bank account for. Or I can get my behind on that ladder, and fix the fucking leak myself.

Determined, I pull my laptop toward me, flip it open and Google do-it-yourself roof repairs.

I'm no wilting flower, goddammit. Not anymore.

Fighting words that come back to bite me in the padded ass only a couple of hours later.

-

I'm feeling pretty smug, having made my way up on the roof. Not really a hero when it comes to heights, my confidence grows with every damaged shingle I pull up and toss over the side, into the parking lot below. I'm thinking I should probably have rented a bin to dispose of old building materials and such. The pile below is rapidly growing and won't be so easy just to haul away and drop off at the dump myself. Not without at least a pickup truck.

This is the problem, when you take on a project with no experience and limited funds. You start out cutting corners from the get go, and that never ends well.

Fuck it; I'll make some calls when I get down.

Another thing, I didn't consider, is that it's not just the shingles that are old and damaged, but in some spots, the underlying materials have been either ripped or rotted away. Like above room seven, even the decking has soft spots and holes where the wood has rotted away. Everywhere else I can get away with replacing just shingles, but this is one spot where I'll have to replace everything, and I don't know if I'm equipped for that. I might be able to get some shingles up on the roof by myself, but I don't think hauling the plywood decking up here is something I can do alone.

As it stands now, I have a hole in the roof and dark clouds rolling in on the horizon. I'm going to need to get that hole covered before it lets loose. The wind is picking up already.

I remember seeing a blue tarp rolled up in the rafters of the laundry building.

Vertigo hits fresh when I swing my leg over the side to find the rungs of the ladder. I take a deep breath to fortify and steel myself for the trip down.

Of course, I have to haul the damn ladder all the way to the other building and hoist it up against the rafters. Swearing under my breath when I feel spiderwebs hit my arms and face, and I pray to God they don't come with spiders. I really don't want to have a major freak-out at the top of a ladder.

The moment I can reach the blue tarp, I yank on it, dislodging it from the rafters. With a wet-sounding thud, it lands on the concrete floor below, sending up a billowing cloud of dust and dirt. That's gonna be a bitch to haul up on the roof.

With a long rope I spot, hanging looped on a peg beside the old generator, I wrap the tarp and leave it rolled up at the bottom of the ladder. I climb up, taking only the end of the rope with me, and using the ladder as a slide, I start pulling up the blue material.

I think I've used every swear word, known to mankind, by the time I manage to finally pull the tarp over the lip of the eavestrough and onto the roof. I let myself fall back and huff it out, when the first raindrops hit my face.

Fucking hell!

In a scramble, I untie the rope, and try to wrestle the material flat. Unfortunately, the wind has other ideas as it gets hold of the edge of the tarp, and I find myself struggling to keep it, and myself, on the damn roof. A corner of the tarp gets hooked on one end of the ladder, and I watch in horror as it slides away from sight. The loud smack of metal against the gravel below is confirmation that my one means on and off this roof is gone.

Adding insult to injury, big fat drops hit my face and drum out a staccato on the roof, mocking the fact that I truly don't have a fucking clue what I'm doing. When a bolt of lightning strikes with a loud crack, close enough I can smell ozone in the air, I drop down on top of the tarp, holding it down, while making myself as flat as possible.

What brilliant irony that would be; *woman attempts roof repair in thunderstorm, dies in process.*

I don't even try to hold back the angry tears and pathetic sobs. It's not like anybody cares, or even sees.

"Get your damn arse down here, you fool woman!"

Roar

I don't fucking like going into town.

Only reason I went was because Charlie called me. She's the only woman I'd drop everything for. Especially after finding out Joe Love was going to charge her three hundred dollars in labour to install her new toilet. That bastard is always trying to capitalize on the fact he's the only plumber in town. He doesn't care that Charlie is on a fixed income. He's a fucking weasel.

I spent most of my morning hauling out the cracked old porcelain throne, and listening to Charlie drone on about her meeting with my new neighbour last week. I'm sure that toilet had been there since they first did away with the original outhouse, and I ended up having to replace some of the equally dated and massively corroded drainpipes. Needless to say, I smell like I just crawled out of the goddamn sewer, but Charlie has a working can again.

I passed on having a shower in her tiny claw-footed bathtub to rinse off the stink, since I was going to have to pull on those same clothes again, but I'm starting to regret that. Even with the windows on the truck rolled all the way down, despite the sheet of rain pouring in, the stench is making my eyes water.

A flash of blue to my left catches my eye, and I almost drive off the road, when I see what I assume is my idiot neighbour, struggling with a tarp on the roof of the motel. In the middle of a goddamn thunderstorm. To emphasize my point, a loud crack accompanies the blinding flash of a lightning strike, and I watch the woman go down. *Son-of-a-bitch.*

I swing the truck around and rush toward the building, getting my teeth rattled when I hit that damn pothole in the middle of the drive. There goes my suspension.

A ladder is down on the gravel, and I pick it up, lean it against the eavestrough, and climb up. I'm not sure what I'll find, whether she's hurt or what. All I can see is one foot wearing a pink sneaker stick out over the edge.

"Get your damn arse down here, you fool woman!" I call up, tugging on the foot, which is immediately pulled back before it kicks out at me violently.

"Don't touch me!" she screeches in a high-pitched, panicked voice.

"Settle down," I yell over the din of the storm, grabbing onto her ankle when her foot comes precariously close to breaking my nose. It wouldn't be the first time that happened; my nose has seen action before. "Let go of the tarp and slide toward me."

"I can't," I can hear her sob. "There's a hole in the roof, the rain will come in."

I take a deep breath and throw a pleading look for patience up to the dark skies when another flash of light crackles the air.

"Won't matter if you get yourself killed first. Now let the damn thing go and slide toward me."

I step one rung higher, so I can see the woman lying face down on the roof. First things I notice, because they're damn hard to miss, are solid legs and a sizable ass in army fatigues. Beyond, just a bright blue ponytail is visible.

"Let go," I urge her on. "Before we both drown or get fried."

She doesn't respond, but sticks her butt in the air as she moves backward toward me. I carefully guide the foot I was loosely holding onto a rung on the ladder, about three above the one I'm standing on, and she manages to swing her other foot down to join the first. I have to turn my head to the side or I'd have my nose pressed into that ass, and that's a bit much for a first introduction, even for me.

I keep my arms braced around her as we slowly make our way to the ground, the blue tarp blowing off the side of the roof. With my feet on solid ground, I put my hands on her hips to help her down the rest of the way, dropping them the moment she turns around to face me.

I barely have a chance to take in her soaking wet, bedraggled appearance, when she throws her arms around my neck and starts sobbing into my chest. *What the fuck am I supposed to do with that?* But before I have a chance to figure it out, she releases me and takes a few steps back.

"You reek," she spits out disgustedly, crinkling up her nose. "You smell like shit."

"You're welcome," I fire back, good and pissed. This is why I don't do women; they're confusing as fuck. Bawling, warm and helpless, in my arms one second and spitting venom the next. "And maybe it's because I just spent all morning servicing Charlie's drain."

A look of shock registers in her blue eyes as her mouth falls open.

"Look," she says, lifting her hands defensively. "I don't know who you are, but I'm pretty sure your Charlie wouldn't appreciate being talked about like that. And also; *eewww!"*

The disgust on her face would be comical if she hadn't already pissed me off. Without a word, I turn to my truck. I have some tools in the box in the back. The woman clearly thinks I'm leaving, because she hurries after me.

"I'm...I'm sorry," she stammers. "Thank you for..."

"Go inside." Her eyes go wide at my growled order and her arms fold defensively around her waist. Arms I now notice are both covered in ink: bold, bright, and colourful ink. *Great, a damn hippie.*

"Rude!" she spits out, closing a pair of full plum-coloured lips into a straight line.

"Lady, just get in the house and get dry."

I turn back to my toolbox to find my staple gun, when I finally hear the crunch of her sneakers on the gravel moving away. It takes me a good forty-five minutes to haul that damn tarp back on the roof and staple it over the hole. By the time I lean the ladder on its side against the wall, under the overhang, I'm soaked down to the last thread. There's one bonus; the stench of sewage is well and washed off.

I haven't seen or heard the woman since she finally marched herself inside, so I go in search of her. I know the house is behind the bar, since I have some good memories there: watching the occasional Sunday night game with Sam and a bottle of *Glenlivet*.

The door to the bar is closed, so I walk around the side of the building and find the side door into the kitchen open. The bar and the house are separated by an industrial-sized kitchen. Sam only used the fryer and the grill for wings, fries, and burgers; the only things he'd serve if he was in a good mood. From the kitchen, I find the door to the living room beyond open and step inside.

Nothing has changed, other than the colour on the walls. The yellowed, old wallpaper is replaced with a putty-coloured paint, that actually makes the space look bigger. The furniture is the same, though. Old and ratty.

On the old, grey tattered couch, the woman is lying curled on her side, apparently sleeping. I'm struck by how different she looks with her face peaceful instead of disgusted or panicked, and I take a minute to look her over. Her hair, which she had in a lopsided ponytail earlier, is now loose and partially covering her face. Dark, almost auburn morphing to bright blue halfway down the strands. Those plum lips, that were clamped shut so tight earlier, are now relaxed and slightly pouted, a perfect focal point in her pale round face. I can't see her eyes, but I know they're a bright blue. The colour of a morning sky.

Goddammit, just what I need; she's fucking pretty.

Without waking her, I turn on my heels, make my way straight back outside, and get into my truck.

THREE

Some lines, once they're crossed, can never be drawn again.

Leelo

"Hey there, it's Travis, right?"

The man in question turns to face me, sporting the scowl I've seen before. Despite the fact he clearly hasn't warmed to me yet, he nods in response. It's progress—of sorts.

"I need some half-inch plywood and tar paper."

I read off the list I compiled at home with the help of a do-it-yourself website. I hope to hell I calculated it all correctly, because I haven't been able to work up the courage to get back on the ladder to measure. Instead, I measured on ground level and guesstimated the rest. Not very scientific I'm afraid, but then I always sucked at math. I don't know half of the tools the site said I need, but I'm sure I can find out their purpose on YouTube.

By the time Travis has stacked up everything I had on my list, it's clear to me that my trusty Jeep will never be able to haul it home. Travis, who has yet to utter a single word, silently leads me to the cash register. My mind is working hard, trying to figure out how to get the materials back to the motel, which is why I don't pay much attention when he rings up my purchases. But when Travis finally speaks, he delivers the heart attack with malicious glee.

"That'll be $973.98."

"What?"

I ask, but I barely hear the explanation, I'm concentrating too hard on getting my heart beating again. A thousand bucks? With what I've spent so far—including getting utilities hooked up and Internet installed, which by the way is not quite as simple as it is in the city—I've already blown through almost half of the total budget.

David had bought me out of the marital home, and I rented a place these past years, so a large chunk of that money was left. Plus, I sold off most of my belongings before I came up here, so I had what I thought was enough to fix up the place and sustain myself until I could start making some money, but at the rate it's flying out the door, I'm not sure I'll manage.

Can't rent out a room that doesn't have a roof, though. I'll just have to suck it up, along with the extra ninety-five dollars he's charging me to deliver the stuff tomorrow, since there's no way I can make it fit.

I scowl at Travis' smiling mug in my rearview mirror as I drive off the parking lot, my Jeep as empty as my wallet.

The sign of the liquor store beckons me when I turn onto Broadway, and who am I to ignore its call? I'm in dire need of some liquid courage so I can get myself back on that roof tomorrow. I have no choice now. There's no money left in the budget to hire out the work.

Besides, a little buzz might help me forget the embarrassing episode from yesterday.

I pretended to be asleep when he walked into my living room. My saviour; the Neanderthal. Only words out of his mouth were either barked or grunted—and the man called me *woman.* Who the fuck does that? Does he think he's the bad boy hero in an HBO feature? Ridiculous.

Although, I have to admit, despite my mild hysteria at the time, the feel of his big body behind mine, and his hands on my hips coming down that ladder, stirred something. He's not bad to look at either, what I could see in that downpour and with that sopping beanie pulled down over his eyes. Reminded me a little of that old Brawny commercial, the lumberjack guy. He was large. Big-boned and a little ruddy looking, but that could've been the cold rain beating down on us. It was running down a largish nose that looked like it had seen a round or two and dripped from the heavy beard covering the bottom half of his face. I have no clue who this man is and frankly, after the vile stuff coming out of his mouth, I don't care to know—but for a moment there, I might've been curious.

Anyway, I'd heard him come in when I was still curled up in a fetal position on the couch, and I feigned sleep so I didn't have to talk to or face him. The experience was embarrassing enough without adding insult to injury.

Armed with a brown paper bag, hiding two bottles on the seat beside me, I head home. Moscato for lighter days and a bottle of scotch for those days when total obliteration is required—like maybe today.

-

"Erm, excuse me?"

I yell up at who is fast becoming the bane of my existence, crawling over my roof, but not before taking a long hard look at that firm ass, clearly outlined in a pair of well-worn jeans. He probably has abs to match, the kind you can bounce quarters off of. Try and do that off mine and you'd need heavy equipment to excavate it.

The moment I pulled onto the property, I recognized the monster-sized pickup truck parked outside number seven. I glance over at the brown paper bag, deciding on the spot that it's definitely a scotch day.

"Hello! What are you doing on my roof?" I try again. This time there is movement.

A head peeks over the side, a familiar beanie pulled low over deep-set eyes. The heavy beard I thought was dark brown is actually more of a rusty colour in the bright midday sun.

"Fixin' a hole," he rumbles in a deep baritone, with a barely distinguishable roll of his eyes. But it's there, in his voice.

"I admit I might have been a bit out of it yesterday, but I'm pretty sure I would've remembered contracting out a job I have every intention of doing myself."

If I wasn't irritated enough by the big lug's mere presence, he really puts a target between his eyes when he barks out a laugh.

"I'm pretty sure I can manage, I've ordered everything I need. They're delivering tomorrow," I throw out there, planting my hands on my hips for emphasis, as I watch him swing his legs over the side and climb down.

"Cancel it," he snaps, stepping off the ladder and into my space. I lift my eyes and instantly bring up my hand to shield them when I'm nearly blinded by the bright sun backlighting his bulk.

"I will do no such thing."

I try hard not to be intimidated by this stranger giving me orders. This is my property, and I don't have to listen to anyone, especially not some random stranger.

"Your call," he says, pulling off his beanie with one hand, while wiping the sweat of his wide forehead with a dirty rag he plucks from his back pocket. "You wanna waste your money, that's your business. Be stupid, though, given I've already got everything you need here."

I'm half registering what he says, too mesmerized by the copper mop of hair, laced with grey, which popped out from under his hat like a damn white rabbit. Luscious, shiny hair that gleams like a new penny in the sun.

"I don't even know who you are," I mutter lamely.

I realize I'm staring when he bends forward to bring his face close and his eyes level to mine.

"Doyle," he rumbles.

Hazel. His eyes are hazel; that blend of brown, gold and green, that looks fucking amazing against the tan and freckled skin of his face.

"Own Jackson's Point. Fishing lodge up on the north shore. Our properties share a border along the northeast side of your land. Consider me your closest neighbour."

"Oh."

"Yeah…"

His drawn out response shakes me out of my stupor.

"Well, Doyle, nice to meet you and all, but still don't really get what you're doing here?"

"Starting to ask myself that," he mumbles in his beard, as he covers those gorgeous tresses with the dull grey knit beanie again.

"Then perhaps you should go," I snap in response. "I don't have the money to spend on labour anyway."

The low growl coming from his chest area has me move back a few steps, but instead of attacking me, he turns around and starts back up the damn ladder.

"Hey!" I call after him. "Did you not hear me?"

"Had some materials left over from a renovation on one of my cabins last fall," he throws at me over his shoulder. "Call Travis, tell him to cancel the order and refund you the money." Without another look he disappears over the edge of the roof.

I'm about to protest again when his head pops back over the side.

"A beer'd be nice. I'm frying like a turkey on Thanksgiving up here."

The gall!

It takes me a minute to will my blood pressure down to manageable levels, before I turn back to my Jeep and snatch the brown paper bag off the passenger seat. With my version of a Xanax clutched in my arms, I march around the side of the bar and into the house, where I first call Travis to cancel my order and have him refund the money to my credit card, and then I sit down at the kitchen counter to pour myself a stiff glass.

Definitely a scotch kind of day.

Roar

She never brought me that beer.

I've been up here in the baking sun for three hours, doing my goddamn neighbourly duty, and not even a bottle of water. Piece of work she is, throwing attitude when I'm saving her from fucking killing herself. I haven't seen her since she stomped her jiggly ass inside the house. I watched it move all the way around the corner.

What the hell is she thinking? She's clearly a city girl, with those tattoos and that hair. Sticks out here like a sore thumb. And getting this damn place up and running again? By herself? She's obviously deranged.

Next time I feel a nudge of chivalry, I'm gonna eradicate it by the root.

I pull the rag from my back pocket and wipe the sweat off my face and neck. It's not even June and the sun is hotter than Hades. One benefit is that the bugs don't like the heat either, not that they bother me much; I've developed thick skin over the years, or maybe they've just gotten sick of the taste of me.

I toss the last of the old shingles she had piled up in the parking lot in the back of my truck and get behind the wheel. One final look in the direction she disappeared, and then I resolutely put her out of my head. I start the truck and turn up the road, where a cold beer and a lazy afternoon of fishing is waiting for me.

Except, when I finally get back to the lodge, after dropping off my truckload at the dump, Patti comes tearing out of the office waving her arms.

"We've got a problem," she says breathlessly when I get out from behind the wheel. "Your guests have stranded their boat on a rock on the far shore." She points out over the water, where I can only just make out the aluminum hull of one of my rentals and one person appearing to stand on the water, waving their arms frantically. I know the rock he's standing on. I had a near encounter with it when I first moved out here. It's large, about ten feet across, and almost invisible, just under the surface when the water is high with the spring runoff. It's the reason I dropped three buoys to mark the spot. Buoys I can usually spot from here, but that for some reason I can't find them now.

"Why didn't you call?"

"I tried, but it went to voicemail," she replies, irritated.

My hand automatically reaches for the phone in my pocket when I remember I left it in the truck while I was on the roof. I reach through the window and snatch it off the console, looking at the screen. Five missed calls, all from my own office.

For some reason that makes me even more annoyed with my new neighbour. Business before anything else, and already that woman is messing with my otherwise good judgement.

I immediately start walking in the direction of the small dock, where my own boat is tied off, Patti trying her best to keep up.

"I couldn't get your boat started," she pants.

"You couldn't steer a boat in the open ocean; what the hell were you thinking? You better not have flooded the engine."

42

"You're an asshole, Riordan Doyle. A class A asshole."

She's right. I am an asshole, taking it out on her. I'm pissed at myself for dropping the ball, for getting distracted by a blue-haired, blue-eyed city girl with endless curves, who has no goddamn place being up here by herself in the wilderness. Playing the goddamn knight in shining armour to a damsel who seems to favour distress. No gratitude either, so I'm done with that.

Patti doesn't do boats, unless someone else is driving and it's moving at trolling speed. I know that.

"Sorry, girl," I mutter, as I climb aboard and mentally cross my fingers she hasn't drowned the engine with her attempts to get it running, but Patti's already stomping off. Luckily the engine kicks right up.

About an hour later, after I plucked Bishop Junior and Senior off the rock, flipped and bailed their boat, and towed it back to the lodge, I go in search of Patti and the first aid kit. Bishop Senior, Adam, cut his leg when he was tossed on impact, and both men are soaked to the core and shivering. The sun is hot, but the water is still freezing. It'll take until July for it to warm up a bit.

"We'll pay for the damage to your boat," the older Bishop says once he's patched up, covered with a blanket and warming up in the sun outside the office.

"Like hell we will," the younger one argues. "That rock should've been marked. We should get you checked out in a hospital."

He turns from his father to me, looking at me accusingly.

"I'm a lawyer. I could sue you for damages," he spouts, and I have to work hard to keep a straight face.

"Oh be quiet, Jamie. You're barely a lawyer, you just spent your first month articling at my firm," Adam scoffs at his son. "Besides, I'm perfectly fine, it's just a cut, and if I recall correctly, I warned you to stay away from any flat spots on the water. You're the one who insisted you wanted to get under the cover of the shoreline there. Now sit your ass down, have a beer, and consider it a lesson learned."

"I'll get the beer," I offer, trying not to chuckle at the way young Jamie is put in his place. I didn't even have to lift a finger.

Patti is waiting for me in the kitchen.

"Do you have any idea where those buoys have gone?" I ask her, as I dive into the fridge for some cold ones.

"Not a clue. I never even noticed they were gone until I saw those two on the rock."

I grab four bottles, close the door, and turn to find Patti standing much closer. I hand her one of the beers.

"You didn't notice anyone out there earlier?"

She takes a swig of her beer and tilts her head. "Nope. I wasn't really paying attention."

I respond with a grunt and move to step around her when her hand on my arm stops me.

"Want me to stick around tonight?"

Fuck.

I knew it wouldn't be easy. Even with her assurances after one lapse in judgement at the end of last season. We'd winter prepped the cabins and cleaned the lodge, and had been shooting the shit over a beer by a bonfire, when once again, even though I'd promised myself not to go there anymore, I didn't put the brakes on. I was mellow, I was looking forward to yet another lonely winter, and I let my dick do the talking. It was a mistake. Especially after seeing her reaction the first time I suggested the occasional *benefits* that came with our friendship might not be a good idea.

I immediately tried to do damage control the next morning, by carefully suggesting this had been a one-off, and that our friendship was too valuable to risk. However, I knew from the brief flash of hurt on her face, that it might not be that simple. During the winter I didn't see Patti that much, only bumped into her a few times in town, but it had been awkward.

Then when she showed up a few weeks ago, ready to get the lodge ready for season, things had felt pretty normal again.

Until now.

"Patti…" I caution as gently as I can. "I just don't think…"

"You know what? You're right," she chirps with a big fake smile on her face, making me feel like an ass. "I've got shit to do at home anyway."

Without another word, she slams her bottle on the counter and rushes past me, out the door.

Son of a bitch.

I seem to be doing well with the ladies today.

FOUR

Both bashful and brass; a walking, talking, tempting contradiction.

Leelo

Drunk is not a good state to be in when you're painting.

I never heard Doyle leave yesterday, because by that time I was blotto on my back on the floor. Thank God for drop cloths because I never would've gotten the paint stain out. As it is, my tee and cargo pants are relegated to work clothing only, given they were drenched in the slate grey paint I'd been in the process of rolling on my living room wall when I passed out.

Hungover is really no better.

Today I'm working on room three, and every time I bend down to dip my roller in the paint tray, I feel like my head's going burst open like an overripe melon. But I have a dwindling savings account, which is why I'm scrambling to get at least one room half-decent so I can generate some income, and there is no one but me to do the work. Hence, I am working hard to ignore the pounding headache.

I'm also ignoring the fact that a complete stranger fixed my roof yesterday, and while he was being a typical redneck, male chauvinist pig jerkwad, he also saved me a thousand bucks. And I never thanked him.

I'm rethinking my decision to steer away from coffee this morning. It's supposed to be dehydrating, and so I chose a large bottle of water instead, but the lack of caffeine is not helping. I step back, look at what I've done so far, and am disappointingly unimpressed with my work thus far. Resolutely dropping the roller in the tray, I move toward the open door to get a pot of coffee going, when I'm startled by a man leaning against a car parked right outside.

This is the real estate guy. The one who accosted me in the parking lot of the grocery store in town a couple of days ago, in much the same way. Once again, the guy's hair is almost as shiny as his car and he's wearing that much too bright smile. This morning, the total effect is almost too much for my delicate senses and I involuntarily squint my eyes against the glean.

"Morning!" he calls out, a little too loud, when I take a tentative step out the door. I flinch at the sound of his voice, but don't stop moving, my attention now focused on the cardboard tray holding two large coffees in his hand.

I mumble an unintelligible response as I bring the cup I snatched from his hand to my lips. My foggy brain is trying to remember his name as I enjoy the first jolt of that warm nectar.

"I have milk and sugar here," he says, pointing at the tray he set down on the hood of his car. "Figured I'd let you doctor your own."

I'm good. I prefer mine black and strong enough to put hair on my chest, so I just wave my hand at him dismissively.

"Kyle Thompson."

My brain finally produces the name he gave me then, along with his business card that probably still lived in the deep recesses of my purse. At the time, he seemed to know I was the new owner of the Whitefish Motel. He even knew my name, which had been a little disconcerting, and I couldn't help feeling uncomfortable.

"Ah wonderful," he smiles even bigger. "I see I've left an impression. Good."

He seems very pleased with himself and I don't have the heart to tell him otherwise. Besides, I should at least be civil to the man who brings me coffee in my hour of need.

Yet I was far from civil with my neighbour, who not only rescued me from the roof in the middle of a thunderstorm, but was back here yesterday fixing said roof. Guilt dulls the enjoyment of the black nectar that is just now hitting my bloodstream.

"What brings you here?" I ask, shuffling over to the lone picnic table I discovered in the back and dragged to the front, so I could sit in the sun to take my breaks.

Kyle follows me and I almost laugh out loud when he pulls an actual handkerchief out of his pocket and tries to wipe the dirt from the bench before he sits down across from me.

"Just checking in with a new neighbour, Lilith." Again with the neighbour. Apparently once you get north of Sudbury, everyone within a fifty kilometre radius becomes one. "Making sure there's nothing you need—nothing you need help with?"

I take in his appearance: dress pants, shiny shoes, button-down shirt, doused in a cloud of aftershave that just now hits my nostrils, but seems to keep the bugs on his side of the table. He's not exactly dressed for manual labour of any kind, so I'm guessing he doesn't mean grabbing a paint roller or say, climbing up on my roof.

"The coffee was good timing." I smile and hold up my cup in salute.

"Looks like a lot of work," he says, looking over my shoulder, mild distaste on his face. "Must cost a sweet penny," he adds, his eyes sliding back to me. His gaze is assessing.

I'm not about to bite at this obvious fishing expedition and just smile over the rim of my cup, despite my growing unease at his intense scrutiny.

"I should take you out for dinner," he says suddenly, the smile back on his face, but forced.

Oh crap. Don't get me wrong, I'm at a point in my life where the prospect of a decent man interested in wining and dining me would be really nice, but I'm not a complete idiot; I know Kyle is neither interested or nice. He's a shark in pretty packaging.

"I don't know…" I hedge, not wanting to ruffle any feathers, and I uneasily shift in my seat.

"Here's my thoughts; if you're determined to make a go of this place, networking is the way to go, and I happen to know everyone in town. I could help. Get word of mouth going. Get you hooked up with the right people and tell you who to steer clear of."

My eyebrows shoot up at the last thing he says.

"Steer clear of?"

He leans over the table and into my space. "Always good to know who your enemies are, especially when they're just next door."

Well, that I can agree on, but this conversation has gotten really uncomfortable, and with my head a little clearer, thanks to the coffee, I should get back to work.

"I'm afraid I'm swamped with work, as you can see," I explain, getting up from my seat. "I simply don't have time for socializing."

"Then call it a business meeting. I don't care, just have dinner with me," he pushes, standing up as well.

"Sorry—I'm still settling in and really need to focus on getting my place up and running." I straighten my back and force myself to look him straight in the eye; instead of cowing under the glare he shoots my way.

"Very well," he bites off, clearly unhappy with my rejection. "I will leave you to it then. Have a good day, Lilith." Without another look, he marches back to his car, his back ramrod straight, and his steps determined.

"Thanks for the coffee," I call out after him, but he just slams his door shut and speeds off down the driveway, wheels spitting up the gravel.

Throwing a wistful look after the disappearing car, I turn back to room three, where a gallon of paint and a roller await me.

-

By the time lunch comes around, I have the first coat up on the walls, despite the slow start. I do a quick rinse of the tray and roller in the room's bathtub, leaving everything to dry in the sun outside.

The fridge in my own kitchen is well stocked with fresh food since my last run into town, but I still grab for the muffins I baked last night, sitting on the kitchen counter. I damn well deserve it after the morning I've had. My secret hope is that the work will offset my love of food, if not help me lose a few pounds. Like maybe fifty.

I always thought I had a weight problem, ever since I was a teenager, but looking at pictures from that time, I have to laugh at myself. All I can see now is a normal girl, slim even, with major self-image issues. Something I probably inherited from my mom who, to this day, is completely preoccupied with her weight, even living in beautiful Belize with husband number five.

There was a period, just after David left me, when I was almost skinny again, insofar that is possible with my pear shape, but that was short-lived. Since then, I've been working hard on learning to love myself and my body for what it is, not for what it could be or maybe even should be. It's hard work. Especially since society, as a whole, judges by external appearance and is quick to slap a label on you.

That's how my tattoos started, and the coloured hair. It was a midlife rebellion, if you will. Not really a crisis, but more like an affirmation of my own identity. Something I'd lost in the years of being a daughter, then a wife and a mother. A middle finger up at uninvited expectations put on me. I have to admit, I enjoy the confusion my colourful appearance creates. The way it makes people slightly uncomfortable because they can't quite figure out where to place me.

I'm learning who I am and what I stand for—and that's the only thing that should matter.

My phone rings, just as I'm washing the crumbs from the two muffins I consumed from my hands. Quickly drying them on the towel, I don't stop to check the display before answering the phone.

"Lilith!" My mother's voice twitters over the line.

"Hi, Mom."

It's been months since we last spoke. She's always been a demanding and judgmental woman, blaming David's extramarital affair, and subsequent leaving, squarely on my shoulders. Apparently, since *I'd let myself go*, it was no wonder I hadn't been able to keep his attention. Oh yes, mother is a prize.

She doesn't even know I've moved up here. Mostly because I'm not in the mood for my mother's version of waterboarding, a relentless flow of words in her case, which leaves me gasping for air in the end. It's no surprise I try to keep contact to a minimum by ignoring most of her calls, and in the next second I'm reminded why.

"I just had to call you to tell you about this wonderful new diet I've discovered. I've gone from a size ten to a size six in two months. You should give it a try, who knows, you might even be able to draw the attention of a nice man."

The woman clearly has a sixth sense, as my eyes shoot guiltily to the remaining muffins, and I feel the bile crawl up my throat. Aside from my obviously poor dietary choices, I've managed to alienate every single man I've come in contact with since moving up here.

Clearly, I'm still a work in progress.

Roar

"Son-of-a-bitch, that hurts!"

I look up from the table where I'm dipping this morning's catch in my beer batter.

Today is their last day here and I took Jamie out on the boat, while his father stayed on the dock, his injured leg elevated. Between us, we had a decent catch and in an attempt to soothe any remaining ruffled feathers from their encounter with the rock, I suggested a fish fry for lunch.

"Cold water," David tells his son, who just burned his hand slipping the battered fish in the hot oil. "Just stick it in the lake, the damn water is probably colder than what you get from the tap."

Jamie follows his father's suggestion, while I slide the rest of the fillets in the cast iron pan over the fire pit. Don't ask me why, but the fish always tastes better when cooked and consumed outside, by the water's edge. You don't need anything else, just a couple of beers, a little salt and a slice of lemon, and a pile of golden-fried, battered perch or walleye. Meal of champions.

I pull the fish from the oil and let it drain on sheets of newspaper I dumped in the middle of the picnic table. Ace, who is chilling in the shade underneath, sticks his head out in hopes of catching crumbs.

"Dig in," I invite the two men, who don't waste any time doing just that. I pull a few cold ones from the cooler and join them.

No plates or utensils required, and after I'll just burn the newspaper in the firepit and throw a bucket of water over the picnic table. Don't want to leave any food scraps behind. This is bear country and they tend to be hungry, this early in the season.

I take a long tug of my beer and am about to reach for my second piece when I hear the crunch of tires. We all seem turn at the same time and watch as my new neighbour climbs out of her old Jeep, a large Tupperware container in hand. I think we're all staring, at least I know I am. Instead of the camouflage pants I saw her wearing before, she now has on some kind of long, flowing top over bright floral tights. The colourful material looks painted on her sturdy legs, and beside me David emits a soft whistle.

I watch as Ace barrels out from under the table and nearly knocks the newcomer off her feet. My mouth is already open to call him back, when I watch her crouch down and greet him.

"Sorry to interrupt," she says, as she approaches the table a little tentatively, my dog at her heels. Her gaze bounces over all three of us before settling on me. "I never had a chance to thank you properly the other day. I hope you don't mind, I just followed the signs here." She looks at the lake and a small smile forms on her full lips. "It's beautiful here."

Nobody has a chance to respond before her focus is back on me.

"Anyway, I baked some muffins last night, and thought maybe you'd like some for lunch." Her eyes land on the remaining pile of fish in the middle of the table and the pink colour, already on her cheeks, deepens to a deep red. "But I see you're already eating. I apologize for barging in."

"Sit."

The order comes from David, who is observing the woman with obvious amusement as she instantly sits down at the other end of my bench. Ace finds his spot underneath the table again.

"Roar here knows how to cook a great fish fry. Have a taste." He gestures at the grease-drenched newspaper on the table. "By the way, I'm David and this here is my son, Jamie. We're just vacationing."

"Nice to meet you," she says, reaching out to shake David's outstretched hand. "I…I'm a neighbour. I mean, I just moved up here recently. I'm Lilith Talbot."

"Pleasure to meet you too, Lilith, now dig in."

She smiles at him before turning her gaze to me, an unspoken question in her eyes. I just shrug my shoulders and reach into the cooler, pulling out another cold one and handing it to her.

"Roar? I thought your name was Doyle?" she asks, after expertly twisting the cap off her bottle and taking a hefty swig of her beer.

A bit of a surprise, I half expect her to ask for wine instead, or at the very least a glass, but she seems as comfortable as the rest of us, drinking straight from the bottle.

"Doyle's my last name."

"Oh." Her eyes go back to the dwindling pile of fish, and I watch with interest as she hesitantly reaches out and grabs the smallest piece, popping it in her mouth all at once.

"Short for Riordan, right?" David pipes up.

"It is."

"Your girl, Patti, mentioned that you were always this communicative, even in high school, and that's why they started calling you Roar," he chuckles at his own joke. "She's right, you don't talk much. You'd make a lousy lawyer."

I pretend not to notice the sudden flash of interest in the woman beside me and instead smile at the older man.

"I talk… when I have something useful to say," I counter, and David barks out a laugh.

"Fair enough," he concedes, before lifting the lid on the Tupperware container and pulling out one of the muffins. "Wouldn't mind trying one of these before we hit the road."

The next ten minutes, I listen as the conversation centers around the motel, while scribbling on a scrap of newspaper. David seems quite impressed that a woman alone would venture into these regions to run a business. Personally, I still think it's a fool's errand, but I have to give it to her, she's got balls just to try.

When Jamie and David leave to pack up their car for the trip home, Lilith excuses herself as well. I automatically follow her to her vehicle.

"Thanks for the fish," she smiles, giving my dog, who seems enamoured, a final scratch behind his ears. "I've never had it like that before, but it's really good."

"Old family recipe. Muffins were good," I add quickly, handing her the empty container back.

"Thanks."

She climbs behind the wheel, closes the door, and rolls down the window.

"You don't look like a Lilith," I tell her, my hand on top of the door. I watch a timid smile form on her lips.

"Only my mother still calls me that. Most people call me Leelo, like my dad used to."

"Leelo," I repeat, the name easier on my tongue. "Suits you much better."

I step back and watch as she drives off, her colourful arm resting on the door like a beacon.

FIVE

*There is no logic in the random pattern of a butterfly,
just an enticing effect.*

Leelo

"He's bad news."

Mrs. Stephens shakes her head adamantly.

"You want well clear of him."

It started with my call this morning.

I've spent the past few days trying to get the bathroom in number three in order, but have run into a snag I can't seem to fix myself.

As if regrouting the loose tiles around the tub wasn't challenge enough, I come to find out the showerhead sprays water in every direction but down. Sure, I probably should've checked first, before I spent a day and a half making the room pretty, but I really don't want to pull those tiles down again. The tap worked fine but when the little lever for the shower was pulled, the bathroom turned into a full on carwash. And I couldn't turn it off. I tried everything, I grabbed the pipe wrench I found in the storage space, along with a bunch of other tools, I tried to tap that lever back into the off position, but it wouldn't budge and finally gave the showerhead a good whack. Not sure what I was thinking, but I was getting desperate. Next thing I know, the whole damn thing breaks off, bringing with it a section of pipe that belonged in the wall.

No more spray, but the gurgling sounds coming from behind the freshly grouted tiles was ominous. I managed to locate the main water valve and shut the thing off, but it was clear I was in over my head on this one. My budget was going to have to stretch to facilitate a plumber.

It was at that point I decided I needed a friendly face and a change of scenery before I suffered a complete meltdown. I was close as it was. I've been teetering on the brink of total failure since I got here, and my dream of independence was suffering serious blows.

Mrs. Stephens answered the phone on the first ring, and after listening to me sobbing incoherently for five minutes, she cut me off and told me to get myself in the car and over to her house where she'd have fresh coffee and Danish waiting.

The Danish did it.

I towel dried my hair, put on some dry clothes, and followed the directions to her place in Wawa.

Sitting here across from her at the kitchen table, with a belly full of hot coffee and pastries, I feel a little better.

"But he's in real estate, surely he knows someone?" I push, but Mrs. Stephens will have nothing of it.

"Kyle Thompson is a slimy weasel who just sees dollar signs," she dismisses, as she pushes back from the table and grabs a phone off the counter.

"How busy are you?" I hear her say to whomever she just called. "I have a friend with faulty plumbing who needs a hand and you're close. It's at the Whitefish Motel. It's urgent"

I have no idea who she's talking to, but in no time she's rushing me out the door, telling me help will be there in twenty minutes.

On my drive home, I manage to get myself back in a positive mind frame, thinking perhaps I'll be able to put that vacancy sign up this weekend after all, when one glimpse of a familiar pickup truck in front of the motel has me groan out loud.

I haven't seen Roar Doyle since I inserted myself in his fish fry. It seemed safer. The way he said my name last week, as I was leaving, had given me butterflies in my stomach. Then I'd beaten myself up over it all the way home.

Sure, he was tempting. Big, manly, and handsome in a rugged way, with his ruddy beard and hazel eyes, but he was also barely civil, bordering on rude. I've been put down enough in my life; I really don't need another man to make me feel inadequate. And I certainly don't need to start drooling over someone who's already taken.

I clearly don't have the best judgement when it comes to men, which is why I steered clear.

Yet there he is, his tall frame standing beside the truck with legs spread and arms folded over his chest, a scowl on his face, looking very annoyed.

"I'm sorry," I start, getting out of the Jeep. "I had no idea Mrs. Stephens was talking to you or I would've—"

"Where is it?" he interrupts and instantly my hackles go up.

"Unit three," I tell him. "But listen, you don't need to…"

I don't even get a chance to finish my sentence before he turns his back and starts pulling a toolbox from the back of his truck.

"Key?" he asks, his hand out, as if I haven't even spoken.

Fine. This is good. He's hammering home what an ass he really is. It'll be so much easier to get the memory of that soft rumble, repeating my name back to me, permanently erased from my mind. *Prick.* I fish in my pocket and pull out the master key; slapping it in his palm and without another word he walks away.

I stand there for a minute, contemplating whether I should make myself scarce or follow him. I finally opt for the latter, since he's got my key.

"*Jesus fucking Christ.*"

The barely whispered curse from the bathroom makes me wince, but still I shore up my courage and step through the door. He's standing with his big work boots in the bathtub, eyeing the hole in the wall where the shower used to be. It, and the length of broken pipe attached to it, lay at his big feet.

"I…" I start again, hoping to explain what happened, but he interrupts again.

"Your pipes are completely corroded."

"What does that mean?" I know what it means; I just need to hear him say it.

I swallow down the bile crawling up my throat as I wait for him to bring the hammer down on my pipe dream. I already know there's no way I can afford to do a major overhaul of all the plumbing. Didn't take long for my lofty plans to take a nosedive.

"Means Sam should've tackled the whole place when he had the work done about eight years ago. He did the house, the bar, but only some of the units from what I recall."

"You knew my uncle?"

Not sure why that was the only thing I got out of that, but Roar looks at me like I'm two cents short of a nickel.

"You don't live next to someone for years up here and not know them," he explains, turning his eyes back to the problem. "And I knew him enough to know he kept tight books. I bet the invoice for the work is still somewhere in that file cabinet of his."

I know what he's referring to. There's a tall file cabinet in the small office space in the back of the bar. I'd looked for a key for that thing, without any luck.

"I don't have a key and he left it locked."

"So we'll open it."

He steps out of the tub and marches right by me, stopping only to grab a hammer and a screwdriver from his toolbox.

"I never understood why he would have people come through the bar to check in," I think out loud, as we make our way through the dark and slightly musty space. I haven't spent much time in here, intent on getting a few rooms up and running before I tackle this.

"Clever, actually," Roar says, as he walks into the back office and bends over to take a closer look at the lock on the filing cabinet. I try not to be too obvious when I check out his ass in those threadbare jeans.

"Clever?"

"Considering most of his guests were travelers, the smell of cold beer would be tempting after a long day

63

behind the wheel," he explains, fitting the tip of the screwdriver into the key slot on the lock and whacking it with the hammer a few times. "Instant customers," he adds, as he twists and jiggles the lock, and with a good yank pulls it free, leaving a hole behind.

"Huh," I manage, watching as he pulls open the drawer, revealing a colour-coded filing system with neatly printed tabs.

"All yours," Roar announces as he grabs his tools, steps around me, and walks out the door.

Roar

I seem destined to be thrown in her path, whether I want to be there or not. The judge is still out on that one.

Charlie seems to like her, and she certainly knows how to bake, but other than that, I have no idea what to make of the woman. From where I sit, she's reckless, impulsive, at times incoherent, and I'm not at all sure I even want to touch the dark shadows in those bright eyes. Yet, I still find myself drawn.

She's got balls, though, I have to give her that. It's clear she bit off more than she can chew, but she's trying—hard.

I feel bad, popping the neatly grouted tiles from the wall she clearly spent some time on, but I have no choice.

"Shit."

I hear her curse as she sticks her head into the bathroom and I turn around.

"Yeah—only way to get at the pipes, I'm afraid."

She walks up and peers over my shoulder at the growing hole in the wall.

"Is that mould?" she asks, pointing at the black crud visible inside the wall.

"Afraid so."

"Fuck—Fuck, fuck, fuck, FUCK!" Her voice rises and I can hear the edge of panic. Don't blame her.

"Did you find anything in the files?" I ask, hoping to distract her. She stares at me, rattled, before she visibly clues in.

"Yes. Yes I did. Units four through eight plus the bar and house were done seven years ago. I just don't get why he didn't have the other three units done."

"Can't recall him ever shutting down to have work done. He may have just kept those open for guests," I suggest. "Or maybe they weren't quite as bad as the rest. Who knows?"

I stop talking when I see her face drop.

"He was my uncle, you know. Sam? He stepped up when my father died. Would always spend the holidays with us," she shares in a soft voice. "And I never once made it up here."

I shift uncomfortably when I see tears brimming in her eyes, but she catches me watching her and quickly blinks them away.

"He talked about you," I offer, remembering conversations over a pint of beer, when Sam would speak of his niece, his only family. I don't think he ever mentioned a name, but I recall him talking about her and her kids. "Spoke of you fondly. Of your kids."

The last thing I expect is the loud snort followed by a giggle.

"He wouldn't have said anything about David," she says with a bitter edge. "Always hated his guts."

I'm assuming David is the husband, or the ex-husband, whatever the case may be. I'm not about to stir that pot, so I keep quiet.

"Anyway..." she drawls, slapping her hands together and forcing a fake smile on her face. "Looks like I've got three units that need work I can't do myself, so I'm going to focus on getting the other five ready. One through three will have to wait." With that she turns and starts walking out.

"You don't have water," I call after her, watching her come to an abrupt stop. Her head drops down.

"*Shit,*" she whispers before straightening her shoulders and turning to face me. "Okay. New plan. If you can direct me to a reasonable plumber, I'll have them fix this one so I can turn the water back on, and *then* I'll focus on the other units."

"I'm here. I've got the tools." I shrug and continue popping tiles off the wall. I can feel her eyes on my back, but just keep working.

"But..."

I swing my head around and give her an exasperated look.

"The sooner you let me get to it, the sooner it'll get done."

I watch her open her mouth, before she resolutely snaps it closed, her full lips pressed into thin lines. She squints so those blue eyes are barely visible as she shoots me a heated look. Without a word, she tosses that blue ponytail over her shoulder and stomps out. My gaze immediately drawn to that round ass swaying out the door.

-

It took me the whole afternoon, a trip into town for materials, a burn on my wrist from the welding torch, and a litany of expletives to get the job done. But it's done. The pipe is replaced, the water is back on, and I put up new concrete board to replace the mouldy drywall I ripped out. I left the tiles I managed to salvage stacked in the tub.

Leelo stayed out of sight the entire time. I heard her drive off early on, but she must've come back at some point, because her Jeep is parked in front of the bar. I'm about to hop into my truck and head out, when I notice partially dismantled furniture outside of one of the units further down and head over to investigate.

The door to six is open so I walk in. She's on her knees on the floor, her back to me, ripping up the dirty old carpet.

"Water's back on," I announce, watching as she whips around.

"Jesus, you about gave me a heart attack," she rambles, pressing a hand in the middle of her chest. I've tried to avoid looking, but it's impossible not to notice those full breasts when her hand is right there, wedged between them. "I didn't want to start painting without water, and obviously cleaning was out of the question, so I thought I'd get a start on the floors. I picked up some laminate flooring on sale. Although maybe I should probably paint before I put it down. Seems like the more logical thing to do," she rambles, struggling to her feet.

67

Nothing to say to that, so I just nod and turn to head out when a thought occurs to me.

"Why six?" I ask. By the look of confusion on her face, it's clear she's not following. "Why start in unit six? You started with number three first, instead of one, and now you pick number six?"

"Well, technically I started on number seven, when I discovered the leak," she reminds me, with a little smirk playing on her lips. "Then I went to three, and you know what happened there, so now I'm in six."

She says it like I'm supposed to follow her logic, except there is none, so I raise an eyebrow in question.

"Seven is my favourite number, but that didn't work out so well. Three is my next favourite, except clearly not this time—and six…"

I hold up my hand to stop her. It's obvious there is no rhyme or reason to be found, so why torture myself further.

"Heading out," I announce, turning back to the door.

"Wait!" I hear behind me. "What do I owe you?" She follows me to my truck.

"I'm taking some guests out on the boat in the morning, but I should be back around eleven. Wouldn't say no to some of those muffins."

Without waiting for an answer, I climb in the cab, start the truck, and back up, leaving her standing on the gravel with her mouth half-open.

An unfamiliar smile pulls at my mouth as I turn up the road home.

SIX

So many layers, it would take a lifetime to reveal them all.

Leelo

"Mom?"

The sound of my son's voice puts an instant bounce in my steps as I juggle my groceries to hold the phone to my ear.

"Hey, baby, how are things?"

"Slowing down a bit. I was wondering if you're going to be around this weekend?"

My heart does a skip in my chest, and my cheeks hurt from the size of the smile on my face.

"All weekend, honey. No big plans, unless you count laying floors and painting endless walls."

Matt's chuckle washes over me like a warm blanket. A lot deeper sounding than it used to, but still familiar and reminding me of the tight relationship we once had. It fills me with hope.

"Want some company? I worked through the last two weekends and Dad gave me Monday and Tuesday off. I can probably get out of here around three."

"Yes! Oh my God—yes, absolutely. I can't wait to see you. Can't wait for you to see the place, you'll love it."

"I'll bring my tools," he offers, and I swear my heart melts a little.

"You don't have to, baby. You've obviously been working hard; you deserve a break. Just come and enjoy. There's supposed to be great fishing here, and the other day I found an old canoe by the edge of the water."

"Okay," he responds, a smile clear in his voice. "I'll bring my rod, but I want to come help too, Mom. I feel bad I wasn't able to get away when you called."

"Oh, Bud, no. Don't worry about that. I ended up getting some help from a neighbour with the roof." I don't tell him the same neighbour had to rescue me off there first, it would only make him feel bad. "He's actually been really helpful," I admit, thinking about the afternoons Roar's been by this week, working on the plumbing. Not that I've seen much of him. His truck just appears parked outside the units. The first day he returned, I looked in on him, tried to get him to quote me a price for the work, but he just shot me down with a sharp look from those deep-set, hazel eyes. Other than dropping off something to drink or eat from time to time, I've mostly steered clear.

It takes me a while to notice the silence on the other side of the line.

"Matt? You still there?"

"Do you know him?" I bite off a grin when I hear the tone of Matt's voice. My boy is growing into a man. A very protective one by the sound of it.

"I do now. He runs a fishing lodge a little further up the lake. Not the most personable guy, he doesn't talk much, but he takes neighbourly to a whole new level," I inform him. "He's good people, Matt."

"I'll check him out when I get up there."

70

"You do that," I concede, barely able to hide the smile in my voice.

"I've gotta go, Dad's calling me."

"Okay, honey. I'll see you tomorrow night, and please, please, drive careful. A lot of moose and deer on the roads up here this time of year."

"I know, Mom. I will."

He ends the call and I tuck the phone in my pocket before unlocking the Jeep and loading in my groceries. *My boy is coming.* A big smile on my face, I climb behind the wheel and check the back seat to make sure I have everything. Four bags—it's not enough.

Half an hour later, I load six more bags on the back seat. Matt is a garborator: a bottomless pit. He's one of those kids who will stand in front of a fully-stocked fridge and proclaim there is nothing to eat. So I bought everything I know he likes.

"Looks like you're feeding an army." I hear behind me, just as I'm closing the back door. I turn to find Kyle Thompson leaning against his shiny car parked beside mine. I hadn't even noticed it.

"Hey, Kyle." I'll be polite, but the guy is really annoying, the way he seems to appear out of nowhere.

"So are you?" he asks, raising a well-groomed eyebrow.

"Sorry?"

"Feeding an army?"

"Oh." I follow his gaze at the pile of groceries in my car. "No, just my son. Although he eats enough for an army."

"I didn't know you had a son."

It's on my lips to tell him there's a lot he doesn't know about me, and I'm not about to change that soon, but I swallow it down. I may dislike the man, but this is a small town, and he's clearly an important part of it. Probably not smart to start pissing folks off when I'm trying to rebuild a business here. So I plaster a smile on my face before I answer.

"I do, and he's coming for a visit." I watch as Kyle folds his arms over his chest and leans a hip against his car.

"He your only child?"

"I have a daughter as well. She lives in Toronto now."

"I see," he says, and I wonder what exactly he thinks he's seeing, but I don't much like this conversation.

"Well, I'd best be going. I've got some stuff in there that needs freezing," I offer, pointing at the groceries. I already have the door in my hand when he speaks again.

"Couldn't help but notice Doyle's truck outside your place for a few days now. Remember I mentioned some people you should probably stay away from? Especially, if you want to build a good name for yourself in this town. Roar Doyle would not be helpful in accomplishing that." The sneer of his mouth when he says Roar's name strikes the wrong chord, and I instinctively jump to his defense.

"For your information, not that it's any of your business, but Roar has been nothing but helpful."

Kyle's derisive snort in response only agitates me further.

"I'm sure he has," he says with a smirk. "He's always been good with the ladies. Someone like you should be easy pickings for him."

I'm so shocked at his words; I don't even have a chance to respond before he's in his car, pulling out of the parking lot. The happy buzz I had just minutes ago evaporated as I stare after his car, disappearing down the road.

Well, *ouch.*

-

It isn't until the next morning that I have a chance to talk to Roar. When I came back from town yesterday, his truck was already gone. I busied myself cooking and baking in preparation of Matt's arrival all last night and finally rolled into bed after midnight.

By eleven this morning, I've had breakfast, finished laying the laminate in unit six, did the laundry, and am putting clean sheets on the spare bed, when I hear the crunch of wheels on the gravel. I peek out the window just in time to see Roar pull his toolbox from the back of his truck and disappear out of sight.

Armed with a plate of cheese biscuits and a thermos of fresh coffee, I make my way over to unit two, the last bathroom left to fix.

"What's with you and Kyle Thompson?" I blurt out, coming in the door. No tact. No finesse. Just a head full of burning questions that plagued me since I watched that wretched man drive off yesterday. Roar is rummaging through his toolbox when he turns around.

"Morning to you, too," he deadpans, a sardonic smirk on his lips.

"Sorry. Morning," I correct myself, duly chastised with just a few words. "I brought you coffee and biscuits." I hold out the plate and thermos as a peace offering.

He tilts his head, his eyes never leaving my face. I set everything down on the dresser, and nervously wipe my hands on my jeans.

"Want to tell me what that was about?" he finally asks, turning his body to face me.

I drop my head, let out a deep sigh, and drop down on the edge of the bed.

"Yesterday, Kyle approached me in the parking lot of the Valu-mart and repeated something he'd said to me once before; about avoiding certain people," I start.

"Let me guess; he mentioned me specifically?"

"Yesterday. Yes," I admit, surprised to see a smile ghost over his mouth. "I mean, he alluded to it last time, but this time he basically said I should stay away from you, if I wanted to succeed making a living here. I told him it was none of his business, that you'd been helping out, but he—"

"You told him off?" The faint smile is replaced with a full wattage grin, as he cuts me off mid-sentence. The effect is stunning. The normally taciturn face is completely lit up. The deep grooves and stern wrinkles on his face are suddenly transformed into laugh lines, bracketing his eyes and mouth.

"I guess I did…" I mutter, almost shell-shocked.

"Bet he didn't like that much."

"Ha!" I bark out a fake laugh. "Not exactly. He mentioned how easy he imagined it would be for someone like me to fall victim to your prowess with the opposite sex."

It doesn't matter that the guy was an ass—*is* an ass—and I should know better than to let it bother me, but the words still left a sting.

"He's an idiot." Roar's deep rumble draws my attention.

His eyes, now deadly serious, lock in with mine and when he says nothing else, just stares at me, I can't help but squirm under the scrutiny.

"But what about…"

"An idiot," he repeats sternly. "He doesn't know his ass from a hole in the ground. Ignore the fucking weasel."

With one last pointed look, he grabs some tools from his box and disappears into the bathroom. I'm left to stare after him, no wiser than I was before.

Roar

The temptation is great to get in my truck, find that piece of shit, and reacquaint him with my fists. It wouldn't be the first time I laid him out. We go way back, fucking Kyle Thompson and I.

We'd been high school buddies, in love with the same girl: Jenny Braxton. I'd been the lucky one to end up with her and married her after I returned from my first deployment. But then I left for a second, and then a third round, during which time Kyle never let up on his relentless pursuit of my wife. Jenny had just found out she was pregnant when I left for Afghanistan that last time, but two months into my tour, she lost the baby. Like a goddamn leech, Kyle latched onto her pain and her loneliness, with me not around to look after her, and she finally took the empty comfort he offered.

Just weeks later I was flown home, injured in an ambush that left my best friend, Tom Jackson, blown to pieces on a dusty road near the Arghandab Dam, north of Kandahar. Jenny was waiting for me at home. She was a mess, and during what was an emotional reunion for a lot of reasons, she confessed to having slept with Kyle.

That had been a hard blow for me, especially on top of the horrors I'd just left behind. We tried. For the better part of a year, we tried. Until I finally lost it on Kyle one day when Jenny and I were out for dinner in town. I'd been successful in mostly avoiding him when he came in, walked past our table, and winked at my wife with a shit-eating grin on his face. Yeah, I lost it. Saw red. I can't remember much beyond kicking my chair back and tackling him from behind, but the end result was an assault charge for me, and Jenny packing her bags and moving out. I didn't stop her. I wasn't the same guy she fell in love with, and the emotional baggage we each toted around was poison to our marriage.

Kyle's taunting never stopped, though. Not even after Jenny was long gone, living in North Bay with her new husband and kids. He seems to have made it his mission to mess with me at every opportunity. Harassing my new neighbour is simply another way of doing that.

He's right, though. Leelo is better off not associating with me, because he could make her life very difficult, if he put his mind to it. He's built a lot of pull in Wawa, and if she wants to make a go of it here, she'll need the goodwill of the town.

-

I toss my toolbox in the back of my truck and go in search of Leelo to let her know I'm done.

76

She's not hard to find, all I have to do is follow my nose right into the large kitchen behind the bar.

"What are you cooking?" I ask her, walking up to where she's standing at the industrial stove. She throws a glance at me over her shoulder, before focusing her attention back on the pan she's stirring.

"Risotto. My son's coming to stay for a few days, and I want to make sure he has something to eat," she says.

She has a son.

"Is he bringing a bunch of friends?" I ask, looking at the various food containers sitting on the counter. She chuckles, following my gaze.

"Nah. Matt likes his food, though. Growing boy and all that, although I probably shouldn't say that anymore—he's almost twenty-one. I just haven't cooked for him in a while. I guess I missed it."

I lean my hip against the counter and watch her do her thing. I realize I know nothing about her other than that she's funny, she rambles when she's nervous or upset, she's a nurturer at heart, and she's got balls bigger than most men I know. Oh, and she has a fucking great smile.

"Only child?" She turns at the sound of my voice and flashes me a small one, shaking her head.

"No. I have a daughter too, Gwen. She's a few years older and works as an IT consultant for a large firm in Toronto." I don't miss the sad look that briefly replaces her earlier smile.

There's a story there. One I'm surprised to find myself curious about, but that would mean spending more time with her, and I just made up my mind that would not be in her best interest.

"You?" she wants to know, drawing me from my thoughts.

"No kids," I answer, feeling the brief pang of loss that seems to surface whenever that topic is broached. "Why are you in here and not the house?" I change the subject, looking around the industrial-sized space. "Something wrong with your kitchen?"

"No. There's just more room here and it gave me a chance to test out the equipment. See if everything is still working, as it should. I actually like cooking in here."

"You should then," I suggest, an idea taking form. "In fact, I don't know what your plans for the bar were, but there's enough space to turn it into a small restaurant instead. Keep the bar, but focus on food."

She pulls the pan she was stirring from the burner and turns around to face me.

"You think that'll work? I mean, I've thought about it, but there are quite a few restaurants in…"

"Absolutely," I interrupt her. "There's quite a bit of traffic along this road. Not all folks want to go into town for a decent meal. You'd have your own guests and then there's the folks staying up at the lodge. I'll do an occasional fish fry, but I don't offer regular meals."

She silently walks past me into the bar and stops, looking around. I follow her and step up beside her, noting how the top of her head barely reaches my chin.

"It could work," she mumbles under her breath as she takes in the space. "A good cleaning, a bit of paint, a few repairs." She points out a table with a crooked leg. "It wouldn't take much."

"No, it wouldn't," I agree quietly, looking down at her. The smile she beams up at me is fucking stunning, and it's all I can do not to take that beautiful mouth with mine.

Instead I take a step away and start moving to the door.

"I've gotta head out. Unit two is ready to go. Catch you later." I quickly pull the door open; intent on escaping before I do something stupid, when she calls after me.

"Wait! How much do I owe you?"

I try waving her off as I walk to my truck, but I can hear the slap of her flip-flops as she follows me.

"Hold on." She breathes heavy when she catches me, just as I'm getting behind the wheel. "At least let me pay for materials," she argues. I'm tempted to dismiss her again, when I see the plea in her eyes. This is important to her.

"Okay," I concede grudgingly. "I'll total it up and let you know."

It goes entirely against my grain, but seeing that smile break through on her face again makes it worth it.

"You're something else, Leelo Talbot," I mutter as I drive off.

SEVEN

Oh, to go where one knows one shouldn't.

Leelo

"Is he a contractor?"

I turn to Matt stepping off the ladder propped against the side of the motel. He just spent the last twenty minutes inspecting every inch of the roof, insisting he make sure the work was all done properly. And that was after checking out the plumbing in the three units Roar had worked on.

"Roar? No. Just a helpful neighbour."

The derisive snort is hard to ignore. An irritating habit both kids seem to have inherited from their father, who was the master of derision.

"Helpful," Matt repeats, his eyes flashing something I can't quite pin down. "I bet. And what kind of name is Roar?" Without another word, he picks up the ladder and takes it back around the side of the house.

I bite off the grin at my son's protective instincts on display and his apparent instant dislike to my neighbour. It'd be interesting to see how the two would react to each other.

Matt arrived late last night and rolled straight into bed, but after he finished breakfast this morning, he announced he was giving the place a good once over, and nothing I said could stop him. Overbearing men seems to be a theme in my life. By merit of his Y-chromosome, even my son in all of his twenty years, feels the need to impart his expertise and wisdom on me.

As if by divine intervention, the well-timed crunch of tires on gravel draws attention to the familiar truck rolling up the drive. Before it even comes to a stop, my son is marching up to it. I lean my shoulder against one of the pillars of the overhang and observe the scene play out. I'm not even trying to hide the amusement on my face as the much larger Roar unfolds himself from the cab of the truck. Even at this distance I can see the firm set of Matt's shoulders slump a little, and the bobbing of his Adam's apple as he swallows hard. His five foot eleven youthful frame doesn't quite measure against Roar's six foot three bulky mass. Still, I watch my son lift his chin and square his shoulders as he offers a hand in greeting. Roar clasps the proffered hand with a serious face, but the hazel eyes that flick in my direction over Matt's shoulder, show a spark of amusement.

"Coffee?" I call out, pushing off the post and walking toward the men. "I have cinnamon rolls," I add and both heads swing my way as I walk into the bar, straight into the kitchen beyond. I'm not surprised when two sets of heavy footsteps follow.

Half an hour later, I head back outside, in desperate need of some air before I do serious physical harm. I leave the two guys, more animated than I've seen either of them before, leaning against the kitchen counter, eating the last of my pastries while making detailed plans for the renovations. No one bothers to run anything by me. Two men, who in my experience manage little more than two word sentences when communicating with me, appear to have no such restrictions when conversing with each other.

Well, the assholes can jabber and plan all they want, but in the end, nothing will happen unless I say so.

Last time I checked, it was still my fucking name on the deed.

-

I'm staining quarter round to finish off the flooring in unit six when I hear the slam of a car door. I half expected Roar taking off again, but instead it's Kyle walking toward me. *Wonderful.*

"What are you doing next Friday?" he wants to know when he's close enough. I straighten up and try to wipe the stain off my hands with a rag.

"Why? What's next Friday?"

"The opening ceremonies for the Wawa Music Festival. As one of the festival's largest sponsors, I'm expected to give the welcoming speech." I take a step back when he leans in close enough that I can smell him, and it's not a pleasant experience. "It would be a great opportunity for you to network. I'll pick you up at six for a bite to eat before."

More than a little irritated with the presumptuous way he lays claim to my time, I open my mouth to object, but someone beats me to it.

"Out of luck, Thompson," Roar's voice sounds from right behind me, as a heavy hand lands on my shoulder. "The lady is coming with me."

I shrug the hand off and swing around. I need to tilt my head back to meet his eyes burning down into mine.

"Really?" I spit out. "I have news for the lot of you."
I swing my arm demonstratively through the air, narrowly
missing a direct connection with the middle of my
neighbour's face. Roar deftly dodges impact as he grabs
my flailing limb in his large fist. That doesn't stop the
tirade I feel bubbling up, though. "Last I checked, I was a
grown-ass woman, more than capable of looking after
myself—" I accompany this declaration with a glare in my
son Matt's direction. "Fully qualified to make my own
decisions—" This with a scowl at Roar, who is grinning
widely but still hanging onto my wrist. "And a woman of
my word," I say this turning my attention to Kyle. "So
when I turn down an offer of dinner, you can bet your
shiny designer loafers that I'm not interested. In the least!"
I add for good measure when I see shock hit Kyle's
features. Better to hammer that shit home, because I don't
feel like having to make the same damn point over and
over again.

I can feel the low chuckle vibrate through the warm
palm of Roar's hand around my wrist, as he makes no
effort to hide his amusement at my outburst. It doesn't
help when my son's distinct snicker joins, and not even
the sharp bang of a car door slamming shut can stem my
hot irritation. I twist my arm from Roar's hold and stomp
off to where another fourteen feet of quarter round is
waiting for stain.

All men can collectively kiss my ass.

Roar

84

I want to kiss that smart mouth.

If not for her son, and that fucking Kyle Thompson; I'd have swallowed that sharp tongue whole. Instead, I watch her decimate my old nemesis and stomp off in her pink Converse sneakers, while he tears out of the parking lot.

"Wow," Matt says behind me, and I turn to face him. He's staring after his mother with surprise on his face. "I've never—not ever—heard that side of my mom. I honestly didn't think she had it in her."

"I'm becoming very familiar with that sharp side of her tongue," I snort, and Matt swings his eyes to me. "Not sure what your mom was like before she moved up here, but this woman doesn't take prisoners."

"No shit. Wish she'd have had a little of this when my dad used to wipe the floor with her."

His tone is wistful and I wrestle to keep my face impassive and my mouth shut. The thought of someone, anyone, wiping the floor with Leelo has the hair on my neck stand on end. With one last look at where Leelo is slapping stain on wood, I turn on my heels and head into unit one.

"What are you up to?"

I look over my shoulder and find the kid has followed me in.

"Last bathroom to finish," I tell him.

"Cool. I'll help."

-

"So what is your interest in my mom?"

I'm leaning against the bed of my truck, grabbing a minute to watch a sweaty Leelo shoveling gravel into the

85

massive pothole in the drive, when Matt walks up behind me. He'd given me plenty of looks all morning, but this is the first time he questions me about his mother.

The kid impresses me. He knows his way around tools and made the job a lot easier. He told me a little about the kind of work he does with his father, which is mostly home and small business renovations. From the sound of it, his dad's a prick. Matt made some remark about hoping to venture out on his own in time, but my impression was that time couldn't come soon enough. He had some neat ideas for the motel. Simple upgrades to the rooms and exterior that would give the place some visual interest, without breaking the bank. Stuff I suggested he bring up to his mom.

Then he mentioned something about fishing and asked for the best places to do that. I told him a little about the lodge and Whitefish Lake, suggested he follow me later and I'd show him some spots.

He talked plenty but this is the first time he puts me on the spot.

I watch the subject of discussion carry another load of gravel in the wheelbarrow, as I weigh my answer. I notice her colourful arms, straining with the weight, and decide to tell Matt the truth.

"I don't know," I say honestly, turning in his direction. "I could tell you I'm being a good neighbour, and perhaps it started out that way, but it's not just that anymore. Your mom is different. She stands out." That gets a loud snort from Matt, and I chuckle myself when I follow his gaze to where Leelo wipes her face with the bottom of her shirt. I try not to notice the exposed wedge of lily-white stomach and quickly avert my eyes. "She's got balls, coming out here to try and build a life. It's hard enough for those of us who've lived here all our lives. She's got every damn odd stacked against her, but I'd really like to see her succeed."

Matt raises his eyebrow. "That's it?"

I shake my head, pull the rag from my back pocket, and wipe my face to hide the grin on my face.

"Why don't you grab your gear, I'm gonna let your mom know we're off," I instruct him.

The moment he starts moving, I head over to the side of the storage shed, where Leelo has been hauling gravel from the pile. I find her shovelling another load in the wheelbarrow. Probably not the best time for her to be doing this, in the midday heat of the sun, but it shows her determination. Besides, she makes a mighty nice picture. The way her sticky shirt is plastered against her body shows off every damn curve and believe me, there are plenty.

Tempting. So fucking tempting, but I resolutely tuck my hands in my pockets, where they're safe, and clear my throat.

"I just—"

I barely get a word out and Leelo jumps and swings around, almost knocking me off balance.

"Jesus, you scared me…" she hisses, slapping a hand to her chest.

Of course, that just draws my attention to some of those curves I mentioned. When a second later she plants both palms against my chest and gives me a good shove, I feel I have no option but to wrap her in my arms.

Then my brain takes a complete detour. I can't tell you exactly what it is, whether the soft press of her warm body against me, or the mix of confusion and heat in those sky blue eyes, but I instinctively lower my head and cover her slightly opened mouth with mine.

The mistake is clear the moment I taste her lips. Soft, pliant, and with a hint of coffee and salt, her mouth is instantly addictive and already I crave more.

Big fucking mistake.

"Heading off to the dump and showing the kid around for a bit," I mutter, keeping a firm grip on her shoulders as I create some much needed distance, all but flinging her aside. "Stay hydrated, you're sweating like a racehorse," I add stupidly, as I try to ignore the look of shock on Leelo's face.

I turn on my heels and aim for the safety of my truck, hoping for a clear getaway, when the sharp sting of a handful of gravel hits me square between the shoulders.

"Asshole!" I hear, just as I climb in and pull the door shut. Matt is already sitting in the passenger seat, a big grin on his face.

"What are you laughing at?" I snap, jabbing my keys in the ignition.

"I'm really liking this new side of Mom," the little smartass replies.

Leelo

What, the ever-loving fuck, was that?

Don't get me wrong; I know exactly what that was. I can still feel the strength of his body, smell the scent of clean sweat and man, and taste the raw heat of his mouth on my lips.

But what the fuck was that?

I'm still fuming when I stomp down the last load of gravel in the pothole that is no longer visible. Nothing like some good old-fashioned physical labour to get rid of anger. Or is it frustration? All I know is it feels like the ground, that started to feel a bit more stable under my feet, is suddenly shifting again.

He is confusing me, and I don't like being confused. Hell, in one of the first interactions we had, the man was boasting about cleaning some chick named Charlie's pipes—I hated him on sight—but then he proved himself to be a pretty good guy, instead. A good neighbour. And I could really use one, given that I was way out of my depth when I moved my life up here. He's been a lifesaver more than once.

Not going to deny that I've looked, and maybe I've fantasized, but there's no way I would've jeopardized a potential friendship. And certainly I have never messed with another woman's man. I've been on the receiving end of that one, and let me tell you, those wounds run deep.

Then he kisses me and fucks it all up.

I tilt up the wheelbarrow to lean against the outside wall of the shed, plant my hands on my hips, and gaze out at the sliver of water just visible through the trees. I've explored the shoreline a little on the other side of the small outcropping of land, but I haven't had a chance to inspect this side. Hot and sweaty as I am, a dip of my toes in cool water holds appeal, and I set off down the narrow, overgrown trail through the bush.

Whitefish Lake is narrow here and I can clearly see the other shore when I get to the water's edge. I'm surprised to spot a small but expensive looking speedboat latched to an old dock on the other side. I was under the impression it was all Crown land over there. Eighty-five percent of land in Ontario is Crown land and falls under the jurisdiction and management of the Ministry of Natural Resources and Forestry. I guess it's possible they've built a dock there for water accessibility, since there are no access roads, but the speedboat looks out of place. Maybe Roar knows something about that.

My mind slips into dangerous territory at thoughts of that man, I turn my attention to unlacing my sneakers, so I can cool myself in the lake. There's a decrepit dock, half submerged under the water, on my side as well. I wouldn't mind seeing that restored and maybe a launching ramp added, so guests can bring their own boats. I may even pick up one or two to rent out.

With my butt on a large rock that juts out, I stick my feet in the lake and don't bother holding back the groan escaping my lips. That feels amazing. Between the thirty plus degree weather of the past few days, and the more frequent hot flashes that have been plaguing me—*something I should probably get checked out*—the cold water is utter bliss. So much so, that I let myself slide fully clothed off the rock and into the lake.

I'm not sure how long I'm floating on my back with my eyes closed, but it seems that dozing off under these circumstance might not be advisable, and I reluctantly make my way to shore.

As I sit down with my back to the water, to put on my shoes, I suddenly hear the soft purr of an engine. I turn around just in time to see the shiny motorboat leave the dock and speed off to the east, leaving a rolling wave in its wake.

There doesn't appear to be anyone steering it.

EIGHT

Imperfections are the vivid details that create beautiful contrast.

Roar

"Awesome!"

I smile at Matt's youthful enthusiasm when he gets his first glimpse of the lodge. The truth is, I still sometimes get a thrill when I see it. Many years and much work has made it what it is now, but the once rundown, turn-of-the-century residence of a lumber baron, has been restored to glory.

Matt had talked a bit about wanting to build himself a log home one day, and I'd told him about the lodge. The massive two-storey structure, made entirely from local lumber, is pretty impressive, especially when you consider it dates back to the late 1800s, when such a large project would've taken a small army of men to build. What's unique about it is the Scandinavian notch used for the joints. It's not often used in North America but the more intricate notching style makes for greater stability for the large logs.

"Found the original plans in an old trunk when I bought the place. You're welcome to have a look at some point. I sure learned a shitload from them."

Guess that's a hit, judging from the big grin on his face.

I like the kid; he's protective of his mom—although he clearly underestimates her—is not afraid to get his hands dirty, and is good with them. Despite being raised a city boy, he'd probably do well living up here.

"Hey, you're back," Patti says, walking down the dock, where I'm just throwing off the last rope on my boat.

"Actually, I'm just taking Matt for a spin on the lake." I notice Patti's got the kid's attention, which isn't a big surprise. She's nice to look at and she works it. "Matt, this is Patti," I tell him and watch the two shake hands. "Matt is down visiting his mom." Patti's expression is blank. "She's fixing up the motel?" I clarify.

"Right," she responds with a bright smile for Matt, but her eyes are guarded when she turns to me. "That's who you've been helping out, right?"

Hearing the edge in her voice, I decide it wiser to stick to an affirmative grunt as I shove the boat off and pull the protective fenders on board.

"Nice to meet you," Matt calls to shore as I crank the engine. By the time I have the boat steered into open water, I find him staring at me with a smirk on his face.

"What?"

"What did you do?" he asks, his smile getting bigger.

"Don't know what you're talking about," I dismiss him, but he's tenacious.

"That woman is all kinds of pissed off at you. The lethal kind, where they pretend to be all smiles, but underneath you can feel the anger seething. Trust me, I know; I have a sister and she mastered in the art of passive aggressive warfare. It's fucking scary."

I can't hold back the chuckle at his description. Especially since it's eerily accurate. Patti is pissed and I could pretend I don't know why, but I do. There's no way she would ever give it to me straight, though, but she sure can make me feel it when she feels I've done something wrong. Jenny was the same way; I had to guess at what had her panties in a wad. It always felt like some kind of test, where I could find forgiveness for my supposed transgressions, only if I could guess what they were. Ask me how successful I was at that. Come to think of it, even Charlie, who is one of the strongest and most capable women I know, can manipulate like a champ.

The only person who seems to lack any guile, who appears to me to be without any pretenses, is Leelo. There is little to no hesitation when she feels the need to put me in my place.

Interesting.

"How did you find this place anyway?"

Grateful for the change of subject, I don't hesitate with my answer.

"I grew up here. My family had a small cabin on the other side of the lake and the old log home was a favourite hangout. I'd borrow my dad's old rowboat and go exploring, any chance I got."

"Borrow?" Matt questions.

"I'd like to think so," I answer with a grin. "Although if my dad were still around, he'd probably disagree. Anyway, when the lumber company that owned the land finally went under, and the property came up for sale, I jumped on the opportunity." I don't mention that it was

Kyle Thompson who tried to pull a fast one on me at that time and almost managed to snag it out from under me. No need to open that can of worms.

"Was it always called Jackson's Point?" he wants to know, unknowingly bringing the conversation almost full circle again.

"No," I answer honestly. "It's named for my best friend. As kids, he and I would fantasize about what we would do with the place if it was ours. When the time came to make that fantasy a reality, it was too late for Tom."

"Why? What happened?"

"He died at the side of a dusty road in Afghanistan." It surprises me how hard it still is to say those words out loud.

"I'm sorry," Matt mumbles, clearly uncomfortable.

"Nothing to be sorry for, kid. We chose to be there."

"You were there, too?"

I ease up on the throttle, letting the boat troll slowly along the far shore, and turn to look at Matt.

"I was. We did everything together. Can't have been much older than you when we enlisted. It was our third tour. Was always supposed to be our last, but not like that. I survived...but came home with my friend in a casket. That had not been part of the plan." I let my eyes drift back over the water, toward the lodge. "We ended up spreading his ashes over the point and I named it after him. It was always meant to be ours."

"We?"

I turn back to face him.

"Patti and I. Patti was Tom's wife."

-

For the last half hour it's been quiet in the boat. All you hear is the occasional splash of water when one of us casts a line.

Matt's questions stopped at my last explanation, but his face shows a level of understanding I would not have attributed to someone so young.

The silence is comfortable though, not forced at all, and I once again consider how well-suited he is to life up here.

A loud splash draws our attention to a familiar dock on shore, where the ripples left behind by a jumping fish spread widely.

"Cool place," Matt says, looking at the old cabin set about two hundred feet back from the shore. It looks a little run down after the winter. A clear reminder I should drive the mower over there one of these days and do some maintenance. "Is it abandoned?"

"It belongs to Charlie. She lives in town, but doesn't get out here much any more. I'm supposed to maintain it."

"She a friend?"

Again with the probing questions. The kid has some great inquisitive skills; he's got me spilling my life to him.

"More like family," I answer with a smile. "This is where I grew up."

Matt opens his mouth with what I'm sure are more questions, when the loud rumble of an outboard motor on the water distracts him. I recognize the hull of the boat approaching from the direction of the channel, leading to the motel.

Asshole.

"Is that the guy who was bugging Mom earlier?"

"That's him," I confirm through gritted teeth, watching the boat slow down as it pulls close to the brand new dock next door. "That's his place."

Leelo

"Mom!"

I no sooner step out of the shower when I hear Matt calling me. Reminiscent of days when I couldn't even pee in peace. Somehow the kids always *needed* me for one thing or another, preferably when I headed for the bathroom.

Despite the warm weather, I'd been shivering by the time I got back to the motel. Dripping wet with the cold lake water, it only took a light breeze to raise goosebumps on my skin. The prospect of a warm shower had me rushing upstairs, stripping off clothes as I went. Water pressure had been sorely lacking before, but Roar had mentioned that once he was done with the units, I would notice the difference. He was right. I stood under that shower for a long time with my eyes closed, hearing nothing but the fall of water, while letting the solid stream massage every sore spot on my body.

"Mom!" Matt's voice is closer as I hear footsteps stomping up the stairs.

I barely manage to cover myself with a towel before the bathroom door swings open and my son barges in.

"Jesus, Bud! What the hell's going on?"

Before he has a chance to answer, Roar's face appears over his shoulder.

"Are you okay?" Roar asks, scanning me over from head-to-toe.

"I'm fine," I snap, pulling the towel tighter around me, painfully aware of my exposed state. "Can you guys please get the hell out?"

"Let's go, kid. Let your mom get dressed." Roar pulls Matt back and reaches around him for the door, but not before giving me a look that sends a shiver down my spine.

The moment I hear the click of one door, I dive through the other into my bedroom. It takes me all of two seconds to yank on some clothes and still drying my hair with a towel, I hurry downstairs.

"What was that all about?" I demand, walking into the kitchen, where Matt is digging a couple of beers from the fridge.

"Has no one told you not to leave garbage laying around outside?" Roar, who's relaxed pose leaning against the counter, is clearly a front as he chastises me. "Or are you trying to draw out every wild animal within a five mile radius?"

I bristle at his tone, but curiosity wins.

"Garbage? I don't know what you're talking about."

"Christ, Mom—when we pulled up just now, there was a massive bear clawing through the garbage bag on the porch outside. And the damn door was open. I thought you were hurt."

"Wait," I plead, shaking my head as I hold up my hand. "A bear? Garbage? I don't understand. I didn't put anything out." My mind is scrambling to remember exactly what I did. "I was cold. I'd gone for a dip in the lake in my clothes and wanted to get in the shower to get the chill off. I'm positive I did not put any garbage outside, but I can't be sure about the door. I can't remember if I closed it or not."

As I'm talking, I move through the kitchen to the closed door, which I pull open. Just outside is a large garbage bag with crap spilling from a large hole, the contents strewn all over the porch.

"That's not mine," I announce, pointing at the heavy-duty black bag. "Mine are cheap: grey, with those yellow drawstring thingies. Besides…" I add; looking around at the stuff spilled everywhere. "I didn't clean any fish. There's at least four fish carcasses out there."

Both guys walk up behind me and look over my shoulder, but it's Roar who moves me aside and steps out for a closer inspection. I'm just going to ignore how nice the weight of his large hand on my shoulder feels.

"Weird," he mutters under his breath, as he rummages with the toe of his boot through the trash. "It's mostly food scraps."

"I know," I tell him. "There's a heavy-duty garbage disposal system in the kitchen, behind the bar, I use to get rid of any organic waste. I never throw food in the garbage."

Matt slips around me with a broom and pan and starts cleaning up the crap.

"You didn't hear or see anything?" Roar asks, looking at me as he moves out of Matt's way.

"No. I worked for a while after you guys left, then went down to the water and took a dip. I can't remember seeing anything when I came back. I'm pretty sure I would've noticed that bag sitting on the porch as I walked in."

-

The guys finish cleaning up the porch and take care of the bag and its contents in the burn barrel out back. I keep myself busy inside, tidying up and running a load of laundry before starting preparations for dinner. But my mind stubbornly returns to the how and who, and most importantly, why.

I pick up snippets of conversation through the open window as Matt and Roar stand by the fire, making sure it stays contained in the barrel. Right now, we have a low fire risk because of the recent rain, plus it's early in the season, but that can change quickly. From what little I can hear, they're mostly discussing some property up the lake before their conversation becomes hushed. No longer able to make out much after that, I focus on the vegetables I plan to roast for dinner to accompany the tenderloin I picked up the other day.

"Want to stick around for dinner?" I ask Roar, when he comes in to wash his hands at the sink.

"Love to," he says, leaning his hip against the counter while wiping his hands on the towel. "But I have guests coming in around dinner time and I should be getting back."

"Why don't you put the vacancy sign up, Mom?" Matt pipes up as he enters the kitchen. "You've got a few units ready to go plus the water's back on now. We can spend the next few days finishing up the rest of them."

"I don't have all the quarter round down yet. Besides, I don't have anything to offer yet, in terms of a working kitchen. I'll need to get that up running first." I do my best to avoid the two pairs of questioning eyes staring at me.

"Bullshit, Mom. No one expects food in a motel unless you offer it to them. And you have two units that only need clean sheets to be ready."

He's right. I know he's right but there's something so definite about putting out the vacancy sign. It's a big step between working up to something and actually doing it. Once that sign goes up, I open myself to failure. What if no one shows? What if they hate it? Or me?

"Not a bad idea," Roar contributes, earning a dirty look from me. "Wouldn't hurt to start generating some income. Plus, the Wawa Music Festival always draws people to these regions. Seems like the perfect time."

"Exactly," Matt agrees. "And if we have some time left, we can start implementing some of those ideas for the bar."

I drop the knife I'm holding on the counter and nudge Roar out of the way to get to the sink to rinse my hands. Snatching the towel from Roar's hands, I swing around to address my son.

"I cannot recall making any plans for the bar," I remind him snippily. "I distinctly remember the two of you deep in conversation in there, but to my recollection I was not included."

With that I wad up the towel and toss it on the counter as I march out, a deep chuckle and a familiar snicker trailing behind.

To cool off, I pull some weeds from one of the overgrown planters separating the parking lot from the walkway in front of the units, when I hear someone coming up behind me.

"I'm heading out," Roar's deep rumble sounds behind me. "I told Matt to call me if you guys need a hand on Monday. I'll be out on the water with the new guests most of the day tomorrow, but they're on their own after that."

I keep my back to him but straighten up and square my shoulders as I sense him closing in.

"You know..." I feel his words against the shell of my ear. "Your son's got a good head on his shoulders, don't dismiss what he says just because you're upset." I swear I can feel the brush of his lips on my skin.

I'm frozen, but whether it's because of his comments or my acute awareness of his proximity, I don't know.

That's a lie. I barely heard what he said, the pounding of my heart too loud in my ears as I wait to see if he'll kiss me again.

The sharp crunch of gravel finally has me turn around, and I watch Roar drive off, a dust cloud in his wake.

NINE

She's the brave new world that draws me in.

Leelo

"Don't cry, Mom."

"I'm not," I lie with my face pressed to Matt's shoulder. It's clear he doesn't believe me, since I can feel his chest move with his soft laughter. I give him a healthy shove as I step out of his embrace. "Not nice to laugh at your mother." The smile on his face cracks open.

"I'm coming back, Mom. I love it up here," he says, running a distracted hand through his unruly mop, as he takes in the surroundings. "Love breathing this clean air. It's quiet. The pace is different. It feels peaceful up here. I feel peaceful up here."

I look at his handsome face and can see he means every word.

"This is as much your home as you want it to be, love," I tell him, putting a hand in the middle of his chest. "All you have to do is show up."

He pulls me back in his arms, tucks my head under his chin, and mumbles, "I know, Mom. I'd stay longer if I could."

"Yeah..." I swallow hard as I soak up the moment. "Best get on the road, kiddo," I finally say, resolutely stepping back as I let go of him. "You've got a long drive ahead, and you have to get up at the butt crack of dawn tomorrow."

I shove the thermos of coffee and the bag of food for the trip in his direction and follow him to his truck.

"Drive safe, and call me when you get to Sudbury," I instruct him, when he rolls down his window and sticks his elbow out.

Matt is about to say something when we both hear someone coming up the drive. The car pulls to a stop beside us. The passenger window rolls down and a woman sticks her head out. A man looks over from behind the wheel.

"Do you still have a vacancy?"

I'd finally hooked the vacancy board onto the big sign by the side of the road, yesterday afternoon. Matt and I worked like dogs the entire weekend, and not only did we get half of the units ready, we also managed to clear and clean the bar. Matt had introduced me to the ideas he and Roar had been discussing, and I had to admit I liked them. A simple lick of paint, a good washing of the windows, and some rearranging of existing furniture left us with a presentable space. It needs a few softening touches, it's a bit bare right now, but those are details that'll come with time.

"I do," I tell the waiting couple in the car. "I'll be right with you." I turn to Matt and mirror the big grin he sports. "Gotta go, Bud. Looks like I've got my first guests."

"Congrats," he rumbles smiling, sticking his head out the window so I can reach up and kiss his cheek.

I watch until he's backed out of his spot and starts down the driveway before turning to my new guests, who are getting out of the car.

"Sorry to keep you waiting. My son was up for a few days, helping me out, and is just heading back home," I smile, as I indicate for them to follow me inside.

After exchanging a few pleasantries, I have them fill out some paperwork, run their credit card with the new Square I picked up for that purpose expressly, and hand them the key to unit seven.

"Are you open for business?" The woman wants to know, looking around the bar. "Or should we find a meal in town?"

"I'm not completely set up yet," I admit, after only a brief hesitation. "But if you don't mind a hearty bowl of chili that's been bubbling since this morning, I'd be happy to share dinner with you. I'll even throw in some fresh baked cornbread."

"We couldn't possibly—" the woman starts, but I dismiss her objection with a wave of my hand.

"Trust me, you'd be doing me a favour," I assure her. "I cooked, not realizing my son wouldn't be here to eat it. I made enough for an army, because he eats like one. I'll have it ready around six?" I smile at both as they exchange a quick look before turning to me.

"Sounds good," the husband answers. "Gives us time for a nap." He throws a meaningful look in the direction of his wife, who rolls her eyes before letting herself be guided outside.

I'd have to be stupid not to know these two are going to have the springs creaking before too long. Thank God I gave them one of the last units. It's one thing knowing someone will be getting some action today, but it's another altogether to have to listen to them go at it. Would make for an awkward dinner tonight.

I smile as I head through the kitchen to my house beyond, to look for some candles or knick-knacks I can use to cozy up the tables.

-

"Whitefish Motel," I answer the ringing phone on the counter. I've just pulled the cornbread from the oven and am clearly getting comfortable in my professional capacity.

"I see you've opened for business," Roar's deep rumble chuckles on the other side.

"I have guests," I announce, smiling big as I wedge the phone between my shoulder and my ear. "Showed up this afternoon, and guess what?"

"What?" he responds dutifully, amusement lacing his voice.

"I'm about to feed them dinner."

"No kidding, eh? Good for you. I won't keep you, I just wanted to see if Matt got off okay." The smile on my face is starting to hurt my cheeks. That's so nice of him.

He hasn't been here since Saturday, but Matt went over to the lodge on Monday, after dinner, to go fishing again. It had been nice just having Matt and I putz around the place, but have to admit, I caught myself listening for the crunch of gravel every time I heard a car on the road.

"He did. Left a little after two. He'll call when he gets to Sudbury."

"Good. That's good. And you?" The smile is gone, but the concern in his voice warms me to the core.

"I'm fine. Sad he's gone, but it was the best time we've spent together in a long, long time," I admit softly.

"I'm glad." His deep gentle rumble gives me goosebumps. "I'm sure he'll be back before long."

"Yeah."

The silence that follows seems loaded, as if we're both unsure what to say next, but not ready to hang up either. It's Roar who finally breaks it.

"I should get going. Call me if you need anything, okay? Any time."

"Sure. Thanks. I'll, uhh…see you around," I add awkwardly.

"Yes, you will," is the last thing I hear him say before the connection is broken.

I don't know how long I'm standing there, dead phone in one hand and an oven mitt in the other, when I hear the door of the bar open followed by a bright, "Hello?"

"I'll be right there!" I call out, reaching for a knife to cut the cornbread. "Grab any table!"

Roar

I drop my head the moment I end the call.

I barely lasted three days.

When I drove off last Saturday, I had a hard-on so fucking uncomfortable it had me shifting in my seat all the damn way home. All from a peek at her barely covered body, a whiff of her freshly washed, ridiculous blue hair, and a light brush of my lips to her skin.

I spent the entire night, and the next day, resisting the temptation to head over there to have another taste of that mouth, and maybe other parts of her progressively irresistible body.

I grab a pen and jot down the words that float to the surface, as they often do.

This is not me. I'm in full control—always—and it's served me well, but this woman unsettles me. Or rather, my response to her does. *Fuck*, I've even taken a shine to her son.

I keep to myself, allowing for minimal involvement, in particular when dealing with women. Sex has for years been more of an occasional physical release than something more—deeper—but it's all I think about now. Sex with Leelo.

I'm obsessed and I've barely even touched the woman. For all I know, we're not sexually compatible at all. But somehow, I don't believe that. Hell, even hearing her breathe on the phone has my body respond like fucking Pavlov's dog.

I've come this far, through hardship and loss, by letting the mind rule over matter. But right now, my *matter* is clearly in the driver's seat, and my mind tossed clear out the window.

I can kid myself and say it was just to see about Matt when I dialled her number, but that would be a lie.

"You okay?" Patti's voice stirs me from my thoughts and I turn to face her, surreptitiously crumpling up the note and stuffing it in my pocket.

110

"Fine," I respond, bracing when she steps right up to me and reaches up with her hand.

"It's getting long," she says, as she runs her fingers through my hair. I do everything not to shake my head free of her touch. "Want me to grab the clippers and give you your summer cut?"

Unable to handle her touch, when my body is still buzzing in response to Leelo, I grab her wrist and pull her hand down.

"No thanks. I'll handle it." I try to be as gentle as I can, but Patti is not good at hiding her hurt.

We've been stuck, she and I, in the years since Tom's death. Bound by the loss, we'd seek occasional solace in each other's arms. Neither of us willing, or able, to move on from where he left us. Part of me must've recognized, in recent years, that perhaps she was more content to settle for me as a replacement in her life than I was with settling for that role. The history we have, as well as the comfortable tangle of our lives, made it easy to slip back into the role of lovers. I love her no different now, as when she was my best friend's girl.

"Sure," she forces a smile, slips her wrist from my hand, and grabs her bag from the chair. "Well, I'm heading out. Are you set for the rest of the week? I'm going to be busy with the music festival coming up. I've been asked to maintain some of the venues."

"That's great, Patti. Yeah, I'm good. We're into weekly rentals starting next week, and I don't anticipate any drop-ins this week, so I'll have lots of time to handle the changeover on Saturday," I assure her.

"All right then," she says, after a brief pause to see if I'm being truthful. "See you next week."

I feel guilty at my relief when she smiles and walks out the door.

-

For the next few days, I stay busy making sure all the boats are running, and all vacant cabins are ready for the Saturday check-ins. Next week will be the first week of school holidays, and although we don't get a ton of families at the lodge, it always seems to herald the start of our summer season.

It isn't until Thursday, on my way home from getting supplies in town, that I can't resist stopping in to see Leelo.

Her Jeep is parked on the side of the bar, and a second car is parked out front of one of the units at the far side. There's no sign of Leelo, but a couple loaded down with luggage is stepping out from under the overhang, heading to the car.

I pull in front of the bar and hop out of the cab, looking around for any sign of her.

"You looking for Leelo?" the guy calls out, as he shuts the trunk of his car.

"Yeah. She here?" I call back, starting to walk in his direction.

"She's out back. Clearing a trail or something, she said."

"Thanks." I nod at the couple as they get into the car and drive off.

I hope to hell they're paid up, because I'd hate to see Leelo stiffed her first week in business.

Making my way around the last unit, I scan the surroundings, but don't see her until a splash of water draws my attention. I can see the lake through the trees and just manage to catch a glimpse of the bright, midday sun hitting the blue hair that's been growing on me.

I find her up to her chest in the lake, muttering and swearing under her breath as she fruitlessly shoves against the dock. I can't see what she's wearing below the water, but her wet shirt is plastered against her body, leaving little to the imagination.

Full, lush, and unapologetic, she's stunning, framed in the bright reflection off the water.

"What are you up to?"

She jumps at the sound of my voice and loses her footing, falling backward into the lake. I'm ready to jump when she immediately surfaces, splashing wildly, while gasping and spitting mouthfuls of water.

"Christ, you scared me," she says when she finally manages to catch her breath, glaring in my direction as she whips the wet hair from her face.

"Sorry," I grin, but I'm not. Not really. That was fun to watch. "Just thought I'd check in and see if you needed help. I can't help notice I came at the right time?" I tease her, earning a dramatic eye roll. "What are you hoping to accomplish?"

"I want to fix the dock and add a boat ramp." She's damn cute, jutting out her bottom lip in a small pout.

"Lofty goals." I nod with my eyebrows high. "I would be happy to lend a hand making those happen after the weekend, but right now I have a truck full of supplies to get home, and no one manning the lodge. We'd need the right tools to do the job right, anyway."

"Hmmm," she hums, pressing her lips together as she wades toward shore. I reach out for her hand and pull her all the way up the steep embankment. My other hand grabs for her hip to steady her when she threatens to stumble back, but all it does is change her momentum forward, and her dripping body lands squarely against my front. I back us up and don't let go of her until we're on level ground, at which point she takes a step back, taking stock of my soaked clothes. She slaps her hand over her mouth but not fast enough to stifle the laugh that gurgles up. I fucking love the sound of it and grin down on her when she raises her eyes.

"I'm so sorry," she mumbles behind her hand, not even close to successful in covering her hilarity. "Let me get some towels." Before I have a chance to tell her it'll probably dry just as fast to the warm air, she shoves her feet in a pair of discarded flip-flops and jogs off.

Now—I noticed that ripe ass maybe once or twice before, but there's no way in hell I miss it shimmying off between the trees toward the house. If I were any younger, I'd file that away in my spank bank, but… Screw that— it's filed.

I amble after her, and catch up when she comes barrelling out of the house, a futile hand towel in her hands. She immediately starts rubbing it over my chest and since that's not helping me at all, I stop her motions by pressing her hand against me.

"It'll dry," I promise her when she sputters in protest. "By the time I get to the lodge, I'll be fine. You're in worse shape than I am," I point out to her, indicating the shirt and cargo pants clinging wetly to her curves. She looks down at herself, turning a pretty shade of pink. "And I do seem to be making it a habit to catch you wet."

I fucking swear no innuendo was intended, but when her head pops up, eyes wide and mouth half-open, I realize how it must've sounded. What surprises me is the deep raw belly laugh that bursts out of her.

"You have no idea," she mumbles, when she finally straightens up and wipes the laughter off her face. At least that's what I think she said.

Temptation plagues me all the way home.

TEN

An innocent smile hides the suggestive twists of her mind.

Leelo

"We'll need them for two nights. We'll be heading home on Sunday."

"No problem." I smile at the man as I hand over the keys for units seven and eight. The only units with a connecting door, plus unit eight is slightly larger than the rest with a small kitchenette. "If you don't mind my asking…how did you find us?"

"We were sent here," he says, pointing at his family, hiding from the steady rain, in the truck outside. "The wife and kids wanted to come up for the festival, and I was hoping to get some fishing done. The fellow at the lodge up the road said he had no vacancies and suggested we try here. Said you were the only other place with water access."

I smile at the mention of Roar. Not that he hadn't been on my mind, but it's nice to find out he's thinking about me too.

"I do, but I have to tell you that I haven't had a chance to put in a proper boat ramp yet, and the dock is in need of repairs."

"No worries," he says, lifting a hand to his face and scratching the stubble on his jaw. "Fellow over at Jackson ' s Point already mentioned that. Told me I could drop the boat in the water there. I just wanted to get the rooms sorted before I head out."

"Feel free to have a look out back," I offer. "You're more than welcome to tie off your boat here during your stay, but I'll leave that decision to you. Next time you stop by, we'll have both the dining room up and running and a place for you to launch your boat."

"Sounds good. Thanks," he replies, grinning as he pulls his baseball cap down over his eyes and heads out the door and into the rain.

Not bad for my first week.

It started raining hard late last night, and I kept my fingers crossed while checking the units this morning to look for potential leaks. Roar must've done a good job on the roof, because there was no sign of moisture in any of the rooms, not even unit seven. I spent a few hours touching up the fresh painting here and there, but by the end of the morning, I was able to put clean linens and fresh towels in the last of the rooms. I couldn't keep the smile off my face as I looked in the bathroom.

I found a small local business that offered organic soaps and shampoos in small, reusable, customized containers. I even ordered a box of small handmade bath bombs to put in each of the bathrooms, and the lemon and thyme scent of the bombs and soap leave a fresh and unobtrusive lingering scent.

I love the idea of doing my bit to minimize waste and reduce my environmental footprint, and it fits with the sparse and rustic decor of the rooms.

Officially open for business.

-

The bar, of course, is still a work in progress, although I managed to bring some of the casual, rustic feel in there as well. Uncle Sam had quite a collection of deer sheds in one of the empty bedrooms upstairs that I scrubbed in the bathtub. I put one on each of the eight small dining tables, and added an eclectic collection of salt and pepper shakers I found here and there.

The space has been otherwise decluttered and stripped, except for the floor. A grey, industrial carpet, which turns out to be even dingier than I first thought now that the grime is off the windows, needs a solution. My preference is to strip it before I even consider opening the kitchen, but I don't know what I'll find underneath.

With my weekend open, I decide there is no time like the present, and grab a claw hammer from the house. Picking the furthest corner, mostly hidden from view by the bar, I drop to my knees. The baseboard easily comes away in one piece, and I slip the claws of the hammer under the edge of the carpet. Pulling back, evidence of old, wide floorboards underneath becomes visible.

"Yes!" My voice bounces through the empty space as I sit back, staring at what I'd picked as my best case scenario.

I didn't hear anyone come in, but a soft chuckle from behind alerts me I'm not alone, and I swing my head around.

"Jesus, Roar…" I gasp, grabbing for my chest. Second time this week that man has me jump from my skin, and the second time he does so with a big grin showing through his beard. "Stop doing that!"

119

His response is silent, but his gaze is intense, the grey beanie pulled low over his eyes.

Turning my back on his big body looming over me, I start tugging at the carpet with my hands.

"What are you doing here anyway?" I ask, as I reveal more of the beautiful old wood underneath.

"Well…" He draws the word out. "I may be a bit early. Still—the floor? Now?"

"Early for what?" I abandon my task, wipe my hands on my old cargos and push myself off the floor. When I look up in his face, his eyebrows are raised high.

"Music festival. Opening night dinner ring a bell?"

I recall the incident with Kyle and Matt outside last week, but I figured Roar just jumped in to save me from dealing with Kyle. I never took that as an invite. Hell, he just barked something about taking me to get that asshole to back off. Didn't look at me once, let alone asked me.

Well and truly steamed, I plant my hands on my hips and take a step closer. Of course, now I have to tilt my head even further back to look him in the eye.

"Well, if that's your idea of asking someone out, you can't be getting around much. No woman in her right mind would've taken that as an invitation."

"I do all right."

His answer, like the man himself, is cocky and provocative, and I don't know whether to laugh or punch him in the nuts. I compromise by shaking my head in exasperation. I don't know why I'm surprised. Riordan Doyle is not exactly the kind of man to lay on the charm and show up with flowers or anything. More the type to knock you out and silently drag you back to his cave by the hair.

120

"Was hoping you could give me a hand," he says, pulling off the knit hat and revealing hair that looks like someone went at it with hedge shears.

The glorious copper and silver waves are now cropped close to the skull over his right ear, but still long in the back. A ditch runs from front to back in the center and on the left side it looks like he tried—and failed—to match the trim on the right. I clap my hand over my mouth to stop the giggle that threatens to escape.

With his lips pressed tight, he produces electric clippers he'd been holding in his hand. Not quite ready to go without the security of my hand pressed against my lips, I reach out with my other hand and take it from him.

"Upstairs bathroom," I mumble from behind my fingers, stepping back to let him pass and lead the way up the stairs.

"What were you thinking?" I finally trust myself to whisper, once I have him seated on the edge of the bathtub with a towel around his shoulders. The question earns me another glare that is now almost at eye level. The hazel is even more pronounced this close by, contrasting with the darker freckles on his suntanned face.

"Thinking I'd get myself cleaned up for dinner." The sardonic tone makes it hard to keep composure. I press my lips together so hard, trying to keep in the snicker, that I inadvertently blow a raspberry, straight at him.

"Oh my God, I'm so sorry," I ramble, mortified, while he calmly covers his face with a corner of the towel.

I can't recall many times when I wished this hard for the ground to swallow me up. I want to puke and step back, when one of his hands grabs me by the hip and holds me firmly in place.

Then I hear it, at first a low rumble growing in his chest, and finally he lets the towel drop, throws his head back, and his loud, booming laugh makes the walls of my little bathroom vibrate. All I can do is stare at the sheer perfection of the man in front of me. I'm already a sucker for a good smile, but a good boisterous laugh filled with a joy, which comes from the very pit of the belly is a thing of beauty.

At some point while he laughs and I stare, his other hand has found its way to my hip and I can feel the tips of his fingers leave indentations in my flesh. A corner of my mouth lifts when he finally lifts his head and his eyes, now dancing in amusement, find mine.

"Come here," he says in an almost whisper.

"I am here," I answer in kind.

"Closer," he orders, spreading his legs wider and pulling me in. "Now bend down."

My eyes don't waver from his. Not even when my mouth finds his. I'm tentative: testing the firmness of his lips with light pressure from mine. He doesn't force, he simply returns the rhythm I give him. The only evidence of a struggle for control is in the flex of his fingers on my hips, and the low rumble of appreciation when I let the tip of my tongue taste him.

It's not until my hands find their way into his hair that I remember where I am and what I'm supposed to be doing.

"Your hair," I mumble against his lips, before straightening up.

"Right," he says, a smirk slowly forming on his mouth. "And just so you know? Anytime you want to swap spit, you just have to ask."

Roar

I'm leaning against the passenger side of the truck, still smiling, when Leelo walks out, closing the door behind her. She made me wait for her to have a quick shower after she cleaned up the massacre I made of my hair, and true to her word, here she is only twenty minutes later. The pretty short-sleeved blouse with the wide scoop neck, leaving her colourful arms and a good amount of creamy cleavage visible, draws my attention first. Obviously. Oh, I don't miss the touch of makeup she put on her face, or the fitted jeans and familiar pink Converse shoes she has on. But the one thing that holds my attention is the softly tousled hair.

"I like this," I tell her, reaching out to tug on a soft curl. A subtle smile forms on her lips.

"A calculated risk," she offers. "It may last a few hours if the next downpour holds off, but the slightest hint of rain will wash those curls right out."

"I see. Guess I'll have to make sure to get you home at a decent time and keep you dry until then."

Leelo's mouth slowly falls open, but I don't clue in until she suddenly bursts out laughing as I help her into the cab of my truck.

"You know you have the worst lines, right?" she chuckles, letting me buckle her in.

"Didn't know it was a line until you pointed it out, just now," I counter, my torso still leaning into the truck. "What I do know is that you have a dirty mind." In case she feels she has to protest, I cup her jaw in my hand and kiss her hard. Before I let her go, with my nose almost touching hers, I quietly add; "I like that."

-

The parking lot at the community centre is already pretty packed when we get there.

The centre allows for both an indoor and outdoor venue, since the sports fields are right behind the main building. Dinner will most likely be inside this year because of today's forecast of rain, and just in case, a large tent is covering the main stage outside.

We're barely in the door, when I see Charlie waving frantically from a table in the far corner. I'd offered to pick her up, but she'd waved me off, insisting she'd already arranged for a ride. She must've kept an eye on the door for us. The woman doesn't miss much. I put my hand in the small of Leelo's back to try and guide her around the hall, but the woman apparently has different plans.

"Wait," she says, stopping in her tracks. "I see Charlotte. Let's go say hello." Without giving me a chance to say anything, she grabs my hand and starts dragging me in the direction I was planning to go anyway.

"Hey!" She waves at everyone assembled at the table, and I hold back a chuckle at her somewhat clumsy antics. It's cute as fuck.

"Let go, you big lug," Charlie barks at me, pulling Leelo's hand from mine. "Let me give the girl a hug."

A heavy wind could blow Charlie over, but that frail exterior holds a powerful punch—as witnessed when she proceeds to smother Leelo in her spindly arms.

"She can't breathe, Charlie," I warn her, earning me a sharp look, but when she reluctantly lets go and Leelo turns to face me, I'm surprised to see shock on *her* face.

"Charlie? This is your *Charlie?*" she stage whispers, leaning in to me.

"Yeah," I point out. "How did you not know that?" She stares at me in disbelief.

"Maybe because the one time you mentioned a Charlie, it was some lewd comment about cleaning her pipes," she hisses in my ear, when I reach around her to pull out a chair. It's loud enough to draw the attention of a few people at the table.

"Oh my," Charlie giggles coquettish, most likely for the benefit of her ride, Bob Duran, former commander of the Wawa OPP detachment, and the most sought after bachelor on the local seniors' scene.

I push down gently on Leelo's rigid shoulders, forcing her to sit as I lean down to whisper in her ear.

"There's that dirty mind again."

Taking my own chair beside her, I shoot a quick glance at the deep red blush on her face. When I try to put my hand on her knee under the table a second later, she forcefully shoves it away.

"Never mind that boy, Leelo. Communication was never his strong suit." Charlie, sitting on my other side, leans over my plate to talk to her. "Chip off the old block," she adds, causing me to roll my eyes, because I know the story that follows well. I've heard it often enough. "My Patrick used as few words as humanly possible, and those he did use, mostly came out as grunts." She takes a quick sip of her wine before continuing. "In fact, as the priest at our wedding was reciting the vows for us to repeat, he had to make Patrick do it three times before he got it right. Every time he'd recite; *I, Patrick Fergus Doyle, take thee, Charlotte Mae Stephens to be my lawfully wedded wife,* Patrick would say; *I take thee, Charlie.*" I chuckle, along with everyone else, at her attempt to match Dad's thick Irish brogue I remember so well, but notice Leelo is not even smiling. Her mouth is slack and her startled eyes find mine. "Anyway," my mother says with a soft smile. "When Father James stopped him the third time, Patrick barked loudly that anyone who didn't know our names by now had no place being in that church. The crowd took some time to settle down, but he finally got it right after that. He never called me by any other name than Charlie, so it's not a surprise Riordan here—when he started talking—called me that as well. Exactly like his dad."

This time, when I slip my hand under the tablecloth and cover Leelo's knee, she doesn't even budge. Instead she turns her face to me and whispers, "*Your mother?*"

I shrug. It honestly didn't occur to me to tell her. Other than my time in the military, Wawa has always been my home. Everyone here knows me—knows my family. It's never really required explanation before.

"I'm sorry," Leelo directs at Charlie. "I guess the last name threw me a bit." My mother chuckles a little before turning serious.

"I'm sure," she says, patting Leelo's arm. "For all the years I had with Patrick, I was known simply as Charlie Doyle—names Patrick gave me. When he passed away, that part of me died with him, so I reverted back to my maiden name. I helped me cope with the loss, reminding me I was a person in my own right."

It's clear Leelo is affected by her words, as she covers Charlie's hand on her arm with her own.

The loud squeal of the sound system startles everyone into silence, as the chair of the music festival committee clears his throat to announce the official start of the evening's program, and servers appear at every table with trays of soup.

By the time dessert is served, Leelo is engaged in a rather passionate discussion about recycling with one of the town's councilman on her other side, and my mother taps me on the shoulder.

"I like her," she says, smiling sweetly.

"I got that." I nod sternly, trying to divert the direction I can see this conversation taking. Charlie, as always, is undeterred.

"No, you don't get it," she insists, putting a hand on my arm. Little does she know, that although I play dumb anytime I think it benefits me, I *get it* all too well. "I like her—for *you*."

And there it is, folks. Date one, and my mother has me safely attached to the first unwitting female. Her favourite pastime of spinning romantic fantasies is usually limited to herself, perhaps one of her friends, but it's been decades since I've given her opportunity to focus on me. The reason is simple; I don't date.

Except, here I am; not only on a date, but on a double date with my mother.

ELEVEN

*The urge to forcibly hold her together when she comes
undone, is hard to resist.*

Roar

When the din of cutlery clanging dies down, and the
last plates are removed, a familiar voice comes over the
speakers. Time for Kyle Thompson, the festival's biggest
sponsor, to give his annual welcome speech. This would
normally be the moment where I'd quietly excuse myself
to Charlie, who is used to me disappearing, but tonight
Leelo is my date, and I'll be damned if I leave her sitting
by herself.

I feel her tense up beside me when she notices Kyle.

At first it's easy to tune out the self-serving drivel he
feeds the crowd, but then something he says draws my
attention.

"I'm excited at the boost this festival gives our local
economy. For the first time, this past year, the number of
small businesses closing their doors was outnumbered by
new ones being opened. I'm proud of that
accomplishment, and I'm pleased to note our latest new
business owner decided to grace us with her presence
tonight," he says, and I snap my head in his direction to
find him staring across the hall at Leelo.

The fucking bastard. I move to shove back my chair, but find myself held back by the women on either side of me. Charlie squeezes the hand she lands on my shoulder and Leelo digs her nails in my thigh.

"Lilith," Kyle calls out with a smirk, beckoning Leelo with his hand. "Join me up here, won't you?"

That's it. I may be pinned to my seat, but no one is keeping my mouth shut, so I use it.

"Hey, Kyle!" I call out, surprising him and his eyes slide to me. "Don't you think it's time to get your own date, buddy? Quit trying to steal mine!" I drop my arm around Leelo's shoulder and pull her close, kiss the side of her head, while keeping my eyes locked on him.

Someone starts laughing and claps, and pretty soon others follow, drowning out anything else coming from his mouth.

"Can we get out of here?" Leelo asks quietly, tilting her head back to look at me.

I hate seeing her eyes are wet, but when I lift a hand to her face, she quickly turns her head away. On my other side, I hear Charlie's deep sigh. That's when I realize she's not just upset with that asshole, but also with me.

"Sure," I tell her, dropping my arm from around her and feeling a twist in my gut. Kyle may have been the first to try and make her feel uncomfortable, but I played right into his hand. My attempt to put him in his place only resulted in putting a bigger target on Leelo. Of course she's upset.

How badly I fucked up becomes clear before we even have a chance to say our goodbyes, when a familiar scent hits my nose, seconds before I feel a hand rub over my head. The uncomfortable knot in my stomach only twists tighter.

"I'm impressed," Patti practically purrs over my shoulder, the smell of alcohol heavy on her breath. "You managed that all by yourself?"

Every eye at the table is turned in our direction.

Son of a bitch. For a night that started so promising, it sure has gone to shit in every possible way.

I purposely keep my back to Patti as I push up from the table, turning to Leelo instead.

"I don't think you've met Patti yet, have you?" I ask, holding out my hand so I can help her to her feet.

Leelo

Talk about mortifying.

First Kyle, then Roar, and now…Patti? So much for easing quietly into a new community, more like being dropped naked in the middle of town square on market day.

It's not that I haven't heard her name mentioned once or twice, I know she works at the lodge part-time, but for some reason I'd envisioned someone a lot older. Not the well put together, intimidatingly pretty, and most definitely tipsy blonde, whose scrutinizing, bloodshot eyes take in my appearance as I put my hand in Roar's and get to my feet. Standing feels a little better, a little less intimidating, but it also makes me conscious of the stark contrast I provide to the much taller, and way better dressed woman, who seems much more suited to the towering man between us.

I've been here before, in a moment like this, where everyone looks at you with a mix of curiosity and pity when you find out how blind you've been.

"I haven't," I finally respond, struggling to keep my voice strong and even. "Hi, I'm Lilith Talbot," I introduce myself with a bright smile, not waiting for Roar to do the honours. God only knows what would come out of his mouth, and I've had about all the discomfort I can handle tonight. As it is, the air is already thick with tension.

"Patti Jackson," she says, giving my hand a squeeze as she leans her body into the man beside her. "Ssso nice to finally meet you. I'm actually—"

"An old friend," Roar finishes for her, effectively cutting the woman off. "She was married to my best friend and helps out at the lodge. And Leelo is the new owner of the Whitefish Motel."

A few random pieces fall into place. Matt had briefly mentioned something about Roar naming the lodge after a friend who passed away. Given her last name, this must be his widow? Yet judging from the way she's leaning against him while eyeing me, something tells me that may not be all she is to him.

"We were just heading out," Roar says, grabbing my hand in his and sidestepping Patti, who briefly wavers on her feet. He stops to drop a kiss on Charlie's cheek and barely gives me a chance to do the same before he drags me out of there.

Not a word is exchanged as he pulls me along to where his truck is parked. Only when he's safely buckled me in, does he briefly rest his forehead against mine.

"That was fucked up," he whispers. "Let me get you out of here."

Dropping a peck on my lips, he backs out, shuts the door, and rounds the truck to get in behind the wheel.

The drive is silent. I open my mouth a few times to say something, but stop myself each time. Better to take a little time to process. Lord knows there's enough there. Not the least of which the woman with the ridiculously tiny waist and the firm ass.

No tight heart-shaped ass here—more like an oversized beanbag.

I know I let myself get swept away with the unexpected attention he gave me, but tonight showed me just how little I know about him. And maybe even more importantly, how easily my newly found confidence is damaged. I'm clearly not the devil-may-care independent woman I try to be. Not yet anyway.

So when the truck pulls into the motel driveway, I already have my hand on the door and a polite goodbye on my lips. Distance. I need a little distance to regain my perspective.

"Thanks for dinner," I rattle off, as I launch myself from the truck the moment it rolls to a stop. All I hear is Roar telling me to wait, but I'm not about to. The tears have already started rolling and there's no way I can hold back the deluge now. A mix of old and new frustration, confusion and hurt come pouring out. Tonight's experience so close to the one from years ago that I thought I'd long left behind me, that the feelings evoked by either blend together in an indistinguishable wave of emotion.

I struggle to fit the key in the door of the bar, when I sense more than hear him come up behind me. Mostly because I'm sobbing too hard to hear anything. He doesn't touch me but his hand reaches around, takes the key from mine, and easily slides it home in the lock. *Fuck him*. Now with unreasonable anger thrown in the mix, I push through the opened door and stomp right through the bar to the sanctuary of my home beyond, determined not to care what happens behind me.

"Go away," I call out blindly, as I flop on the couch and pull the quilt over my head. I'm tired, I'm worn, and I just want to be left alone. When I don't hear anything in response, I safely assume I'm alone and finally completely let loose, burying my cries in the couch pillow.

It's surprising how cathartic it can be from time to time, to fling open the floodgates and hold nothing back. Like a good cleansing, letting the toxins just pour out of your body. Everything, past and present emotions tripping the other like domino stones as the neat rows of tight control slowly disappear. And with each stone falling, a little pocket of tension is relieved.

By the time I've purged enough to be able to draw a normal breath, the pillow is soaked, my eyes are burning, and my head is pounding with the beginnings of a doozy of a headache. *Lovely*. But a weight has lifted and my body is relaxed as I drag the quilt away from my slobbery face.

"Wipe with this."

The sudden sound of his voice, along with the cold wet cloth he drops on my face, scares the shit out of me.

134

"Again?" I screech; scrambling up in a sitting position with the quilt clutched to my chest. Roar just manages to catch the washcloth as it falls to the floor and instead of handing it back; he uses it to gently mop up the mess on my face himself. Stripped of any remaining dignity after the night I've had, I let him, keeping my eyes closed until he's done.

"Drink this," he orders, placing a mug with something warm in my hands.

"*Bossy*," I mutter, but I dutifully bring what smells like tea to my lips and take a sip, and then another.

"When I came back from my third tour in Afghanistan, injured and escorting the dead body of my best friend home, Kyle Thompson had finally found his way into my wife's bed. That day I lost everything."

My eyes shoot up only to find Roar staring into the distance, lost to his thoughts.

"I'm sorry," I whisper, wrapping my hands tighter around the warm mug.

"It's a game to him. Always has been, since we were friends in high school. Everything had to be a competition. I usually just shrugged it off, but Jenny changed that. He used her, and when he got what he wanted, dropped her to deal with the ravages of our marriage. Any other time we might have found our way through, but with what I'd just been through, the stretch just wasn't there." He finally turns his head to face me, and it's all I can do not to reach out and let my fingers run along his cheek and beard. "What I'm trying to tell you is that I have lived here my whole life. There's a lot of history, and some of it might bubble to the surface before I have a chance to catch you up. Tonight's a prime example of that." He unfolds one of

135

my hands, still holding the mug, and brings it up to his lips, kissing the back of my fingers. His eyes never leave mine.

"And Patti?" I can't stop the question from forming. "Is she an example of that as well?" I hear the deep sigh and instinctively pull my hand from his, tucking it protectively around my waist, but I don't back down. "I'm sorry if I'm overstepping, but I got the impression there's some history there that is not quite as simple as just an old friend. I haven't always had my eyes open in the past, and the consequences have done damage, which is why clarity on that particular subject is important to me."

The silence that follows is unsettling, and I almost get up to start pacing when I feel his hand on my knee.

"There was more. We were both stuck in our loss, not looking for anything new, and occasionally turned to each other for—"

"I get it," I say quickly, cutting him off, not really wanting to hear more. But he twists in his seat and cups my face in his hands, forcing me to look at him.

"I ended it quite a while ago. Could be I sensed it had started meaning more to her than it did to me. Her friendship is more valuable to me."

"I get it," I repeat, before softly adding, "I'm just not sure she does."

Roar

Her face is still red and puffy from her earlier meltdown, but her red-rimmed eyes are steady on mine as I gently stroke my thumbs over her cheeks.

I'm not sure why it felt important to let her work through that emotional collapse on her own, or how I managed to keep from interfering, but forcing myself to stay in the background while listening to her come apart was pretty fucking brutal. But I can feel the calm coming off her now, even after plodding through a few difficult topics.

Christ, how I hate talking, but after tonight, I feel I owe her at least that.

"I know," I finally say.

Not easy to finally admit something I didn't want to see. If not for Leelo broaching the topic, I would never have gotten into the whole Patti thing, but now that it's out there, it's a bit of a relief.

Her hands come up to cover mine, bracketing her face, as I drop my forehead to hers.

I'm wiped. My body is buzzing with awareness at the smell and feel of her, and I'm sure is game to explore those further, but my mind feels sluggish, like it's been through the wringer. I'd prefer to pay attention to what I'm doing, instead of letting instinct take over and blindly fucking that soft, warm body on the couch.

"I gotta go," I say instead, pressing a kiss to her lips. But when I pull away, her hands shoot out and tangle in my beard, tugging me back. My own fingers slide back, twisting into her hair until her head tilts further back, and I slam my mouth down on hers.

Her lips open immediately and my tongue invades, the hot throb of my blood flaming the surge of hunger. It

137

feels like I'll burst out of my skin as I devour her mouth. *Fucking hell,* she tastes good.

Feels good too, as her body twists, and with her fingers still tangled in my beard, drags me down on top of her, without ever taking her mouth off mine. The next second, my hand is tugging down her neckline and bra, to lift one lush tit from its confines. The sharp sting when I pull my beard from her hold barely registers, when I bend my head to run my tongue over the creamy flesh.

I pluck lightly at the tight pink nipple with my teeth, before taking it between my lips.

"*Yesss...*" she hisses, her body restlessly shifting under mine.

Fuck! Not like this.

I drop my head to her chest and try to regain some control.

"I really should go," I repeat, feeling her body freeze at my words.

I lift my head and drop a kiss on her nipple, before gently covering her back up. She tries to scramble upright, her face a tight mask, but I shift my body to keep her in place.

"Been quite a while, sweetheart," I explain, my nose just inches from hers, even though she avoids looking into my eyes. "Combine that with the kind of night we've had, I know I wouldn't be able to do you justice," I push on, pressing my hard-on against her hip and a thumb under her chin, until her eyes finally meet mine. "I know you feel that."

When I finally push myself off the couch and let her sit up, her sass returns when she treats me to a dramatic roll of the eyes. I'm grinning as I walk toward the door.

"I'm not blowing you off, Leelo," I promise, stopping to turn around in the doorway.

She's pulled the quilt back over her and is holding it bunched in her fists, under her chin. Her eyes sparkle bright blue, her hair is mussed, and her face is deeply flushed. She needs to know she's much more than a quick grope on the couch. So I tell her.

"I'm saving you for a special occasion."

TWELVE

Her soft curves contrast as well as complement her strong spirit.

Leelo

Son of a bitch!

I drop the pile of dirty sheets I just collected from the empty units on the ground outside the shed. I normally keep the separate doors to both the storage space and the laundry room locked. Guests are told when they check in that they can come borrow the key if they wish to use the facilities. Not that anyone in their right mind would walk off with the equipment. The two washers and dryer are massive industrial-sized machines, which is why I'm dragging the sheets over here. I can wash them all at once, instead of running the regular washer and dryer at the house all day to get them clean.

But this morning the laundry door is hanging open, and judging by the state of the doorpost and lock, I'd say someone was eager to get in.

Crap. After the debacle Friday night, I'd had such a good weekend.

I may have woken up Saturday morning feeling all kinds of hungover and sorry for myself, without the

141

benefit of getting drunk first, but after my second cup of coffee things started turning around.

Shaking off the drama and shoving Riordan Doyle firmly from my mind, I grabbed my keys and headed to the Valu-Mart in town. My objective was their garden centre. The large planters in front of the motel, I had painstakingly rid of weeds, needed something.

Late afternoon, a sore back, buckets of sweat, and two hundred fifty dollars in annuals and potting soil later, the facade of the motel was sufficiently beautified to put a bright smile on my face.

I just stepped back to admire my work when two cars rolled onto the parking lot. A group of travelers stopping for the night on their way to Thunder Bay. Apparently with the festival in town in full swing, mine was the first 'Vacancy' they'd seen.

That night I slept like the dead; my body deliciously sore from a productive day and four of my units rented out.

Yesterday I spent ripping up the carpet from the bar. Disgusting work, and at the end of the day, I had decades of dirt covering my body and my fingertips were bloody stumps from pulling up a truckload of staples. The wooden boards I uncovered were worth every last drop of blood and sweat, though. So Sunday ended much the same way Saturday had, with me rolling sore and satisfied into bed.

My guests left yesterday, but I didn't want to stop what I was doing and clean the rooms. That had been on the agenda for this morning. I got up early so I could get it done before Roar shows up to get going on the dock.

And now this, putting a damper on my good mood.

I gingerly nudge the door open wider with my foot, and at first glance all I notice is laundry detergent covering the floors, the folding table. But when I shove the door all the way open, the stench hits me. It's so thick and putrid; I slap my hand over my mouth and back right up before I lose my breakfast. *Jesus.* Smells like something died in there.

Walking far enough away to get some fresh air, I contemplate my options. There really aren't any, other than going in there, finding and removing the cause of that godawful stench. I take a few deep breaths, and yank the neck of my T-shirt over my mouth and nose, before stepping back inside.

Good God. Determined not to let the smell get to me, I focus on breathing through my mouth, while I search for the source of that pungent aroma.

Nothing is immediately obvious, but then I see the doors of the two washers, as well as the dryer, are closed. I know I left those slightly open so they wouldn't start smelling musty. Flicking on the light for a better look, I spot dark smears on the white enamel of the dryer, and something is visible against the inside of the porthole door. A quick glance at the two other machines shows the same dark smears on the top-loading lids. Something tells me this is not going to be pretty, but with one hand pressing my shirt against my mouth and nose, still I reach out to open the dryer door.

The instant the latch releases, it swings open and something unrecognizable falls half out of the opening. A wave of rancid air has tears blur my vision, and I have to blink a few times before I'm able to identify an eye, dangling from the socket of what looks to be a deer head, by a single strand.

The violent surge of my stomach has me running out the door, away from the sick carnage, and straight into a solid mass of muscle.

"What the hell?" Roar's voice barely penetrates the pounding in my ears as I bend over and deposit my breakfast all over his dusty boots.

-

"A prank?"

I'm well aware that my voice is pitched at a level that could be considered painful to some, but I don't give a flying fuck.

Some sicko decided to stuff a carved up deer carcass in my washers and dryer, which is disgusting and vile enough by itself—but it also rendered the machines useless, and this damn OPP officer calls it a prank?

"You call that a prank?" I repeat, a little less shrill this time.

Roar's large hand wraps around the back of my neck. I'm not sure if it's to calm me down or to prevent me from charging the snot-nosed, uniformed punk who seems to find the whole situation quite amusing.

"Ma'am," Constable Williams drawls in a condescending tone that has me grind my teeth. "I'm sure it's not something you're accustomed to, coming from the city, but it wouldn't be the first time some kids played around with roadkill for a giggle."

I bite my lip to keep from screaming my frustration, but apparently Roar has heard enough as well.

"Hardly the same as poking a stick at a dead opossum on the side of the road," he growls, as he moves me out of

144

the way and takes a step closer to the much smaller officer, who wisely loses the smirk from his face. "A full report better be on your staff sergeant's desk by tomorrow. Bill said he'd pop in this week anyway, it's been a while since we've been fishing."

The blanching of the young punk's face is almost comical as he backs away, mumbling an apology of sorts.

It had taken the OPP cruiser forty minutes to get here. Enough time for my nausea to subside and the shivers to stop. I tried apologizing to Roar for puking all over his footwear, but he waved it off. Unperturbed he grabbed the hose and rinsed his boots off, while I gathered up the sheets I dropped and carried them inside the house to wash. The subsequent wait, for the constable to show, had not done the overall mood any good.

"Grab me some garbage bags?" Roar turns to me after watching the police cruiser drive off, his tone still angry.

Not in the best of moods myself, I swing around wordlessly and stomp off inside. Grabbing the box of bags behind the bar, I also pick up the work gloves and bucket I used yesterday, before marching back out, and without looking at Roar, head in the direction of the shed.

"*Fuck me.*" I hear him mutter behind me as he follows. "I'll take care of it," he barks when he catches up with me, trying to snatch the bucket from my hands.

I'm not sure why I'm suddenly so angry. Perhaps it's the fucked up events of this morning and the realization that no matter how much cleaning we do, my laundry facilities are a write-off, but I don't think that's all. It's Roar I'm pissed with.

All weekend I've shoved him to the back of my mind, determined not to obsess about the fact I didn't hear from him after he left me hot and bothered, not to mention emotionally wrung out, last time I saw him. My initial relief, when I quite literally, ran into him, is fast disappearing at his less than companionable mood. The last thing I need is him ordering me around.

"Shit, woman!" he snaps, letting go after a fruitless tug of war on the stupid bucket. "I said I'd take care of it. Why the fuck are you so stubborn?"

I can almost feel the steam shooting from my ears as I swing around and fling the bucket at him.

"Stubborn?" I start, poking a finger in his chest. "You know what? I've had it! You're just another typical asshole, who can only feel the size of his dick by going caveman on some hapless creature he can order around, yet feels it shrivel in the presence of a self-sufficient woman, who knows what she wants and when she wants it!"

I don't realize I'm waving my arms around like a crazy person until I find myself suddenly restrained, my front plastered to a, by now well-acquainted, chest and my hands pinned behind my back. My attempts to struggle free are easily thwarted by the steel bands of his arms that hold me in place.

"You done?"

Roar

It shouldn't, but the snarling, spitting, and royally pissed-off woman in my arms turns me on faster than a spark in a haystack.

"You done?" I grind out through clenched teeth and her body stills instantly.

She seems to have wasted all her energy on that spirited rant, because she doesn't answer, but I let go of her arms anyway. The moment I do, she steps away from me. All I get is a death glare before she turns on her heels.

I let her go, following her with my eyes as she walks off with her hands fisted at her side.

She's pissed all right.

I have some time to think as I stuff the rotting remains in garbage bags, fighting my gag reflex the entire time. By the time I remove my tools and lumber from the back of the truck, toss the garbage bags in, and drive the putrid load straight to the dump, I've come to the conclusion that, although the infuriating presentation left much to be desired, she may have a point.

Coming to the rescue is something I don't think about, I just do. It comes natural and it makes me feel good. I may grumble when Charlie calls me to fix something, but I'm pretty sure she keeps calling me because she knows I like doing it. And for reasons that are slowly becoming clearer, I like being that person for Leelo as well. Especially when something happens like this morning.

She scared the crap out of me when she came barrelling out of the shed, like the devil was on her heels, and when I saw what she'd been running from, the hairs on my arms stood on end. This wasn't some innocent prank, more like malicious attempt at scaring Leelo senseless for whatever reason. Something that worries me and I'm gonna do my damnedest to get to the bottom of.

What she's way off base on, is her assumption I'd rather have her be helpless than the capable person she's proving herself to be. It's her strength I find attractive, and I thought that would've been clear, but given that tirade, I'm thinking it might require reinforcing.

There's no sign of Leelo when I get back and hose down the laundry room, as well as the bed of my truck. For good measure, and because the stench is lingering, I strip down to my shorts, throw my clothes and boots in the bed of the truck and wash those down as well. Leaving them to dry in the sun, I fetch the wheelbarrow, load it up with my supplies, and head barefoot to the back of the property.

It isn't until I have dismantled the lopsided and rotting portion of the dock, that I spot Leelo. Wearing only a pair of cutoffs and a tank top, her pale legs stand out for their lack of colour. The tattoos covering her arms have clearly not made it that far. Yet. She's carrying two bottles in one hand, and keeps her gaze focused on the ground in front of her feet, allowing me a chance to observe.

There's something about the way she carries herself that is at the same time defiant and oddly self-conscious. Both even more obvious when her eyes peek up from under her lashes to find me staring, and immediately her back and shoulders straighten in a silent challenge.

"Hey," I throw out as a peace offering, when she gets close enough.

"Hey yourself," she replies, wading into the waist-deep water to hand me a beer. "Thought you deserved a cold drink after all that."

I keep my eyes on her as I take a long tug from the cold bottle to watch her do the same. While setting the bottle on the dock with one hand, I reach out with the other and slide it around her neck, pulling her close for a quick kiss on the lips, clearly surprising her. The instant I let her go, her free hand comes up to touch her lips.

"Tough day," I offer with a tilt of my mouth that grows into a full grin when she snorts unceremoniously in response.

"Ya think?"

And just like that, it seems like balance is restored, as we spend the rest of the afternoon working side by side.

It's not until much later, when it gets close to dinner time and I get ready to leave and check on the lodge, that she makes a subtle reference to this morning's scene.

"Lock everything tight after I leave," I tell her, pulling on my jeans over my wet shorts.

"There you go again," she says, amusement lacing her voice. "Bossy—again."

I straighten up to find her quickly averting her eyes from where she was staring at my chest. The grin is involuntary. I'm far from gym-worthy, and I show every one of my forty-five years, but I can't help feeling pretty good about the sturdy, work-honed body I have.

"Concerned," I correct her, tugging on a strand of hair that escaped her ponytail. She looks good. Healthy and a little sunburned, with a relaxed smile on her pretty face.

"If you say so."

149

"I do," I confirm. "Although I will admit it might come across as bossy."

"So noted." She smiles as she looks down at her feet. "And ditto," she adds, glancing up before clarifying; "my impression of a banshee this morning."

"Point taken." For a moment the two of us stand there, just grinning at the other. "I should get going," I finally say, although I really don't feel like going. "Call me if you need me."

She lifts up on tiptoes, puts her one hand in the middle of my chest, and with the other pulls down on my beard until her mouth can reach.

"I will," she promises with a brush of her lips against mine, before she turns and heads inside, her round ass beckoning me with every step.

It takes a will of steel.

THIRTEEN

All it takes is the ghost of a smile in her voice to sustain me.

Leelo

To say I slept soundly last night would be a lie.

Every time I closed my eyes. I could see that bloodied head toppling out of the dryer. The dark swollen tongue sticking out of the side of its mouth, and that eyeball swaying from a thin string of tissue. Each time my eyes would shoot wide open and I'd lay staring at the ceiling in the dark.

It's funny how suddenly you analyze every little noise you never noticed before: the light creak of the house settling around you, that slight scrape of a branch against the outside wall. I did exactly that until I finally fell asleep, exhausted, as the first light of morning softly filtered into my room.

Needless to say, coffee is my friend this morning. Although last night I wished for a motel filled with guests, right now I'm glad for the absolute silence as I sit on the steps of the little porch at the side of the house, sipping the fresh brew.

I can't see the work we did on the dock yesterday from here. It's just on the other side of that copse of trees jutting into the water. From this side of the property, I have a pretty decent view in the opposite direction, where the early morning mist comes rising off the water. Already feels like it might be a scorcher today.

Roar said he'd be back today. We managed to shore up the remaining fixed part of the old dock and replaced some boards that were rotted. He already hauled a stack of lumber to the waterside yesterday and mentioned bringing over four large barrels today. I didn't question him, he generally seems to know what he's doing, but last night I did Google some DIY pages online to educate myself. He mentioned something about getting the barrels framed today, and at least now I know what the hell he's talking about.

It'll be nice, once it's done, to just take my morning coffee out on the dock and watch the day wake up.

We worked well together. That is, when I wasn't staring at his mostly naked body. Who knew that chest hair could be so goddamn sexy? He's not covered in heavy fur, thank God, but he's not baby-butt bare either. David was, and the odd hair that would grow on that milk white chest he would pluck. David would probably have been well-served with a good mat of hair to hide his weak chest.

No weak chest on Roar. No scrawny arms either. A workman's body with big hands and strong long legs, and to my surprise, he had a decent tan on him. For some reason I'd expected the pale skin associated with redheads.

It was hard not to stare at his chest. Every now and then, the sunlight would play off the water droplets clinging to the silver and rust coloured curls, and I'd be so mesmerized, Roar had to call my name twice to get my attention.

When my cup is empty, I hoist myself up on the railing. I desperately need a refill to clear the cobwebs, or at this rate, I won't be much help today at all.

The storm door creaks when I open it, and closes with a satisfying bang behind me. I'll always associate that sound with growing up. When my dad was still alive, we'd rent a cottage on a lake somewhere for a few weeks, and those inevitably had a storm door that squeaked. Something my mother loathed but my dad insisted on. As an only child, vacation time was precious to me, because it would mean Dad got to spend time with me. He doted on me. Where my mother was constantly trying to improve me, my father adored me just the way I was. I know he'd be proud if he could see me now.

The unexpected wave of emotion blurs my vision, and I wipe impatiently at my eyes and nose. Lack of sleep, that's all it is.

I'm pouring myself another coffee when my landline rings. My eyes shoot to the small clock on the stove to see it's barely seven.

"Whitefish Motel," I answer.

"Leelo?" Roar's voice rumbles over the line. "Is everything all right?"

"Yeah...why?"

"You sound upset."

"Nah. This is my normal morning voice," I joke, hoping he'll drop the subject.

"Something to look forward to," he fires back, and I can hear the smile in his voice.

"Promises, promises."

153

I honestly don't know where that came from. One minute I'm bawling in my coffee because I miss my dad so much, and the next, I'm joking and flirting with a man I didn't even know six weeks ago. And flirting? Last time I tried that was in high school when I tried getting Jeff Stokes' attention by showing off my dance skills. Problem was, I had none, and it resulted in a trip to the emergency room and a cast for six weeks. I gave up on it then.

"You're killing me here," he growls, making me grin even bigger. I may have picked up some skills over the years after all.

"You're the one who called at seven in the morning."

"Yes, right. And that kills me too. I was planning to head out to your place in an hour or so, but it appears three of my guests are having problems with their boats. I've gotta work on getting those fixed and back out on the water as soon as possible."

"Sure, of course," I reply immediately, but I have to fight the wave of disappointment washing over me.

"If I don't make it out there today, then tomorrow?"

"Tomorrow is fine. Gives me a chance to run into town for supplies today. Good luck with the boats." I put as much cheer as I can muster into my voice.

"Thanks." I hear him clear his through before he continues, "And Leelo?"

"Yeah?"

"I'd rather be there."

I open my mouth to say something back—probably *me too,* or something equally stupid—when the soft click in my ear tells me he's already hung up.

I've barely put the phone down, when it starts ringing again. Convinced it's Roar calling back—who else would

154

it be at seven in the morning—I answer with a chuckle. "Miss me already?"

The heavy silence on the other side is a warning that it was clearly not who I thought it was.

"Hello?" I prompt, to which I finally get a response.

"Mom?"

"Gwen?"

"Last time I checked," comes the deadpan reply. The sarcasm is strong in my daughter.

"Hey, baby, how are you?" I know I'm gushing, but I can't seem to help myself. It always slips out before I can check it; in my eagerness to set the right tone in our somewhat strained relationship. And like always, I can almost hear the roll of her eyes at the endearment.

"Pretty sure I lost that title when I learned to pee on the potty, Mom, but I'm fine. Thanks." Her tone is snippy, as it often gets when everything I say seems to rub her exactly wrong. The harder I try, the more irritated she gets.

It's been months since I spoke to her. A conversation that did not go well, since my girl thinks I'm an irresponsible twat—and told me that in so many words—when I told her I was moving up here. It wasn't for lack of trying on my part. I must've left half a dozen messages since then, but so far without response.

Until now, and already tension crackles the air. Not a promising start.

"Who were you expecting?" she wants to know, an edge to her voice.

"Oh, just a friend," I offer dismissively, hoping to avoid deeper probing, but I should know better; Gwen rarely lets go when she gets a whiff of something.

"Must be some friend if you're on top of the phone at seven in the morning, waiting for their call."

And there it is, the accusation clear and the sting no less than all the times before, when she found ways to remind me of a brief period of time after her father left me. I'd been hurt and lonely, and my judgement had been temporarily absent when I tried forgetting my sorrow in the arms of another man. Or a few men. Not sure what I was thinking, but for a while I could feel less alone and a little more desirable.

I'm still not sure how she found out, but she did, and the whole experience left me labelled with a big scarlet letter on my chest. Never mind that her father had fucked around on me for a year before he finally decided to dump me for her.

I swallow hard, trying not to become defensive or even react to the clear taunt. I've been there, I've done that, and it's never worked out well for me.

"Are you on your way to work? How is it going?" I firmly change the subject.

Gwen found a great job, straight out of university. She's always been a bit of a tech nerd, and working with computers was a dream of hers.

"I am," she says after only a moment's hesitation. "The job's good. I'm still loving it."

"Great. That's great, honey. I'm glad."

"Yeah. Anyway, I talked to Matt over the weekend, we're helping Jess plan a surprise fiftieth for Dad, and he mentioned he'd been up to see you."

I bite down the bitter, "That's nice" that I'd like to vent at the perfect family picture she paints with just a few words. Instead, I settle for a non-committal hum.

"He says he really likes it up there."

"I'm glad," I say cautiously, not quite getting where this conversation is going.

"Yeah, well, I'm not," she counters, her voice raised and gathering steam. "He's talking about moving there, Mom. Quitting his job with Dad and buying some land. What have you been filling his head with? And who the hell is Roar? It's one thing for you to throw your life away in the middle of nowhere, but Matt has a future here, Mom. A future where in maybe ten years he'll take over Dad's company and be settled for life."

"Whoa..." I breathe out slowly, when her rant ends on a sob. "Hold your horses, kiddo. I know Matt really enjoyed himself, but I know nothing of him quitting his job or any plans to move up here. Are you sure he's not just fantasizing out loud?"

"Of course I am," she sniffs. "We got in a fight over it. This whole family is falling apart and all because you had to move all the way up there."

I could point out to her that the family fell apart long before that, and I was as much a victim to that as she was, but I've been down that road and I won't go there again. I understand her better than she thinks. Gwen has a strong, determined personality and she is harder on herself than I could ever be. It may not show on her polished surface but she feels deep too. She sees it as a weakness. The sensitive side she's fought her whole life to hide, but I know is there. Her defense has always been anger, and often that was, and is, directed at me. Probably because I see all of her.

"Sweetie," I try gently. "Don't forget you moved to Toronto yourself. Something I supported because it was what you wanted, but that doesn't mean I enjoyed it. Whatever I chose to do, or Matt might end up choosing for himself, distance doesn't make us less of a family, unless you let it."

"Whatever, Mom. I've gotta go, I'm at the office." Before I have a chance to say goodbye she's already hung up.

That's twice already today, and it's not even eight o'clock yet.

I'm thinking it might be a good morning to check out that tattoo place I saw in town.

-

"Nice sleeves." The girl behind the counter points at my arms and smiles. "Looking to add?"

"Maybe," I answer, shrugging my shoulders as I look around the place.

The place looks spotless. Smooth plywood paneling on the walls, polished to a high sheen, and plywood and steel dividers, creating a little privacy around each of the stations. The only contrast a single, deep plush wine-red couch and richly coloured tattoo designs decorating the walls. Very minimalistic and very attractive, as is the girl addressing me.

"You know this might not be the best time of year to get new ink, right? Sun exposure and all that?"

"Yeah, I know. I'm thinking of something small, though. Simple. Something that would be hidden from the sun," I say, thinking out loud as I pull the binder, open on the counter, toward me, an idea forming on the spot. It doesn't take me long to find an example, since it's a tattoo I've seen quite often. "See this one? I like that concept, except I'd like it customized."

It takes me only a minute to explain what I want, and a further five for Ginnie, as the girl introduces herself, to sketch.

"Where are you thinking?" she wants to know.

"Over my heart." Is my immediate answer.

Roar

It's taken up all fucking morning to replace the fuel lines on three of the outboard motors.

At first it looked like wear and tear, small cracks all along the hose you sometimes find with age and exposure. The last motor I'd just serviced two weeks ago though, and the fuel line was brand new. When I went back to check the other two, it was clear these were not cracks, but small slits, made by something small and sharp, like a box-cutter maybe.

In any event, it was enough to have me toss all three of the damaged hoses in the back of the truck and head over to the office to warn Patti I'd be going into town. A visit to the OPP detachment seems in order.

I haven't talked to Patti since last Friday night. I was with Leelo yesterday and she was gone when I got back to the lodge. And I just saw her car pull in an hour or so ago, while I was busy on the dock. Her back is to me by the open file cabinet, when I enter the office.

"I'm going into town," I announce, and she slowly turns to face me. "Keep an eye on the phone." I realize I'm curt, but I'm still pissed at her.

"Look," she starts. "I'm sorry about Friday night. I may have had a little too much to drink. I didn't mean to—"

"Knock it off," I interrupt her brusquely. "You absolutely *meant to.* You heard what I said in that pissing contest with Kyle, and you decided to come over and try to stir that pot a little more by staking your claim." I lean a little closer. "A claim—I clearly need to remind you—that you don't have, or ever had." I watch as her eyes fill with tears and one tips over, rolling down her cheek. She makes no effort to hide them now, and I feel like an ass, but I can't back down now. "I don't want to lose a valuable friendship over this, but this shit has got to stop." Then I add a bit more gently, "I really like this woman, Patti. I don't expect you to be BFFs, but I hope that if this goes somewhere, I'm not forced to make a choice."

With that I walk out of the office, wincing at the muffled sob behind me. *Fuck.* This is why I don't like talking.

-

"Yup," Bill Prescott confirms, dropping the fuel line on the table and scratching his head. "What I don't get is who? Think it might be one of your guests?"

"Why? Doesn't make any sense," I point out. "I'm thinking it might be someone local."

Bill's eyebrows shoot up and he leans forward with his elbows on the table.

"How so?"

"Two weeks or so back, those buoys I have marking that flat rock across the lake suddenly disappeared, and one of my boats ran into it. One of my guests got injured. Then there's the stuff that happened at the Whitefish

160

Motel. Did Constable Williams file his report yet?" I can tell from the crease forming between his eyes that this may be news.

"Not aware of any incident at the motel. I'll make sure to check with Williams, but in the meantime, why don't you tell me what that was all about?"

I spend the next twenty minutes telling Bill about Lilith Talbot inheriting her uncle's motel, about the work she's been doing to it, and about the sick games someone seems to be playing by leaving her dead animals.

"Did you look for anything identifiable in the garbage left on her porch?"

"I did. There was little other than fish waste. In hindsight, I should've called you guys in for that as well, but it didn't seem that significant at the time," I admit.

"And the deer?" he prompts.

"The deer cranked it up to an entirely different level. From what I could see, the doe had been dead for a while. She was hacked up, with something crude, an ax maybe. Pretty gruesome discovery for her. I'm thinking that's not something she'll likely forget, and if you ask me, that's exactly what he wants."

"He? Sounds like you might have an idea who did this," Bill points out astutely.

"Nothing more than a suspicion," I offer, knowing better than to start spouting accusations I can't substantiate.

"Wouldn't have anything to do with that little disturbance at the community centre the other day, would it? That cockfight half the town was witness to?" I keep my mouth shut, and Bill doesn't seem to expect an answer. "This Talbot woman…you like her," he says with a grin.

It's not so much a question as it is a statement. Yet this time I choose to respond.

"What can I say? She's likable."

FOURTEEN

Peaches & cream; every rich and succulent inch.

Roar

"Whitefish Motel."

I like her voice.

She has the kind of warm, expressive sound that belies everything she's feeling. I could listen to her recite the phonebook and it wouldn't be boring. Mind you, there's little about her I find boring.

I'd been tempted earlier.

Hell, I even slowed down, ready to turn left into the motel lot, when I spotted a couple of cars outside two of the units. A loud honk behind me from an approaching truck made the decision for me, and I took off toward Jackson's Point.

Patti's car was already gone when I pulled into my parking spot, and I have to admit it was a bit of a relief. I hadn't been in a hurry to get back. I figured if I was in town anyway, I might as well run a few errands, and ended up at Charlie's. I took her for some pierogies at her favourite restaurant around the corner. Nothing fancy, the place looks more like a hospital cafeteria than a restaurant, but their food is great.

"How was your day, Sunshine?" I ask by way of introduction. Leaning back in my chair, I prop my feet on my desk and watch the sun go down over the lake. I smile at the sound of her soft chuckle on the other side.

"Productive," she answers, as I listen to the clang of pots in the background. "How about yours?"

"Not sure you could call my day productive, but I stayed busy all the same. What are you up to?"

"Breakfast prep," she says without hesitation, and my eyes shoot to the clock on my office wall.

"At nine thirty at night?"

This time I can feel her responding low chuckle hum through my body, and I shift slightly in my seat.

"I have guests," she offers by way of explanation. "I promised them a full breakfast tomorrow, so I'm baking."

"That's great."

"I figured I'd offer breakfast daily and a simple dinner only on the weekends. Home cooking, you know? No menu, just a big blackboard with a few daily choices. Stuff that's easy to prep and can be set up buffet style. I'm not too keen on running a bar when I'm just by myself here, so I figure I could use the actual bar to set out the food. I'm still trying to work that out in my head." The whole time she's chattering, I can hear her move around her kitchen. She sounds happy. "Anyway, I'm sorry, I'm being rude. I'm sure you didn't call to listen to the sound of me yammering on."

"Actually, I did," I admit. "I like listening to you talk."

"Oh."

"And for the record, I think it's a good idea."

"You do?"

"Sure."

There's complete silence on the other side of the line, and then I hear her take a deep breath in.

"So…breakfast is between seven and nine. If you're interested," she quickly adds.

"Oh, I'm interested," I grin, hanging up the phone.

Leelo

"I'm stuffed."

The woman who introduced herself as Lesley last night, shoves her plate toward the middle of the table. She and her travel companion, Jane, mentioned being on their way to a school reunion in Timmins.

"Would you like more coffee?" I lift the thermos I just refilled with fresh coffee. My other guest, a middle-aged gentleman in town for business, just left with the last of the previous pot in his travel mug.

"Please. We're gonna need all the reinforcement we can get, right, Jane?" she says, smiling at the other woman across the table, who only nods in reply. Clearly the quieter one of the two.

"How so?" I can't help ask, filling both their cups before setting the coffee pot in the middle of the table and gathering up their plates.

"I imagine we'll be shocking quite a few old classmates tonight." She reaches over to grab Jane's hand off the table and entwines their fingers before turning to me. "We've been best friends since ninth grade," she explains. "And lovers since grade eleven. Not something you would broadcast at sixteen in a predominantly Catholic small northern community. Our families had a hard enough time accepting it. This will be the first time in twenty years we're going back as a couple."

"A married couple," Jane adds in a much softer voice, her eyes focused on her wife.

"Congratulations, that's fantastic. I'm so happy for you," I gush, moved by the obvious devotion between the two.

"Thank you. We are too," Lesley replies, when her attention is drawn to something behind me. "But we should head out. We're keeping you from your other customers."

I turn around to find Roar walking in the door, his focus on me as he grabs a seat a few tables down. The smile, already on my face, only gets bigger when he pulls off his beanie with a wink and runs his hand over his head.

"Yes, we should," Jane answers behind me and I hear the scrape of chairs on the floor.

I barely manage a half-assed "Good luck. Hope to see you back," and small wave of my hand, before my attention is right back on him.

After he hung up last night, I hadn't been able to get the sound of his voice out of my mind. That deep rumble calling me *Sunshine* did all sorts of things to me. I blush remembering the frantic search for two double A batteries, upon discovering I'd somehow managed to drain the ones in the discreet little toy I kept in a small bag in my nightstand. A toy that had seen little to no action until I moved here.

166

"I'd love to know what you're thinking about right now." The sound of his voice spurs me to action.

"Morning!" I chirp, sounding shrill, even to my own ears, as I turn toward the kitchen, completely ignoring his words. "Let me grab you some fresh coffee." There is fresh coffee still in the pot, but I need a minute to compose myself.

Dropping the plates in the sink, I brace myself on the counter, leaning my head down. I take a few deep breaths and will my heart rate to slow down, when I sense him walking up behind me. Before I can turn around, two large hands land on my hips and do the turning for me. I don't even have a chance to look at him before his mouth descends on mine, and he steals every single thought from my mind. I taste the mint of his toothpaste, with a heat that is all him, and all I can seem to do as my body becomes a slave to his force, is hang on to stay standing.

"That's more like the good morning I was hoping for," he says when he finally releases my lips.

"Amen…" is all I can manage.

-

"Hold this," he instructs me, brushing Ace's nose aside before handing me one end of the waterproof rope, while he starts fastening the other end to the outside frame.

We've been working on dry land, building the frame that holds the barrels we unloaded off of his truck this morning. Roar's dog, who'd been patiently waiting in the cab of the truck earlier, is now romping around the property, and breakfast is a distant memory, as my stomach rumbles in loud protest.

"Can you hang on for twenty more minutes?" Roar smiles at me, having clearly heard my body's loud plea for sustenance. "I just want to get this part done."

"Absolutely," I say with more conviction than I feel. "Let's get this done."

He's already explained that once the barrels are strapped to the frame, it'll need to be flipped over and moved into the water to start laying the top boards.

"Will we be able to get it in the water ourselves?" I ask a bit later, as we sit side by side on the porch steps, eating a quick sandwich, with Ace stretched out at our feet, waiting for crumbs to fall.

"I think so. I brought a heavy tarp we'll flip it onto. The ground is pretty level, we should be able to slide it easily," he explains. "Besides," he adds, grinning as he looks me up and down. "You're made of pretty sturdy stuff."

Self-consciously, I put my sandwich down and start pulling at the men's T-shirt plastered against my sweaty body. Not my first choice in this heat, but it hides my new ink nicely, and now I'm extra grateful for the added coverage.

"What I meant to say," Roar clarifies as he plucks my hand away from my shirt. "Is that I've seen how strong you are. You've been hauling those beams around all morning."

"Oh."

"Hmmm," he rumbles, before he shoves half his sandwich in his mouth, leaving a drop of mustard in his beard. I can't help staring as it moves when he chews.

"You've got…uhh…" I mumble, unable to help myself as I finally lift my hand and wipe at it. "Mustard," I explain, holding up my finger in evidence.

His gaze shoots from my finger up to my eyes. He grabs my wrist and excruciatingly slowly, brings my finger to his mouth.

"Good sandwich," he says, after slipping my slick digit from his lips. "Back to work."

I watch him walk off, Ace loping after him, while I wait until I'm sure my legs can hold me.

-

"I'm exhausted," I moan, flopping on my back beside Roar, who is letting the sun dry him off. The new floating dock bobs gently on the water, safely tethered to the old fixed section. I close my eyes to avoid being tempted to check out his long body beside me, clad in only the swimming trunks he changed into at some point.

"Too bad."

His deep rumble comes from above me, and I peek through squinted eyes to find him—leaning on an elbow with his head resting on his hand—looking down on me.

"How is that?" I whisper, my throat suddenly dry, making my voice sound raspy.

"Because I've been thinking up ways to get you out of those clothes," he replies, his eyes drifting down my body and back up again. The close scrutiny has me suck in air, something that he doesn't miss, as his gaze gets stuck somewhere in the vicinity of my boobs. "I'd love to see what you're hiding…" I can't seem to catch my next breath when he traces a finger from the hollow of my throat, straight down, taking my shirt with it. The rasp of his calluses tease the sensitive skin between my breasts.

169

"…Right here," he finishes, flicking the corner of the protective bandaging that covers my new tattoo.

"Oh *fuck*!" I scramble to my feet, causing the dock to pitch dangerously, but I'm already gone, hustling toward the house.

That dressing was supposed to have come off sometime this morning so I could clean the fresh ink and put some Tattoo Goop on. Instead I've been sweating buckets all day in the heat, letting God knows what kind of breeding ground for bacteria develop. I'm cursing myself under my breath, as I manage to step over Ace, who is lying on the porch, tear into the house, and strip off my shirt the moment I hear the storm door slam shut.

By the time I get upstairs, I'm out of breath. In the bathroom, I pull away the cup over my left breast and carefully peel the tape loose.

Dammit, dammit, dammit. The patch of skin surrounding the small innocuous tattoo is shaded a deep red and looks inflamed.

I turn on the cold tap and shove a clean washcloth underneath, when the door behind me opens. Covering myself with the wet cloth, I find a slightly concerned looking Roar looking at me in the mirror.

"How bad is it?" he wants to know.

"Not sure," I mutter, surprised that I'm not more upset. At him at least. I'm upset enough with myself.

"Show me," he says, stepping into the bathroom and I turn to face him.

"Look, Roar," I protest weakly. "Maybe you should—"

"Show me," he repeats more sternly. "It's not the way I'd envisioned you getting naked, but it was gonna happen anyway. Now let me see."

My hand still holds most of the washcloth in place, but I let him lift away the part that covers the red swollen skin. I feel more than a little exposed as he turns me into the light and bends down to take a closer look.

"Pretty," he says, his breath brushing against my skin. The resulting goosebumps don't go unnoticed as he leans in and presses a kiss on my collarbone, before he straightens up. "Did you get it done at that place town?"

"Yes. I forget the name, it's on the instruction sheet I left on the coffee table."

"Why don't you have a quick shower while I give them a call," he says, not waiting for confirmation as he turns and walks out.

I don't think about protesting, I'm too busy watching him leave—still wearing only a pair of board shorts.

Roar

After talking to Ginnie at Slick Skin—who suggests marking or recording the inflamed area, but otherwise to follow regular aftercare—I head out to the porch to grab the clothes I left there earlier and give the dog a quick scratch behind the ears.

I'm still buttoning up my fly when I hear the bell over the bar entrance go off and quickly pull on my shirt.

"Can I help you?"

"Yes. Would you happen to have a couple of rooms?" The older, bespectacled man, dressed head-to-toe in camo turns around from where he was looking out the window. "I'm afraid we don't have a reservation," he says, chuckling a little at himself. "My fault, my wife assures me. We've got our grandsons for a week and since it was my idea to take them fishing, I guess it was my responsibility to book, and it would appear I forgot. There is no reservation, or a vacancy, at Jackson's Point. I was redirected here."

I bark out a laugh and offer my hand in greeting.

"Peter—how are you? Was wondering when you'd be up this way again." Peter Walters grabs my hand with a smile, giving it a firm pump.

"Mr. Doyle—good to see you, although I'm a little confused to find you here. Patti told me a woman had taken over Sam's old place."

"His niece, actually," I clarify. "I'm giving her a hand with some repairs."

"I noticed it looked much improved since I drove by here last year," he says, looking around the bar when a car horn sounds outside. "Right, that'll be the wife. So about those rooms?"

"Why don't you put your wife's mind at ease, I'm pretty sure she has rooms for you, let me just check which ones."

"I'll be outside then," he says, smiling as he pulls the door open. "Oh and, Doyle? You may want to do something about your shirt—it's inside out."

I shake my head as the old man steps out, cackling as he lets the door fall shut behind him.

"Leelo?" I call up from the bottom of the stairs. I can still hear the shower going so I run up, two steps at a time. "Leelo?" I try again, knocking on the bathroom door.

I hear a wet thump, a muffled "*Fucking hell*," and then the sound of the shower curtain being moved aside.

"What?" There's a rattling I imagine being the towel bar and some shuffling. "Yes?" This time her voice is much closer to the door. Finally the door opens a crack, a single, clear blue eye staring at me through the opening.

"You've got guests," I announce, biting my lip so I don't laugh when that blue eye widens dramatically, and I refocus over her shoulder.

"Oh, oh, give me a minute," she sputters, her fingers clasping the edge of the door. "I'll be right there."

"Just tell me if I can put them in seven and eight. It's an older couple with their grandkids. I know them. They're good people. You can take care of the paperwork after, I'll vouch for them."

"Sure. Okay, that's fine," she says, a little more of her face visible now as she smiles. "Thanks."

"No problem.

During that entire exchange—and until she clicks the door shut—my gaze never once leaves the reflection I catch in the strip of mirror visible over her shoulder.

FIFTEEN

A careful touch has the power to wipe the battle from her eyes.

Leelo

I'm doing what I do whenever I have excess nervous energy. I bake.

I tell myself it's because there are guests, and I'm supposed to be offering them breakfast in the morning. However, that's not the real reason I'm kneading dough for fresh buns in the morning, when my arms feel like they'll fall off after the kind of exercise they received today.

No.

I'm jittery. Restless.

Ever since Roar left, Ace in tow, right after he checked in my new guests.

He cited the need to check in on the lodge and feed the dog. I couldn't fault him for that. After all, he'd spent all day working here. The lodge is booked up for the week, and despite the fact the cabins are mostly self-sustaining, as he explained, it would probably not be a bad idea to show his face.

I'd been hiding out in my bedroom when he came knocking the second time, to let me know he had to go. I wasn't exactly ready to face him. Not after that scene in the bathroom, when I clicked the door shut, twisted my head around and realized my ass had been on full display in the mirror.

There had definitely been something brewing before that. The whole day seemed to build up to something, and then apparently one glance at my pale, cellulite riddled expanse was too much for the man.

So I'm left with a build up of energy, and a head full of thoughts I don't want to explore. About to jump out of my skin. So I bake.

There's something therapeutic about massaging the slightly warm dough, squishing between my fingers, only to pound it into submission a moment later. When I have the texture where I want it, I take my sharpest knife and cut the dough in sixteen equal pieces, placing them on a greased baking sheet with the edges tucked under. I lightly grease the tops and cover the whole tray with plastic wrap, and a towel, before sliding it in the bottom of the large fridge where it will slowly rise overnight.

By the time the sun starts going down, I have the kitchen clean again, but I'm still restless.

I love the way the dock moves under my feet as I walk to the very end, half a bottle of wine tucked under my arm. Who needs a glass? I sit down on the edge and let my toes play in the chilly water, while I bless the introduction of screw tops on wine bottles as I take a healthy swig.

It's a beautiful evening. The water is still, and the sounds of the night slowly come to life as I watch the last streaks of remaining sunlight disappear behind the trees.

Ouch.

I slap my thigh where a mosquito just bit me. I wipe at another one that lands on my arm, and pretty soon the buzzing is loud around my head, and I'm frantically waving my hand around my face. A blood-sucking army is out tonight, and I scramble to my feet, snatch up the now empty bottle, and hustle toward the sanctuary of my house.

My heart lodges in my throat when I see a figure detach itself from the shadows of the porch.

"Was wondering how long it would fucking take before you came running."

I bend over, gasping to get air in my lungs, when I hear the voice.

"I swear, Riordan Doyle...one day you'll be the death of me."

"Not what I had in mind," he chuckles easily, as he grabs my arm, drags me inside, and out of the way of the charging mosquitoes.

"What are you doing here?" I ask, as he takes the bottle from my hand, sets it on the counter, and pulls me into my living room. There he drops down on the threadbare couch and tugs me down beside him. "I thought you went home?"

"I did," he confirms, throwing his arm over my shoulder and tugging me to his chest. "And I was just putting my feet up on the coffee table when I realized I didn't want to be there."

"No?"

"No," he repeats. "Couldn't relax. Started thinking about this...*thing*...between us. And you know what? Waiting for the right time is for the fucking birds."

"It is?"

"It absolutely fucking is," he says with conviction, curving his free hand along my jaw and turning my face toward him.

His hazel eyes are almost black in the scarce light of my living room, his heavy-lidded gaze roaming my features before settling on my lips.

"I'm thinking right now sounds like the right time."

I can feel the deep rumble of his voice down to my toes, and my own drops a few octaves lower as well.

"You do?" I mutter breathlessly as his head bends down.

It's clear from my distinctly unimaginative responses that my brain cells have signed off for the day. I'm starting to sound like a goddamn parrot, but Roar doesn't give me time to linger on that thought. His mouth is already on mine and his tongue is demanding entry.

One moment I'm tucked beside him on the couch, and the next I'm on my back, Roar's heavy frame covering me, his lips still firmly fused to mine. Good God the man can kiss.

My arms wind around his neck and my fingers look for purchase in his hair, finding only short stubble. The one semi-coherent thought I have, before I let myself be drawn under, is that I wish he still had those long tresses for me to hold onto.

My brain doesn't know what to focus on, as he thoroughly explores my mouth with hungry lashes of his tongue, and his restless hand skims every inch of my body he can reach.

"Bed," he mumbles against my lips, and I groan in protest when he rolls off me, pulling me up with him.

I try to stay in the moment, I do.

I want this, my body clearly wants this, but my mind can be a real shit disturber. The moment we reach my bedroom, reality hits, and the blissful cloud of lust I was drifting on dissipates.

"What is it?" he asks when I freeze just inside the door.

"I'm...I'm just not sure this is a good idea," I blurt out, bracing for the anger I expect to be unleashed at me. Instead, he gently tugs me close enough to wrap his arms around the small of my back.

"Why?" His voice is gentle, without any trace of the irritation I anticipated, at the very least.

His hold on me is comfortable, comforting even, but still my thoughts are hard to voice.

"Because I don't want to be a disappointment. I've been one for too long already."

When I see him get ready to respond, I press my fingers to his mouth.

"Let me finish," I plead, earning me a nod. "It took a lot for me, moving here, making a new start at this point in my life, but I did it anyway. I lost so much already in my quest to find myself. My family, my friends—those who stuck with me after my divorce—they all thought I was crazy coming here." I pause, taking in a deep shaky breath. Roar uses the moment to guide me to the bed and encourages me to sit down. Then he crouches down in front of me with his hands on my knees, and quietly waits for me to continue. "I like it here. I like working with my hands and seeing the results every day. I'm proud of the person I'm becoming, and I like that I am building friendships with people—with you— willing to see me that way." My voice wavers a little, and I swallow hard, determined not to start bawling. "But I'm afraid that if I open myself up, if I let you in, that you'll see the person I tried to leave behind."

His fingers flex on my knees, and I see a muscle in his jaw hard at work, but I don't stop him from talking this time.

"And who would I see?"

I pause, because this isn't just a question—and he's not looking for a simple answer—he's asking me to take a leap of faith. To show him exactly what it is I'm afraid he'll see in me. He's asking for full exposure.

With the slight burn of my new ink a reminder to let go, I take a deep breath and jump in, with both feet.

"A flawed person," I start. "Someone who still has a hard time looking at herself in the mirror, because she can see every single one of her shortcomings reflected. An overweight, middle-aged housewife, who allowed herself to be belittled for years before she was cast aside, and who so completely lost it after that, she managed to alienate her children in the process. A woman who battles a constant fight to love and accept herself the way she is, but can't bring herself to believe others ever will."

There's no holding back the tears now. Resigned, I just let them roll out from under my closed eyelids.

Roar

She's killing me.

Not that all of what she said is a complete surprise to me, but the harsh clarity she paints herself with is as telling as the words themselves.

I asked for this, but I'm not sure I know what to do with the outcome.

"Hey." I wipe at her wet cheeks with my thumbs, encouraging her to open her eyes. "Lie down with me," I suggest, and that seems to do the trick, as her eyelids shoot open. I have a hard time keeping my grin in check at her disbelieving glare. "Come on," I prod carefully. "Give an old guy a break; any more time on my knees and I may never get up again."

The corner of her mouth tugs slightly at my lame joke, but it's enough to have me flip on my back across her bed, and hold out my hands in invitation. After just a moment's hesitation, she plants a knee in the bed and crawls in my arms. With her hand on my chest and her head tucked in my neck, the words come.

"Want to know what I see?" I smile when I feel her nod, her hair snagging in my beard. "A real person, someone undervalued and then duped by an asshole, who didn't take the time or effort to appreciate the beautiful creature sharing his bed. A mother working hard to show her kids that you're not weak for falling, but strong for getting up again." I hear her sniffle and tighten my arms around her, before sliding one hand down to palm the curve of her ass. "Earlier, I saw a woman in the mirror; warm, soft, resilient, and utterly tempting. So much so, that the image of that glorious ass had me pull on my boots, hop in my truck, and show back up on her doorstep, not two hours later."

"*Shit,*" she mutters in my shoulder before I hear her snicker. "You saw me."

I plant an elbow in the mattress and easily roll her over.

"Bet that fine ass of yours I saw you." I smile down in her flushed face. "And it's not nearly enough."

She blinks a few times but doesn't move when I raise her arms and stretch them over her head. Not even when I pull her shirt up and off over her head.

"Stay still," I whisper, receiving the slightest of nods

I run my hand from her neck, down to her soft belly, before slipping it behind her back to undo the utilitarian bra she's wearing.

For all her pretty ink, it's clear Leelo prefers comfort.

She doesn't resist when I pull the straps down from her shoulders, and kiss the newly exposed skin, while slowly uncovering her breasts. Her shallow breaths flutter against the tip of my tongue as I lazily lick her distended nipple. Lifting up on my knees, I make quick work of her shorts and panties, sliding them down and off. I watch her struggle not to squirm when I run my hands slowly from her ankles up her legs, spreading them open as I go.

Fucking phenomenal.

Her pale, ripe body, open and vulnerable, stirs a raw need in me. A basic urge to claim and conquer.

"I don't think…" she whispers, trying to close her legs against my hands.

"*Shhh.* Stay still," I remind her, before sliding off the mattress, kicking off my boots and stripping myself naked as fast as I can.

Her eyes follow every movement, finally coming to rest on my engorged cock, already an angry purple, jutting out from my hips. With her focus on me, and not on herself, I palm my erection and pump a few times, easily drawing a bead of precum I rub around the head with my thumb.

I don't miss the tip of Leelo's little pink tongue brushing a quick lick of her bottom lip, or the slight press of her ass into the mattress, looking for friction.

"Mouth or cock?" I ask her, letting go of my dick and her eyes shoot up to mine. Her mouth slightly opened, it's all I can do not to climb over her and feed her my length, but this is not about me.

At least not all.

"Tell me what you want," I push her. "I'm starved either way."

"*Cock.*"

I would've missed the soft whisper had I not been looking at her closely.

"Cock it is," I confirm, as I deliberately climb up between her legs.

Unable to resist a quick taste, I slide my thumb through the wetness clinging to her curls, probing for the small bundle of nerves I know is hiding there. When I feel the hard smooth surface, I add my other thumb to spread her open for my mouth.

The hot, spicy, distinctly nuanced taste of her is a surprise. A really fucking good one.

I don't often volunteer going down on a woman, let alone crave it. Only if I know it's something that will help get off the woman I'm with, and even then the list has been a dramatically short one. I know guys who get off on it, but I've never been one of those.

Until now.

I'm really fucking happy I gave into my curiosity, when Leelo's hands find the back of my head, breaking the pose I'd ordered her to keep. Her hips buck off the mattress and the scratch of her nails over my scalp only add to my indulgence.

"Holy shit," she breathes, when I drag myself away from her warm heat. "I didn't ask for that, but I'm glad you didn't listen. I doubt your cock can make me feel all that."

I lift up on my arms and grin at her from between her legs. It's the most she's said since we got naked, any self-consciousness clearly forgotten.

"Now there's a challenge I can't walk away from," I growl, climbing up her body. She snickers as I lower my hips in the cradle of her thighs, but the grin disappears when I slick the crown of my dick along her slit and carefully probe her opening.

"Yesss," she hisses as I test her tight fit around me.

I spread and pull up my knees, lift her ass with one hand, and ignoring the aches and pains of a hard day's work at my age, I set about the task of proving her wrong.

SIXTEEN

She's the place where fantasy and reality meet.

Leelo

"What do you mean, the dock is gone?"

Roar's voice, which had been distracted when he first answered, snaps with sudden focus.

"Gone—just gone. As in, it's no longer attached and I can't see it anywhere. So can I borrow a boat? I need to go look for it."

"I chained that sucker down, Leelo. No way it could've just floated off. Are the chains still there?" he asks, completely ignoring my request.

"How else would it've disappeared? Not like someone could've hauled it out and carried it off without me noticing," I bite off, already irritated and not just about the missing dock. "I wouldn't have bothered you if I didn't need to borrow one of your boats. I could—"

"Do you even know how to drive a boat?" he cuts me off, leaving me with my mouth gaping open.

Talk about insult to injury.

I woke up this morning; still a little sore after the vigorous paces Roar put me through last night, in an empty bed. Sometime during the night, or early morning, while I was still sleeping off the evidence that his cock indeed could make me feel *all that* — and more — he disappeared on me. No goodbye, no note, no nothing.

Now I'm not asking for a goddamn lifelong commitment, for Pete's sake, but a note might've been nice.

It was after I put on breakfast for my new guests, the Walters, that I went out with my favourite travel mug to enjoy my morning coffee on my new dock, to find it gone. And given that he snuck out sometime during the night, I didn't particularly want to, but couldn't think of anyone else to call.

"Look," Roar says in a calmer tone that does nothing to soothe my ruffled feathers. "Just sit tight. I've got a bit of a situation here, but I'll head out to look as soon as I can."

I exhale sharply when I hear the click on the other end. Not quite the *morning after* I had imagined, and most certainly not the same man who had slain me with his words, and then his body, last night.

This one just pisses me off.

With a head full of steam, and restless energy to burn, I figure now is as good a time as any to find that insurance policy Henry Kline, of Kline, Kline & McTavish, was supposed to have transferred to my name.

I've got a claim for two wrecked washers and a dryer, and now possibly a missing dock.

Roar

"What do you want me to do with these numbnuts?"

I put the phone down and turn to Bill. I'd called him out of bed this morning, opting to forfeit the OPP switchboard and have them send an idiot like that Constable Williams.

For the mess I found when I got here this morning, I needed someone I could trust.

I woke up to my phone buzzing in the pocket of my jeans beside the bed. Leelo's warm naked body was wrapped around me like cling wrap, but she didn't even stir as I untangled myself from her limbs. I snagged up my jeans and walked into the bathroom, shutting the door behind me.

I couldn't understand everything the woman on the other end of the line was saying, since she was crying hysterically, but got enough to know I needed to get my ass over to the lodge right away. I told her I'd be there shortly, pulled on my jeans, grabbed my boots and shirt off the floor, and with a last glance at the still sleeping form of Leelo, I rushed out the door.

Four-thirty in the goddamn morning, and I had bodies bleeding all over my property when I pulled into my parking spot.

I'd warned the group of five Toronto yuppies, up here for a week's fishing, on two previous occasions already, when their drinking got a little too loud. They clearly did not get the message.

The idiots decided it was a good idea to build a bonfire in the middle of the goddamn night, blasting their music out over the water. Their loud, inebriated party woke up guests in neighbouring cabins, who tried to shut things down. Inevitably voices got raised and before long the fists had been flying and things got out of control fast.

The wife of one of the guys, involved in the brawl, ended up finding my number tacked on the message board beside the office door when she couldn't get an answer knocking at the lodge.

The fight had already died down, but left three people in need of proper medical care. The woman's husband was bleeding from a nasty gash to his head, sustained when one of the idiots slammed his head on a rock, knocking him out cold. The other two were partiers, one with a mangled hand that will likely require surgery to repair, and the other drunk moron was spitting up blood, after a well aimed kick to his ribs.

An hour later, the flashing lights of emergency vehicles were bouncing off the mirror surface of the lake, as the three guys were loaded up into two ambulances and the rest of the assorted cuts and bruises were being checked out. By then just about every last guest of Jackson's Point was wide awake.

Bill had been the first to get here, followed closely by a second OPP patrol car, and he and the officer had jumped right in, trying to sort through the mess. With interruptions to get medical attention for those who needed it, they took until Patti showed up half an hour ago to get the stories straight.

"I want to send them packing," I tell him, referring to the three guys from the Toronto group still left. "Get them gone. I don't have time to babysit their asses the rest of the week. My other guests paid good money for a relaxing vacation, I don't need these yahoos causing any more disruption than they already have."

"Fair enough," Bill says, scratching his head as he stares out over the water. "Out of curiosity, though—how come you didn't nip this in the bud?"

I take in his profile and notice the corner of his mouth twitch. *Asshole*.

"Wasn't here."

The twitch turns into a shit-eating grin as he turns his gaze to me.

"Oh?"

"None of your goddamn business," I bark, but I can't help the smile tugging at my own lips at the memory of the warm bed and lush body I left behind.

"Shit, that reminds me; I should get going. The floating dock went missing from behind the motel sometime between last night and this morning."

"The motel, huh?" Bill looks at me smugly.

"Don't be a prick. Leelo called just now. It's brand new. We built it yesterday and I made sure to latch that thing down with chains. This morning it was gone."

"Well then," Bill says, suddenly all business. "Let's get those city boys out of your hair, and we'll go hunting for your lady's dock."

Fuck Me.

-

"There it is," Bill calls out an hour later, pointing at the overhanging brush on the far end of the old pilings on the north side of the lake. Almost immediately across the water from the motel.

Tucked under the branches, a corner of the brand new floating dock is still visible. On closer inspection, we notice one end of it is caught on a rock on the water's edge.

189

"Weird," Bill remarks. "Didn't think there was much wind to speak of last night?"

"There wasn't," I confirm, grinding my teeth. "Water was smooth as glass."

I loop a rope around one of the pilings and lower myself into the water, Bill doing the same beside me. Between the two of us, it doesn't take long to pull the dock free from where it's stuck and tie it to the back of my boat.

"What do you say we drag this thing back to where it belongs, and have a look at those chains you mentioned?"

With just a nod of agreement, I start the engine and steer the boat away from the shore, aiming it for shore on the far side.

She must've seen my boat from her window, because by the time I lower the throttle and let the boat coast into shore, Leelo is walking toward us.

"Nice." I hear Bill mumble under his breath behind me, clearly seeing much the same thing I do when I take her in from top to bottom. The blue hair, usually tucked in a ponytail, is bouncing freely around her face. The white slouchy shirt hangs loosely down one shoulder, exposing the strap of a bra and the hint of ink on her shoulder. And finally, her slim ankles and bare feet sticking out of the rolled up khaki cargo pants. Casual, unapologetic, and totally Leelo.

I'm not sure if it's Bill's quietly voiced appreciation, or the curious glance Leelo shoots over my shoulder, but I don't hesitate jumping out of the boat, marching right up to her. With a hand on either side of her face, I tilt her chin, and don't allow for any doubt when I thoroughly claim her slightly pursed lips.

"*Caveman*," she whispers when I pull away.

"You bet." I growl my response.

The clearing of a throat interrupts the moment, as Bill walks up behind us.

"Since Doyle here seems to be busy wielding his club, I might as well introduce myself," he says, stepping around me and reaching out his hand. "Bill Prescott, at your service."

"*Jesus Christ*," I mutter at him. "You're OPP, not MI-5." Turning to a snickering Leelo, I add by way of explanation; "Bill is the staff sergeant for the local OPP detachment."

"I see," she says, grinning at *him* as she shakes his hand. "I'm Lilith Talbot, but my friends call me Leelo."

"A pleasure, Leelo." The asshole smiles big at her. *Fucking Bill.*

"Now that we know who we all are, maybe we should take care of that dock?"

I hustle back in the water where the floating dock, caught in a current, is starting to pull my boat away from shore.

"Oh, shit," I hear Bill behind me as he splashes into the water to help me reel it back in.

Leelo

It's almost as good as watching an old *Three Stooges* episode.

Except, there's only two, although these guys are a shitload better looking than Larry, Curly and Moe.

I sit down on the old portion of the dock, dangling my feet in the cooling water, watching them struggle to pull the boat back to shore. The occasional verbal barbs they exchange put a grin on my face.

I'd lost most of this morning's bad mood when I was putting away my laundry, looked out the bedroom window, and saw the boat towing my dock from the other side of the lake. It wasn't hard to make out Roar's tall form, although I didn't know who the second man was.

There was still some lingering disappointment to find him gone without a word this morning, but hunting down and bringing me back my dock goes a long way to alleviating it.

"Sunshine, can you pull the chain up from the water?"

I scoot over the to end of the dock and reach down to fish it out. The locked padlock is still on there, its key in the lockbox in the office, where Roar left it.

He wades over, pulling the dock along behind him, and I hold it up for him to see.

"Fuck," he says, looking at the cut link dangling at the bottom, before hauling himself out of the water and turning to his friend. "Don't let it float off this time, I'm just gonna grab the key."

"I knew it was a good idea for me to come along," Bill comments, watching Roar stalk off toward the house.

"Someone cut it." I state the obvious.

"Looks like," Bill agrees.

"Where exactly did you find it?" I want to know.

"It got stuck on a rock beside the remnants of an old dock straight across the lake," he answers.

I look in the direction he's pointing, remembering the boat I'd seen there.

"Someone was out there last week. One of those sleek speedboats. I saw it tied up when I went for a swim and then it took off," I recount. "I remember it striking me as odd, since I didn't think there was much of anything out there. Just Crown land, right?"

"Did you tell Doyle that?" he probes, his face suddenly serious.

"Tell me what?"

Roar wades into the water to where Bill is holding onto the dock, and holds his hand out to me for the length of chain. While he makes short measure of latching the errant dock back down, Bill repeats what I told him. The two share a look in some kind of silent language I'm not privy to.

"See anyone in the boat?"

"Nope. I remember thinking that was odd. Almost looked like one of those remote control things. Or..." I add pensively. "Whoever was driving it was ducking out of sight."

"Right," Bill mutters, as the two men finish securing the floating dock in silence.

"Do you have coffee?" Roar asks when they're done.

"I can make some," I offer.

"That'd be good."

-

Thirty minutes later, we're sitting at a table in my makeshift restaurant, the guys putting a dent in this morning's leftover muffins.

"So why would anyone have it out for me?" I ask. "And who? I haven't even had time to make enemies."

Bill spent the past half hour questioning me about any little incident that might have happened since I arrived. Both men seem of a mind it's likely one person behind the dock, the poor deer, and even the bear incident.

"I mean," I continue. "I had a bit of a rough start with Travis at the hardware store, but I think we've gotten past that, since I'm in there all the time now. Everyone else has been nice." I shudder when I think of Kyle Thompson. "Almost too nice," I add.

My words are met with silence and both guys are staring at me.

"What? The real estate guy? Kyle Thompson? Why in hell—"

"He's the only one on the lake with a boat like the one you're describing," Roar points out. "He's also tried unsuccessfully to get in your pants on several occasions, and believe me when I tell you, the man does not take rejection well."

"But—"

"Timing is interesting too," Bill adds his two cents. "From what I can gather, every confrontation you've had with him was followed by an incident."

"But I haven't seen him since his speech at the community centre," I challenge. "By your logic that incident resulted in the mess in my laundry room, but what about the dock? What would his motivation have been for that?"

"Me."

I look at Roar who is calmly staring back.

"What about you?"

"Look," Bill answers instead. "Kyle and Doyle here have somewhat of a history."

"So I've been told."

"Right, well then you know that if Doyle has it—Kyle wants it."

I sit back and let that percolate, because that would mean he's been watching. *Closely.*

"But the dock…" I protest feebly, looking down at my hands to avoid Roar's eyes for fear the blush crawling up my neck will ignite all over my face.

"Wouldn't have been hard for him to figure out Doyle spent the night," Bill suggests gently.

His astute observation does little for my complexion, which I'm sure is a deep shade of beet red now.

I hear the scrape of a chair and then a mumbled, "Gotta make a call," from Bill before his footsteps move away from the table. The moment I hear the door close, I let out the deep breath I'd been holding.

"Come here."

"Why did you sneak out?" I ask him, ignoring his demand, and to my surprise, he answers without hesitation.

"A messy situation at the lodge I had to sort out. My phone woke me up. You were deep asleep and I didn't want to wake you."

"Oh."

His quick response makes me feel a bit better. All morning I hadn't been able to shake off the thought that perhaps he regretted what happened last night. Or, God forbid, it had been a big disappointment.

It irritates me that I still do that, putting myself down, but I can't seem to stop it. Years of conditioning is hard to break out of.

"Come here." His deep rumble pierces my thoughts, as he reaches over the table, grabs my hand, and pulls me up.

I can't help casting a quick glance outside to see if we're being watched, but Bill's back is turned and he's talking on the phone. Roar tugs me close to stand between his legs, his hands on my hips. Even with him sitting, and me still on my feet, I don't have to look too far down to find his eyes on me.

"I had to call Bill in this morning. A fight broke out between some guests and people got hurt. I kinda had my hands full when you called."

"That's okay," I mumble.

"Anyway, Bill heard my side of the conversation and guessed," he explains. "We've been friends for many years, and he's one of the few people who knows me best. Didn't take much for him to clue in."

For a moment, I just look down in his face; not smiling, but his eyes are soft on mine. I lift my hand and run my fingertips over the worry grooves between his eyes.

"I'm sorry that happened," I voice. "I hope everyone is okay?"

"Had to kick out some guests with Bill's help, but yes, everything should be okay."

He grabs my hand and tugs me down, hooking me behind the neck as soon as he can reach. When he lifts his chin in invitation, I don't hesitate to give him my lips. His kiss is soft—conciliatory. When he lets me go, he has one hand cupping my face, his thumb gently brushing my lips.

"Next time, I'll leave a note."

SEVENTEEN

When did she become my measure?

Leelo

"Hello?"

I stick my head out of the kitchen, when for the fifth time today; I'm interrupted.

I've been busy all day, setting up the buffet and preparing the leek and potato soup and stuffed peppers for dinner tonight. I was going to wait opening up the restaurant until the motel got a little busier, but yesterday when Bill got wind of my plans, he pushed me to just go ahead. He promised to spread the word, and would personally show up with his wife.

Roar mumbled something about putting a sign up on the message board.

I haven't heard from either one since they took off in the boat yesterday, but I hope they come through, or else I'll have thirty stuffed peppers and almost four gallons of soup to freeze.

"Smells good in here."

I smile at the fifth new person to walk in the door. The previous four were looking for rooms, and I'm guessing this guy is too.

"You're smelling tonight's menu," I share. "What can I do for you?"

"Well," he mutters, pulling his ball cap off his head and twisting it in his hands. "This used to be my overnight stop when Sam was in charge 'ere. Name's Tucker. I drive copper from the mine in Sudbury to Thunder Bay on Fridays. Had a hell of a time finding another spot to park my rig overnight, since Sam shut the place down."

I look over his shoulder to where he's indicating the massive eighteen-wheeler taking up half of the parking lot.

"Sam was my uncle," I say by way of introduction. "Nice to meet you, Tucker, my name is Leelo."

The grin I get back is missing a couple of teeth, but that doesn't dull its warmth.

"Well, I'll be darned," Tucker cackles. "You sure is nuttin' like your uncle said."

This time my smile is bittersweet with regret again. It's clear my uncle thought enough of me to have mentioned my name to one or two people. I should've come up here while he was still alive.

"Where would Sam usually have you park?" I shake off the sudden sadness, and get down to business.

"Had me pull it in beside the shed," he says without hesitation. "So's not to block the parking lot."

"Sounds good to me. You staying the night then, Tucker?"

"If you've got me a bed, I'm hanging around. Wouldn't mind me some of whatever it is you're cooking either."

"I've got unit two open. Let me go grab you a key so you can settle in. Buffet is open at five," I say, after taking a quick peek at the clock. I have an hour.

Five rooms rented between noon and four. Seven in total when you add the Walters family. Only one left, not too shabby.

I'm smiling when I head back into the kitchen.

Half an hour later, I hear the bell over the door once again, immediately followed by heavy footsteps coming in this direction. I barely have time to put the lid back on the soup and turn around, when a pair of arms circle my middle.

"Hey," Roar's voice resonates in my ear.

"Hey yourself." I turn around in his arms to look at him but barely get the chance before he's kissing me.

"Smells good. I'm starving," he says, reaching around me to lift the lid and peek in the pan.

"Save it," I order, smiling. "I need a hand transferring the food into the buffet servers."

Without a word, he moves me aside and takes charge. Doesn't take long before my buffet is set up. Three servers with fresh biscuits, soup, and stuffed peppers respectively.

"Can I eat now?" Roar says, his mouth full of biscuit.

I grin, just shaking my head as I carry the standing blackboard with tonight's menu outside. I've barely set it up when Tucker steps out of unit two.

By ten minutes past five, I've got a small line, up at the buffet, and I'm starting to get worried I might not have enough. Tucker alone has downed two large bowls of soup and is on his third stuffed pepper.

Almost every table is occupied, and I'm busy enough to consider I might need to hire someone to help me out the three nights I plan to be open.

"Aren't you glad I suggested not putting everything out all at once," Roar leans over and whispers in my ear.

"Whatever." I roll my eyes at him. We'd bickered earlier when I wanted him to put everything out and he told me that wasn't a good idea. "Smug is not a pretty look on you," I throw over my shoulder, on my way to the kitchen, listening to him chuckle behind me.

-

"So what are we eating tomorrow?" Bill asks me, wiping a trace of tomato sauce from his lips.

"Bill!" his wife, Nancy, whom I was introduced to earlier, admonishes him.

"What?" he reacts, a look of fake innocence on his face, before turning to me with a wink as I clear away their plates. "I'm just looking out for you, honey. Gives you a nice break from cooking."

The two bicker their way out the door after being the last ones to say goodbye.

I'm still shaking my head a little later, carrying the last stack of dirty dishes to the kitchen, where Roar is leaning his hip against the counter.

"What about you?" he asks, as I dump the plates in the large sink.

"What about me?"

"You haven't eaten," he points out.

"I've been inhaling the smell of food all day. I'm not hungry right now, I'll probably grab something later," I assure him.

"You'll be busy later." There's no mistaking his meaning, when I turn around and catch his look. "Don't want you wasting away," he adds.

I snort. Loudly.

"I doubt you haven't noticed that me wasting away isn't something you'd have to worry about."

Instead of answering right away, he looks me over—thoroughly—before wrapping me up against his chest, his beard tickling my face.

"But I do," he finally says. "I haven't had a chance to properly explore some of those curves—yet."

Roar

I force my eyes open so I can see her.

As promised, I explored every curve, every crevice, every inch of her body, with my hands, lips, and eyes. Without words, just with touch, she slowly relaxed and gave herself over.

Her face is turned to the side, lips open and swollen from my kisses, strands of blue are plastered to her face, and her arms are stretched out wide on the mattress, their colour a sharp contrast to the white sheets.

She's a picture of surrender, trusting me to bring her to that edge, and over.

The only sounds are our heavy breathing and the sharp slap of skin, each time I drive my cock into her, until I can't hold back the groans.

I know she's close too, when her fingers curl in the sheets and her body strains for release. I cover her back with my front, slipping my hand between her hip and the mattress. Her clit is slick and distended, easily found, as I roll it firmly under the pad of my middle finger. It doesn't take long for her body to spasm underneath and around me, and I follow her over, my legs trembling from the effort as my hips buck with little control.

"My God…" she manages, as she tries to catch her breath

I take a little of my weight off her with my arms, but am not ready to lose my connection with her.

"Hardly." I smile when her eyes pop open and she twists a little to look at me.

"Really?" The incredulous look on her face is priceless, and I chuckle as I roll off her, onto my back. "You know," she says, lifting her arm across my stomach and her chin on my chest. "It strikes me that as someone whose verbal acuity can be lacking at times, your body certainly has the better communication skills."

"Just better?"

"Fine," she grins. "Do you like *outstanding* better?"

"Much better," I growl, rolling her over and proving my point with my mouth on hers, before planting a final kiss on her stomach and getting up.

I clean up in the bathroom, and grab a wet washcloth for her.

The clock on her nightstand shows only nine forty-five, but tomorrow is Saturday; when most of the cabins need to be cleared and cleaned before the next load of guests arrive. Besides, since Friday night is the last night for most guests, it can get a bit rowdy at times. I don't want any repeats of the other night.

"Are you off?" she asks, pulling a nightie from under the pillow and slipping it over her head.

"Busy day tomorrow and I'd best keep an eye on things tonight," I explain, as I pull on my jeans before walking over to where she is fiddling with the hem of her nightshirt. I take her face in my hands and tilt it up. "I'd much rather stay here, or drag you off to my bed, but we both have a full house." I press a hard kiss to her lips before I step back to pull on my shirt. "We'll figure it out," I add with a wink.

"Yeah." Her voice is soft and her smile is wistful. "I know."

I really fucking like her.

-

"Hey, buddy."

Ace comes barrelling from the lodge the moment I open the door. I didn't want to bring him tonight, people tend to frown on dogs in restaurants, so the poor animal's been cooped up for hours.

He trots in front of me, marking every grass blade he comes across, as I do my nightly round of the property. It's quiet. Seems much more subdued than I would expect a normal Friday night during the summer to be. I'm guessing everyone is treading lightly after Thursday morning's incident.

I check to make sure the doors are secure on the single empty cabin—the one those yuppie idiots were staying at—before I head over to the small campfire next door.

"Hey there," I call out to the woman, who's roasting marshmallows with her kids.

"Oh, hi," Elaine says, smiling when she recognizes me. Ace immediately saunters to the kids who give him some loving.

"How's Steve?" I flip a log on its end and sit down beside her.

"Good. He'll be released tomorrow. No bleeds, no swelling, just a severe concussion."

"That's great to hear. Have you decided yet whether you're staying for your second week, or are you heading home?"

"Steve wants to stay," she answers, smiling. "The kids love it here, and he says he still wants to get some fishing in."

"And what about you?" I ask, noting she doesn't say anything about her own preference.

"Oh, I'm happy as long as Steve and the kids are having a good time," she says, and suddenly Leelo comes to mind.

I could see her not giving a second thought to her own needs, her focus on making sure her kids were happy and her husband was taken care of. As commendable as that may be, I much rather see the woman I've come to know, who seems to be slowly discovering what it is she would like out of life.

"Well, let me know should you need anything" I smile at Elaine, nod at the kids, and slap my leg to get Ace's attention.

There's one more small group gathered around a fire behind one of the other cottages, but the rest of the point is quiet.

My last stop is the main dock, where my Bayliner is tied off. There I sit down, pull the cigar from my shirt pocket where I tucked it earlier, and give in to my weekly indulgence.

There'd been a time when I smoked cigarettes, close to a pack a day. It was a habit I'd gotten into overseas. There was little else to do in the mountains of Afghanistan once nightfall came, and we hunkered down for the night. In the first year after I got back home, I used smoking as an excuse to step outside, away from the constant strain that was palpable in our house. It wasn't until well after my marriage had completely imploded, that I decided to quit, only allowing myself this one cigar on Friday nights to get my head focused on the week to come.

Almost as good as a weekly session with a shrink, I use the time to process and read through the thoughts I scribble down on pieces of paper during the previous week.

I pull my billfold from my pocket and fish out the seven random scraps: a corner of a newspaper, a piece of a napkin, a page torn from a small notebook. Scraps in all shapes and sizes that hold one prevailing thought for every day of the week.

Another habit I picked up while deployed, while others would scribble entire entries in journals or letters to loved ones, I would try to summarize my day into one single thought. There had been times when my life in those conditions became so overwhelming—my brain was so overloaded—it would not stop churning at night.

I learned to compress the crap I saw and did, on any given day, into one single line. By jotting it down, I could clear my head enough to get a decent night's sleep. My own version of a journal, with the lone entries for each day painting a timeline through the ups and downs of my life.

Odd as it may sound, reading through my scraps at the end of a week gives me a sense of where I am. A touchstone.

As I flip through the pieces of paper, I notice again, as I've done more frequently in recent weeks, that my focus has become almost singular.

Just about every entry is a reference to the woman whose bed I reluctantly left earlier tonight.

Leelo

I have no idea what time it is when the insistent ringing wakes me up.

My hand knocks my book off the nightstand before it finally finds my phone.

"Hello?" I mumble sleepily, as I reach for the switch of my nightlight with my other hand and note the time on my alarm clock.

Eleven fifteen.

"Hello?" I repeat a little more firmly, when I don't immediately get an answer.

"You know, I always knew you were a miserable bitch, but this is low, even for you."

It takes me a moment to register who is on the other line, but when I do, I scoot straight up in my bed.

"What? Why are you calling—how did you get this number?"

Although, even as I'm asking, I know who would've passed it on. And I don't really expect an answer anyway.

"You're asking me why I'm calling? Are you out of your fucking mind? This is about my son, goddammit!"

"Our son," I interject as if by rote.

David always liked to refer to the children as his, as if it wasn't me who carried them for nine months, and birthed them, and raised them practically by myself because he was so busy building his business and fucking his goddamn bookkeeper. But David is on a rant; he doesn't even hear me, which is not news either.

"It's one thing for you to move your worthless ass out to the boonies, but for Matt, it's throwing away an entire future. He's making the biggest mistake of his life by listening to your irresponsible, idealistic bullshit ideas."

I stopped listening at the mention of Matt's name.

"Wait. What? Mattie is coming here?"

EIGHTEEN

She stills my mind and wakes my instincts—I'm falling.

Leelo

"He's an asshole, Mom."

I look at my son, agreement on my lips, but I keep the words from rolling off. For him. Because I won't sabotage their relationship—not again. The last time I did that, it didn't work out so well for me, and I seriously hurt my kids in the process.

I'd been angry with Matt when I finally saw his headlights pull into the parking lot at close to six o'clock this morning. Furious, actually, and terrified. I'd been trying to call him from the time I got off with his father. I didn't get much useful information from David as to what happened, he was too busy raging at me. I ended up hanging up on him, in hopes Matt could explain, but he didn't answer his phone the entire night.

Not like I could go to sleep after that phone call and without knowing how, or where the hell my son was.

So yeah, when he first walked in, I was ready to tear a strip off him, but then I saw his face. All I did was open my arms and let him cry on my shoulder.

We're sitting on the dock, watching the sun come up with a cup of coffee. I'm going to have to get breakfast started soon, but my kid comes first.

"What happened, Bud?" I probe when Matt just stares out over the water.

"Last night was Dad's surprise fiftieth birthday party," he starts, dropping his eyes to the mug in his hands. "I overheard Dad say to someone that he was hoping to hand over the business to me in five years. I choked it back until everyone had left but, Mom, I had to say something. I don't want that." He looks up at me with tears in his eyes. "I don't want to take over his business, his life. That's not me."

"I know, baby." I put a comforting hand on his knee.

"We got into a big fight when I told him that. It was ugly, and by the end, Jess walked out and Gwen was crying, trying to smooth things over. But, Mom, he said and did some pretty fucking shitty things."

"Oh, honey…" I reach for his face, but he twists away.

"Anyway," he says, getting up. "I grabbed what I could off the lawn and got out of there. Been driving all night and I'm tired. I'm gonna crash."

"Wait…" I call out when he starts walking down the dock. Something he said just registers. "Why was your stuff on the lawn?" I demand, getting to my feet.

Matt doesn't stop, or answer, and I rush after him. Grabbing him by the arm, I repeat my question.

"Matt, why was your stuff on the lawn?"

He slowly turns to face me, and I can see the answer on his face even before he gives me the mumbled words.

"That's where he threw them."

212

With a sharp jerk of his arm, he slips out of my grip and continues inside. This time, although my heart hurts for him, I let him go.

-

Apparently rage can be very productive.

My first instinct had been to call the prick. Seemed like fair payback, calling him out of bed on a Saturday morning, when I know he likes to sleep in. Just like he knows I go to bed early most nights, but that didn't stop him either when he woke me up last night.

Rather than to follow my usual pattern, to react first and think later, I've been in the kitchen mostly, feeding the guests who started drifting in for breakfast.

It's after eleven now, and other than the Walters family, as well as the couple in unit three, everyone has already checked out. Matt is still sleeping upstairs, and to keep my head from exploding or making an already bad situation worse, I've baked.

Muffins, sausage rolls, apple turnovers—my entire stainless steel island is covered with baked goods, and I've run out of eggs. Maybe I can borrow some off Roar; it's closer than going into town.

At least that's what I tell myself as I dial Jackson's Point.

"Good morning, Jackson's Point."

Crap.

I didn't even consider Patti being there, but of course she would be. It's a busy day in the hospitality industry. At least it is for most.

"Hi," I start hesitantly. "Is Roar there?"

"Who can I say is calling?"

I cringe. I was hoping she'd just hand over the phone, now I wish I hadn't called. *Eggs*, such a lame excuse to hear a friendly voice.

"It's Lilith Talbot. Whitefish Motel?" I add

"Yes, I remember," she says, curtly. "Let me see if he's available."

"Thank y—" I start, but the sharp impact of the phone hitting a hard surface cuts me off. All right then.

I'm still waiting ten minutes later, wondering if I should just give it up, when a click on the line indicates a call waiting. Checking my call display, I make a snap decision.

"Hey, sweetie," I greet Gwen, switching calls. "Matt is here. He's safe. If that's why you're calling. He mentioned turning off his phone last night."

"And he couldn't call when he got there? Jesus, Mom—you could've picked up the phone too. I've been worried sick."

I swallow down the accusatory tone; reminding myself she was scared, much like I was all night.

"I'm sorry, honey. I'm still trying to get a grip on what happened. Your father wasn't very helpful when he called last night, and Matt just gave me some basics this morning, before crashing. He's still sleeping."

The sniffles on the other end of the line cut me to the core. Matt has always been the sensitive one of the two, but Gwen tends to keep her emotions tightly locked away. This is the second time in as many months I hear her crying.

"It was so ugly, Mom," she finally says, using much the same words her brother did earlier this morning.

"So I gather," I offer gently, ignoring the call-waiting click in my ear.

"Dad…he completely lost it. I've never heard him be so deliberately hurtful." She pauses briefly before continuing. "Except perhaps with you," she finishes softly.

"Right." It's all I can think of to say. It brings a lump to my throat because in all these years, this is the first time my daughter acknowledges her father may not have been perfect in his treatment of me. I don't know why it matters so much, especially in this moment, but it does.

"Is Mattie okay?"

"Sad, I think. Exhausted for sure. He seemed a little shell-shocked, but I'm sure fatigue had something to do with that as well."

"What are we going to do?" she asks.

"Nothing," I immediately reply. "Nothing but listen and not get in the way of them working this out."

"But, Mom—maybe if we could—"

"Trust me when I say this, sweetie, let them work it out. If you try and meddle in some way, it will just come back to bite you in the butt. If not from one, it'll be from the other."

She seems to be processing what I'm trying to tell her, because it takes her a while to speak.

"Is Matt going to stay?" she asks in a small voice.

"He's welcome if he wants to, but I'm not going to put pressure on him, one way or another. He has to find his own way."

"If he does, can I maybe come visit next month? I have some vacation time coming."

"Of course," I assure her. "Whether Matt is here or not, I would love for you to visit."

Again I'm met with silence, but I wait it out despite another click on the line.

"Dad told Matt he'd never amount to anything on his own. That he was glad he had at least one child with half a brain." I try to stifle the involuntary gasp, but Gwen doesn't miss it. "I never knew how mean he could be."

"Sorry, honey," I tell my second child this morning. I can't help feeling some responsibility, if only for not being able to shield my kids from their father's brand of nasty.

"Can you ask Matt to call me? I'm home. I drove back to Toronto first thing this morning."

"I will. As soon as he wakes up," I promise.

After she hangs up, I ignore the state of my kitchen and slip out the side door and sit down on the porch steps, where a large maple provides welcome shade on an already hot day.

Roar

"Who was it?"

I wave the dead phone at her, whoever had been on the line had hung up by the time I picked up.

Patti looks up from where she's filing away last week's paperwork.

"Lilith Talbot."

"Leelo?"

She shrugs her shoulders and returns her attention to the stack of bills, while I call back. No answer. I try again with the same result. Weird. My first thought is that something else has happened.

"Did she say why she was calling?"

Patti drops the stack of papers back down on the desk and whirls around.

"She didn't exactly share," she snaps, disbelief clear on her face. "Asshole," she adds for good measure, before slamming the file drawer shut with a bang, and marching out of the office.

"Wait!" I hurry out, catching up with her outside. "I'm sorry that you're pissed, but she's over there alone. She's had some really disturbing shit happen recently, and I'm worried."

I catch a flash of guilt before she turns her eyes to the water, in the direction of the motel.

"I didn't know," she mumbles. "I left her waiting for a while before I called you."

Fuck.

Without a word I dive back in the office, grab my keys and phone, before charging back outside.

"Gonna check on her. I've got my phone," I tell Patti as I brush by her.

On the short trip over, my mind manages to conjure up one scenario after another, each more disturbing than the next. So by the time I walk into the bar and look toward the kitchen to see a wide set of shoulders about to disappear into her house beyond, I'm primed for a fight.

"Hey!" I yell, following him in, but I grind to a halt when I recognize her son, Matt.

"Hey," he says, barely looking up as he sits down at the dining table and shoves half a sandwich in his mouth.

"Where's your mom?"

"Don't know. I just woke up." He shrugs and turns his attention back to the plate in front of him. "She can't be far," he says, holding up a muffin. "This is still warm from the oven."

I find her sitting on the porch steps, her arms wrapped around her knees.

"You okay?"

She looks up, surprised, as I lower myself on the step beside her.

"What are you doing here?" she asks, answering my question with a question.

"Checking on you. Wasn't sure what I'd find, after you apparently hung up on me."

"Oh shit." She slaps her hand over her mouth. "I forgot. I'm so sorry," she says, grabbing my arm. "It's just…things have gone to hell in a handbasket since you left last night." She blushes at the reference. When I left her last night, she was well and sated in her bed. I'd made sure of that.

"Anything to do with Matt being here?"

Leelo's head drops down between her shoulders, and I automatically reach for her, sliding my hand up her back. Without thinking I start rubbing the tense muscles in her neck.

"Everything," she sighs, before turning her face to me. "I'm sorry I hung up. I just wanted to talk to you when Gwen called, and…well, I kinda forgot to call back."

"Wanna talk to me now?"

218

-

Part of me wants to drive eight hours, just so I can smack some sense into that asshole ex of hers, but I can't. I have a business to run. So instead, I give Leelo a last hug and quick kiss, ignore the looks Matt throws me through the window, and head back to the lodge with the promise I'll be by for a bite tonight.

After hearing the whole story, I can see why Matt was surly, but I'm already thinking ahead. The kid is good with his hands, and there sure as hell is enough work for him up here if he wants it.

The motel may be as good as done, but other than a bit of paint, nothing has been done to the house. There's still the boat ramp Leelo wanted put in and plenty of other odds and ends to work on just here. Hell, I have a whole to-do list of things at the lodge I could use help with. And that's just off the top of my head.

Between the motel and the lodge, we could keep him busy all summer. Give him a chance to find some steady ground under his feet, earn a bit of money. Who knows; maybe when folks get used to him around town, see the kind of work he does, he'll have more jobs coming his way.

Something maybe to broach with him tonight, when he's had a chance to get his bearings.

The afternoon flies by with only minor snags to resolve; a dripping tap in one of the units, a busted AC window unit in another. Nothing out of the ordinary, so when five thirty rolls around, after I just gave the last guests a tour of their cabin for the week, I get ready to head over to Leelo's.

Patti left for home earlier. I'm pretty sure she avoided me this afternoon but fuck, I can't exactly say I'm sorry about that. Don't get me wrong, I feel bad she's disappointed, but I don't know how to fix that. There's nothing I can say to make her feel better.

After a quick shower and change, and feeding Ace his dinner, I pull the door closed behind me, when my phone rings.

"Bill," I answer, with a quick glance at my call display.

"Guess who I just ran into," he jumps right in.

"I give up."

"You're no fun," he chuckles. "Our favourite local real estate agent."

"Thompson?"

"One and the same. Spotted him coming out of the tavern in town. He seemed a bit unstable when he got into his car, so I decided to pull him over. Point zero eight."

"You screened him?"

"Hey, I observed the guy swaying with my own eyes," he sputters. "Told him with that reading I could take him into the detachment to make sure he wasn't over the limit. He seemed, for lack of a better word, a tad reluctant, so I offered him an alternative."

"I bet you did," I snort.

"Had a little chat, he and I. Oh, he did a good job of looking surprised when I mentioned the missing dock and the deer carcass. But when I pointed out how curious it was that both his boat and his car might have been spotted around the time of those incidents, I swear I could see him blanch under that fake tan of his."

"You lied," I conclude with a grin.

"Not at all," he denies firmly. "He was seen driving off the motel property several times by several people, and his boat was spotted right where we found the dock."

"Not necessarily on the same day, though," I point out.

"Yeah…but *he* doesn't know that."

By the time I walk in, four of the tables are already occupied. The blackboard outside lists grilled chicken and pineapple kebabs, peanut sauce, and something called quinoa salad. I'm not sure about fruit with my meat, and I don't have a fucking clue what *quinoa salad* is, but I'm willing to try anything Leelo puts in front of me.

I'm glad to see Matt is pulling his weight, serving drinks to a few tables before he spots me and walks over.

"Am I gonna like it?" I ask him, catching him off guard.

"Like what?"

"Whatever the fuck your mom has on the menu for tonight?"

I'm rewarded with a lopsided smile.

"It's the bomb. You'll love it," he grins.

"Okay. I'll take your word for it. I'll have a Moosehead, if you have one cold?"

While he fetches my beer, I grab a plate and load up at the buffet. I try to peek into the kitchen, but don't see Leelo.

"Where's your mom?" I ask when Matt delivers my bottle.

"Back porch. Barbecuing the kebabs. I'm sure she won't mind your company." I look up from my plate at his words.

221

"Good to know," I say cautiously. A whole lot was said with that single sentence, but it pays to make sure. "I like your mom."

"Figured that when I was here last time, and it was kind of hard to miss when I saw you sucking face earlier. It's cool," he adds with a shrug. "She seems to like you, too."

I don't know the proper protocol here—not like I'm well-schooled in the whole dating thing, let alone dealing with kids in that mix—so I decide to go with my gut. I pick up my beer and plate and with a, "*Thanks, man*" to Matt; I head out back.

I'm greeted with a smile the moment I step out on the porch. One that stirs the blood in my veins.

"You're back," she says when I sit down on the steps, set my beer down, and take my first bite of chicken. It's fucking delicious.

"You keep giving me more reasons to come back," I tell her around my mouthful.

Her bright boisterous laugh settles warm in my chest.

NINETEEN

From sunshine to moonlight goddess.

Roar

"I'm sorry if I get in your way," Matt says, casting his line in the water.

The sun is dropping and traffic on the lake is dying down at this time of night. Ace is in his usual spot in the bow of the boat, his head hanging over the side, looking for fish. At Leelo's urging, we left her with the cleanup after the third dinner in a row I showed up for. She's a good cook, much better than I am. So why would I mess up my kitchen when I can get a good meal five minutes down the road? Besides, it gives me a chance to see her, since the weekends are generally busy for me at the lodge.

No sleepovers though. Not last night and probably not tonight either. It would be a bit awkward bumping into her son in the middle of the night. The logistics may be a bit of a challenge, but I'm sure we'll find ways to make it work. In the meantime, having Matt there during the nights, makes me sleep a fuck load better in my own bed.

"You don't, I'm actually glad you're here," I admit. "Not sure if your mom's had a chance to fill you in, but it looks like someone enjoys messing with her."

Credit to the kid, his eyes immediately flare as he looks up.

"Messing with her, how?"

Tension radiates off him as I remind him of the bear incident before filling him in on what's happened since.

"That sleezy dude in the Italian loafers? The one she ripped a strip off?"

"As I recall it, she ripped a pretty good-sized strip off all of us, but yes, that's the guy."

"So why isn't he under arrest or something?" Matt demands to know.

"First of all, we may believe it's him, but no one actually saw him do anything, and there's no real evidence. Secondly, what he did constitutes vandalism at most, not generally something they lock you up and throw away the key for," I explain, understanding the kid's frustration.

I feel it, too. Kyle Thompson worries me. It's not normal for a grown-assed man to resort to those kinds of vindictive antics unless he's unbalanced to begin with. That's something I've come to learn about Kyle, he's got a mean streak a mile wide, and when he doesn't get what he wants, there's no telling how far he'll take things. Which is why I feel better knowing Matt is around.

"We should probably head back," Matt says, looking over my shoulder in the general direction of the motel.

"Sure thing."

"And for the record," he adds, pulling in his line as I start up the motor. "Appreciate you looking out for Mom."

I bite down a smile. "Not a problem."

"I gathered that," I hear him mumble under his breath and this time I don't hold back, I throw my head back and bark out a laugh. I like the kid.

Leelo

"Tomorrow night, I cook."

I look up from the rock I've been trying to move, unsuccessfully I might add.

"Fish fry," Roar offers.

"What's in a fish fry?" Matt wants to know, walking up with the wheelbarrow.

"Fish."

"Cool."

"Actually," I clarify, in hopes to lift the dialogue from the monosyllabic exchange I've been listening to most of the afternoon. "Technically there's a bit more than just fish in Roar's fish fry. He dips the fish in beer batter before he fries it."

"What's in beer batter?"

"Beer," Roar grunts.

"Cool."

"Oh, for Pete's sake!" Ready to pull my hair out, I toss down the shovel and take off toward the house. I have a large bottle of wine in the fridge.

It's boiling hot out here, my SPF 50 is sluicing off my body, leaving me exposed to the scorching sun, and I don't burn pretty—think lobster. I'm sweating like a

225

goddamn faucet and I'm sick and tired of the less than stimulating conversation. *Men.* They either barely take a breath when yelling at you—like David's done twice more since Friday night; before I decided to ignore his subsequent calls—or they can barely string two words together.

It's possible I may also be more than a little frustrated that in the past four days since Matt showed up, I've barely managed to catch a moment alone with Roar. He doesn't seem to mind, spending more time with Matt than with me.

"Was it something I said?" I hear Roar ask Matt, as Ace follows behind me, hoping for food, no doubt.

"Nah, Gwen says it's menopause. Mood swings worse than PMS, apparently."

I swear if ever there was an excuse for filicide, surely this is it. Instead I throw my head back and scream at the sky.

Fuck the wine—this is a scotch kind of day.

-

"Is everything all right?"

I'm sitting on a kitchen chair in front of the window unit, sipping my second glass of scotch, promising myself that if there is any way I can work it in my budget, I'm installing central air, when Roar walks in.

"I'm fine," I grumble, lying as I usually do when giving that answer. Ace barely lifts his head from where he's lying at my feet, he doesn't like the heat either.

I'm not fine. I appear to be stuck in the mother of all hot flashes, near tears, and will surely lose that battle with the next kind word. I try to ignore the sounds of Roar rummaging around the kitchen behind me, until something blissfully cold is pressed against the back of my neck.

"My God, what is that?"

"Peaches and cream corn, I think. Just grabbed the first bag from the freezer and wrapped it in a towel."

Frozen corn, I never thought it was worth crying over until now.

"Are you crying?" I can vaguely make him out through blurred eyes as he crouches down to look at me. "Sunshine?"

"You h-had to go and b-be nice, didn't you?" I accuse, feeling him laugh as he pulls my head forward to rest on his shoulder. "I'm a puddle."

"I've noticed," he deadpans, as his big hand presses the cold compress firmer to my skin.

After sitting quietly like that for a bit, I can feel my body cooling down. In hindsight, my grab for the scotch may not have been such a brilliant idea; I really didn't need the added flush of alcohol. I'm feeling better now, though, and I gingerly lift my face from where I've left a giant damp spot on Roar's shirt.

"How did you know to do that?"

He shrugs his shoulders and with his free hand brushes a strand of hair that is stuck to my face. "Charlie," he says. "I remember her walking around with bags of frozen peas draped around her neck. Thought it might help."

"Sorry," I mumble, suddenly embarrassed. I'd carried on like a lunatic. "I've been a bear."

I've barely finished my sentence when his lips are brushing mine.

"Hush," he rumbles. "It's been a rough couple of days."

Yes. Yes it has. All of a sudden something occurs to me and I sit back to look at him.

"Is that why you've been keeping your distance?"

"You had a lot going on, thought I'd give you some space."

"Well, you can stop that now," I suggest a tad snippily.

"So noted." He smirks, not in the least impressed with my foul mood. It almost has me in tears again.

"It'd be nice to have one man in my life who's not grunting or yelling at me."

I can feel the air chill around me as Roar goes completely still, the smile gone and his eyes narrowed.

"Who's yelling?"

"It's nothing," I say quickly, putting what I hope is a calming hand on his arm. Last thing I need is David to have another reason to be pissed at me, and that is exactly what will happen if Roar gets involved.

"Who the fuck is yelling?" he repeats forcefully, and the dog lifts his head, ears perked up.

"Dad," Matt says, walking in the door. "He's been calling me since you stopped answering your phone." He looks at me, shrugging his shoulders like it's all the same to him.

It's not. I know my boy better than that. He hates confrontation, always has.

"I'm sorry," I offer, but Matt sharply shakes his head.

"Don't. Don't take responsibility for this—for him. You've done enough of that."

"You going to start crying again?" Roar asks, a hand curled under my chin when my eyes fill at Matt's words.

"Nope," I answer, blinking my eyes furiously and breathing deeply.

"He calls again, I wanna talk to him."

"Oh no, no, no. I don't think that's a good idea," I sputter, noticing the grim set of his mouth.

"He wants to talk to you, he does so respectfully or he deals with me. No room for negotiation on that."

I'm about to protest, when I spot Matt hiding a smile behind his hand, and promptly close my mouth.

Roar

I make sure Charlie is buckled in before I get behind the wheel.

There was a time this would be a weekly occurrence, but I can't get her to come up to the lodge often anymore. First she'd still drive out on her own, before she had a close encounter with a moose one night, but even after that, I'd swing by to fetch her almost weekly for a fish fry. She hasn't been out here yet this season, but when I told her Leelo and her son would be there for dinner, she was game.

"How's the motel coming along?" she asks, as I pull onto the road.

"Good. She's pretty busy. The rooms are all done and she's mostly converted the bar to a dining room. Food is good too. You should come try it "

"Would love to," Charlie smiles before turning her gaze out the window.

She seems a bit distracted. More than usual and I'm worried about her. Eighty-one years old, and there was a time I thought for sure she'd live forever. She's by far the strongest person I know, but lately she's been withdrawing a little. When I asked her the other day about Bob Duran, she didn't even remember he'd been her date at the music festival a few weeks ago.

I should make more of an effort to get her out of her apartment.

"What's that?"

She points out the window when we pass the motel.

"Bobcat," I answer. They must've dropped it off this afternoon.

We'd done as much clearing as we could by hand yesterday, but we needed that piece of machinery to level the trail properly. Leelo's already ordered a precast slab to be delivered the end of this week, so in order for the truck to be able to get to the water, we need that trail done.

"She's installing a boat launch," I clarify when Charlie looks at me confused. "That thing can clear rocks and tree stumps we can't do by hand."

"You've been helping out then?"

"When I can," I concede.

"Do you think she'll hack it up here?"

Charlie's question surprises me and I turn to find her looking at me intently.

"I think so. She's tough, and she seems to love it here."

"Good. That's good." Charlie leans her head back in her seat and closes her eyes.

Not entirely sure what that was all about, but I decide to leave it alone and let her have her catnap.

-

"So tell me about your plans?"

Matt, who just walks up with a few fresh beers from the office fridge, is pinned by Charlie's question. His eyes flit over to his mother before turning back to Charlie.

The remnants of dinner are burning up in the fire pit, and we're all sitting back, enjoying the substantially cooler night.

"They're still developing," he says carefully. "I'd love to make a life here. Build a business, and eventually a house, if I find the right piece of property."

"Sounds like plans to me. I'm sure your mother won't mind having you underfoot in the meantime."

I hear Leelo's barely suppressed snort and have a hard time keeping a straight face myself. Although Charlie appears oblivious, Matt isn't and chuckles out loud.

"Maybe in small doses, but I have a feeling Mom may have a newfound appreciation for her empty nest. Ouch," he says in the next breath, ducking to avoid a bottle cap Leelo deftly twists off her beer and aims at his head.

"I imagine she does," Charlie mumbles, not half as clueless as I thought she'd be, before continuing a little louder. "I'm getting a little tired. Would you mind terribly driving me home?" I'm ready to get up but her eyes are firmly fixed on Matt.

"Sure," he agrees before I have a chance to jump in. "Be happy to drive you home."

"Excellent." My meddling mother is virtually rubbing her hands together as she gets up from her chair. "Gives me a chance to pick your brain about a few repairs I'd like done to my cabin across the lake."

"Wait," Leelo jumps up as well. "Let me just grab my purse. Matt can just throw me out at home."

"Nonsense," Charlie says resolutely. "I'm sure Riordan can drive you home at some point."

Effectively manipulated by an octogenarian and a man-child, Leelo and I watch as Matt's taillights disappear down the road.

"You said nothing!" She swings around, punching me in the arm.

"Fuck no. Not gonna hear me complain." I pull her against me and wrap her in my arms.

"Jesus, Roar...your mother and my kid...this is embarrassing," she mumbles into my shirt.

"Just so you know, your son doesn't begrudge you this."

"How would you know?" she asks, tilting her head back.

"Because he told me in so many words. As for Charlie, I'm guessing she likes the idea of us." I let go of her, grab her hand, and snag my bottle from the picnic table. "Now grab your beer and come with me."

The night is quiet and the only ripples on the water are those made by my boat and the odd fish. I'm heading north to a quiet inlet, a ways up the lake, where I often go in the early morning hours because it has the best bass fishing. The heat has killed off a lot of the bugs, so it's a

232

perfect night to do some stargazing. Especially up here, where there is no light pollution.

A lot of the land on the north side of the lake is only accessible by boat, and it's easy to imagine we've left civilization behind.

I glance over at Leelo, who is leaning back in the captain's chair, her eyes fixed on the sky and a ghost of a smile on her lips. The quarter moon paints her face a pale blue, making her look almost ethereal.

When I turn off the engine, she lazily rolls her head in my direction.

"Where are we?"

"My favourite place." Her smile gets wider as she redirects her gaze back up at the stars.

"Come here," I invite her, climbing on the bow of the boat, deep enough for me to stretch out, with my back propped against the windshield. I grab her outstretched hand and help her settle in beside me.

"This is perfect." Leelo's voice is soft, almost reverent.

I love that.

I love that she seems to feel the kind of awe that sometimes comes over me when I'm out here. A humble appreciation that someone of my insignificance gets to be witness to a beauty this grand.

"Thank you for bringing me here," she says, sitting up and twisting her body to lean in, brushing my lips with hers. Soft at first, tentative, until she deepens the kiss, and my cock instantly hardens in response.

Next thing I know, she is straddling me, her cut-offs tossed somewhere behind me in the boat. My shirt is off

233

and twisted around my arms, keeping them trapped above my head.

"Stay still," she whispers against my lips, as her hands make fast work of the buttons of my shorts, eliminating the last barrier between her heat and my dick.

It's hard, holding still, not touching her, and allowing her to set the pace. I want to touch.

"Uh-uh, use your other senses," she suggests when I shift, raining kisses on my face, my neck and down my chest. "Let me make you feel."

I *feel* all right. The moment her eager hands release my cock and her lips close over the crown, my hips involuntarily surge up from the deck.

"Mmmmm," she hums, only enhancing the sensation and it's all I can do to keep from tangling my fingers in that blue hair. She's not in a hurry, leisurely exploring me with her mouth and tongue until she has me panting like a racehorse.

"*Please.*" I don't think I've ever begged before. "*Fuck*, Sunshine—you're killing me."

The soft peal of her laughter bounces over the water when she releases my cock. Straightening, she reaches up, untangles my arms from the shirt, and places my hands on her hips. She holds on to my shoulder with one hand and with the other guides me inside her.

"Get naked," I growl when she's fully seated, helping her get rid of her shirt and bra, before leaning back and taking in the view.

She's fucking gorgeous, her full body on display like some lush, erotic porcelain doll. The colours of her ink fade out in the moonlight, leaving only a blue-tinted intricate pattern of lines down her arms.

The newest tattoo, two small birds taking flight from her heart, stands out in stark contrast against the pale skin of her breast.

TWENTY

She cares and it's as intimidating as it is heart-warming.

Leelo

"My apologies again."

Henry Kline finally called me back. I'd left a few messages on his direct line last week, but I should've called the firm's main number. If I had, I would've discovered he was on vacation.

Henry was my uncle's lawyer and good friend, although he and I didn't get off on the right foot. When he first got in touch to notify me my uncle had left me the motel, he'd assumed I would sell and had papers ready for me to sign, but I didn't want to rush any decisions.

He'd seemed genuinely surprised when I called him back a few weeks later to let him know I'd decided to get the Whitefish Motel up and running again. He'd voiced concern it might be too much to manage on my own, but I made it clear my mind was made up, and since then he's been very helpful.

"No worries," I reassure him. "Entirely my fault. It's a relief you were able to dig up the policy. I should probably have a copy on hand."

"Probably," Henry agrees. "In any event, before you call the insurance company, make sure you have a copy of the police report on hand. They'll want to see that."

"I'll make sure. I'm eager to get this sorted out. It's no fun trying to do the motel linens in my small washer and dryer. I have to run them all day, every day."

"I bet," Henry says, clearly uninterested in my laundry. "Out of curiosity, how is business?"

I spend the next twenty minutes filling him in on the improvements already in place, the steady flow of guests, and the success of my little restaurant. He seemed pleased and promised to drop by some time soon to taste my food.

Outside the morning is heating up. Thunderstorms are expected this afternoon, finally breaking this blasted heatwave. The guys are out there to finish the last stretch of the trail down to the water before the weather hits. It has to be ready for tomorrow morning when the concrete ramp will be delivered.

Grabbing a few cold bottles of water, I head down to where they are working.

"Hey," Roar calls out when he sees me approach.

At some point he's taken off his shirt and I do my best not to ogle his sweat-slicked chest. Since our little late night excursion on the lake a few nights ago, I've wondered when next I'd have a chance to get him naked. However, with my son just feet away, operating the Bobcat, the timing is clearly off.

I hand Roar the cold water, but he grabs my arm and pulls me in for a kiss. That's something new these past few days. Before he'd barely touch me with Matt around, but now he does so freely. Aside from a few pointed looks the first couple of times this happened, by now, Matt barely seems to notice.

"Do I call Bill for a copy of the police report?" I ask Roar when he lets me up for air. "Henry just called with the insurance information. I want to get this ball rolling, so I can at least get those appliances out of there and give the space a good scrubbing."

Instead of answering, he lets me go and pulls his phone from his pocket.

"Bill?—Yeah, Doyle. Listen, Leelo needs a copy of the police report. You gonna be in the neighbourhood?— Yes, the carcass.—Fine, I'll let her know."

He ends the call and slips the phone back in his pocket. I doubt that conversation even lasted a minute.

"He has to check on a report of an abandoned vehicle up the road anyway, so he'll drop it off sometime in the next hour."

"You don't waste words, do you?" I tease. "No *hey, how are you doing*, just straight to the point."

"The phone is for relaying messages—not for casual conversation," he says, taking a drink of water.

"Says who?"

"Me," he responds instantly, an arrogant smirk behind his beard, but his hazel eyes dance with humour.

"I'm pretty sure I remember a phone call or two where—"

"Tell me you brought me a water," Matt interrupts, climbing out of the Bobcat, but before I have a chance to answer, Roar picks up the bottle and tosses it in his direction. "Sweet," he says, twisting off the cap and downing half the bottle in one swig, before wiping his mouth with the back of his hand. "It's hot as balls."

"For now," Roar says, grinning. "Look north, system coming this way."

I look in the direction he's pointing and sure enough, I can see a dark ridge of clouds and the sky beyond is almost black.

"Yowza," Matt blurts out, dropping his bottle in the grass. "Best get this done, that looks like it's coming fast."

"Another hour if we're lucky," Roar says before turning to me. "They're predicting heavy rains and high winds, so check you've got all windows and doors secure, and make sure you have enough fuel for the generator. These summer storms can pack a punch up here, and it's not unusual for power to get knocked out. You want to be prepared."

"Shit. Okay, I'll check. But what about you? Shouldn't you be doing the same at the lodge?" I ask him.

"Got ready before I came here this morning," he explains, throwing an arm over my shoulders and tucking me close. "I'll head over to keep an eye on things as soon as we're done here."

He kisses the top of my head, gives my shoulder a squeeze and picks up the shovel he dropped earlier. With one last eyeful of his strong back and tight ass, I reluctantly turn back to the motel to get it storm ready.

-

I'm just pulling a load of sheets from the dryer when I hear a loud boom outside, followed by an ominous crunching noise before a heavy crash shakes the house, and the next instant everything is dark and eerily quiet.

The storm hit about thirty minutes ago. Fat raindrops started hitting the roof and windows, drumming out a loud staccato. Not long after that, the wind started howling, almost drowning out the sound of the TV I had tuned to the Weather Network. When the rain stopped falling hard, the sky lit up with lightning.

Matt went down for a nap after Roar took off. He mentioned they'd probably need to give the trail one more pass tomorrow morning, depending on what the storm will leave behind.

I've just been putzing around since he disappeared. Doing laundry and looking into upgrading the poorly executed, single-page website Uncle Sam apparently put up years ago. One look at it and I decided to start from scratch. Already have a landing page built and was just working on a rates page when the dryer dinged. I'll need to replace the default images with actual pictures of the motel, maybe of one of the rooms, but that will have to wait for a nicer day.

Fuck!

I drop the laundry and run to the computer. The screen is dark.

You know that slightly nauseating gnaw in your stomach when you wish you could go back just a few minutes and change what you now know to be a disastrous outcome? Right. A few hours of work down the drain because yours truly didn't save. Not a damn thing.

Loud knocking on the door separating the house from the bar interrupts my self-flagellation, and I rush to pull it open.

A very bedraggled Peter Walters stands on the other side, dripping water all over my floor.

"So sorry to barge in on you like this, but you may want to come have a look."

Something tells me the loss of a few hours of work is going to be the least of my problems. I shove my feet in a pair of flip-flops just inside the door, grab a slicker, and follow Peter through the restaurant to the front.

The rain is still coming down steadily and even though it's only four o'clock in the afternoon, it's almost dark outside. I'm surprised to see the rest of the Walters family sitting in the car in front of unit eight, but when I get closer I see why.

One of the tall pine trees lining the east side of the property is down, taking with it the hydro pole leading in power from the road, and caving in my roof.

"Jesus! Is everyone all right?"

I rush to the car parked out front and peek inside. Mrs. Walters rolls down the window a crack.

"We're fine, dear. Just a little plaster dust," she says, patting her wet hair.

"The kids?"

"Not a scratch," she assures me.

"Come inside where it's dry," I suggest but she firmly shakes her head.

"Not sure that's a good idea," her husband pipes up behind me. "We should probably call the fire department."

I whip around to look at him.

"What?"

"You have live hydro cables on your roof," he points out.

242

Roar

"*Phone!*" Patti is standing in the open office door, yelling through the storm.

She tried heading home earlier, but a downed tree in the road effectively cut us off from the main road, so she had to turn around.

I took my truck and went to see if I could chain it to my truck and drag it to the side, but the thing is huge, covering the road from one end to the other, and wedged in the trees on either side.

There's no simply pulling it out, it requires a chainsaw, which is why I'm back at the lodge, loading up whatever I think I might need when Patti calls out to me.

Pulling my beanie down over my eyes, I trot over to where she's leaning out, my cell in her hand.

"Yeah?" I answer, stepping just inside the door.

"Tree down at the Whitefish. Took out the hydro lines and part of the motel," my chief at the Wawa volunteer fire department barks without any introduction. "Head straight there. We'll bring your gear on the rig."

The last five years since the lodge has gotten busier, I've not been active as a volunteer firefighter, unless extra bodies are needed in case of major emergencies or when there are a large number of calls, which is probably the case now with the storm. There will likely be trees and power lines down all over the place, but the mention of the Whitefish Motel has me rushing out the door.

"Where are you off to?" Patti calls after me.

"Hydro lines down at the motel," I call back, already jogging back to my truck.

"You can't get out!"

Fucking hell. The road is blocked.

"Taking the boat," I yell, changing direction to the dock.

"You're crazy! You don't go out on the water in this weather!"

"I'll be fine, just keep the dog inside!"

She's right, but I don't slow down. I'll stick close to the shore, but there's nothing that will stop me from getting out there.

Once on the water, I pull out my phone and try contacting Leelo but I end up with voicemail. Over and over again.

By the time I slide alongside the dock, after a harrowing trip across the lake with the storm raging around me, I'm about to lose my shit. I lash the boat to the dock cleat and take off toward the motel.

You can't miss the damage. The top of a large pine has caved in a portion of the roof over a few of the units, and I can see the exposed hydro cable hanging down the back of the motel. I head around the building on the other side, by the house, and run smack into Matt, almost knocking him down.

"Whoa! What's going on? Where's your mom?" I fire off, grabbing onto his shoulders to keep him upright.

"I have no idea, I just woke up," he mumbles, somewhat disoriented.

Peter Walters is standing next to his car in front of the motel, but there's no sign of Leelo. In the distance I can hear the siren of one of the station's two fire trucks, as I make my way over.

Just as I'm about to tap him on the shoulder, I see Leelo darting out of unit eight, her arms full of what looks like laundry.

"What the hell do you think you're doing?"

She stops dead in her tracks on hearing my booming voice.

I swear that woman can get my blood boiling in more ways than one.

"What is it about storms that makes you reckless and lose all common sense?" I snarl, my hands itching to shake some sense into this woman. "For your information, that room is half caved in and there are live wires dangling off the roof. Where in your head do you figure this might be a good time to collect the laundry?"

Leelo has been quiet so far, but her eyes have been narrowing to angry slits. Silently she turns to Peter, hands him the pile of whatever the hell it is, which he swiftly deposits in the trunk of his car. *Ah*.

Swinging around, she faces me with her hands planted on her hips, but before she has a chance to tear into me, the department's rig turns into the parking lot.

-

"So you never mentioned you were a volunteer firefighter," Matt says, standing beside me as we watch the fire truck turn back on the road three hours later. The bulk of the storm has passed, leaving only an occasional roll of thunder.

The Ontario Hydro crew showed up twenty minutes after the fire truck to secure the live wires and cut off power from the road. They won't be able to make the necessary repairs until tomorrow, so the motel will be without power until then. We managed to cut the tree and clear the pieces before pulling a tarp over the hole in the roof.

The Waters family left shortly after my crew showed up, deciding to head home a day early, and the occupants of the other two rented units were shipped off to a hotel in town.

"I'm not active. I only get called in when they're short bodies." I turn around to see Leelo slip into the restaurant. She hasn't spoken a single word to me since I got here. "You guys should grab a bag and come with me. I have a couple of spare beds and the power is still on at the lodge."

"Not sure Mom will go for that," Matt says, smirking. "You pissed her off good."

"We'll see about that," I growl, heading after the source of my frustration.

I find her in the restaurant kitchen, pulling stuff out of the fridge.

"You're better off leaving that door closed instead of letting out the cold."

"Is that so?" she snarls, ignoring my words and diving back into the fridge.

"You need a new generator. Won't be the last time you'll lose power up here, and that old thing in the shed hasn't worked properly in years." I lean my hip against the counter and fold my arms over my chest, perhaps unconsciously bracing for the fireworks heading my way.

"You're just full of wisdom, aren't you?" With a slam, she closes the fridge door and steps right up to me, her finger poking my chest. "Lecturing me on my *stupidity*, when all I tried to do was help my guests retrieve their belongings so they could be on their way.

And now, when all I'm doing is trying to throw some sandwiches together so I can feed us." She turns to the food she piled on the counter and I feel a niggle of doubt enter my self-righteous mind.

"I have food and power at the lodge," I offer. "Just grab an overnight bag and we'll head out."

"Not likely," she snorts, her back still turned to me as she starts slathering mustard on some slices of bread. "I'll just stay here."

"They're expecting more cells to pass through tonight and you have a hole in your roof," I plead my case. "Come on. We'll hop in my truck, and I'll bring you back here tomorrow before the hydro crew gets here."

"Your truck?"

Shit.

"Right. Yours then. I have a tree down blocking my road and I came in the boat," I explain. "Matt can help me clear the tree on my property so we can get through." It's then I notice her hand frozen in midair, mustard dripping from the knife she is clenching.

"You came by boat?" The knife clatters to the stainless steel counter as she whirls around. "You are lecturing me about reckless behaviour, and you took a boat out on the lake in the middle of the mother of all storms?" Her voice has steadily risen to a near screech, and I unfold my arms, resisting the urge to slap my hands over my ears.

"That's different," I protest without much conviction.

"Really? Different? How? You are somehow immune to the forces of nature? Your sheer masculinity makes you untouchable? Give me a fucking break!"

With a frustrated growl, she turns back to the food, viciously slapping cold cuts and cheese on the bread. I stand there, watching her without a damn thing to say, when Matt marches in and snatches a sandwich off the counter.

"Awesome—food."

TWENTY-ONE

She almost saw inside my heart.

Leelo

"I'd like to go to bed."

Two heads swivel around. Both have their eyebrows up in their hairline.

"Mom," Matt is first to react. "It's not even ten."

I know this. I've been staring at the clock in Roar's kitchen for the past forty minutes, while the guys are making drawings and schematics of the repairs they're already planning for the motel.

Matt was the one who finally convinced me to get in his truck. The guys had already loaded a chainsaw, I had no idea was in the shed, and other assorted tools needed to clear the road by the lodge. I'd still been in search of candles, so I would at least have light for the overnight vigil without electricity in my own damn home.

Then I went to the bathroom, with the single tea light I managed to unearth, only to discover that without electricity, there's no water. Matt explained that the well water pump runs on electricity, as does the water heater, so I could kiss my nice warm shower to wash the day off me goodbye too. It wasn't such a hard decision to make after that.

Small bag packed, I took a seat in the truck, and found myself wedged between the two large men, and I'm not exactly economy-sized myself. When I suggested, perhaps with a hint of attitude, that my Jeep might be the more comfortable option, I was shut down. No trailer hitch on the Jeep, which might be needed to get the tree out of the road.

It was then I decided to just shut up and suck it up. No one was listening anyway.

That only became easier when we finally got to the lodge, after a twenty-minute delay to clear the tree, to find Patti waiting in the doorway with Ace. Awkward doesn't seem an adequate descriptor for that situation. Painful is better.

It was all over Patti's face when she saw us getting out of the truck. The smile meant to greet Roar, I'm sure, dropped the instant she spotted me. She recovered quickly, I'll have to give her that, when she invited Matt and me in and offered us warm soup she had bubbling on the stove. Roar's stove, in Roar's kitchen.

I was afraid if I opened my mouth, nothing good would come out so I limited myself to nodding. Safer that way.

Patti took off almost immediately after, with the road passable. Since then I've been sitting here, the dog at my feet, quietly stewing while the guys ignored me.

"I know it's not quite ten, Bud," I tell Matt, with as much patience as I can muster. "But I'm wiped. I'd like a hot shower, and a bed." Only then do I dare look at Roar, whose face seems impassive behind his beard. "If that's possible?" I add.

Roar doesn't miss my tone, but to his credit, he doesn't call me on it. "Sure." He gets off the kitchen stool and starts walking to the door. "Are you coming?" he says annoyed, when he notices I'm not getting up.

The temptation to throw a little tantrum is great, but I catch Matt, who probably has a good read on where my head is at, giving me a barely noticeable shake of his head. To try and avoid being the subject of another discussion on the dangers of my hormonal recalibration, I press my lips together, hard, and follow Roar's broad back out of the kitchen.

The lodge really is gorgeous. The exposed log beams give it a cozy, rustic feel, despite its substantial size. The sleek, stainless steel kitchen works surprisingly well against the rugged backdrop. The foyer is quite bare, with only a simple glass hall table with a mirror in the entrance, and the only splash of colour a blue earthenware bowl on top to catch mail and keys.

I'm quickly distracted from the beautiful rough-hewn stairway by the view of Roar's tight ass going up it, right in front of me.

The landing upstairs has two doors on one and three on the opposite end.

"There's clean towels on the shelf," he says opening the door to a nice-sized bathroom with a walk-in shower, which immediately catches my eye. It's big and inviting, and I struggle not to groan at the sight. "And the bedroom is through there." He indicates another door in the bathroom. "Bed's made so you can get right in," he adds before backing into the hallway and shutting the door.

The shower is fabulous. It takes me all of two seconds to strip and step in, pulsing streams of water massaging me from three different shower heads. I let go of the groan I've been holding back, as the strain of the day is kneaded from my muscles.

I'm not sure how long I stay in, without any regard for the size of his hot water heater, but I don't care. By the time I grudgingly turn off the shower and step out, I'm so relaxed; I just want to pour myself into bed.

Wrapped in a towel, I open the connecting door to the bedroom and come to a dead stop. Greeting me is a massive king-sized bed, with my overnight bag placed on top. It's not hard to figure out this is Roar's room. A pair of hiking boots and leather flip-flops are tucked under the foot of the bed, a small dish with change is sitting on the dresser, and a large flat screen TV is mounted on the wall opposite the bed.

What most intrigues me is a bookshelf against the wall between two large windows. Somehow he never struck me as someone who would read, but as I walk closer to look at the substantial collection on the shelves, I'm surprised at the wide diversity of books. From *An Introduction To Composting*, to Dumas' *The Count Of Monte Christo*, and from *Che Guevara:A Revolutionary Life,* to a copy of Stephen King's *The Stand.*

I trail my fingers along the mostly worn spines, an assortment as random as the titles. Leather-bound, hardcover, and paperback are lined up in completely random order. They all have one thing in common; they've all been read.

On top of the bookshelf I spot a large glass jar, filled with an odd collection of what appears to be scraps of crumpled up paper. I reach for it to get a better look, when I'm startled by a noise behind me and swing around.

252

"I'll take that," Roar growls, crossing the room in big strides, to grab the jar off the shelf. He opens the closet on the far side and shoves the jar on the narrow overhead shelf before firmly closing the door.

"I'm sorry…" I start, not quite sure what just happened but feeling responsible nonetheless.

"It's nothing. Just some receipts."

"I didn't mean to—"

"You didn't," he quickly interrupts before changing the subject entirely. "I'm just gonna grab a shower myself."

"This is your room," I point out the obvious, when he starts kicking off his boots and pulls his shirt over his head, aiming it for the laundry basket by the bathroom door.

"Yeah?" He seems confused by my conclusion.

"I can't sleep in your bed."

"Why not?"

"Because…my son's under the same roof."

"So?"

"It wouldn't be responsible," I snap, getting frustrated.

"Look," he says, walking up to me and putting his rough, calloused hands on my bare shoulders. The resulting shiver is involuntary and I watch as his mouth twitches. "Your kids are grown."

"He's a boy," I counter.

"He's a man," he insists. "And he's not stupid. He knows which end is up. Now get in bed, you were tired."

"Stop ordering me around." I'm not sure why I'm picking a fight. This whole night has sent me for a loop. The storm, the damage, the bank account I'm not sure can handle the cost of repair, and then to top it off, the sight of Patti. Playing hostess in *his* house. At home in *his* kitchen. And I'm sure in his bed. The bed he's now ordering me to get into.

Without warning I burst out into sloppy tears.

"*Fuck me.*" I hear Roar mumble, as he wraps me in his arms, his hand to the back of my head pressing my face in his chest.

His very naked chest.

For some reason this makes me cry even harder. Blasted hormones.

"Wanna tell me what's going on?" he says, pulling me down on the edge of the bed beside him. "You've been in a snit all day."

Nothing could've dried up my tears faster than those words.

"A snit? Let's recap, shall we?" My voice is dripping with sarcasm as I push him away to create some much-needed distance. "This afternoon you show up in the middle of a crisis, and the first thing you do is dress me down and embarrass me in front of my son and my guests, when I'm trying to be helpful. Then you proceed to ignore me, and the fact you've upset me, for hours, only to lecture me like a three-year-old, in my own kitchen. Next," I continue, working up a good fume as I get up and start pacing the floor. "You presume to know what's best by dragging me to your house, where a woman you are involved with, is welcoming us at the door with a fucking pot of soup!"

"*Were*," he says with a straight face. "*Were* involved with. Past tense, and even then it's an arguable statement."

I swear.

"What-*ever*!" I lean down to shout in his face; pretty sure I have steam blowing from my nostrils. "And finally, like a nail in the coffin of my seriously fucked-up day, you want me to crawl into bed with you. A bed, I might point out, I'm sure Patti is quite familiar with as well!"

With that I stomp off, clutching the towel I'm still wearing to my body, determined to find myself a bed or comfy couch elsewhere in this house. But before I even get to the door, I find myself lifted off my feet by a set of strong arms, and tossed on the bed. Roar's large body lands on top, pinning me effectively to the mattress. His hands come up and frame my face, holding it still as he leans down, his eyes shooting fire.

"Are you done?"

Roar

I swear.

I'd like nothing more than to flip her over my lap and tan that ass of hers, but I'm pretty sure at this point *that* won't be received well.

Still, when I look down at her, seeing tears swimming in her eyes again, my frustration with her just slides off me.

She's right. This day has been one big gigantic fuck up from beginning to end. A lot that was beyond my control. Except for the way I reacted, and I'm not particularly proud of the way that went down. Up to and including finding her in here, reaching for the jar.

Leelo just sniffles in response to my question and does her best not to look at me straight.

"I'm sorry," I whisper, my forehead touching hers. That gets her attention, and her eyes focus on mine. "I was worried. Scared," I correct quickly. "It's not an excuse but it's all I've got. My blood ran cold the moment I got the call from the station, and then I couldn't get to you fast enough. I yelled because I was scared. Please, don't cry," I sigh when one tear and then another escapes her eyes. "I'm sorry I was an asshole, and I'm sorry I didn't stop to think Patti being here might be awkward. All I thought about was having you safe." I pause when I see her close her eyes, giving her a minute before I push on, to tackle what I realize means more to her than it ever did to me. "I can't change what happened in the forty-five years before I met you, and I'm not sure I'd even want to when all it did was bring me to this point. All I can tell you is that nothing means as much as having you sleep in my arms, in my bed, so the last thing I feel before I fall asleep, and the first thing I feel when I wake up, is your breath against my skin."

I know I've made headway when her arms wrap around and she buries her face in my neck. After a while, I hear her breathing even out as apparently exhaustion has taken over, and she's fallen asleep without saying a word.

I carefully roll off her and cover her up with the sheet. Her wet hair is creating a wet spot on the pillow, but I don't have the heart to wake her.

Stripping off the rest of my clothes, I head into the bathroom to have a quick shower. I'm pretty sure I smell after today, and although I plan nothing more than to sleep tonight, the promise of waking up with Leelo's body pressed against mine is incentive enough to make sure I don't smell like ass when I snuggle up to her.

I curse myself for conjuring up images of her, naked in my bed, because now my dick decides to make its presence known. Realizing full well that I'll be awake all night in this condition with her beside me, I wrap my hand around my cock. With my head leaning against the tile, and my eyes closed, I recall Leelo riding me in the moonlight. Deep long strokes, along with the memory of the faint roll of the lake under me, and the sight of her heavy breasts swaying above me, is enough to draw my balls tight between my legs. My hand is moving faster now, and I bite my lip not to groan when I jerk myself to completion.

By the time I come out of the bathroom, Leelo has curled up on her side, the towel she had so tightly wrapped around her somewhere by her feet. Forfeiting my boxers, I slip in behind her, curving my body around hers.

"When's your birthday?" I hear her mumble.

"What?"

"You said forty-five years, so when do you turn forty-six?" She rolls over on her back as her heavy-lidded eyes find me.

I rise up on my elbows, gaping at her.

"That's what you retained from all I said? My age?"

"I want to know," she insists, a small smile breaking on her sleepy face.

"September tenth," I tell her, watching as her smile gets bigger.

"Yay," she cheers softly.

"Why? When's yours?" I ask.

"I turn forty-six on July twenty-ninth," she says, rolling over on her side and tucking the sheet under her chin. I have to strain to hear her next words; "I've always wanted to be a cougar."

TWENTY-TWO

She bounces back…and forth.

Leelo

"No. We're talking two separate claims. One for a washer and dryer, and that one is accompanied by a police report. The second is new, the roof was damaged yesterday in the storm."

I swear I've aged five years since I got on the phone with the insurance company. The woman on the other end doesn't seem to be the sharpest hook in the tackle box. I've tried to explain twice already that these are not claims resulting from the same incident. Apparently they have different adjusters for the different types of claims, and she is unsure what to do next.

"Look," I add, exasperated at the silence on the other side. "Why don't we just start with the more recent one: the roof, since that clearly is something that needs to be addressed right away."

She finally is able to decide who to put me through to, and I spend another thirty minutes with that guy on the phone, explaining in detail what happened and what is damaged. By the time I hang up, I have one claim activated and a promise that an adjuster will be by before the end of today. We'll see.

I grab my coffee and step out the side door, onto the deck. It's nice out. Beautiful, really. No more rain is expected until next week.

The boys are out back, finalizing the boat launch. The concrete ramp was dropped off this morning and luckily the storm hadn't done more damage than a few branches they had to clear, so the delivery truck was able to get in and out quite easily. With the ramp in place, the guys are sloping the soil around it, so the transition will be smooth.

Roar woke me up this morning, when it was still pretty early, with his face in my neck and his hands all over my body. Apparently I'd fallen asleep naked and he made it obvious he had no objections to that. He rolled me almost to my stomach, pushed up my top leg with his own, and slipped inside me from behind.

His lovemaking was unhurried and gentle. His lips pressed to the back of my neck, mumbling sweet nothings against my skin.

It wasn't until later, when I disappeared into his bathroom to clean up, that I noticed my hair had frizzed into a bird's nest overnight. *Charming*. Roar went downstairs to fix us a quick breakfast, while I woke Matt up.

The bacon and eggs was about six hours ago and I'm getting peckish.

"You guys want some lunch?" I call out in the general direction of the water, and I smile when I hear Matt yell back.

"Hell yeah! Food!"

There's been no sign of the hydro crew, so Roar brought over an old camping percolator for coffee. I brewed it on the barbeque. First time I ever made coffee that way, but it actually tastes great. Since the temperature in the fridge is slowly rising, I took out all the meat and tossed it on the grill as well. So I have the counter full quickly with ground beef patties, a couple of chicken breasts, and a foil packet with a few halibut filets. I'd skewered large chunks of vegetables along with cubes of halloumi cheese and grilled those as well.

I've barely pulled down the plates when Matt comes barrelling into the kitchen, grabbing a beef patty with his hands and eating it like a cookie as he dives into the fridge for a drink. Force of habit, because we actually put the drinks in the cooler, with some ice from the lodge, to keep at least those cold.

"Close that door. Drinks are in the cooler," I remind him. "And there's cutlery on the table, ya know?"

I shove a plate at him, just as Roar comes in the side door, with Ace on his heels. He grabs a drink from the cooler first, but then also snatches the beef with his hand.

"Cheers," he says, smiling at Matt as he touches his patty to my grinning son's, before shoving half the meat in his mouth. "Any word from Hydro? Did you try to call?" he asks, his mouth still half-full.

I give both of them a dramatic roll of the eyes, making Matt chuckle and leaving Roar with a grin on his face.

"No. Not yet. I've been on the phone with the insurance company and they're sending someone out, hopefully today. Hydro is next on my list."

Outside I can hear the crunch of wheels, and I gesture for Roar—who is ready to check it out—to keep eating while I go look.

A young guy, maybe thirty at most, is standing beside a newer-model pickup truck, looking up at my damaged roof. He appears a bit out of place in his dress pants and tie, but at least he has his shirtsleeves rolled up. It's hot today.

"Can I help you?"

The guy turns at the sound of my voice, smiles, and walks toward me with his hand stretched out.

"Brian Dinker," he introduces himself when I shake his proffered hand. "That's some nasty damage. I'm guessing last night's storm?"

"Yes," I state simply. The man still hasn't told me what he's doing here. "How can I help you?" I repeat.

"More to the point," he says, ignoring my question. "How might I be of assistance to *you?* Have you heard of the Northern Lights Group?" He doesn't wait for my answer. "We've purchased and successfully developed several unique northern properties along the Trans-Canada Highway. We're interested in your land. It's close to the highway and yet gives off that secluded vibe people look for. We heard you might be in the market to sell."

"I'm not sure where you heard that," I snap. "I'm not selling."

"Actually—" The smarmy smile on his face makes me want to haul out with my fist, but instead I keep them clenched at my side. "I was given to understand that recent unfortunate events might have changed your mind."

"You heard wrong," I answer, feeling the hair on my neck stand on end. The grin slides right off his face and he looks almost confused when his eyes dart over my shoulder.

"Is there a problem?" Roar's deep voice rumbles behind me and I feel the heat of his body at my back. Ace, who must've come out with Roar leans his weight against my knee and growls softly.

"No problem at all," young Mr. Dinker sputters, holding up his hands defensively. "Just some misinformation we apparently received."

"Let me guess," Roar snorts. "Kyle Thompson is your source of that misinformation?"

At Kyle's name, Brian Dinker visibly startles.

"Actually—" he starts before Roar cuts him off.

"Don't bother," he says, his hand in the developer's face. "I think the lady was clear enough the first time. I'm sorry you've wasted a trip, but she's clearly not selling."

"Of course, but in case you change your mind." He sticks out a hand holding a business card to me, but I don't even get a chance to take it. Roar grabs the younger man by his outstretched arm and marches him back to his truck, waits for him to get behind the wheel, start the truck and drive off before he turns back.

"Call Hydro One," he says as he walks up. "I have a sneaky suspicion fucking Kyle may have been busy."

Ten minutes later, his suspicions are confirmed. The hotline received a phone call early this morning from a gentleman cancelling the scheduled crew. I finally get off the phone with their apologies and assurances that a crew will be here before the end of the day, to find both Roar and Matt leaning on the counter, thunder in their eyes.

"I'm gonna pay that son of a bitch a visit," Roar growls ominously, and I quickly put my hand on his arm.

"Let me call Bill instead. I don't know what he can do with the information, but let him handle it. We've got a ramp to put in."

After a brief but intense staredown, Roar nods, leans in to kiss me, and walks out of the kitchen, slapping Matt on the shoulder.

"Let's go, slacker, the boss has spoken."

Roar

"Call me later," I mumble against Leelo's lips.

I don't like leaving her for the night, but weekends are busy at the lodge, and I have to show my face when the new guests come in tomorrow.

I'd asked her to come to the lodge again, even though the Hydro crew had come and gone, restoring power to the motel, but she insisted on staying. It made me feel marginally better that she wouldn't be alone and promised to sleep with her phone by her side.

The claims adjuster had been and gone as well. Matt had done his own assessment of the damage, assured the guy he could do the work and gave him an on the spot quote for materials and labour needed. The man, pleasantly surprised at the low number, okayed it right away. Unfortunately, materials won't be delivered until Monday. Matt won't be able to do all the work by himself, and I won't be able to help out until after the weekend. So for the weekend, they'll have to keep the motel closed, to Leelo's great disappointment.

The guy was nice enough to make up a claim report for the industrial washers and dryer as well. All it took was for him to stick his head inside the laundry room, take a good whiff of the rotting stench lingering inside, before also signing off on that.

Having that assurance did wonders for Leelo's demeanour.

I made sure she woke up with a smile on her face, but that only lasted as long as it took us to get to the motel. The sight of her caved in roof wiped the smile right off.

So far I haven't had a chance to ask about her finances—it's not really my business—but I know she was on a budget and having to close down the motel and pass up on income, has got to hurt her bank account.

When she heard she would get money back, it went a long way to putting that smile back on her face.

Matt and I just finished loading each of those heavy fuckers in the back of our trucks, and are off to the dump before I head home.

"I will," Leelo promises, squirming a little in my arms.

She's still a little uncomfortable with public displays of affection when her kid can see, but I'm determined to cure her of that. I don't have the fucking restraint to keep my hands off her and the kid is old enough. Besides, he may turn his head away every time I kiss her, but he does it with a grin on his face.

Matt follows me to the dump where we interrupt a couple of black bears in the middle of a meal. Unloading is easy enough; all we do is back up to the edge of the garbage ditch, drop the hatch and heave the machines over the edge. The bears, already backed up a little cautiously, run off into the woods at the loud impact.

"Look after your mom," I tell Matt as we get into our respective trucks. He doesn't answer, just gives me an affirmative chin lift.

The kid's going to fit right in here.

-

"Love to, Charlie, but she's had to shut things down after the storm. I'm pretty sure she'll have the restaurant open next weekend."

My mother is looking for a Saturday night dinner date, and apparently, I've just squashed her hopes of checking out Leelo's buffet special.

"Oh." That single syllable speaks volumes about her disappointment and pulls on my conscience. I haven't spent that much time with her since Leelo moved up here. Not that she minds me spending time with my neighbour; if anything, she's pushing me to move faster. But I can tell she's a bit lonely.

"As soon as my last guests arrive, which should be any minute, I'll come and pick you up. Take you to Kinniwabi Pines." Her responding squeal makes me grin. She's like a teenager sometimes.

"I should probably dress up then, right?"

I shake my head. Charlie, who is generally dressed to the nines at any time of day, will grab any opportunity she can to dial it up a notch. Chances are, she'll show up ready for opening night gala, when we're just going to a nice restaurant, not even all that fancy. It used to irritate me, but these days I actually get a kick out of her antics. I don't embarrass that easily anymore. Besides, she's old; she deserves to be a little eccentric.

"You probably should," I answer, playing along.

"Wonderful! I'll give Leelo a call and make sure we're coordinated," she titters excitedly.

How this went from me taking my mother for a bite on a Saturday night to a full out dinner date with two women, I have no clue, but such are the powers of Charlie.

Somehow it doesn't surprise me that by the time I swing by the motel to pick up Leelo, she's already waiting with Matt by her side. Her boy cleans up well, in dress khakis and a white dress shirt, but Leelo takes my breath away. Wearing a vintage dress with a large pink rose pattern, the bodice formfitting and the skirt wide and billowing, she looks like one of those mouth-watering 1950s pinup girls, with curves from here to eternity. Her cleavage is nothing if not impressive, and already I can tell I'll have a hard time looking anywhere but there.

Fuck me.

"Your mom says we should take my Jeep so we'll all fit," she says when I get out of the truck.

Figures. Trust Charlie to need only half an hour to get everyone in line and organized.

"Sure," I give in easily, plucking the keys from Leelo's hand and tossing them to Matt. "You drive, I'll be in the back seat with your mom."

"Roar!" Leelo objects indignantly as I bend her over my arm and plant a resounding kiss on her plum-coloured lips. Matt just chuckles, rounds the Jeep, and without argument gets behind the wheel. His mother is a different story altogether. She doesn't go meekly in the back seat.

"Stop it," she hisses when I try to slide a hand up her skirt. Matt has his eyes glued to the road and easily recalls the way to Charlie's place.

"Relax," I whisper with my face buried in her hair. "Let me take all of you in. You're stunning."

I guess it was the right thing to say, because she stops resisting. When she realizes I don't do anything more than stroke the soft skin of her leg, she snuggles a little tighter in my hold.

As expected, Charlie is decked out like she's headed for the Queen's Plate, or the Kentucky Derby, complete with large brimmed hat and little white gloves. Matt tries to hide his grin and Leelo can't stop her soft giggles as I open the car door and help Charlie in. She has to sit with her head slightly tilted away from poor Matt, or the brim would block his vision, and I'm not quite sure how we're going to fit around one of those small tables at the restaurant.

The Kinniwabi Pines is considered a fine dining restaurant by Wawa standards, but the ambiance is rustic. Log walls and ceilings, and plain wood furniture and white linens, it's nothing special, but a treat for Charlie. The views are spectacular. Set high above the Dead River and looking toward the provincial park right on the edge of Lake Superior, the scenery is worth the drive. I make sure the drive is worthwhile in the back seat of Leelo's Jeep, with my hand on her knee and her head on my shoulder. Of course, Charlie tries to crane her neck to see what's going on behind her, but the ridiculous hat prevents sufficient movement, to her frustration and my amusement.

"This is stunning," Leelo exclaims once we're all seated.

"Isn't it?" Charlie answers before I have a chance to respond. "You know this is the prime spot for locals to go for a romantic dinner?"

"Charlie…" I warn, sensing where this is going. "It's hardly a romantic dinner when your mother is at the table."

"Well," she says, pseudo offended. "I just want her to be prepared next time you invite her here."

I ignore Matt's snickering and Leelo's soft chuckle and try to burn Charlie with my glare.

"Prepared for what exactly?"

I know I made a mistake not dropping the subject, when a superior smile settles on Charlie's face, and she answers with smug satisfaction.

"Good grief, for a ring on her finger of course!"

TWENTY-THREE

I don't believe in destiny, but there's not a doubt in my mind that she is mine.

Leelo

"I'd sell it to you."

My mouth falls open at Charlotte's declaration.

We've been discussing the visit from the guy from the Northern Lights Group since Matt noticed Kyle Thompson sneak out of the restaurant, shortly after we sat down. Charlotte mentioned that she was approached by him several times over the years, hoping to purchase her property from her. She explained that he eventually managed to get his hands on her neighbour's, when he discovered she wouldn't budge. It's clear he's been after the lodge as well, and Roar suspects him of sabotage, listing several incidents.

Matt mentioned that he could see why someone would be interested in getting their hands on any of these properties when Charlotte drops that bombshell on him.

"To me?" he says, incredulously.

"Sure," she says, shrugging her shoulders when even Roar looks taken aback. "I'm never there. I'm too old for the upkeep, which means Roar has to do it, and he doesn't need the added responsibility."

271

"But I thought you didn't want to sell?" Roar says carefully.

"Not to that idiot," she spits out, and I can't help giggle at her obvious disgust at the local real estate agent. "But to someone who will appreciate the land and wants to build a life on it? Someone I like? In a heartbeat," she says, with a wide smile for my son, who in turn is beaming.

"I would totally be interested," he says, sounding more like the teenager I remember, instead of the level-headed man he's growing into.

"We'll discuss it some more, but not over this wonderful dinner," she says, patting his hand.

I snicker at his look of near worship at the innocent-looking, grey-haired lady with the ridiculous hat. She may look innocent, but I'm starting to discover that Charlotte, for all her 'little-ole-me' airs, is in truth a shrewd, conniving, manipulative operator. I laugh out loud when she blinks her eyes a few times at Roar's low, warning growl. He doesn't stand a chance in hell.

-

Matt chatters all the way home, after we drop Charlotte off at her place. Full of ideas and plans for Charlotte's cottage, his mind is running a mile a minute, and I'm a little concerned he's getting ahead of himself. After all, he doesn't even know whether he can afford it.

He's only twenty, how much can he have saved up?

I'd love to help him out, but I'm currently living on a prayer as well. Anything I had saved up has gone into the motel, and there have been times over the last twenty-four hours, where I've wondered whether I'm not biting off more than I can chew and would be better off just selling. Only momentary lapses of my usual optimism, but still.

"Son of a fucking bitch!"

I twist my head to see what Roar, who is sitting beside Matt in the front seat, is looking at when we turn onto our driveway. It takes me a minute, but then I notice the awkward slant of Roar's truck and the busted windows of the cab.

"Jesus, mine too!" Matt pipes up, staring straight ahead where his truck is parked.

Sure enough, Matt's truck looks like it's received the same treatment.

"Stay here," Roar orders me when my Jeep rolls to a stop, and both he and Matt jump out.

Part of me wants to argue, but I have to admit that I'm a little shaken. My determination to build a life here had already been wavering a little after fate, in the form of the storm, decided to dump another disaster on me. You can only take so much before you start to wonder if a higher force is trying to tell you something.

In this case it's screaming; *go home.*

Except, home is here now. It's surprising how little I miss the conveniences of city living. Instead, I've really come to love my life in the relatively short time I've lived here. I have never really been someone who needed a gaggle of friends, and the few I've made here accept me just the way I am. I don't think I've ever known anyone who didn't have expectations for me, a role for me to fill.

I watch as Matt inspects his truck, while Roar walks up to the bar and tries the door. I'm shocked when he pushes it open. I'd locked it just a couple of hours ago.

Just a second later, he steps back out, closes the door, and pulls his phone from his pocket.

I'm out of the Jeep in a flash and try walking past him, but one of his long arms shoots out, blocking my path.

"Don't," he mumbles at me, his eyes solemn. "Yes, get down to the motel. We've got a break-in and extensive damage," he barks into the phone. At his words, I pull from his hold and shove the door open.

The devastation takes my breath away. The only windows intact are the ones facing the street, but every other window has been smashed. The large mirror behind the buffet-bar is in pieces on the ground. My dining room tables and chairs were a motley collection at best, but it still makes me sick to see it reduced to kindle littering the floor. Not a single intact piece of furniture is left.

And the trail of destruction doesn't stop there; it runs back to the kitchen and I'm fearing for my house beyond. A pained groan escapes from deep in my chest when I think of what I might find there. I don't have a chance to move further inside, because a pair of strong arms wrap around me from behind, and pull me back outside.

"Come on, Mom," my son's gentle voice sounds in my ear, as he moves me around so I'm looking at the parking lot instead of my ransacked building.

Roar is a few steps away, still talking on the phone but his concerned eyes are on me. It's then I notice I'm crying.

Roar

"Doesn't look forced," Bill says, checking the door I found open. "Do you know who all has a key?"

He'd been in his car when I caught him earlier, so we didn't have to wait long. I'd barely managed to convince Leelo to get back in her Jeep, with Matt standing guard, when his OPP cruiser pulled onto the property. He'd wasted no time.

Of all the previous incidents, the deer carcass had been pretty gruesome, but still it had nothing on the utter wreckage left behind this time. It's gone from some serious pranks to outright maliciousness. I can't help think that had someone been here, the person who did this would not have stopped at busting up windows and furniture.

Sadly, on the brief walk-through I just did with Bill, we found both the restaurant kitchen and the main level of the house in much the same state; windows broken, furniture destroyed. Very little was left intact.

The upstairs was left alone, which led Bill to surmise that we may have interrupted whomever was here. The next logical conclusion was that they must've left either on foot or by water. I did recall hearing a boat's engine, shortly after we got here, but at the time I'd only seen the state of the trucks. I hadn't been inside yet.

Bill's theory was supported by the wide open side door to the house.

It didn't take long for two more cruisers to drive onto the parking lot. The team Bill called in. He immediately sent them to the back to see what, if anything, they could find.

"I'm guessing Leelo and Matt, but I don't know who else. You should ask her," I answer his question.

"I will." He straightens up and directs his attention to the side of the building where his two men appear. "But let's wait to see if they found anything out back," he says.

One of his constables holds up a coiled rope.

"Is this your rope?" he asks, looking at me. "I found it tied to a cleat on the dock, the rest floating in the water, which seemed a little strange."

"No it's not. I had my boat tied off there earlier and keep my ropes on the boat. There weren't any others."

He hands over the blue and white striped rope to his boss. "Could be in their hurry to take off, they quickly released rope from the cleat on the boat instead of the dock," Bill muses as he examines it. "It looks pretty new."

"My boats all have plain white rope," I offer as my thoughts immediately go to the one person I know on the lake who has a relatively new toy. "Maybe check—"

"On it," Bill says, interrupting me. "Roberts, you stay here and tape off the building. Don't let anyone in or out until I get back. McGillicutty, come with me. We're going to pay Mr. Thompson a visit."

It's clear Bill's thoughts run in the same direction mine do.

"Do you need Leelo and her son here? It's getting dark and I'd like to bring them back to the lodge."

"I'll find you," he says, lifting two fingers at me as he walks off with his constable.

Once again, Leelo needs a little convincing, but she quickly concedes when I point out the fact they won't be able to enter the house until it's been properly searched.

276

"Where is Bill off to?" she wants to know, when I climb behind the wheel of her Jeep.

I explain the rope they found, and what it might imply, which seems to lift her mood a little.

"So that would be cause enough to have him arrested?"

"If he has only one matching rope on his boat, it might. It's pretty distinct. By itself it might not hold, but there are other ways to know whether his boat has been on the water recently."

"The engine would still be warm?" she suggests astutely.

"Possibly, or perhaps it's been seen. Either way, the sooner Bill gets out there the better."

The drive to the lodge is mostly silent, but when we pull up in front of the building, Leelo speaks up. "You think he spotted us all at the restaurant and saw his opportunity?"

"Something like that," I confirm, unbuckling her seatbelt before doing my own.

When I get out, I notice she's still in her seat, staring straight ahead through the window. Walking around the car, I encounter a much more subdued Matt, who is distractedly kicking the gravel at his feet. Without saying anything, I just clap his shoulder and give him a nod when he looks up.

Leelo hasn't moved when I pull the passenger side door open, and she doesn't turn to look at me when she says; "I don't even have a bag this time. All I have is this dress."

"Come on," I urge her, taking her hand in mine as I help her from the Jeep. "We'll find you something to wear."

I'm a little concerned at her defeated tone. It's not something I'd associate with her; she's a fighter—tenacious—and has been able to roll with the punches. Lord knows she's had a few since getting here, not to mention in her previous life.

She meekly lets me guide her inside and resumes her motionless staring when I sit her down at the kitchen table. Her hand automatically reaches down, to where she knows Ace is, at her feet, as he always seems to be when Leelo is around.

"Have a seat," I invite Matt, walking straight to the liquor cabinet and pulling down a three-quarters full bottle of Canadian Club whiskey and three tumblers. I pour each of us a stiff shot and set them on the table.

"I usually have scotch after a particularly shitty day," Leelo says after taking a good swig.

"Surprised you can even taste the difference," Matt says after doing the same, a look of distaste on his face that makes me grin. Took me until my late twenties before I could appreciate anything but beer and tequila shots.

"I'll make sure to have scotch on hand for the next shitty day," I tell Leelo, tossing back my own drink. Despite the fact it's not her drink of preference, the alcohol puts some colour on her face and some life back in her eyes.

Forty-five minutes later, with Leelo dressed in one of my flannel pajama pants and an old shirt, her face washed clean of any makeup traces, Bill shows up.

"Bingo," he says, the moment I open the door for him.

"Yeah? Fucking moron," I spit out as he walks past, and I follow him into the kitchen.

Bill snickers. "You have no idea. Not only was he missing one of his tie-down lines, the idiot left the hunting knife and the baseball bat in the bottom of his boat. He tried to talk his way out, saying he just got there and didn't use his boat all night, but the keys were still in his pocket when we searched him," he says, leaning on the back of the chair beside Leelo.

"Did he say anything?" I want to know, holding up the bottle of whiskey, but Bill shakes his head.

"He asked for his lawyer before we even got him in the cruiser. I explained he was being premature, since I haven't even charged him with anything—yet. McGillicutty is taking him to the detachment, letting him stew for the night. I just wanted to come by to keep you in the loop, but I have to get back to the motel to help process the scene. We likely won't question him until tomorrow morning, but I'm pretty sure he'll insist having Ian McTavish there."

I notice Leelo's head shoot up at that name.

"Of Kline, Kline & McTavish?" she asks.

"One and the same," Bill responds, a questioning look on his face. "Why? You know them?"

"Henry Kline is my lawyer. I just wonder if that will be a conflict of interest or something."

"Not sure. Kline is civil law and McTavish is the firm's criminal lawyer. I'll check it out."

Bill leaves shortly after that and when I come back to the kitchen, I catch Matt barely stifling a yawn.

"Just grab the same room," I tell him. "You can get Netflix on the TV in the armoire up there."

He walks over to his mom, leans down to give her a kiss, and with a chin lift to me, heads upstairs.

"What about you?" I ask her. "You want to go upstairs now, or wait until I get back from doing the rounds of the property?"

It's something I don't do every night, but on Saturdays when we have a load of new guests, I like to make myself seen. Just in case some of the general rules of conduct need enforcing.

"I think I need another one of these," she says, waving her tumbler. "If I want any chance of sleep tonight."

Leelo

I quickly get restless once Roar is gone.

With my tumbler in one hand and the bottle of Canadian Club in the other, I wander out into the foyer. There are four more doors, besides the one I just came through, and I feel a little like Alice in Wonderland, unsure which one to explore first. The kitchen is the first door to your left when you come in the front, so I start with the one right beside it. It's a powder room, pretty nondescript, with a simple white porcelain sink and toilet, in stark contrast with the dark wood of the walls and floor.

Across the foyer, beside the stairway going up, is only one door, directly across from the kitchen. I try that one next, only to find a short hallway to the small two-room office beyond. That doesn't yield much of interest either, other than a bunch of filing cabinets, a few utilitarian chairs, a couple of desks piled high with paperwork, two computers and a phone.

Two more doors are left, immediately opposite the front door. The first one opens up to a large spacious living room. I flick on the switch and soft, diffused light bathes the room in a warm glow. A large, worn, light-brown leather couch sits at an angle, facing a massive lake stone fireplace in the corner, with two oversized club chairs upholstered in a pale kelim pattern on either side. The smell of the fireplace permeates the room.

I drop down in one of the club chairs and have a sip of my whiskey, letting my eyes wander around, taking in the oversized windows. Beautiful Inuit prints hang on the walls, and on the thick slab of wood that serves as a mantel for the fireplace, rests a massive painting of a wolf. A pile of do-it-yourself and hunting magazines is stacked on the rustic coffee table, yet as fabulous as this room is, and clearly suited to Roar, it holds little to no personal items. No books, no photographs, no knick-knacks—nothing to identify Roar as its owner.

I could see myself here, though, curled up with a book on a cold night, watching the flames in the fireplace. Except at this point in time, I don't even know if I'll still be here this winter.

I furiously wipe at the single tear rolling down my cheek and before I drown in self-pity, I determinedly get up, flick off the lights and head for the final door.

Jackpot.

The walls in here are lined with shelves, jam-packed with books as far as the eye can see. Shelves even run under and around the large windows and the door I came through. I can smell the paper and ink alongside another scent, something slightly smoky but sweet and very familiar.

Another fireplace, this one smaller than the one next door, is in the adjoining corner of the room. Its mantel is covered in picture frames. A love seat, matching the couch in the other room, is facing it with a large ottoman in front. On the side table is an open book, facing down, with a pair of reading glasses perched on top. On the same table sits an ashtray with two pipes and a pouch of Amphora tobacco. My father's favourite brand.

This time it's nostalgia that has my eyes tear up as I set down my glass and the bottle, pick up a pipe, and hold it to my nose. With the scent of my father soothing me, I walk up to the mantel and check out the pictures.

Charlotte as a young woman, beside a larger than life, robust-looking man, with a beard much the same colour as Roar's and a pipe clenched between his teeth. His father, no doubt.

Several photographs of Roar as a young boy, with freckles and white blond hair that slowly turns a deep red as he ages. In one picture, he has no front teeth, and is proudly holding up what looks to be a huge trout. I can't help but grin, having an almost identical shot of Matt with his first catch.

The last photo to catch my eye is a group of young soldiers; arms slung around each other's shoulders and smiling wide for the camera. Except the two in the center, they are smiling at each other.

One is clearly a younger Roar, and if I would venture a guess, the second man is Tom Jackson. The man this place was named for.

"Taking up smoking?"

His voice startles me, and I swing around to find him leaning his shoulder against the doorway, his arms folded over his chest, and a small smile tugging at his mouth.

"This brings about some sweet memories," I tell him, as I sniff the bowl one last time before laying the pipe back in the ashtray. "And I wasn't aware you smoked."

I watch as he slowly stalks into the room, his eyes kind.

"Very occasionally," he replies. "And purely for sentimental reasons."

"The Amphora?"

"My father's tobacco of choice," Roar says, and it makes my heart do a little skip in my chest.

"Mine too," I smile, cursing the blasted tears that threaten again.

TWENTY-FOUR

She is now embedded in my senses and entwined with my warmest memories.

Roar

I didn't realize seeing her in my sanctuary would have such a visceral impact on me.

My instant reaction had been anger at the invasion, but the longer I watched her from the doorway, lightly touching each of the pictures, while carrying my dad's old pipe around in her other hand, relief followed right on its heels. Funny, this is a room I don't ever socialize in. Other than Charlie and Bill, no one else comes in here. Even Patti knows this is off limits. I've always assumed she respects my wishes.

Having Leelo touching my things, my memories, it feels right.

The thought of sharing everything with her is not as scary as I thought it might be. I've been very protective of my privacy ever since my best friend, as well as my marriage, blew up within mere months of each other. There's no danger of feeling that kind of bone-deep loss when you barely let people under your skin. The only person who still has that power is Charlie.

Until now.

Until Leelo.

I watch as she blinks away the tears from her eyes. What are the odds the smell of Amphora tobacco would come with similar memories for us both.

"Every now and then I'll sit here and miss him," I admit, stopping right in front of her and cupping her face in my hands. "I'll pack and light one of his pipes until the smoke brings the good memories to the forefront. It helps me."

She takes one step forward and does a face plant in my chest. My hand cups around the back of her head and I rest my chin on her crown.

"Would you like me to light one?"

I feel her body freeze under my hands, after a moment, she lifts up her face and what I see there has me swallow hard. Her eyes big and shiny, gazing up at me with such beautiful pain and hopeful trust. A look like that settles deep in a man's heart.

"*Please.*" I barely hear her whispered plea, but I see her lips form the words.

I pull her down on the couch with me, settling her in the crook of my arm. With my other hand, I grab the pouch of tobacco and the pipe she was holding, and with her in the circle of my arms, I pack the pipe, and hand her the lighter. She expertly touches the flame to the bowl when I clamp the pipe between my lips and pull in air.

"What's in those?" she asks, her eyes on the narrow shelves between the windows where I store my jars filled with notes and scraps. "More receipts?"

"Something like that," I mumble, pulling her close with my free hand.

She settles in, tucking her head under my chin, and her left hand splayed in the middle of my chest, as I take the first few drags, blowing billowing clouds of smoke around us.

"I miss him," she says softly after maybe five minutes. I rub my hand down her arm and up again.

"What was he like?"

Leelo sighs deeply beside me and takes such a long time, I'm not sure she's going to answer.

"He was wonderful. He worked hard, but on the weekends and during his vacation, he was all about his family. He taught me to love the outdoors, even though Mother was never a fan. She had a conniption fit when he came home with a tent and sleeping bags one summer. Forced him to rent a cottage, so she could have her indoor plumbing, her ice cubes, and a proper mattress, while he and I pitched the tent beside the cabin and slept there the entire week. He would cook on a wood fire and showed me how to clean fish. He used to say that Mom needed looking after, but like him, I'd be able to survive on my own." She sniffs the air and sighs. "And he'd always ask me to come sit with him on the porch steps while he had his nightly pipe, because mother didn't like him smoking in the house."

"And he smoked Amphora," I fill in, and she lifts her face and smiles at me.

"And he smoked Amphora," she confirms. "What about your dad?"

I take a deep pull from the pipe and blow a few perfect rings in the air before answering.

"Very similar to yours, by the sound of it. Loved the outdoors, taught me everything I know, and adored

287

Charlie and me. We weren't ready to lose him. Not by a long shot. And I don't think Charlie ever got over him."

"My mother was married to the first of my stepfathers within six months."

"*Fuck me*," I mutter, imagining how that might have been for a young girl, who just recently saw her father buried.

"I'd love to," she deadpans, and my reaction is immediate. My eyes drop down to see her dancing ones shine up at me, and my cock is instantly awake.

"You sure?" I ask, already tapping the embers from the pipe bowl into the ashtray. Leelo nods by way of answer and twists her body toward me, tugging my face down by my beard.

"Positive," she says, her breath brushing my lips.

Leelo

I understand his reluctance.

It's been a shit day, and both of us have just lost ourselves in bittersweet memories, but something makes me want to deepen the connection. Claim this moment and make it ours—own it.

I don't hesitate. I press my mouth against his and slip my tongue between his parting lips. His hands grab my hips and guide me to straddle his lap. For a man in his mid-forties, Roar's body is incredibly responsive. The prominent ridge of his already hard cock feels delicious between my legs.

With his hands now kneading my ass, as he encourages me to rock against him, I feel sexy.

Don't get me wrong, I look like shit warmed over—I'm wearing an old worn shirt and flannel pants, and my face is a mess—but to feel the almost involuntary physical response he has to me is powerful. I've never felt more wanted.

His breath under my lips comes in small grunts, with each grind of my slick heat along his length, and I don't hold back my own sounds of pleasure. Mindless and natural, the way we move together. *Beautiful.*

He lets go of my mouth and drops his head back on the couch, lips wet and parted and his heavy-lidded hazel eyes almost black with heat, the focus intently on me as his large hands continue to work my cheeks.

"I love your ass," he growls, digging his fingers into the most noticeable part of my anatomy. "I'd love to flip you over this couch, pound my cock into you from behind, and watch the soft flesh jiggle every time I bottom out inside you."

Holy shit. My nether parts just did an involuntary Kegel at the mental picture that conjures.

I quickly dismiss the inner voice—the one that sounds surprisingly like my mother's—reminding me of the occasional, unsightly red bumps on my ass. Those burning eyes fixed on mine tell me I am beautiful, bumps and all.

I crawl off his lap and grab for the hem of my shirt, when he holds up his hand, stopping me.

"Stay right there," he grunts as he gets up, adjusting himself in his pants.

I watch as he walks to the door, flips the lock, dims the lights, and prowls toward me, pulling his shirt off, and dropping it on the floor. I let my eyes feast on his strong body, not chiselled but solid, steady, and supremely sexy with those big shoulders and muscular legs. By the time he stands in front of me, he's left a trail of clothes behind, and is as naked as the day he was born, his fierce-looking cock jutting out straight from the dark red patch of tight curls.

Magnificent.

"Let me," he says, brushing my hands that are still clutching the hem of my shirt away.

Without taking his eyes off mine, he whips off my shirt, dropping it carelessly, and then pushes down the flannel pants along with my panties, helping me step out of them. Only then does he let his eyes wander up and down my naked form.

Instead of making me feel self-conscious, he makes me feel desirable and my body tingles in response.

Wordlessly, he guides me around to the side of the couch, where he turns me and pushes me down over the armrest, his large hand between my shoulder blades. He bends his body over mine, his cock teasing my ass cheeks as his voice rumbles in my ear.

"I always imagined you sitting on my face would be a fantasy come true, but having you bend over for me, your ass up for the taking, beats all."

I can feel the rumble of his voice like electricity buzzing under my skin, and when his hand slips around and between my legs, fingers probing the wetness gathered there, a shiver runs down my entire body.

"So ready for me," he groans, right before I feel just the blunt head of his cock press inside me.

He straightens up, and at first I perceive the sudden cool air on my back as exposure, but when I twist my head, and see the heat in the way he looks down on me, I feel alive.

With his free hand, he takes a firm hold of my hip, while the fingers of the other slip around our connection between my legs, and with a deep satisfying grunt, he drives inside me.

-

Sweaty, satisfied, and replete, I snuggle into his body, my knee pulled up over his legs.

We are on the couch, watching the moon outside the large window of his library. My fingers play in the curls on his chest while I listen to the beat of his heart, steady once again.

"I've never been fucked like that before," I admit, slightly embarrassed.

It's true, despite my age; I've had little in the way of creative sexual experiences, but not for lack of a vivid imagination. I've probably explored them all in my fantasies. Riding Roar on the deck of his boat was definitely one, but the sheer animalistic surge in our most recent session is by far the most exciting and the most liberating.

"You weren't fucked now," he says, his voice low but clear. "I know the difference. I've fucked before, but, Sunshine, every time with you I've been making love."

I lift my head and prop my chin on my hand covering his chest, so I can look at his eyes on me.

"Making love…" I repeat dreamily, feeling myself fall even further.

"The way I feel about you, it can't be anything else."

I'm the first one to look away at the message I read clear in his eyes, but I do it with a soft smile on my lips.

I hear him. I don't need words when everything he says and does is evidence of how deeply he feels for me. I may be insecure at times, but I'm not stupid.

The sappy smile still on my face, I drop my cheek back on his chest, my fingers once again playing with his chest hair.

"Me too," I tell him, my eyes already closing.

"I know," is the last thing I hear before I drift off.

Roar

"Mom?"

"Roar? You in here?"

I wake up to loud pounding, surprised to find myself buck naked on the couch in the library, with Leelo's soft body half covering me. The pounding on the door resumes, and she stirs in my arms, her sleep-swollen eyes blinking against the morning light streaming in.

"Mom?"

Matt's voice can be heard outside the library door. Thank God I had the presence of mind to lock it before I bent Leelo over the couch last night. The memory puts an instant smile on my face and a rise in my dick.

"*Fuck,*" Leelo mutters, scrambling off the couch.

"We'll be right out!" I yell, enjoying the view of her ass as she bends over to grab at the pile of clothes on the floor, tossing mine in my direction.

"*They're here,*" I hear Matt telling someone outside the door.

I chuckle at the look of panic on Leelo's face as she frantically tries to straighten her hair that teeters in a tangled mop on her head.

"It's fine," I assure her, pulling her hands down and running my own fingers through it, to loosen some of the snags. "You're fine. We just tell him the truth…" I snort when her eyes threaten to roll from their sockets. "That we fell asleep on the couch while talking."

Her little fist is sharp as it meets my midsection, eliciting an involuntary, "oomph".

"Pull your shirt down," she hisses, pointing at my happy morning dick clearly outlined in my pants.

"It's natural," I defend, but she's already tugging at the hem of my shirt, trying to cover the bulge. I don't have the heart to tell her that she's not helping matters.

When I finally pull open the door, I'm surprised to find not only Matt and the dog, but Patti waiting outside as well.

"What are you doing here?" I ask, none too graciously. But instead of looking hurt, Patti narrows her eyes and plants her hands on her hips, glaring at me.

"I was worried, you idiot," she spits out, but her face softens when she spots Leelo hiding behind me. "Sunday mornings I clean the OPP detachment in town. Bill

293

mentioned your place got ransacked," she directs at her. "I came to see if you needed help, but you weren't there and the place is still cordoned off with police tape. I figured I'd find you here."

"Thank you," Leelo mumbles behind me, and I step aside to guide her forward.

"Anyway," Patti continues. "I got here and found this young man roaming about, looking for you as well."

"We fell asleep talking," Leelo sputters beside me, and I can't help the grin on my face. She couldn't sound guiltier.

Matt rolls his eyes and saunters off to the kitchen, and surprisingly, Patti smiles kindly at Leelo before completely changing the subject.

"Why don't you two freshen up and I'll get some coffee and breakfast going? That boy of yours looks like he could use something."

"Thanks, Patti," I manage to call out as she too disappears into the kitchen.

-

"She's nice," Leelo says, after spitting out her toothpaste.

We're in my bathroom, sharing the sink.

"Yes, she is," I confirm, grinning at her reflection in the mirror, toothpaste dribbling down my beard. I quickly duck down and rinse my mouth and beard, before I continue, "She's always been a good friend, first and foremost. You'll find that up here, in a small community where you often have to depend on each other whether you like it or not, good friends are important to your survival." I watch as she slowly nods, taking in what I'm saying. "Take her at face value, Sunshine. She heard about what happened and came running. I understand why she makes you uncomfortable, but it would be a shame if you let that colour your view of her." I reach out and stroke the backs of my fingers down her cheek. "What are you thinking?"

"I could use another friend," she says softly, but I can see it's not easy; she has to swallow hard.

"Come here." She steps into my arms without hesitation and circles my waist with hers. "Remember what I said about the difference between fucking and making love last night?" I feel her nod her head under my chin. "Good. Then I won't have to repeat myself."

She snorts into my shirt, mumbling; "Aye aye, Sir."

Fuckin' A.

TWENTY-FIVE

She is da bomb.

Leelo

It's a little less awkward this time when I walk into the kitchen to find Patti behind the stove.

Especially when she shoots me an almost apologetic smile.

"Hope you don't mind," she says, clearly conceding control to me. Something I'm grateful for.

"Not at all," I reply with surprising honesty. "I'm starving." Bacon is sizzling in a large skillet and Patti expertly flips blueberry pancakes on the griddle. "Maybe I can return the favour some day," I add, and she casts a curious glance over her shoulder. "Stop by the motel, and I'll cook you breakfast one morning."

The motel. *Shit.* My restaurant. *Jesus*—my fucking kitchen.

I sink down in a kitchen chair at the table, a heavy weight landing on my shoulders. If not for Matt walking up behind me, leaning over my shoulder, and kissing my cheek good morning, I might actually have burst out crying at the sympathetic smile Patti sends my way.

"Bill mentioned he'd call as soon as his guys have all they need from your place," Patti says, forcing through that awkward moment. "I have a bulk-sized box of garbage bags, buckets, mops and cleaning materials in the back of my car. We'll get that place back in decent shape in no time."

"Okay. Plans," Roar says, sitting down beside me with a pen and pad. "Bill just called, he'll meet us at the motel in thirty minutes to take pictures for your insurance and note down anything missing. So eat up." He turns to Matt, who sets down a plate Patti just handed him, piled high with pancakes, in the middle of the table. "We're measuring windows. Today every broken pane gets replaced. As will every lock, including the ones for the units." He scribbles on his pad and looks at me. "You and Patti take detailed notes of everything inside that is beyond repair, take pictures and then toss it. I'm having a bin brought in later this morning."

"Travis doesn't open until after church, you know that right?" Patti says to Roar, while she pours me a coffee.

"He will today. Bill already called him first thing this morning."

And just like that the floodgates open.

Tears are streaming down my face as I listen to Roar and Patti organize the cleanup. With every word I hear, a little of the heavy load is lifted off my shoulders. Myself, I haven't done anything but worry and yet around me people are jumping into action. I never had to ask, they just do what is needed.

It's overwhelming. The past few days have slowly eaten at my resolve, but the way this community steps up to support someone they barely know is humbling. So I cry, because I don't know what else to do.

"Awww, Mom," Matt, who notices, mumbles as he comes around the table and crouches beside my chair, wrapping his arms around me. I gratefully bury my face in his shoulder as I let it all hang out.

It's cathartic. Cleansing.

But it really sucks when the sniffles subside and you realize you've just made a spectacle of yourself in public, and you're going to have to show your tear-streaked face and red nose. I'd rather keep my head buried in Matt's shirt.

"Mom," he nudges, trying to untangle himself from the desperate hold I have on him by now. "Let go, Mom. My shirt is soaked."

I keep my eyes closed as I feel myself plucked away from my son, turned and hidden in another chest—another shirt.

"Dresser in my bedroom. Second drawer. Grab a clean shirt and bring a few more down," I hear Roar say to Matt. "We'll all probably need one by the time she's done."

"Hey!" I protest, planting a fist in his stomach as I rear up.

I instantly know I'm had when I see his teasing grin.

"There you are."

"I hate you," I pout.

"Nah. You don't," he drawls arrogantly.

I cautiously look around but I can't see Patti. Roar notices.

"She had some calls to make," he explains.

I know it's a lie and it says volumes about the kind of person Patti really is, and when she walks in moments later, with a wet washcloth she hands to me without any fuss, it almost has me back in tears.

"Oh hell no." Roar puts his hands on either side of my face and forces me to look at him. "That's done now," he orders, pissing me off and at the same time drying my tears, which is exactly what he's aiming for.

Smug bastard.

-

I watch Bill drive off with a memory card full of date-stamped pictures of the carnage inside and a list of missing things with exactly one item on it; my laptop.

Everyone seemed to be looking at me, waiting for another meltdown when I first walked inside. But as I took in the full extent of the devastation left behind, I got angry instead. I kicked at broken furniture while cursing up a blue streak, making up swear words on the spot that had Patti snickering and Matt in stitches. The only weak moment was when I couldn't find my old laptop. Like everything else, it could be replaced, but not the folders of digital images of the kids growing up, or the file with pages and pages of entries I made over the past three years while I was pulling myself up by the bootstraps. A document I often flip through when I need a reminder of how far I've come.

The thought of those items in anyone else's hands makes me cringe, but the fear they might be lost forever cuts deep.

"He'll find it," Roar says behind me, dropping his arm around my shoulders.

He's referring to Bill, who promised to obtain a search warrant this morning, as soon as he has a chance to interview Kyle Thompson. He apparently still refused to talk without a lawyer and now they're waiting for Ian McTavish to get out of church.

"Let's get this place cleaned up," I say resolutely, turning my head so I can kiss the top of his hand that is resting on my shoulder.

I already feel a bit better, having had a chance to change into my own clothes, and I manage a smile for Roar before I head inside, in search of Patti.

I've barely started on my living room, when I hear Patti call out a, "*Oh hey!*" from the restaurant kitchen. I follow the sound of voices and find four more women, varying in age from about thirty to substantially older than me.

"Hi," the eldest of the four walks toward me with her hand stretched out. "You must be Sam's niece. I'm a little embarrassed I haven't had the chance to come say hello yet, but I didn't want to intrude while you were still getting the place together. I'm Deena Filmore, Patti's mother? Sam was a dear friend."

I see the resemblance, as I take her hand and smile.

"Nice to meet you, Deena."

"This is my youngest daughter, Natalie," she says, introducing me to the youngest member, blonde like her sister. "And I think you've met Nancy Prescott? Bill's wife?"

"Of course," I confirm, turning to the woman I knew looked familiar. "Good to see you again, Nancy."

Finally I turn to the fourth woman, and am surprised to find her a lot older than she initially looked.

"They were leaving me at home," she says, her English slightly accented and her tone insulted. "But I jump in the back seat. I am Zhao Lin, but you may call me

Lin. I live next to the Filmore house. Noisy." The small oriental woman makes me smile, and I reach out to take her hand in mine, surprised to find her grip much stronger than her stature would imply.

"Pleased to meet you, Lin."

"Now," she says, clapping her hands sharply. "We clean, yes?"

"Never mind her," Patti whispers in my ear. "She's moody, she complains a lot, but underneath that nasty attitude lives a heart of gold. And just so you know, she may not act it, but she adores us."

A loud snort comes from the older woman on the other side of the kitchen, who clearly has superior hearing. "That what you think," she snaps at Patti, before her eyes shoot to me and she throws me a wink. I can't stop the giggle that bubbles up.

I don't know how, and I don't know why, but I do know that I'm laughing more than I ever thought I would, all afternoon, working side by side with these women I didn't even know before today.

And the best part? Every time Roar would walk by, or our paths would cross, he would grab me by the scruff of the neck and plant a hard kiss on my lips.

Not once do I feel victimized—instead I wonder how the fuck I ever got this lucky.

Roar

"Last one, kid," I tell Matt, handing him the new lock for unit eight.

We've been working steadily all afternoon.

You could've knocked me down with a feather when Mrs. Zhao stepped out of Deena's car. Like oil and water, those two. Years of quibbling over a cherry tree dividing their properties will do that. I've always suspected Mrs. Zhao had too much fun riling up her neighbour, but I've never said that out loud.

As expected, despite her diminutive stature, Mrs. Zhao took charge of the cleanup like a general. Not even Leelo's input was acceptable, even though this is her place. The old woman simply doesn't care. I get such a kick out of her.

I purposely avoided calling Charlie, because I didn't want to upset her, but with Patti's troops here, she's certain to get wind of what happened soon enough, and then I'm sure she'll rip a strip off me for keeping it from her. Can't win for trying.

Travis showed up earlier with sheets of plywood and helped us board up the broken windows. I thought Leelo was going to pass out when she saw him wielding a hammer. Unfortunately, he didn't have the right glass in stock, so we had to order it in from Sault Ste. Marie, and it likely won't get here until tomorrow afternoon.

The boards will at least hold animals at bay.

It looks like Leelo and the kid will be spending another night at the lodge. Not that I'm complaining.

The sound of a horn has me swing my head around, only to meet my mother's furious eyes through the windshield of her antique Hyundai Pony.

Well, shit.

"Give me a sec," I tell Matt and walk up to the car, pulling the driver's side door open. "Hey, Charlie."

She doesn't even look at me, just gets out of the car, marches right past me, with only a kind hello for Matt. I'm clearly in the doghouse, and I wonder whose ass I have to kick for filling her in. I follow behind her as she heads into the restaurant, where the five women are tossing broken furniture in the wheelbarrow. We've made a makeshift pile of trash in the parking lot, until the dumpster is delivered, which could be any time.

"You!" Mrs. Zhao hisses when she spots my mother.

With senses sharpened from an entire afternoon between a harping Deena Filmore and Zhao Lin, Leelo immediately jumps in when she hears the tone. I stay back and watch as she puts an arm around Charlie and kisses her cheek.

"I don't know what I did to deserve all of you, but I appreciate every one of you."

Charlie hugs Leelo back while Mrs. Zhao looks on. The old lady smiles sweetly at my girl, but there is no mistaking the tip of her sharp tongue sticking out at my mother, right before she turns back to what she was doing, leaving everyone to wonder if they saw it right.

"I came to offer you the use of my cottage until you've got this place back in order," my mother offers Leelo with a sneaky, saccharine smile in my direction. The wench. She's upset and she's smart, so she's making me feel her displeasure. She knows she's sabotaging my plans and is taking great pleasure at bringing her point home.

"All right, Charlie," I intervene. "Let's talk, you and me, okay?"

"Oh? You want to talk now?"

Leelo is looking over my mother's shoulder, pressing her lips together to keep from bursting out laughing. She's missed nothing.

"Please," I plead, trying to ignore the curious eyes of every woman in here. Clearly my mother chooses her audience well, since even Mrs. Zhao glances at me with disapproval.

I'll never get it. Women can be mean-spirited creatures amongst themselves, but cross one of them and the rest will be quick to form a lynch mob, no questions asked.

"I was going to call you," I start feebly, once I have her outside and out of earshot.

"Was that before or after you decided to call in the help of everyone else?" she snipes.

"I fucked up, Charlie," I admit, feeling guilty for upsetting her.

"*Language.*"

"Fine, I messed up. For the record, I didn't call anyone—Patti did. I didn't know they were coming until they got here. By that time, I figured you'd already be piss...I mean angry. Who told you?"

"Bill Prescott came by, asking about Kyle. Wanting to know whether I've had any troubles with him at the cottage, seeing as he's my neighbour."

"Did you tell him?"

"Of course," she huffs, insulted that I'm questioning her.

"Listen," I coax gently. "I'm sorry if I upset you. It's the opposite of what I wanted. I know you adore Leelo and would be concerned, so I figured if we could get things under control here first, it would be less of a worry."

"You thought wrong," she answers, her head still turned away, so I turn her around and wrap her in my arms, dropping my cheek to the top of her head.

"So noted, Mom." I rarely ever use that term, except when it's very important she hears me.

And she hears me.

Leaning back, she scans my face with squinty eyes. "I know you didn't mean to, but you have to remember, I was rolling with the punches long before you were even a sparkle in your father's eye. I would've worried—heck, I *will* worry—but that's my prerogative. I worry for the people I care about. I can handle it. I'm made of sterner stuff. However, what brings me to my knees is being left out of the loop because my son doesn't trust my ability to cope."

Jesus fucking Christ.

Talk about getting cut off at the ankles and left bleeding. I can't remember the last time I was made to feel like the rotting slop at the bottom of the lake. Only she can. And maybe Leelo.

"So noted," I repeat. "Love you, Charlie," I add for good measure, and it earns me a little pat on the cheek like when I was ten years old.

"I know, my boy. And I you." She smiles, turns, and starts walking toward her car.

"Where are you going?"

"Into town," she says as she opens her door. "It's clear no one has thought about food. Someone has to."

I snicker at the triumphant gleam in her eyes.

"Food?" Matt sticks his head out of the door of unit eight, clearly finely attuned to that word.

"Absolutely," Charlie says. "Anything in particular you'd like?"

"I'd kill for a pizza," the kid says with a broad smile.

"Done. And without any need for bloodshed." She gets behind the wheel and immediately rolls down the window—by hand—and calls out. "Oh and, Matt? Why don't you stay at my cottage for a bit," she says, tossing him a bundle of keys that he deftly catches. "Best way to decide if something is the right fit is to try it on for size, right?"

With a jaunty wave at a slack-jawed Matt, and a sneaky wink in my direction, my mother—clearly a force to be reckoned with—spins the wheels of her old heap of a car on the gravel, before speeding recklessly toward the road.

I shake my head after her.

"Your mom is da bomb," Matt announces, grinning ear to ear.

You have no idea, kid.

TWENTY-SIX

I can't remember what I did before she filled every one of my days.

Leelo

"Doesn't look like it was tampered with," Bill says, handing me my laptop.

I don't know whether to laugh or cry with relief as I quickly thank Bill, tuck the computer under my arm, and rush to my bedroom. On my bed, I flip it open, type in my password, and assure myself that everything is still as I left it.

"All there?"

Roar is leaning against the doorway, having clearly followed me upstairs. I smile my relief at him.

"Come see."

I pat the mattress next to me and watch as he saunters over and sits down beside me, his hip butting up against mine.

I click on the folder that holds a lifetime of memories and give him a first row seat into my life. The world around us disappears for a while, as I flip through picture after picture of my history.

"Your daughter is very beautiful, does she know she looks just like you?" Roar comments when I show him Gwen's convocation photo, and I laugh.

"Oh, hell no. She doesn't like being compared to me, in any way. In fact, I think she goes out of her way to prove to the world she's not like me at all." I grin, flipping through the pictures taken by Matt at the ceremony I was asked not to come to. I've looked at them so often; it barely stings anymore. All I feel now is pride for the independent, capable person she has become.

"She could do a lot worse," he mumbles under his breath.

"Thank you, but she's always marched to her own drummer, that one. I think she's so determined to carve her own path; she doesn't want to be compared with anyone. It's not just me."

"Pizza!!" Matt's voice sounds from downstairs.

"We should grab some before he eats it all," I warn him, closing my laptop.

"Hang on. Let me see that?"

Roar lifts the lid back up and points at the small thumbprint beside the filename—*Daddy.* A melancholy feeling washes over me when I double-click on the file, and the screen fills with an image of my dad, sitting in his favourite chair, a half-smile on his face, and his pipe stuck in the corner of his mouth. He's watching eight-year-old me, sitting on his knees, reading my book, completely oblivious of the sheer adoration on his face.

If this picture was in print, it would be grey by now from all the handling.

Funny how an image can invoke such seemingly contradictory feelings, so maybe melancholy is not the right word. There's sadness, absolutely, but also a deep gratitude that I had a father, who could love in a way that showed in everything he did. Even just watching his daughter read.

"Great picture," Roar says simply, but his eyes show the deeper understanding.

"It is," I agree, slapping the laptop shut. "But that's enough of that, we're missing out on the food and I'm starving."

When we get downstairs, Lin is complaining loudly about the *'cardboard pizza,'* but she does it while shoving another piece in her mouth.

Charlie took no half measures, there's a stack of five large pizza boxes and an assortment of drinks on the bar in the restaurant.

"Jesus, Charlie," Roar remarks. "Who else did you invite?"

"Don't you be a smartass, Riordan," she scolds him, waving her index finger. "Between Matt and Zhao Lin, it'll all get eaten." That remark, of course, starts another tirade by the older woman.

I take a seat on an upside down bucket, eating my slice, and smiling as I listen to the three older ladies disagree on everything, *including* the colour of the sky.

Somewhere I lost the time, and I'm surprised to notice the shadows quickly getting longer as the sun is setting, painting the sky a warm gold.

Although, Lin claims it's red, and Charlotte insists on yellow.

I shake my head and reach for another slice from the box Roar brings around, his eyes crinkled in a barely-there smile.

311

There are five beams and thirty wood planks that make up the ceiling in Roar's bedroom.

I've been counting.

The clock on his nightstand reads three-thirty, and I've been lying here, staring up, and counting boards for over an hour.

Oh, I fell asleep. Well, more accurately, I was fucked into oblivion by Roar, who had my legs bent up in ways I didn't know were possible. Although I'm sure he would disagree on the *fucked* part.

I passed right out after that and slept blissfully for a few hours, but woke up in the dead of night, and now I can't get back to sleep.

The past twenty-four hours have left me with so many impressions that my mind seems unable to properly process them. Add to that the things that are left to be done over the next days and weeks before I can even feel back on top of the game again. Not to mention my budget, which is blown to smithereens. Even if I get a decent chunk back from insurance to cover damages—something that remains to be seen, given that this would be my third claim in a very short time and bound to raise suspicions—I'll still run short.

I was supposed to capitalize on the summer so that my income could last at least partway through the winter, but the summer is about half gone, and I really have no income to show for it.

"You think loud," Roar grumbles sleepily. "Go to sleep."

"I'm trying."

"Not hard enough," he complains, reaching over to pull me onto his chest. His large hand cups the back of my head, and I instantly feel more restful, breathing in his warm scent. "It'll be all right," he soothes and I feel the words vibrate in his chest.

Already my eyes feel heavy.

"Everything's gonna be fine."

-

"Should we go check on Matt?" I ask, stacking our breakfast plates and walking them over to the sink.

Last night, I tried to get my son to stay at the lodge one more night, but he was gung-ho to try Charlotte's cottage. Armed with her keys, the leftover pizza, and driving her little old car, which she let him use after he dropped her home, he left with a big grin on his face. I chuckled when I noticed how he had to fold himself behind the wheel, but watching him drive off, I wondered when my boy had grown up.

"He's got Charlie's car and food. He'll surface when he's ready."

"Pizza isn't breakfast food," I sputter.

"If you're a twenty-year-old kid it is," Roar claims.

I run water over the dishes and squirt detergent in the sink, when I feel him walk up behind me. He brushes the hair away from my neck and presses his lips to the sensitive skin behind my ear. It sends a current over my skin that leaves my nipples achingly pebbled.

"*Honey…*" I sigh, not sure whether it's a plea to stop or to continue. The deep chuckle against the shell of my ear is not helping.

"I like it," he says straightening up, and I feel the immediate loss of his heat.

"What?"

I'm playing coy, knowing full well he likely took note of my hard nipples, as he doesn't really miss much, but his reply is a surprise.

"The way your body responds to just a little touch. But I really like when you call me *that*."

"What—honey?" I ask, turning to face him.

"Yeah," he drawls, a look of contentment on his face. "I like that."

"I'll keep that in mind," I concede with a smile, putting my hand in the middle of his chest and leaning in for a kiss.

He covers my hand with his as he kisses me back, sliding it down over his stomach, to the hard bulge behind his fly.

"My dick likes it, too."

Roar

That fucking picture of a little, chubby girl, her tongue peeking out between her lips as she's reading a book on her father's lap is messing with me.

So innocent, so blindly trusting that her daddy had her back.

I felt the same trust from her last night, as she sat beside me and took me on a guided tour of her past.

Christ.

There are times I wish it was easier for me to say the words I feel, instead of scribbling them down on scraps of paper. Somewhere between my brain and my mouth, they tend to get mangled. So more often than not, I say nothing, gathering them up throughout the day until a single thought floats out above the rest—and that one I write down. Jars full of them. Years of thoughts, memories, and feelings, reduced to random scratches on bits of paper.

"Roar?" Matt's head sticks out of the side door, waving my phone. "It's ringing."

I drop the large shard of windowpane I just managed to pull free from its frame in the bucket at my feet and reach over to take it from him.

"Yeah?"

"Prosecutor brought down charges," Bill announces. "Thompson's not going anywhere for a while. We found evidence in yesterday's search of his house, that he may have blackmailed the previous owners into selling him their property at a ridiculous price. So there'll likely be more charges coming down. Tell your girl she can rest easy, he may not be talking, but his house of cards is coming down, one way or another."

"Good to know," I say with some relief. "Is anything else required of her?"

"Prosecutor's office will likely get in touch with her at some point, but that could be a while."

"Sounds good. Anything else?" I want to know as I watch Leelo round the corner at the back of the house. She was on the dock with a cup of coffee, needing some Zen time to let her mind settle. Her words, not mine.

"Nope, but I'm off in an hour and a half and am coming over with Travis to help put those windows in. I just saw him at Tim's and he says the truck is on its way."

"Not gonna say no."

"I figured as much," he fires back.

"Asshole," I grumble, but I do it grinning.

"Yeah," he drawls, a smile in his voice. "But I'm *your* asshole."

Leelo slips her arm around my waist just as I end my call.

"Who are you calling an asshole at ten in the morning?"

"Bill," I tell her, slipping my phone in my back pocket before wrapping her up in my arms. "He's always an asshole, but especially so at the end of an overnight shift."

"Don't be mean," she scolds. "He probably needs his sleep. He didn't sleep the night before either."

"I know. Yet he's still got it in his head that he's coming straight here to help install the windows."

"For real? But that's so nice."

I grin into her smiling face, knowing that the next words from my mouth are going to wipe the smile right off.

"I know, especially since he's bringing your good friend, Travis."

I chuckle as I watch a frown start between her eyebrows.

"You're kidding right?"

"Afraid not."

"Asshole."

I laugh as she wiggles out of my hold and stomps off inside, throwing me the bird before she lets the storm door slam shut behind her.

-

"Add a shim on that top corner there, Matt, it's still off by a hair."

I hand him the small strip of wood.

We were able to replace just the glass in most of the windows, except the large one in the living room, overlooking the water in the back. Matt is the one who suggested putting a new window in there. The new ready to install frame, with double-paned glass, would help keep down the cost of heating in the winter, with the way the winds can blow off the lake.

With the window now plumb, it takes only seconds to fill the remaining gaps with foam insulation before we finish off the inside framing. I hand Matt—who is still standing on the ladder—the moulding for the top, when I notice he's looking over his shoulder, his eyes focused on something beyond the open door to the restaurant. He's down the ladder and out the door before the sound of raised voices reaches my ears, and then I'm tearing out after him.

I don't see them at first, hidden by the bulk of a brand new, shiny, GMC Sierra Denali. A typical city boy's idea of penis enhancement. Safe to bet the owner is lacking in the schlong department. It never fails; it's always the smallest guys who drive the biggest trucks.

When I round the front end, I find that Matt has already joined in the confrontation between Leelo and some penny-loafered asshole. So he's not quite as short as I thought, but judging by the formfitting shirt and too-

317

tight-to-be-comfortable pair of jeans he is wearing, he isn't hiding much else.

So this must be David, judging by the way Matt edges his way between his father and his mother, drawing the man's obvious ire to him. I knew I liked that kid for a reason.

Rather than jump in, which would be my normal response, I instead lean my shoulder against the fender, and let Matt sort this out while I listen in. Something goes wrong, I can always move fast.

"What the fuck, Dad? What the hell are you here for?"

"What kind of question is that? Your idiot mother gets it into her crazy head she wants to move to the boonies, where, might I point out, she is clearly failing, not that I expected anything else, only to drag you down with her? You want me to stand by and let that happen?"

It takes everything out of me not to wipe his sissy metrosexual ass all over the parking lot, but I want to give Matt a chance.

"Get lost, Dad. You come here and give off on Mom, when it's me you're mad at, just like always. You're an asshole!"

"Don't you talk to me like that."

"Why not? You're the one who taught me!"

I watch as Leelo plants her forehead between Matt's shoulder blades, both in support and perhaps an attempt to help him keep his cool.

"Son," he says, in a clear attempt to calm the waters, although by the stubborn set of Matt's shoulders, I'm not sure it has any effect. "You walk away from a future many a boy your age would gladly sign for, of course I'm going

318

to be worried. You pack up and disappear without a word and don't answer my calls, of course I have to come to make you see reason."

"Are you for real?" Matt hisses, leaning forward to the point where Leelo is physically holding him back. "I didn't disappear without a word, which you well know, since you're the one who held open the door to make sure my ass was walking out. As usual though, you've chosen to rewrite fucking history, so that you come out the innocent victim. And don't even pretend that it's my well-being you are concerned with, because I know that fucking snitch of a bank manager called you the minute I got off the phone with him. Go home, Dad. I'm making a life here and there's dick-all you can do about it."

I'm so impressed with the kid; I almost miss the hot glare the asshole is sending my way. I raise my eyebrow in challenge.

"Who the fuck are you?" he barks, trying to come around Matt, who sidesteps to block him, but I take it as an invitation to join the discussion.

Walking up, I lightly tap Matt on the shoulder to let him know to step aside, and make sure I tuck Leelo safely under my arm.

"Who is this bozo, Lilith?"

She just looks up at me with a small smile tugging at the corners of her mouth, and places a proprietary hand on my stomach.

"David, meet Roar, my—"

"Are you kidding me?" he interrupts rudely. "Not wasting any time fucking the local handyman for favours now, are you? Although, you might've saved it for

319

someone with balls—this one doesn't appear too eager to come to your defense, leaving a boy to do a man's work."

That triple stab signals the end of my patience.

"Few things," I finally say, working hard to keep my voice level. "Matt here may only be twenty, but in the past five minutes has proven to be more of a man than you ever were or will be, during the course of your miserable life." The weasel opens his mouth to speak, but I snap my fist up, index finger out just a hair from his nose, effectively shutting him right the fuck up. "Next, you must be the dumbest fucker on the face of this earth to let this woman here walk out of your life. She has more balls than you'd even know what to do with, but perhaps that's why you couldn't hack it—maybe you knew all along she was your superior in every way that counts and simply wasn't man enough to keep up." I ignore the barely contained snort coming from Matt, because I'm on a fucking roll here. "And finally, the only reason I stood back and let these two handle you, is because there's not a doubt in my mind that either one of them could wipe the fucking forest with your skinny ass."

I can tell most of the fire has gone out of him as his eyes flick from his son, to me, and to the woman he discarded, but as usual, someone cornered has no choice but to come out swinging and this time he aims for Matt.

"Good thing I have *one* child who takes after me with common sense *and* some brains. One who isn't destined to become a loser like his mother."

I use the index finger I've been waving under his nose to poke him in the chest once, hard, to get his attention.

"You don't deserve any of them, and I believe you've been asked to leave politely, but let me make sure you understand clearly."

I lean in, my nose almost touching his.

"Get the fuck out of here. Fuck…off!"

TWENTY-SEVEN

I never wanted more—until she made me want to give her more.

Leelo

I hadn't even been all that surprised when David showed up.

Part of me had been expecting it ever since Matt arrived. The phone calls had just been the warm up for the main event. He never could stand being ignored and that's what Matt and I had been doing after that first call.

The contrast between the two men was never as clear. David would demand attention with his air of superiority and his temper, mostly to compensate for what he lacks in charisma and confidence. Roar doesn't need to yell or throw attitude, he could stay silent and his mere presence would still claim any attention he needed. He has no need to yell; because his quietly spoken words deliver all the impact he is looking for.

David may scoff at the other man's rough exterior, and clearly jumped to the conclusion he was dealing with some backward hick, but the truth is, with his unkempt beard, sleeveless flannel shirt, ripped jeans, and old work boots, Roar is keenly intelligent and has more class in his pinky than David's shiny truck and carefully put together ensemble could buy.

"You okay?" Roar's arm comes around me as David's truck speeds over the gravel, almost spinning out when he makes the turn onto the road and leaving a trail of dust billowing in the air.

I could see the struggle on David's face when Roar told him to take a hike. He speared me with a dirty look before turning to Matt and shaking his head. Matt turned on his heels and marched right around the house. By the time I looked back, David was already getting in his truck while Roar calmly looked on.

I'm sure it's killing my ex to know he was bested by a man he considers beneath him, but who is clearly superior.

In every fucking way.

"I'm good," I tell him, grabbing the hand he has draped on my shoulder and pulling him toward the restaurant, or what's left of it. "Not wasting another thought on him. We've got better things to do."

-

Yesterday, Patti and her crew made piles on the stainless steel counter in the kitchen of everything that survived. Mostly utensils, pots and pans—stuff that doesn't readily break—but there were also some linens, some china, and glassware. I'm cleaning and packing everything in the large plastic tubs Matt went and picked up this morning to keep it safe. I'll stack the bins in the shed, where the washers and dryer used to be. I haven't even had a chance to look at new ones. Not with this persistent shitstorm raining down on me.

The guys' trucks were hauled off on a large CAA flatbed truck for repairs, new tires, and windows, and may not be ready for a few days. So between us, we just have my Jeep for transportation, a borrowed cottage for Matt, and a warm spot in Roar's bed for me. Can you say up shit creek?

You'd think I'd be ready to throw in the towel. I mean, this kind of bad luck surely can't be normal. Oddly, the thing that would once have sent me over the edge, David's derision, seems to have the adverse effect now. It's driving me forward with determination to make my dream a reality, no matter what other calamities lay ahead.

It's ridiculous how calm I am.

"Where's Matt?" Roar asks, as he sticks his head around the door.

"My guess, he's sitting on the dock cooling down." I close the bin I was working on and shove it to the end of the counter. "I'll go get him, if you wouldn't mind putting this in the shed in the meantime?"

I let the storm door slam shut behind me, the familiar squeal of the spring putting a little smile on my face. It's warm, as it has been most of the summer so far. Very little rain has fallen and fire hazard warnings went from moderate to high along the roads. There have been some fires, small ones, mostly started by stupid people who toss their cigarette butts out of the window or don't cover off their campfires at the end of the night, but nothing major, and nothing close. Still, having such a large body of water nearby is a safe feeling.

As I suspected, Matt is lying on his back on the floating dock, his feet dangling in the water. His boots are standing next to him with his shirt on top. He's probably trying to get some colour on that white chest of his. He has his forearm covering his eyes, and doesn't move when I start walking down the dock toward him, but I'm sure he knows I'm there.

"I'm sorry, Mom," he says when I kick off my sneakers and sit down beside him, sticking my toes in the water as well.

"For what, Bud? You got nothing to be sorry for. Your father is an ass. Always was and I'm afraid he always will be."

"I'm sorry for taking so long to see it. For giving you such a hard time, when I should've been protecting you." He lifts his arm away and I see his eyes swimming in tears.

I lean over and kiss his forehead, before turning to the water, looking out at the raw beauty of this place I've chosen to make my home, while I search for words.

"No, Matt. That's not for you to be sorry for. It's not your job to look after me, it's mine to look after you, and let's be honest; I didn't do such a great job of that myself. What you don't do, is let things that you had no control over in your past, dictate how you are today, or will be in the future. You learn from it, and then you let it go. We all have to let this go. I'm not sure what your Dad thought he would accomplish by driving all the fucking way up here, but we're not going to let his actions today, or in the past, have impact on the path we've chosen. Me on mine, and you on yours."

Matt is quiet beside me and I let him be. Give him time to process what I'm telling him. That this is his life. That the only person who should be in the driver's seat is him.

I feel a tug on my arm as he pulls me down on the dock beside him. Curling his arm around my neck, he kisses the side of my head.

"I like you, Mom," he says, and I'm happy to hear a smile in his voice. "You're pretty smart for an old broad."

That earns him a sharp elbow in his side.

"I like you too, Bud."

-

I'm not sure how long we lay there, bobbing on the water and watching a few clouds drift by above, when a familiar heavy tread sounds on the dock and a familiar voice pipes up.

"Room for one more?"

A hand with three cold, dripping bottles of beer comes into my line of vision, and I automatically reach for one as I sit up. Matt grabs one too as Roar kicks off his dusty boots, strips off his socks, rolls up his jeans, and sits down next to me, sticking his feet in the water as well.

"Doesn't matter how hot the summers can get at times, this water always stays cool," he mutters, wrapping his lips around the beer bottle and taking a swig. I scoot closer and lean my head against his shoulder. "You guys good?"

"We're good." I tilt my head back a little and smile up at him.

"Yeah," Matt adds before he continues. "I'm thinking of putting in an offer on your mother's property."

I lift my head and look at him in surprise, but Roar seems unfazed.

"Figured you might," he says, matter-of-factly, without even looking in Matt's direction. "Figure she's waiting for it, too."

327

Roar

"I was looking at some comparable properties," Matt says, more animated now than he was earlier. "I mean, I know what I can afford based on what I have saved up, and what I used to have coming in, but I'll have to see if the bank would give me a mortgage based on what I used to make or what I'm hoping to in the future. Maybe I should wait until I've had a chance to build up my business."

I bite off a smile at Matt's excited ramble and throw Leelo a wink.

"Talk to her," I calmly tell him. "There's more than one way to skin a cat. Financing might not be the best option at this point, but there are others."

What I don't tell him is that I already talked to Charlie; she may be old, but she's also sharp as a tack. She already researched a rent-to-buy contract that would require a nominal amount as down payment, but after that, only monthly rent payments to cover the cost of maintenance, plus a set amount to go toward the principal amount owing.

I think Charlie likes the idea of keeping the cottage in the family, so to speak.

But I don't tell Matt any of this; I can sense how important it is for him to forge his own path.

"Okay," the kid says with a small grin on his lips. "I'll give her a call."

"Better yet," Leelo pipes up. "Why not finish up what we need to here, you drop Roar and me off at the lodge, and go see her. Take her for dinner at the Embassy on Broadway, she loves their pierogies."

There's another reason I can't resist this woman. She sees, she listens, and she remembers all the big and little things that are important. Not for herself, but for the people she cares about.

I look down on her two-tone coloured hair and wonder what I've done to deserve her. I don't even notice Matt getting up until he speaks.

"Let's go then," he says, already walking down the dock.

I reach over to grab Leelo's pink sneakers before she can, and pull her feet from the water, one by one, drying them on my shirt before I tie her shoes for her. Then I quickly slip on my socks and boots, and get up, holding out my hand to help her up.

"Last time someone tied my shoes, I was in grade four and my dad was in a rush to get me off to school," she says, a melancholy smile on her face.

I tilt up her chin with my forefinger and brush my lips over hers. Once, and then again a little longer. Her response is immediate as she wraps her hands around the back of my neck and holds me in place. An image of me taking Leelo right here, on the dock, is clear in my head, but it's quickly thwarted when Matt calls out.

"Come on, you guys! Enough time for that later!"

-

I clink my glass to Leelo's.

To her delight, the bottle of scotch she saves for special occasions survived the baseball bat. It had rolled under the lower shelf of the steel kitchen counter, and she kept it cradled in her arms all the way to the lodge.

"To a scotch kinda day," I say, earning me a warm smile.

"You've got that right."

She lifts the glass to her lips and takes a cautious sip, while rocking gently in one of the rustic rocking chairs on my porch. We came out here to see the sun go down on yet another tumultuous day.

When Matt dropped us off earlier, I noticed a couple of outdoor fires in front of some of the cabins.

Usually, when the fire hazard warning is high, I choose to restrict open fires on my property. I've seen it too many times; people think they're safe as long as they're close to the shore, but the truth is, the wind can be unpredictable coming off the lake. Most people don't realize that a single gust can carry an ember up to a kilometre, if not further, into any direction.

After telling Leelo to go ahead, I check in with the guests at the two adjoining cabins. Neither was aware the warning had been raised to high and immediately shovelled dirt on their respective fires without argument.

By the time I got back to the lodge, she was already going to town in the kitchen. A frittata, she said she was making, which was fine by me. If it has eggs and cheese or meat—or better yet, both—it's good enough for me. I walked up to where she was chopping vegetables next to the sink and kiss her neck—something that seems to get me an instant response every time—before leaving her to check mail and messages in my office.

Now, with the motel windows replaced, my emails caught up on, my stomach full and my feet up on the railing, this day can be marked off as productive.

I reach out my hand and Leelo places her palm against mine, entwining our fingers, as we quietly watch the moon come out over the water.

"I was thinking," I start, breaking the silence, as I gently stroke the back of her hand with my thumb. "Tomorrow we start on the roof, but given that half of this summer is already gone, maybe instead of rushing to put things back the way they were, you should put some thought into what you want to end up with."

"What do you mean?"

"Well…" I shift a little in my seat so I can look at her. "What if you spent the rest of this summer making the Whitefish into exactly what you hoped it might become someday? Let me finish," I warn her, when she opens her mouth to protest. "Think about it; you could provide ongoing work for Matt for the foreseeable future, and along with realizing your own dream, help him realize his."

Her eyes soften a little as she lets that sink in.

"That *would* be wonderful, except for the fact that the insurance company doesn't pay for improvements, just for repairs. Besides, my bank account is so depleted, I don't know if I'll make it to next month, let alone next summer." She leans over and places a hand along my jaw. "I love that you want that for me, and for Matt, but I just don't—"

"What if there's a way to make the finances work too?" I offer carefully, sensing her resistance right away. "A way that would have everyone come out ahead?"

331

"Like what?"

"The lodge is booked solid for the remainder of the summer. Next year is quickly filling up. Every day I get new inquiries, and every day we turn people away who take a chance and drive up." I watch as Leelo gets up and starts pacing—she's listening. "I've thought about adding a few more cabins, but I'm hesitant," I continue, knowing I have her attention. "One of the main attractions here is that the waterfront is not crowded. You on the other hand, have a decent chunk of waterfront, with only the one single dock in a prime spot with just Crown land on the other shore. We could partner up." This idea has been percolating all weekend, but today it all seemed to gel.

"Are you suggesting we join forces?" She stops right in front of me, her hands on her hips, and her head cocked to one side. "We've know each other all of what? A few months? And you're expecting me to believe that you want to go into some kind of business deal with me as equals?" You'd think she's Italian with the way she gestures as she talks. "I want independence, Roar. I want to stand on my own two feet."

"I'm not suggesting anything else," I assure her. It's not like I didn't know this might be a hard sell. "I have no interest in taking your independence. What I'm suggesting is—"

"What he's saying is that he'll invest the money, you provide the land. Let me guess," Matt says to me, walking up the steps. Neither of us heard him coming, but it's clear he's heard enough. "You foot the bill for any upgrades on the motel, then you want to expand with three or four cabins on Mom's waterfront, and the two of you share in the proceeds of those. Oh, and of course, you'll hire me to do all the work."

I can't help grin at the smug smile on Matt's face. Smart kid.

"And we'll have a proper contract hammered out by your lawyer if that makes you feel any better," I direct at Leelo, who is looking at her son, slightly puzzled.

"Did you know about this?" she asks him pointedly, and Matt vehemently shakes his head.

"I didn't, but that doesn't mean I didn't think about it. Although, I admit that was mostly in terms of me investing money, but now it looks like I won't have a dime left."

It takes Leelo a minute to catch on, and then she squeals.

"You got it?"

"Rent-to-own. She had an agreement drawn up and everything, wanted me to take it to a lawyer to look over, but she cautioned me to stay away from that local firm. Suggested I find one in Sault Ste. Marie, like she did." He turns to me with a shit-eating grin, cracking his face wide open. "And can I just say, your mom is a shark." I chuckle at the description. Charlie would get a kick out of that. "She gave Dad a run for his money."

"Wait," Leelo interrupts, swinging him around by the shoulder to face her. "Your father?"

"Was there eating dinner," he explains, clearly struggling for patience. "He must have seen us come in, because we barely sat down and he was standing at the table. He started giving me a hard time when Charlotte, cool as a cucumber, stood up, offered her hand like they were meeting at a tea party, and proceeded to tell him she'd expected a *much* more substantial man, given that his son is such a strapping boy. Should've seen his face." Matt snorts. "Looked like he was going to blow a fuse. He started to; slammed his fist on the table. Your OPP buddy, Bill? He was there too. Heard the whole thing. He came right up to the table, grabbed Dad by the scruff of his neck, and marched him out of the restaurant."

"No shit." This from Leelo, who's listening with her mouth hanging open.

"Shit," Matt shoots back, his eyes dancing. "Bill came back, said he gave him directions back home and told him not to stop until he was safely back there."

"I need another drink," Leelo says, dropping back down in the chair beside me and holding out her glass. "This is all gonna take some time to process."

When Matt gets back from grabbing a glass for himself, I pour all of us a shot. We raise our glasses.

"To your first house," I toast Matt.

"To your expansion plans," he in turn toasts his mother and me.

"To your shitbag of a father being run out of town by a five foot nothing octogenarian," Leelo puts in her two cents, and before I can comment on that, she tosses the contents back in one swig.

"You go, Mom," Matt says laughing and she holds up her empty glass for a refill.

"Definitely a scotch kinda day."

TWENTY-EIGHT

Her softly whispered words wipe the remaining shadows from my soul.

Leelo

"Mom, grab me a bottle of water?"

I look up to see him peeking over the edge of the roof.

"Roar want one, too?"

"Sure." I hear his voice but I can't see him. This is the second day the guys have been working on the roof. The materials were dropped off early yesterday morning, and they've been at it for two days, while I've been wandering around rather aimlessly.

Two days have gone by.

Two days and my head is still trying to adapt to some of the new realities.

I came to the Whitefish Motel determined to give my life new content, and with every step I've taken it seems I've had roadblocks thrown in my path. I never thought my son would follow me here, and I certainly never expected to find a neighbour who would become such a permanent fixture in my daily existence.

There is nothing that's really gone according to plan, so I'm not sure why I'm so reluctant to let go of the vision

335

I came here with. If anything, I've proven these last couple of years that I can be in the moment.

Shit, my ink and my hair colour are evidence of that.

Yet here I am, agonizing over a proposal that secretly excites me with possibilities, but it requires a leap of faith. Again. I already took a giant one, moving here in the first place. I find myself, once again, on the edge of a cliff with nothing but beauty in front of me, but afraid to let go of the crumbling stability under my feet.

All I have to do is leap. Grab hold of the new opportunities opening up. God knows I want to, but years of practicing conventional wisdom and the sound of my mother's voice in my head get in the way. I imagine it spouts every caution and concern that has been grinding through my head, and I'm about sick of myself.

No one is holding a gun to my head. No one is forcing me into anything. The choice is all mine, and if I don't go for it; I know I'll regret it forever.

I'm the only one holding back.

I walk back out with a couple of frosty bottles of water and drop them in the bucket underneath the ladder. Matt's head sticks over the edge at the sound and immediately pulls the bucket up by the rope attached to the top rung of the ladder.

"I want a proper restaurant, a diner," I call up, surprising myself. "I want to gut the living room and kitchen of the house, and I want to incorporate that into the dining area. I want the main kitchen opened up, so everyone can see what goes on in there. I want to open from breakfast to two o'clock every day and do boxed lunches for those who want it. I don't want to do dinner.

336

I'm sick of doing dinner. It gives me a headache trying to think up meals."

I keep talking when Roar's head appears beside Matt's, both men looking at me strangely, but it doesn't matter, the cork is out of the bottle and there's no stopping now. "The top floor of the house can be converted into a one-bedroom apartment with a multi-level walk out deck that also serves as separate entrance. I'd like to see if it's possible to turn units one, two and three into two housekeeping units with full kitchen facilities like number eight. One less unit, but twice the opportunity for long-term rentals. Also," I continue, as I tick off the mental list I seem to have accumulated. "That ugly plastic siding has to go. I want that replaced with beams, or something that makes it look rustic, like the lodge." I watch as Roar slowly comes climbing down the ladder and stops in front of me, putting his hands on my hips, a half-smile on his lips. "And I'd really like this parking lot and driveway paved, I'm sick of gravel."

"Matt?" he calls up to where my son is still hanging over the edge of the roof, but his smiling eyes never leave mine. "Can it be done?"

"Some things easier than others," my son says with a grin. "I would need a few guys, a licensed plumber and electrician, and we'd have to get proper drawings done up and permits sorted. It would have to be done in a certain order, but I think it can be done."

"Good," Roar says, a full smile cracking his face wide open, as he wraps his arms around my middle and lifts me clear off my feet, shoving his face in my neck. "Are you planning on renting out that apartment?" he mumbles softly, and now it's my turn to smile.

337

"Eventually."

-

The next afternoon the three of us are piled into my Jeep and on our way back from Sault Ste. Marie.

We sat on Roar's porch last night and hammered out an agreement. Matt was there to give practical feedback on the construction timeline and an off-the-cuff cost projection, so we'd have an idea of the kind of money needed. I was surprised to find out that Roar didn't even flinch at the number Matt spouted off.

As luck would have it, Matt had already made an appointment with a lawyer in Sault Ste. Marie for noon today, as per Charlotte's suggestion, and he apparently was able to fit us in right after. It was my choice not to go with Henry Kline, mainly because he's really more Uncle Sam's lawyer than mine, and I still didn't feel quite right that his firm represents Kyle Thompson.

"Oh my God, this is so good," I groan, licking the foam from my Starbucks caramel macchiato off my lips. "I missed it."

I made Roar pull in when I saw the familiar logo. Wawa doesn't have one. I know, because I looked. Tim Hortons is more Wawa's speed and normally I don't mind, but nothing beats the foamy sweet treats Starbucks has to offer.

He went through the drive-thru and almost choked when the girl told him it would be almost fifteen dollars for three coffees. Matt ordered his cafe latte in the back seat and of course Roar just wanted a regular coffee. A term the girl at the window was not familiar with, so I ordered him an Americano. It really threw him off when I explained what an Americano was.

"So basically you ordered me a regular coffee," he pointed out, confused, which made me giggle.

"They don't do regular coffees at Starbucks," Matt piped up from the peanut gallery.

"Apparently they do," Roar grumbled. "They just don't know it."

I didn't say another word, and avoided even looking at him while he paid the girl, but couldn't hold back the moment that nectar of the gods hit my taste buds.

"So good," I repeat, with a sideways glance at Roar who takes a sip of his cup. "And?" I prompt.

"Not bad, but not five fucking dollars worth of good, either."

"Think of it as our version of champagne, a celebratory drink," I tease.

"That's overpriced, too."

I leave him alone the rest of the drive, and listen while he and Matt make plans. Sounds like they're going to be busy for the foreseeable future.

Suddenly it hits me; I have nothing to do. The motel will be under construction and I'll be twiddling my thumbs the whole time. It's gonna drive me around the bend. *Fuck.* I don't even know if I'll have a place to stay.

"I should've thought this through more," I mutter and can feel Roar's eyes turn to me.

"Second thoughts? Already?"

His eyes scan my face and I'm sure the panic I feel is all over it.

"What the hell am *I* supposed to be doing?"

I see him bite the inside of his cheek to stop from laughing, but before he has a chance to answer, Matt leans forward between the seats.

"What do you think you'll be doing?" Matt fires off. "Sitting on your ass watching us? Hell no. A project this size needs all hands on deck. You wanted to be equal in everything, right? Well, then get ready for bruises and blisters, because you'll be covered in them after the first week."

With that he scoots back in his seat, a smug grin on his face as Roar barks out a laugh.

Well, that stuns me silent. Roar puts his hand on my knee and gives it a squeeze.

"You okay?"

I'm sure when I look at him it's no longer panic he sees on my face, but excitement instead. My wheels are spinning.

"I need a tool belt," I blurt out. "And I really want to use a nail gun."

I hear Matt groan in the back seat and beside me Roar sighs deeply. Guess my guys don't like the idea of me handling power tools, but they'll just have to suck it up, because I can't wait.

Roar

Fuck me.

This has been a frustrating week.

I know it takes time to get a project like this off the ground, but I'd hoped we could at least start knocking down some walls. That, however, requires the original building plans so we can make sure not to rip out a load-bearing wall or damage any pipes. Those plans, including any upgrades or changes Sam made since, are at Kline, Kline & McTavish, but they've been giving us the run around.

My guess is Henry found out Leelo went to the big city to see a lawyer and he's not liking the loss of her business.

"You've reached Kline, Kline & McTavish. Our opening hours are nine to five, Monday through Friday. If you know your party's extension, please dial it now. Or you can leave a message in our general mailbox."

I slam the phone down on my desk. I don't even know why I tried, it's not like I didn't get the same damn answering machine all day yesterday as well.

First time I called was Friday morning, and the woman who answered explained that I would have to speak with Henry Kline directly but sadly he was in meetings all day. That started a discussion around what might be a good time to call back and resulted in me losing my temper, at which time Leelo grabbed the phone and tried. She didn't get much further, only able to leave a message for him to call her back as soon as possible. Of course that didn't happen.

By the time four thirty rolled around on Friday, we were back on the phone, only to be told Henry Kline had left for the day, and although he might pop in over the weekend, she couldn't make any promises. We'd have to wait until Monday.

It's Sunday, and yesterday wasn't so bad, with the arrival of a bunch of new guests at Jackson's Point, but today pretty much sucks.

Thank God Matt and I got our trucks back last week, because sharing one set of wheels between the three of us was getting old, and with his truck back, Matt's been using the time to do some small projects at his new place. We haven't seen much of him.

Leelo has been hanging out here, with me, bored out of her gourd and therefore baking in my kitchen. I just hope my guests don't think the baskets of muffins she delivered to each cottage this morning are the norm, because they'll be in for disappointment.

To top it all off, what was a small fire at the northeast edge of Lake Superior Provincial Park is steadily growing in size and moving fast. There's a chance our small Wawa volunteer crew is going to be mobilized to assist and when that happens, it'll be all hands on deck and that includes me. Timing sucks.

I can smell her before I hear her. Cinnamon with the subtle undertones of banana. Her colourful arm comes around me, setting a plate on my desk with a thick, steaming slice of what I assume is banana bread, lathered with melting butter. I lean back in my chair until I can feel her body and she drops her arms over my shoulders, hugging me from behind.

"Hey, Sunshine," I mumble in greeting, dropping my head back so I can look up at her.

"Hey yourself." She smiles, before leaning in for a peck.

When she starts to pull back, I raise my arm and catch my hand around the back of her neck, pulling her head back down. This time I kiss her properly, slipping my tongue between her lips and tasting her deeply. Cinnamon, banana, and Leelo. *Fucking delicious.*

Without breaking the kiss, I swivel my chair around and with my other hand pull her onto my lap. Now I can have both my hands free to explore. Her hands come up, tangle through my beard, and along my jaw, before sliding over the short hair on my head. She gasps in my mouth when my fingers find her hardening nipple and lightly twist. My girl likes a little edge. Something I discovered when I slapped her naked ass getting out of the shower this morning. Her mouth, already swollen from taking my cock, fell open, and for a moment, I thought she was pissed, but the next thing I know, a deep flush spread over her chest and that pink little tongue of hers slipped out for a leisurely lick.

"Honey," she mumbles breathlessly and I love the sound of that word from her lips. She uses it more and more.

"I want to strip you down, and have you ride me in this chair, those fucking fantastic tits bouncing in my face," I growl, getting harder at the thought.

It wouldn't take much either. Already I have one hand shoved down the back of her shorts, my palm full of her glorious ass and fingers teasing her crack, while the other is kneading her tit under her shirt. Despite the flash of heat in her eyes at my crass suggestion, she puts a restraining hand in the middle of my chest, gently shaking her head.

"*Honey*, it's the middle of the afternoon, someone could walk into your office any time."

"We'll lock the door," I suggest, but she's already leaning away, grabbing the plate off the desk where she placed it.

"It's not why I came in here. I need you to try this banana loaf."

I open my mouth to tell her I've already tasted it and deemed it delicious, but I don't get a chance. She takes the opportunity to shove a piece of the bread between my lips. I have no choice but to chew.

"It's good," I manage around the bite and barely swallow it when she pops another piece in my mouth.

So it's not hot bouncy sex in my office chair, but having Leelo sit on my lap and feed me her baking by hand is not altogether bad either. Until the phone rings.

"Jackson's Point," Leelo answers, since I'm still chewing. "One moment, please." She hands the phone to me, a concerned look on her face.

"Got the call, Doyle. We're heading out from the station in an hour. Don't make me wait." The chief hangs up without waiting for an answer or giving me a chance to ask any questions.

This is the first time in a couple of years I've been called in. I've missed the adrenaline rush, and part of me is excited at the prospect, but I certainly don't miss having to leave behind loved ones with only worry to keep them company.

"Fire's getting out of hand, Sunshine. I've gotta go."

I watch her close her eyes and take a deep breath in, exhaling through flared nostrils, strain already visible on her face.

"*I love you.*"

At least that's what I think she says, I could barely hear it.

"Leelo?"

Her eyes pop open and she cups my face in her hands, leaning in so the tip of her nose is touching mine.

"If you're going out there risking your life, you should do it knowing that I love you."

I mirror her hold as I lift my hands to hold her face.

"*I know,*" I whisper, pressing my lips against hers. "But it feels so fucking good to hear you say that."

TWENTY-NINE

I'd forgotten how hard it was to miss someone — or did I ever know?

Leelo

"I'll miss you."

It's been four days since Roar mumbled those hurried words, his face buried in my neck as we were standing by his truck.

He had only fifteen minutes left to get to the fire station. The rest of the time since he received the call was spent making arrangements to have Jackson's Point looked after. Matt was on board, sticking around the lodge to see to any hands-on needs, and I got a crash course on his computer so I could access the booking site and emails. Patti would be by at her regular times, but Roar assured me I could call her with any questions. His last call had been to give Charlie a head's up, and I promised him I'd check in on her regularly. He had no idea how long he'd be gone.

I didn't expect him to reply in kind when I blurted out my feelings. I did that for me, because one thing I've learned in my years is that you never leave things unsaid. Life can be cruel, and I don't want to be living with the regrets of missing a chance to let someone know how much they mean to me. I also don't want to pretend I don't know that his whispered "*I know*" and "*I'll miss you*" convey he feels the same for me.

Roar's feelings for me are clear in his actions, it's just a matter of recognizing them, and I'm learning.

One such example is his request that Matt stay at the lodge as well, while he's gone. Initially I'd balked, suggesting I'd be fine by myself, but now, after last night's incident with a bunch of drunken guests disrupting the peace, I'm glad Matt was there to back me up. Sometimes my stubborn drive for independence gets in the way of common sense.

"Mom," I hear behind me and I turn away from the computer screen. "Gwen wants to talk to you," he says, walking in holding out his cell phone.

I haven't spoke to Gwen since the incident with my ex last week, not really eager to get slammed with a regurgitated version of David's interpretation of events. It would just cause more aggravation on both sides, which is why I'm reluctant to take the call.

"Hey, love," I greet my daughter anyway, since there's no way I could've refused her or the puppy-dog face Matt is giving me.

"We need to talk," is the first thing out of her mouth, and I can feel the hair on the back of my neck standing up. Only the encouraging smile on my son's face holds me back from reacting.

"Sure," I offer cautiously.

"I have a week's vacation coming up and I want to drive up."

My mouth literally falls open, torn between elation and sheer panic. My daughter is a city girl, who needs her creature comforts. Plus, she wasn't impressed with the ink I had last time I saw her, so I'm a little concerned with how she'll respond to the additions since then, let alone the blue hair. She can be quite critical of me.

On the other hand, I love my Gwen, whatever way she comes, and I can't wait to wrap my arms around my girl. If she'll let me.

"Of course," my mouth says before my brain has a chance to process. Where the hell am I going to put her? The motel is a shambles right now, and I feel awkward putting her up at the lodge.

"I'm staying at Matt's cottage," she volunteers, undoubtedly reading my mind. She's good at that. "I hear he bought one."

That last was a bit of a dig, but I guess I'd be a little pissed off at being out of the loop too, if I were in her shoes.

"He just did. Great, right?" When I don't get a reaction I forge ahead. "So I guess he told you we're staying at the lodge for now, right?"

"Yes, Mom, I heard all about *your man*." The last doesn't sound very friendly, but I decide to bite my tongue. "And not just from Matt."

Ah, so I guess her father's been in touch with her. It shouldn't surprise me. He was always quick to launch complaints about me to the children.

"I see. Is he back home?" I ask carefully and listen to Gwen sigh deeply on the other side.

"Yes. Look, I really don't want to do this over the phone, but that was a dick move by Dad, and had I known he was planning it, I would've given you a head's up." Another deep sigh and this time when she continues, I can hear a hint of vulnerability in her voice. "For the record, he wasn't too impressed with me either when I told him as much."

Typical of David, when he doesn't get the affirmation he expects, he'll turn on you. I'm sure that must've been a sobering experience for Gwen, and I'd love to offer her my ear, but she's right, this isn't something to be discussed over the phone.

"Sorry, sweetie," I offer instead. "When are you coming up?"

"I should be there early evening tomorrow."

"That's a long drive, Gwenny," I caution gently, knowing that she doesn't usually take it well when I question her.

"It's fine, Mom. I'm leaving at the butt crack of dawn. I can drive ten hours," she scoffs, as expected.

"Just make sure you take regular breaks." I can't stop myself, it's a mom thing and it works like a red flag on a bull with Gwen.

"I said it's fine," she snaps, effectively cutting off any further concerns I might have.

"Okay, love. Can't wait to see you." I don't even try to tell her to drive safe, I assume she knows I'm thinking it though, as I hear a click on the other side.

My daughter may have a bristly exterior, but I *know* her. I know most of that hard facade is a defense mechanism to protect her sensitive heart. She has difficulty trusting people, especially those who've already violated her trust once. Sadly I fall under that category. I let her down when I couldn't be strong enough for me, let alone her and her brother. I guess, in a warped way, it's a tribute to me that my transgressions felt so much more of a betrayal to her than the stunts her father pulled. I take it to mean I always had the power to hurt her more, and therefore she will make me work so much harder to win her trust back.

But I will.

Roar

Jesus.

I spit out the coffee, which tastes more like engine oil. It's probably been sitting in that big thermos all day.

A truck comes into the makeshift camp every morning, bringing bottles of water, sandwiches and coffee. If you don't get a break until later in the day, like me today, the coffee tastes horrible, and if you're lucky there's only tuna on rye left. Nobody fucking likes tuna on rye. Especially not with the flavour of smoke permeating every bite, since it's been sitting out all day.

"Doyle!" I turn around to see Rick, our fire chief, head toward me. "How are you guys doing on that firebreak up on the ridge?"

"Slow," I tell him honestly. Our job since we got here on Sunday has been to try and contain the northeast edge. The winds have been mild and coming from the northwest, but according to the forecast, there's a system coming through from the west that could drive high winds in north-easterly direction. Toward Wawa.

The past five days we've been clearing brush and cutting down trees to create a four to six foot wide trench uphill from the fire. The plan is that if those winds turn, a backfire will be lit along the break. It's easier to control than the main body of fire coming up the hill.

I'd honestly expected to be home already. I'm too old for this shit. Every fucking muscle and bone in my body is screaming, and I'm dying to take in a deep breath that is not thick with smoke and ashes. I'm rank too. Fucking five days of splashing yourself at the back of a water truck, with cold water dribbling from a little tap, is not very effective.

"We don't have much time," Rick reminds me, not that he needed to, I know damn well the kind of time constraint we're working under. "I'm sorry, I don't think I can miss you on Saturday. Looks like the system is moving faster than we thought, it could get here as early as midday on Sunday. We've gotta get that firebreak done, Doyle. I'm sorry."

It isn't really a surprise, but that doesn't mean it's not a disappointment. I'd wanted to surprise Leelo on Saturday, help out with the new guests checking in, but it looks like that's not gonna happen. Worst part is that I don't seem to have cell reception here. No towers nearby. Not that it matters, the battery ran out on my phone two days ago.

The chief has a satellite phone but that's kept open for communications. He just uses it to check in with the fire station in Wawa every night. He did pass a couple of messages for us through the dispatcher there, who in turn relayed it to our families, mainly just letting them know everyone is fine.

I pull my sleeping bag in the shadow of one of the smaller trucks used to transport firefighters, and lie down on top of it. It's too hot to crawl in, and I pull a T-shirt over my face to block as much of the light as possible. It doesn't really matter what time of day or what conditions, when you have a chance to sleep, you take it. There's no telling when the next opportunity will come along.

I don't fall asleep right away though. My thoughts are on Leelo. I want to hear her voice, want to know how she's holding up and what is happening at the lodge. I really fucking wanted to see her this weekend.

I shouldn't have left without telling her I love her, too.

Leelo

"It's done, Mom," Matt says, handing me the first few of the building permit applications he's been working on. These are for the three added cabins along the water's edge.

Roar had shown him the drawer in his office that held all the blueprints for the cabins at Jackson's Point, as well as copies of the permit applications he had to submit at the time, and told Matt to "have at it" while he was gone. I'd been surprised, and Matt a little flustered, with the show of trust, but once my son got over his initial shock, he dove right in. It's amazing what a little show of faith can do for someone's confidence.

My boy has only been here a few weeks but he is flourishing.

"So what now?" I ask, unsure what is expected of me in addition to my signature at the bottom.

"Not sure," Matt says. "But I think it's safer if you drop them off yourself. I can stay here and man the office."

"I'll get some more groceries too, we're running low. Let me make a list."

This would be the third time already I go grocery shopping this week. Matt's appetite hasn't waned yet, and I want to replenish what we use up. I have no idea when Roar is going to get back and I don't want him to find empty cupboards. From what I understand from the updates I get from the firehouse, they're still battling to get the fire under control.

Now that I have Gwen on her way, I should probably grab some stuff that she likes as well. Matt is a meat and potatoes kind of guy, but my girl has slightly more refined taste buds, so I cater to her on those very rare occasions where I can. Matt couldn't care less. Like I said, as long as it's got enough meat and carbs, he'll eat anything.

Ace trots hopefully beside me to my Jeep. He likes rides apparently. I was over at the motel yesterday to grab a few more clothes, and he jumped in the driver's side the moment I opened the door, so I let him come for the ride. Shopping is another matter. I doubt that he can come inside the Valu-Mart, and leaving him in the car with this ongoing heat would just be cruel.

"You stay here, buddy," I tell the fierce-looking, but sweet-natured dog, whose pout is almost irresistible. "Tell you what—how about I bring you back a special treat?"

354

Silly mutt is wagging his tail furiously like he understands what I'm saying.

"You're gonna have him so spoiled, he won't even know who Roar is by the time he gets back."

I turn around to find Patti coming toward me. She must've just arrived.

Since the break-in at the motel, when she was the first person to reach out to help, we've been getting along surprisingly well. Still, we've never really addressed the awkward situation we find ourselves in.

"I'm sure Roar will hold his spot as alpha without much problem," I suggest with a smile.

"Have you heard anything?" Her smile slowly disappeared to show the strain of worry underneath and I could shoot myself. I never even considered she might be worried about him, too. I've been faithfully keeping Charlotte up to speed with what little information I get, but have not once mentioned anything to Patti.

"Oh good Lord, I'm so sorry. I didn't even think—" I try to apologize, but Patti shakes her head sharply, cutting me off.

"You couldn't have known," she says, a kind smile on her face. "They used to contact me, years ago, when he was still more active. Roar felt it was better should something happen, that I pass the news to Charlotte. It's been quite a few years since the last time he was called out, and I honestly never thought I'd be this worried—but I am." Her sheepish grin warms me even further to her.

"He's fine," I quickly tell her. "They hope to get the fire under control soon, and when that happens, Roar's unit is likely to be the first to head back home."

"Hope so," she says earnestly. "You know, I know I didn't take it well at first, but I'm actually grateful you came here."

To say I'm surprised would be the understatement of the century, but I keep my reaction level and try not to blurt out, "*You are?*" Instead I nod and wait for her to go on.

"I'm starting to see that I was desperately trying to hang on to Tom's memory, by staying as close as possible to the only other person who could still feel his loss as acutely. I suspect Roar was doing the same, except he came to that conclusion long before I did." She takes one look at me and buries her face in her hands, and I see her shoulders shaking.

I don't quite know what to say. Standing in the parking lot of the lodge, in the middle of the day, having a really fucking deep conversation with my lover's emotional ex-lover is well out of my comfort zone, but I shouldn't be surprised. Everything in my life recently has been well out of my comfort zone, and I'm getting better at rolling with the punches. I dig through my purse and come up with a packet of tissues.

"Here," I say awkwardly, shoving them at Patti, who lifts her red face from her hands. She takes one look at the tissues, then at my worried face, and promptly shoves her face back in her hands.

Well, that went well.

"No-oh," she hiccups, reaching out with one hand to clasp my wrist. "I'm not crying. I'm laughing," she explains, and I finally clue in. "It was your face. I've never seen someone look so utterly uncomfortable as you did. It was hilarious."

I dropped the applications at town hall, and went to quickly check on Charlotte, who was busy beating some hapless seniors—*young 'uns*, she called them, since they were only in their seventies—at euchre, and didn't need anything from the store. I just finished my groceries, another two hundred dollars later, and am pulling onto the street when something occurs to me. I'm only two blocks from Henry Kline's office.

Despite repeated attempts to get hold of him, we haven't been able to so far. Either the man is supremely busy, we are very unlucky, or someone is doing a fabulous job at avoiding us. My money is on the latter. The problem is, I can't figure out why.

I just spoke to the secretary yesterday, and she mentioned Henry would be out of town on business for an undetermined time, but when I pull into the firm's parking lot, I clearly see his car parked in its marked spot. Why would she lie?

I park the Jeep in a vacant spot, throw a worried glance at my groceries on the back seat because I have frozen yoghurt in my bags, before I decisively get out of the car and head for the front door.

"Hi," I greet the girl at the front desk with the friendliest smile I can muster, even though I feel like throwing a tantrum. "I'd like to see Henry Kline right away?"

"Let me call his assistant and see if he is available."

The girl picks up the phone on her desk and in an on the spot decision, I reach over and place my hand over hers on the receiver.

"You know what?" I smile at her, hoping I look disarming and not slightly maniacal, like I feel. "I'll just head up and talk to her myself. That way I can make an appointment if he's not free."

Her mouth is moving like a fish out of water, and I'm not about to wait until she finds her words. I rush past her and up the circular stairs to the first floor where his offices are. I'm rushing because I'd like to catch him and his assistant unaware, before they have a chance to come up with another excuse.

Pushing through the tall double doors I see at once Henry's assistant rising up from behind her desk, and the door wide open to his office.

"Hi there!" I chirp nervously, waving as I hustle past the woman's desk and into the office beyond, before she has a chance to stop me. "Henry!" I call out when I find him sitting behind his desk. "What a surprise. I was told you were out of town, I took a chance and look…here you are." I hear a rustle behind me as his assistant finally catches up with me.

"I'm sorry, sir. She rushed right past me."

Henry's face which had been frozen in shock at my unconventional entrance, smoothed out in front of my eyes, and with a pleasant smile he turns to the woman.

"It's fine, Rebecca. Close the door behind you?"

With just a few words and a flick of his hand, Henry is firmly back in control. Always with the impeccable manners—except when he doesn't return my calls—Henry pushes himself up behind his desk and gestures at one of the visitor's chairs. I take his silent invitation and sit down, and he lowers himself back into his seat, folding his hands on his desk.

"Now Ms. Talbot, what can I do for you?"

THIRTY

She's my Polaris — my North Star — my home.

Leelo

I'm sure the disbelief is plastered all over my face.

I've been chasing after him for over a week, his office telling me he's out, or in meetings. Almost daily messages that went completely unanswered and the latest out-of-town excuse that turns out to be untrue.

You'd fucking think it should be clear by now what he can do for me.

I have to grab a firm hold of the temper I'm in danger of losing before I answer.

"As I mentioned in my voicemails and the messages I left with your staff, I would like the copies of the original drawings for the Whitefish, I understand you have on file here."

"Ah, yes, that's right. You'll have to forgive me; it's been incredibly busy. It's true, it's not unheard of that we sometimes keep copies of blueprints on hand for our clients in our archives. I believe my assistant, Rebecca, had an intern look, I simply haven't had the time, but I don't think they had much luck. Let me check." Before I have a chance to say anything, he pushes a button on the phone on his desk and his assistant's voice comes through.

"Sir?"

"Yes, those plans for the Whitefish, any luck finding them?"

"Uh…I don't believe so, sir."

"That's unfortunate, I suggest you have look yourself next week, Rebecca. I'm sure they're there."

"Of course, sir. Will that be all?"

Without even responding, Henry ends the call, rests his elbows on the table, and tents his hands, tapping his fingertips together as if he's thinking hard about something.

"You know," he says to me. "It is always possible that they have copies at the municipal building. I know Sam applied for a few permits over the years, he may have been asked to supply them."

I was just at the fucking municipal building.

Frustrated, I get up and grab my purse.

"That information would have been handy last week, Henry," I point out. "Could've saved us both some time."

"Yes, I wish I'd thought of it sooner. Talking about time," he says, looking at his watch. "I have a meeting in a few minutes I need to get ready for."

"That's okay, I was leaving. I'm heading straight over to the municipal building." I'm already halfway out the door when his voice stops me.

"I'm afraid they're closed as of five minutes ago," he says, tapping his watch. "Summer hours; they close at one on Fridays."

-

My day didn't get much better from there.

By the time I got back to the Jeep, I found my frozen yoghurt melted all over the back seat and my air conditioning stopped working on the way to the lodge.

There I found a present left on Roar's bed when I went to lay down to fight off a headache, after putting away the groceries and cleaning the car seat. Apparently, Ace had managed to sneak a rabbit inside the house and chose the master bedroom to pull the poor little creature apart and left its carcass on the bed.

"He does that sometimes, when Roar stays away for longer periods," Patti explained, while helping me change the bedding.

It was three before I finally got the nap I was craving, and by that time, my head was one big throbbing mass, so it took me a while to get to sleep.

"Mom?"

I peel my eyes open to find Matt leaning over me.

"What time is it?" I ask, rubbing the sleep from my face. Fortunately the earlier sharp headache was now just a dull nag, feeling more like a heavy fog.

"Seven," he says and I shoot upright in bed. I've slept away the whole damn afternoon.

"Gwen?"

"On her way. She's just south of Wawa." He sits down on the edge of the bed. "Mom," he starts. "She said there's a lot of smoke coming across the highway a few kilometres south of the airport. She said she could smell the fire."

"*Jesus.*" I knew when Roar left it could be dangerous for him, but hearing this makes it so much more real. Scarier.

"I know, Mom. Gwen does too, I told her when she called yesterday where he was. That's why she called, she was concerned."

363

I swing my legs over the side of the bed and run my hands through my hair, trying to get rid of the last threads of sleep clouding my thoughts.

"I have to call the station."

"Just did," my son says, gently smiling. "Was told the crew is fine. Apparently, the wind started to shift, and the smoke that was blowing mostly south before is now being reported blowing in more northerly direction. The woman at the station promised if there was anything to report, she has all our numbers."

I'm relieved the guys are good, but I don't like the sound of the shifting wind. If smoke is now traveling north, that means the fire likely is too, in our direction.

"Thanks, Mattie," I tell him, pressing a kiss on his forehead before I head to the bathroom to freshen up. By the time I come out, the bedroom is empty but I can hear voices coming from downstairs. Sounds like Gwen arrived.

"Sweetie…" Her head snaps up at the sound of my voice, and for a moment I see my little girl, happy to see me, before her carefully cultivated mask slips back into place.

"Hey, Mom," she says, allowing me to crush her in my arms, but reluctantly so.

"How was your drive?" I ask when I finally let her go.

"Long, and I'm starving."

I smile at the hint of drama in her voice, for all her level-headed maturity and drive, she still can have those moments of teenage theatrics. Except now I don't cringe at them, I embrace them, treasuring anything and everything I get from my kids. Even if it's attitude.

"Why don't you let Matt show you around, while I whip something up for dinner?" I suggest.

"Actually, Patti cooked chili while you were sleeping," Matt says, with an almost apologetic shrug. "It's good too, I already had some."

It's odd, where not that long ago I was upset to find Patti cooking in Roar's kitchen, this time I just feel grateful.

"Hope you left some for us," Gwen says, thumping her brother in the shoulder. He reacts by putting her in a headlock and ruffling her nicely styled hair. "Asswipe," she swears at him, but he just laughs as he lets her push him off. "By the way, who is Patti?" she wants to know as she hooks her arm in his and allows herself to be dragged into the kitchen.

I barely hear his answer as I follow behind, a big grin on my face.

Dinner is a casual affair at the kitchen table and I enjoy the kids ribbing each other. They used to be best buddies when they were young, but adolescence put an end to that quickly. Now, both more mature with adult problems and responsibilities, they seem to be finding each other again and that brings tears of gratitude to my eyes. Despite the many screw-ups on their parents' part, our kids are fucking awesome.

"What breed is this anyway?" Gwen says, watching as Ace follows me outside, a tray with cups and a teapot in my hands.

If he's looking for handouts, he'll be disappointed. He's still in the doghouse.

"I think Roar said something about part timber wolf, part hound? Not sure," Matt says, already camped out on one of the rockers on the porch.

"Wow," my girl says, getting her first glimpse of the night sky up here. "I'd forgotten how many stars there really are."

"Beautiful, right?" I offer, as I pour us all some tea.

"Mmmm," she hums noncommittally, but the little smile on her face when she takes the mug from my hand says enough.

"Apparently, it's not unusual to see the aurora borealis up here when the conditions are right," Matt pipes up. "It's supposed to be better from the lake, if you take a boat a bit further north. Roar says a lot of the land there remains untouched because there is little access, except over the water."

"Cool." Gwen shrugs. "You should take me out there this week."

"Need to buy a boat first," my son announces, a fat grin on his face.

"Maybe you can borrow one of Mom's boyfriend's?"

It takes me a minute to catch on to Gwen's reference, because my mind is still stuck on what she said before.

"You're staying here the whole week?" I ask, doing my best not to sound too frigging excited and failing miserably.

"I thought you got that when I said I had a week off and was driving up." I ignore the sharp edge to her voice, the way it gets when she's irritated.

"Yes, I did hear that, but I've learned not to make assumptions. You could've planned to stay just for the weekend before heading somewhere else," I point out calmly. "Regardless, I'm excited you will spend your whole week here."

Gwen looks intently out at the night sky, visibly focused on something else.

"Can you smell that?" she says, and I immediately sniff the air.

"Smoke," Matt says before I have a chance.

Roar

Five more hours.

I heave the last piece of the tree stump I just dug up onto the dump truck that will remove it. Looking back down the gully I'm standing in, I can see how much work we've accomplished today. Good thing too, since with the shifting winds, I can feel the heat from the fire pushing in this direction.

Five more hours, of cutting up some of the larger tree trunks and stumps into more manageable pieces before clearing them out, left in my sixteen-hour shift. I am so far beyond the point of exhaustion, I can't even tell you if I'm hurting or not. The only thing that keeps me going is knowing that this stupid firebreak we've been working on, for God knows how many days, may be the only thing between this angry fire and my home—my loved ones.

There is progress though, and a plan of action that might actually work, by using the power of nature against itself.

Winds are supposed to pick up during the course of the day tomorrow, assisting the crews to the south in driving the fire in this direction. A backfire will be lit along the south side of the clearing we created to burn out the fuel in front of the fire. North of the break, crews will be stationed to control any flare-ups, and waterbombers will dump their loads along the south, east, and west sides of the fire. Crews coming in behind will put down any remaining flames so it doesn't have anywhere else to go.

It's a perfect plan, provided the execution is flawless and there is no change in conditions. The only thing in the equation that is controllable is the execution, and because of that, I am ignoring the soot and the dirt coating my hair and skin, the stench of sweat and smoke I can't get out of my nostrils, and the toll my body is taking.

Five more hours and I will hoist my tired, filthy body to my truck parked two kilometres from base camp, and I will not stop until I can wish my girl happy birthday.

Leelo

"You guys." I smile when both kids barge into the bedroom, singing "Happy Birthday" and carrying a tray with breakfast.

I can't remember the last time I had breakfast in bed. Maybe some Mother's Day, when the kids were little.

"You know that's way too much for me, right?" I point out, looking at the stacks of pancakes and entire plate of bacon.

"Duh," Matt replies. "We've got to eat, too."

Forty-six years old, and I find myself sitting in bed, bracketed by a kid on either side, sharing pancakes and bacon. Already it's the best birthday I've had in years.

I'm about to tell my kids so, when suddenly Ace, who snuck in behind them, jumps up and runs out of the room, barking. Matt moves to get out of bed when a dark shadow fills the door.

Literally.

He's barely recognizable with all the black crap covering him, but that doesn't stop me from leaping out of bed and launching myself in his arms, completely forgetting about the kids.

"Happy Birthday, Sunshine," Roar's familiar voice rumbles in my ear as he gingerly lowers me to my feet.

I'm to busy kissing his face to respond.

"Baby, I stink and there's two more people in my bed, staring at us."

"Are you okay? Tired? Do you need something to eat? I can make more bacon," I rattle off, but I can't stop myself.

"Leelo," he stops me sternly. "Maybe introduce me first? I'm thinking this is Gwen?"

I swing around to find Matt popping the last of the bacon in his mouth, grinning widely, while Gwen has her arms folded over her chest and her head tilted to the side, watching with cautious curiosity.

"Shit. Right, okay. Roar, this is my daughter Gwen. Gwenny, meet Roar Doyle. Actually, it's Riordan, but he's called Roar. Or Doyle. I guess whatever works for you."

"Mom? You're rambling," Gwen kindly points out, with a smirk, and Roar chuckles behind me. "Nice to meet you, Roar," she adds. "Although, I still have no idea what you look like, seeing as you're covered in guck."

"Right, I should probably grab a quick shower. It's been a while."

"That's our cue, Sis," Matt announces, jumping out of bed. "Let's go cook up some more breakfast, I'm guessing Roar might be hungry."

Gwen follows him right past us out the door, throwing a little smile in my direction before she turns to her brother and stage whispers; "Judging by the way he looks at Mom, breakfast may not be the only thing he's got an appetite for."

Roar

"I won't be long," I promise, pressing a kiss to Leelo's mouth. It's been six days and there's nothing I'd rather do than have my way with her, but I'm filthy and I reek, her kids are around, and my time is very limited before I have to head back. With any luck, I can be home maybe Monday.

I strip out of my dirty clothes and step into the shower, groaning when I feel the strong warm stream of water hit my parched skin. God, that feels fucking

370

fantastic. With my forearms leaning on the shower wall, my forehead between them, I let the water pressure massage my neck and shoulders, feeling the tension slowly ebb, leaving a dull ache in its wake.

I don't move when I hear the shower door open and feel Leelo slip in behind me. I don't object when I feel her soapy hands on my back, washing away a week's worth of dirt and grime. I groan, feeling her fingers dig and her nails scrape my skin, followed by soothing kisses from her sweet lips. When her arms slide around me to the front, I feel her body bracing mine from behind. Soft pliable curves that gently cradle my battered body, as her hands wash my chest and stomach, before sliding down further between my legs. With one hand massaging my balls, and the other firmly wrapped around my rock hard cock. I drop one hand over hers to still her stroking.

"You don't have to," I say, my voice hoarse with fatigue and need.

"I want to," she assures me, her soft voice brushing my back.

I don't resist and let go, completely and quite literally in Leelo's hands, I have no reserves. It takes her no time at all to have me shooting cum over her hand and the wall, my breathing ragged and laboured, and my knees near to buckling.

I let her minister to me as she washes my hair, guides me out of the shower and dries me off, and finds me clean clothes to wear. I'm little more than a rag doll.

"There are so many words I want to give you," I tell her when I find my voice again. I watch her turn around from dropping my dirty clothes in the laundry hamper. "Much I want to say. That I've wanted to say. This

371

morning I was out in the gully we've been clearing and I couldn't see the stars anymore. It scared me." She slowly moves toward me, taking the hand I'm holding out and I pull her between my legs. "Not because of the smoke getting thicker and the fire closing in, but because the stars made me feel connected to you. Reminding me that you were close. It's strange how detached you become from everything when you are out there, fighting this bitch. It demands all your attention, needs all of your focus, and sucks up all your energy." I drop my head between her breasts and her hand finds the back of my head, holding me in place. "It used to be it didn't matter. The ultimate rush of adrenaline made it all worth it. But that has changed. This will be my last fire. I won't let myself be scheduled on the reserve list again. I'm done. I want to give you my attention, my focus, and all of my energy."

"Love you."

I hear her clearly this time, and pressing my lips to her stomach, I lift my eyes so I can look at her. I carefully move her aside and walk into my closet, grabbing the glass jar from the top shelf.

"And I you," I tell her, handing her the jar. "My birthday gift to you is all the reasons why."

THIRTY-ONE

Her light filling my eyes, I would die a happy man.

Leelo

"You okay, Mom?"

The second best birthday present is my daughter slipping her arm around me, as I watch Roar's taillights disappear, in an uncharacteristic show of affection. I swallow hard, already on the verge of tears with hormones all over the fucking place, and another year older, with my guy heading back into danger, and my girl being all nice.

"I'm good." My voice sounds strangled as I force the words out, squeezing her hand resting on my shoulder.

"I still need to talk to you."

"I know, Sweetie, just give me a couple of minutes, all right?"

"Sure," she says easily, removing her arm from my shoulders and I instantly feel the loss. "Matt and I were going to head into town to pick up some supplies for dinner anyway. We can talk while he and I cook?"

I smile in response and watch as they too drive off. I turn away and walk back into the lodge to grab another ice tea. It's starting off a hot one today, but there's a stiff wind blowing that comes along with a cold system that's supposed to be rolling in. As is usual, the instability will probably cause thunderstorms to pop up, and I just pray that we're spared any more damage anywhere. I try not to think what it could mean for those men battling that fire, but according to Roar this weather change might be a blessing.

It's been a great birthday. Best in a long time, and it's not even over yet. I got everything I wanted. Fuck, I got more than I deserve. Both kids here, doting on me and helping out this morning, clearing the cabins so I could spend some time with Roar before he had to head out. It was interesting to see him and Gwen dancing around each other. Sizing each other up. Both protective of me but in different ways. Hopefully, there'd be more time for them to get better acquainted later this week.

Then of course there's that jar. So tempting to hide out in the bedroom and dump the contents on the bed, reading each snippet of paper at leisure. But Roar asked me to wait until bedtime tonight, so he'd know I was reading them. Like I'm going to refuse a request like that?

The sign in for new guests is at three, but according to Patti, who's been cleaning cabins all morning, they often arrive early. It's barely one thirty and already someone is driving up in a pickup, toting a boat. I hold the door to the office open, waiting for the portly guy who is jogging toward me.

"Afternoon," he says with a big grin.

"Hi there. Come in, you're a little early, but depending on how far housekeeping is, we might be able to get you settled in. What name is the reservation under?"

"Porter. Jeff Porter, been coming up here for damn near twelve years now."

I hear a distinct American accent but I'm not sure if I can place it.

"Where are you from, Jeff?" I ask, as I log into the computer and pull up his reservation.

"Saginaw," he says with a smile. "Not the prettiest city in the state of Michigan, that's for dang sure. That's why once a year; we take the easy six or seven hours straight up the 75 and stay at Jackson's Point for a week. Been knowing Doyle all this time. He around?"

"Sorry, we're hoping he'll be back soon, but he's helping fight that forest fire along the highway? You probably passed it on your way up."

"No shit? Pardon my French." He chuckles sheepishly. If only the man knew how much I swear, to my daughter's great distress. "Say, are you new here?" he asks, looking a little suspiciously at my ink. "There was usually a pretty blonde here when we checked in. Penny? Always wondered if there was something going on between—"

"Patti is the name. Close enough though, Jeff," she says from right behind him, throwing her arm around his shoulders. "And no, Doyle and I just are old friends, but Leelo here, she's his fiancée," she elaborates a *tad* introducing me, throwing me a saucy wink.

"Well, I'll be damned. Fiancée. Huh, I never would've pegged Doyle for—"

"You know what?" Patti interrupts him again; before the man has a chance to put his other foot in, something he seems particularly talented at. "I knew you'd be early, since you are every year, so I finished your cottage first. It's all ready for you."

"Yes, of course. Much obliged." He tugs at the bill of his cap. "And nice to meet ya, Lili."

I just wave, because really, what can you say to that?

"Sorry about that!" Patti comes back in, minutes later, after showing Jeff out. "He's a bit of a redneck, but he's really a decent guy. His wife is nice, too. He just isn't the smoothest, so when I saw him pull in, I ran as fast as I could."

"Tattoos and blue hair are clearly not his cuppa," I observe, chuckling. "And you have to admit, Roar and I are not exactly an obvious match."

Patti tilts her head to one side, scrutinizing me closely.

"You know what? Maybe not, but I've seen you together, and it works."

-

It's near five when Gwen comes looking for me and finds me still in the office.

"Is everyone checked in?"

"All but one. Not sure when they'll be here and Patti had to leave, so that's why I'm waiting," I explain.

"Well, come and wait in the kitchen. We can see through the window if someone pulls up. I have a bottle of wine with your name on it."

I smile at my girl, turn the computer and the lights off, and follow her through the foyer and into the kitchen, where Matt is doing his best to massacre fresh asparagus.

"Jesus, Mattie. I said chunks, not minced," Gwenny scolds, as she takes the knife from his hands. "If you want to mince, grab that little jar with the truffle, and take half of that. The other half can go back in the jar and in the fridge."

"Truffle?" I ask, an eyebrow raised. My daughter, who never ate more than a handful of things growing up, has turned into a regular gourmet cook.

"It's a truffle, asparagus, and mushroom risotto with asiago cheese." I catch the little curious glance she shoots me, hoping to catch a reaction.

"Colour me impressed," I say, smiling big. "I don't think I've ever had such a fancy birthday dinner."

"Don't worry, Mom," Matt pipes up. "There's lots of meat, too. She has two bacon-wrapped pork tenderloins in the oven."

My boy. A meal is not a meal unless there is meat. And lots of it.

"Two? For just the three of us?"

"Four actually, I promised Charlotte I'd pick her up. Besides, I don't see a problem," Matt says. "It'll make for a great midnight snack."

I warm at the thought of the kids arranging for Roar's mother to join us for my birthday dinner, as I watch Gwen throw a little look of concern in his direction before looking back to me, a light blush on her cheeks.

"Actually," she says. "I thought since your guy is not here, and we *are* using his kitchen, it might be nice to save him some of your birthday dinner too. I can easily freeze it."

"That's really thoughtful. I think Roar would appreciate that."

"Yeah, well, whatever. If it gets eaten, it gets eaten," she responds, making both Matt and I laugh out loud, because it's so typical.

"God forbid we think you're doing something nice, right, Gwenny?" Matt teases.

"Shut up." She tries to keep a straight face, but loses miserably, soon laughing right along with us. But it isn't long before her expression sobers. "So, since my rep is busted anyway, I might as well rip the Band-Aid off completely and tell you I'm sorry, Mom."

"About what, Sweetie?"

"Dad's a prick. He's always been a prick, to you anyway, and I know that. I just…well, I guess I just didn't realize how big of one. First the stuff with Mattie and then driving up here to give you a hard time. I mean that's seriously messed up."

"Yup. It is, but that's not your cart to tote," I tell my daughter. "It's his. I don't want you apologizing for your father. Not ever. Just like I don't want you apologizing for me either. Not your monkey, honey."

"Yeah, but, Mom, how can he do that? Say that shit to you, and to Mattie? That's his son. And you're the mother of his kids. It's not right."

I can tell she is getting agitated so the hug I wanted to give her, I'm putting on hold. Instead I give her some reality.

"I remember one of the hardest realizations I ever came to was when I discovered my parents weren't perfect or infallible. God, you've met your grandma and her collection of exes. We all mess up. We all do stupid things. There's no doubt in my mind you two will fuck up on a regular basis, just like the rest of humanity."

"Hey, I resemble that remark!" Matt interrupts jokingly, and at the same time I get a stern "Language!" from Gwen.

"Your father was always good at making it look like he had all his ducks in a row, and a lot of the time he did, except when he didn't. Maybe that's where we were fundamentally different; me so blatantly fallible, it clashed with his sense of perfection. Who knows? Point is, we're here, we got through, and we're all trying to find our way. Just because your father and I happen to be a few years older doesn't mean we're not looking, just like the two of you."

"You're pretty smart for middle-aged, wannabe sideshow headliner." The look on Gwen's face as she delivers that line, with a saccharine smile, has Matt doubled over laughing.

"Hey!" It's my turn to protest her jab at my hair, my ink, and my choice of clothing, none of which she's a big fan of.

"Mom'd be a great addition to any travelling carnival," Matt taunts, grinning. "She's like a multifunctional attraction."

I sit back and take a sip of my wine as my kids proceed to roast me, while they cook me a gourmet birthday dinner. *There are worse things*, I smile to myself

"How do you figure?" Gwen bites.

"Blue-haired lady, tattooed lady, pinup of the month," Matt ticks off on his fingers. "And her newest act: bearded lady."

Immediately my hand goes to my chin where I've recently discovered a few pesky whiskers I keep trying to pull.

The kids are still laughing loudly when my phone rings.

"Hello?" I get up and out of the kitchen to hear who is on the other line.

"Ms. Talbot. It's Henry Kline calling."

"Mr. Kline? What can I do for you?"

"A little bit embarrassing on two accounts, I'm afraid. One; I was sorting through some boxes in my home office today and I found the drawings for the Whitefish, and two; I'm standing outside the motel but no one seems to be here."

"Oh, yes, no, actually, I'm staying…up the road."

"In that case, why don't I drive up to meet you?"

"You know what?" I make a split-second decision. "Stay put, I'll be there in a few minutes. Don't go anywhere."

I push back from the kitchen table and face my kids who are both looking at me curiously.

"You'll never guess," I say, mostly for Matt's benefit, since I haven't had a chance to fill Gwen in on all the details surrounding the motel. "That was Henry Kline. He found the drawings. He's waiting at the motel."

"Why?" Matt asks right away.

"He seemed surprised I wasn't there," I clarify.

"Okay, I'll go with you," Matt offers, wiping his hands on a towel.

"There's no need for that. I'm just picking up the plans from him, I'll be back in ten."

"I was about to go pick Charlotte up anyway," Matt says, determined to follow me out it seems. "You'll be all right for a bit, right, Gwenny?" he throws over his shoulder, already on the move.

"Go right ahead!" Gwen calls after us. "I'll just take care of the home front!"

Matt trots up behind me when I get to the Jeep.

"I'm just going to follow you there, wait for your thumbs up, and then I'll head on to Charlotte's. Okay?"

"Do what you gotta do, Bud."

It's not even that late, there's plenty of daylight left when we hit the road. As promised, Matt is sticking to my tail, making me smile. Roar's overprotective nature is starting to rub off on my boy and I'm liking it.

When we get to the motel, I turn up the driveway and Matt stops at the bottom, letting his truck idle. Henry's black Audi is parked in front of what is going to be the restaurant, but I can't see him. Still, I pull in beside his car, get out, and give Matt the thumbs up. I wait until I see him slowly drive off, then I go in search of the lawyer.

"Hello? Henry?"

I try the door to the restaurant, but it's locked and I wonder if he's gone around the side of the house. I head around the corner, but I can't see any sign of him.

The side door is also still firmly locked, but still I peek through the windows to see if anyone's inside. This is really weird and I'm starting to question my decision not to have Matt wait with me.

Unless…I look toward the dock, and as if by rote, start walking in that direction.

The wind is stronger, the closer I get to the water's edge and the only thing I see out on the lake is a loon about twenty feet from my dock, ducking under to fish. Nobody else in their right mind would be out there right now. At least not for fun.

On the off-chance perhaps Henry's fallen in the water, I walk the length of the dock, up one side and down the other, checking the water lapping against the sides. No sign of him.

Weird.

Perhaps I should've checked his car. I never even looked inside. God knows if he's had a heart attack or a stroke, and needs help.

I rush back up the trail to the house and round the building to the front. It's hard to see inside from a distance, but the closer I get, the clearer it becomes that there is no one inside that car. What I do see lying on the passenger seat is a roll of drawings.

Goddammit, Henry. Where the hell are you?

I pull open the passenger door of the Jeep to grab my phone, only to find it died somewhere between the lodge and here. *Wonderful.* I slam the car door shut and with my keys in hand, walk over to the restaurant. The phones downstairs may be out of commission, but the landline beside my bed upstairs should still work.

Inside, sheltered from the wind, it's surprisingly quiet. Hollow even, as I make my way through the now empty space to the house beyond. It's better once I get upstairs: no sound echoing off the walls.

I round the bed and pick the handheld from its base, but there's no dial tone when I try calling. Another dead phone. Exasperated, I toss it on the bed and swing around to look out the window. My bedroom faces the back of the property and the views from up here are beautiful. Looking out now, I notice that from up here, I can see the property from a different vantage point.

I hit every window up here, scanning the property below for any signs of Henry, but I don't see anything. Nothing either from the spare bedroom window, overlooking the front, and I'm starting to wonder if I wouldn't be better off just driving into town to get help, or wait at the end of the driveway for Matt to come back around. He should have collected Charlotte by now.

Decided on a course of action, I take one last look over the property below when my eye catches on the laundry shed.

The door to the shed is open a crack. *That's odd*. I'm pretty sure it was locked, along with every other door, but it's always possible one of the guys left it open at some point. I know they stored some tools in there while they were working on the roof.

Heading downstairs, I notice it getting a little darker outside. Clouds are moving in just as the sun is setting. We were warned we might get some thunderstorms tonight. I just hope they hold off until we're all safely home. Roar included.

I lock the door, and step on the gravel, hearing it crunch under my feet as I make my way over the shed. One day soon, all this dirty, dusty gravel will be smooth asphalt. I have a smile on my face when I place my hand on the frame and call inside.

"Henry? You in there?"

I stick my head around the door and reach out to flick on the light switch.

"Jesus, Henry," I rush to the crumpled form of the older man on the floor. "Henry, are you okay?"

The sound of a door slamming shut has me spin around.

"Not exactly. I'm afraid Mr. Kline was unable to keep up his end of what could have been a mutually beneficial bargain, Ms. Talbot. He had every opportunity but sadly failed to execute, so I was left with no choice but to execute him."

I can't breathe.

I'm on the floor of my shed, sitting beside a dead man, and a gun is pointed at my head.

Fate, or karma, or whatever the hell it is that's been screwing with my life, really fucking went all out on this one.

Roar

"Doyle!"

I can hear my name called but I can't seem to move.

I'm not even sure what happened. One minute we're doing cleanup, taking down a couple of tall pines that sparked a fire north of the firebreak and the next I'm pinned to the ground.

"Doyle," Rick says, his face floating in and out of my vision.

"What?" is all I manage to get out.

"Stay put, you lucky bastard. We're going to lift this sucker off you and then we'll see what the damage is. Can you hang in there?"

I try to nod but my helmet is restricting my movements. I instinctively try to wiggle my toes, successfully I think, and next my fingers, also with positive results. The heavy smoke from moments ago is starting to dissipate, and I see a trunk about three feet in diameter is keeping me pinned at the bottom of a small gully. I'm soaking wet and I'm having a hard time breathing.

"What happened?" I try again.

"You had a burning tree land on you, ya moron. Fucking luck of the Irish had you land in a gully full of runoff water, bought us enough time to douse the fucking torch laying on top of you before you turned into bacon crisp. Fucking shamrock up your arse."

"The fire?"

"She's controlled, my friend. It worked."

I lay my head back and stare straight up, through the curling drifts of smoke to the darkening sky above, where only one single star is visible.

Polaris—the North Star.

THIRTY-TWO

*The longest night of my life lasts only a second if she's
on the other side.*

Leelo

"You took long enough," the man, leaning his back
against the door says, right before he takes a step forward
and the light from the small window catches him across
the face.

"You're the developer."

I remember seeing that baby face before.
Brian...something. Roar chased him off.

"You could call me that. My boss considers me the
last line of attack. I'm only called in when all else seems
to fail, as it has done in this case."

"I'm not sure what you're talking about, what case?"

"It doesn't usually come to this, I want you to know.
Mostly some well-executed pressure is enough, often
using local talent, and I'm able to procure my boss his
next pet project. Unfortunately, our local associates here
in Wawa have not fared so well. In fact, as you well know,
Mr. Thompson is currently in jail awaiting trial, and our
Mr. Kline here became too much of an albatross around
our necks." I watch as the young thug starts pacing from
side to side, but the gun never wavers. "My boss is not a

387

patient man, Ms. Talbot, and it is in my best interests to keep him happy. He's had his eye on this property for as long as your dear uncle was in the nursing home. Mr. Kline assured him the beneficiary in his will—that would be you, Ms. Talbot—would be eager to unload it upon his death. I simply took it upon myself to help matters along."

I can't help my shocked gasp, when the reality of his words hits.

"You killed my uncle?" I watch in disbelief as he smiles and shakes his head at me dismissively.

"No need for drama, Ms. Talbot. I simply added a little extra to his medication to help him from his suffering." He waves it off like it's nothing, and that is almost more terrifying than sitting on a damp floor next to a corpse having a gun waved in your face. Brian...whatever, just keeps on talking. "It was fast and painless. But you, Ms. Talbot, have been an even bigger obstacle. I haven't quite decided whether it is stupidity or sheer tenacity that keeps you coming back, but I'm afraid we're done trying to coax you into making the right decision. I will make the decision for you. My boss will be extremely appreciative when the property unexpectedly comes available, due to a second unfortunate death in the family. I'm sure, under such horrendously sad circumstances, your darling children will be eager to grab the first decent offer they receive and readily leave the Whitefish Motel in their rearview mirror."

I'm listening to his words, almost frozen at the almost polite way he tells me he's about to kill me, but I'm also counting his steps, trying to find his rhythm as he paces from side to side. If I get even the slightest opportunity to distract him enough and get that barrel out of my face, I'm gonna try for the door. He's not letting me walk away, and I sure as hell am not going to make it easy on him.

Mere seconds later such an opportunity presents itself, but at an expense much greater than I would ever have been willing to pay.

Just as Brian…whatever his name is, moves away from the door, it slams open.

"Mom!" Matt cries out when he sees me on the floor.

"Watch out!" I try to warn him, launching myself at the man who now has the gun pointed at my son, but it's already to late. I see the flash of the barrel an instant before I hear the bang, just as I slam into his body at full force.

I don't know what drives me to continue fighting, using every fucking ounce of my overweight body to keep the much slighter man from turning the weapon on me. He's strong, though, much stronger, with a similar desperation feeding him. I try to resist, but he manages to flip me on my back, straddles my chest, and pins my arms down with his knees. Then he sits up, and calmly aims the gun at my forehead.

Nothing left for me to do but close my eyes and be grateful my kids know I love them, Roar knows I love him, and my father waiting for me on the other side.

Roar

"Please try again," I plead with Rick, who is in the ambulance with me en route to the small hospital in Wawa. Initially, there was talk of airlifting me to the larger facility in Sault Ste. Marie, to be on the safe side, but that was quickly nixed with Rick's support, who is a licensed EMT himself. Smoke inhalation at this point is my biggest problem. My ribs might be bruised, but nothing has punctured my lungs, and thanks to landing in a gully of water, the burns I sustained to my chest and upper arms appeared to be mostly second grade. Stuff our local clinic can easily handle.

My main concern now is Leelo hearing through the grapevine that a local firefighter is down, and thinking the worst, instead of being calmly told that I'll be fine in a couple of days at most.

"I've tried, man. I'm not getting through."

"Call Bill. He can go by and tell her. Bring her to the hospital."

I'm a little calmer when Rick hangs up and confirms Bill is already on his way.

The EMT riding in back with us covers my mouth with an oxygen mask and places an IV in my arm. Then he starts cutting away whatever is left of the shirt I was wearing, and I hiss when he pulls at a strip that seems to have fused with my skin.

"Not all second degree burns," he says sternly, throwing Rick a scowl.

Rick, as expected, ignores him and waits until the guy's attention is back on me before he throws me a wink.

The small hospital has only a handful of emergency beds, and apparently there's only one other patient in there. It's fairly quiet and I've got my eyes closed, enjoying the lack of noise and fresh air, despite the discomfort of being poked at.

Suddenly, I hear commotion outside in the hallway before the doors fly open and a gurney is wheeled in. I don't see much more than that, because one of the nurses working on me quickly draws the curtain around my bed. But then I hear a woman's voice yelling and every hair still on my body stands on end.

"Leelo?" I call out, ignoring the hands that are trying to hold me down in my bed.

"Roar?"

Leelo

I can't breathe.

A heavy weight is covering me and I can't get any air.

"Stop yelling at me and help me roll him off her. She's gasping!"

Charlotte.

My five foot nothing saviour.

I thought the next thing I would hear was another gunshot, but instead it was Charlotte's voice, yelling at the gun-toting maniac to "Leave my girl alone!" before swinging a long piece of wood at his head. Knocked him right out, she did. Right on top of me, and now I can't fucking breathe.

391

I don't know how she got here, but I was so happy to hear her voice.

In the next moment, my chest is free and I take in big gulps of air.

"Are you okay, honey?" Charlotte asks, hovering over me as I try to catch my breath.

"Leelo?" Bill's voice sounds from behind her as his face comes into view. "You good?" I barely have a chance to nod before he turns on Charlotte. "Next time I tell you to wait in Matt's truck, you wait. You hear me? Racing in here, brandishing nothing but a two by four. Did you not hear the shot?"

"Mattie," I manage, struggling to get up.

"Lucky kid," Bill says, stepping aside so I can see my son carefully lifting his head, blood streaming down one side. "Bullet just grazed his scalp. Can knock you out and bleeds like a stuck pig, but he'll be fine. Just a cool scar to show off to the girls."

"You okay, Mattie?" I ask, sitting up, holding my side where I hit the ground when I tackled the guy who is beside me, out cold. Matt just nods, holding his head in his hands.

Jesus.

"Drove up right behind them," Bill explains, as he puts handcuffs on the unconscious man beside me, before moving over to Henry to check his pulse, shaking his head when he finds none. "Charlotte was sitting in the cab with the window down, waving in the direction of the shed. Told that woman to stay put while I checked it out, but when that shot sounded, she came running past me like a mad woman. She picked up that length of wood and disappeared through that door before I had a chance to pull my sidearm."

"You're just getting slow, Billy Prescott," Charlotte taunts him, sitting with her back against the wall in her summer dress and pearls. She talks a good game but I see the shock in her eyes as she takes in the scene. "Best get into shape before your wife finds out an old biddy like me ran circles around you. She'd have you on a diet so fast, your head would spin."

In the end, Matt and I are loaded in an ambulance Bill must've called. Brian Dinker—Matt remembered his name—was checked out by the EMTs and was sent off in one of the OPP cruisers that had been arriving, and would be closely monitored for a concussion at the OPP detachment.

Bill promised to follow us to the hospital with Charlotte, undoubtedly bickering with her all the way there.

"You okay, Bud?" I ask Matt, who is lying on the gurney. I'm strapped into a chair next to him. I insisted.

"Yeah. My head hurts though," he says, wincing before throwing me a sheepish grin. "Some kind of hero, right?"

"Don't joke, Mattie. He'd already killed someone. Had you not stopped to check on me, I would be on the floor of that laundry room, lying beside Henry Kline: just as dead. Don't you tell me you're not a hero." I wipe angrily at the tears suddenly streaming down my face. "Stupid? Absolutely, and as soon as your head is better I'll cuff your ear for taking a risk like that." I pinch my thumb and forefinger together and stick them in his face. "This close. This close you were to losing your life. Let me tell you, losing you would be a worse fate than death, my boy. Don't you ever do that again!"

"Ma'am, please stay calm or I'll have to sedate you."

"Don't you dare," I hiss in the young EMT's face.

The only thing that calms me is the big hand that wraps around mine, holding on tight all the way to the hospital.

-

"Please, ma'am, sit down in the wheelchair."

The same EMT is trying to get me to sit down, but I want to follow Matt's stretcher that's already heading through the doors.

"So help me, if you take me anywhere else than where my boy is going, I will castrate you with my bare hands."

"Ma'am, please stay calm or I'll have to restrain you."

"I will. I'll behave. Please, just take me to my son," I plead, folding my hands in front of me as I watch the stretcher disappear down a hallway. This damn wheelchair can't move fast enough.

I stay calm too, just like I promised, right until I'm wheeled into the emergency room and the EMT hands me over to a nurse.

"Patient is emotional and combative," I hear him say and it's like a red flag.

"I will have you know I was just held at gunpoint, and my son was shot. Am I allowed to get a little emotional?"

"Leelo?" I hear a familiar voice from behind one of the curtains.

"Roar?" I call out, already getting up out of the chair.

"She's just menopausal," I hear my son call out, and I make a note to murder him in his sleep.

Roar

"You know what they say about relationships forged under extreme circumstances. Do you think that applies to us?"

I turn my head on the pillow to where Leelo is lying in the bed beside me.

She's been checked out. Thoroughly—I made sure—and aside from a few bruised ribs, bumps, and scrapes, she should be fine, although perhaps a little sore for the next few days.

Matt's been stitched up and will be kept overnight for observation, because he'd lost consciousness.

As for me, I was very lucky. I'm being kept overnight as well for smoke inhalation, my burns will heal and the two cracked ribs will as well.

But I'm done firefighting. The fear on Leelo's face when she ripped aside that curtain earlier: if I hadn't already made the decision to stop, I would've done it in that moment. Seeing me lying in that bed, after all she'd apparently already been through, it was no wonder her knees buckled under the weight.

Personally, I was glad I was lying down when Bill walked in with Charlie and recounted all that I'd missed.

I just looked at my mother and shook my head.

"I have a feeling life with you will always mean living on the edge, Sunshine," I tease Leelo. "You guys throw quite the birthday party."

"Oh shit!" she shoots upright in her bed, wincing as she grabs for her ribs. "I need a phone. Gwenny."

"Use mine." Rick, who's been here the whole time, hands his phone to Leelo.

"Hey, Sweetie," she coos in the phone, looking pained as she listens to what I'm sure is a very upset and confused Gwen on the other end. "Yeah, I'm sorry, there was a little incident."

Rick chuckles along with me as I listen to Leelo trying to downplay events to keep her daughter calm.

"Do you want me to send someone to pick you up?— Okay, Gwenny. See you soon."

"She okay?" I ask, reaching for her hand.

"She says she is. She says she's already fed Ace, is going to lock up and head over."

"All right, if you don't mind," Rick says, running a hand down his face. "I'm heading home. I haven't seen my family in over a week and I'm bushed."

"Of course." I grab his offered hand, giving it a solid squeeze.

"I'll check in with you tomorrow, Doyle. Nice to meet you guys. I'm sure we'll be seeing more of each other." He lifts a hand in Leelo's direction before disappearing down the hall.

He's barely left and Bill walks in. He left earlier to take Charlotte home, once we knew we'd all be here overnight, and would check in with his crime scene boys at the motel.

Before Bill has a chance to say anything, Leelo pipes up in the bed beside me.

"You realize, as soon as you're done with the laundry shed, I'm tearing that damn thing down, right? With my bare hands if I have to."

THIRTY-THREE

Sometimes you let her battle, and other times you battle for her.

Roar

"Some more risotto?"

I look up from my plate to find Gwen handing the pot across the table. I grin at her, taking the serving spoon and adding another pile to my plate.

It's my second serving and I already know that unless someone else finishes it first, it likely won't be my last. This stuff is fucking delicious.

When Leelo first mentioned the risotto Gwen was cooking for her belated birthday dinner, I have to admit I was a little worried. I'm not one for fancy food, it didn't even look all that appetizing when I first looked down at my plate, but it sure as hell tastes good.

"This is great, Gwen," I mumble around a mouthful and watch as a pleased blush stains her cheeks. So much like her mother.

Things have been a little awkward since we all came home early this afternoon. I don't think I've ever had this many bodies in the lodge all at once. Charlie was already here, and so was Patti, making sure the guests were looked after. Bill and Gwen were the ones who drove us home.

I could tell right off the bat that Leelo's girl felt out of the loop, unable to get a handle on all the different dynamics playing out in this crowd. She seemed confused by Patti, and kept looking back and forth between her and me. Calling my mother Charlie didn't help things either, and when Bill pulled open the fridge and got out a beer, handing one to Matt, she was completely lost.

Leelo noticed, and tried to quietly get her up to speed, but that seemed to irritate Gwen more than it helped.

Bill left immediately after he finished his beer, promising his guys would drop Matt's truck and Leelo's Jeep, which were still at the motel, back here some time this afternoon. Patti didn't hang around long after that.

Things had settled down since then, with Matt heading to the spare bedroom for a nap, Leelo and I relaxing on the couch in the living room, and Charlotte disappearing into the kitchen to see what Gwen was up to.

Rick called earlier to let me know that all of our crew had been pulled and were on their way back home, and one of the guys was driving my truck. The weather had really played a huge factor. After an intense thunderstorm last night, the rain had started and it had come down steadily overnight. Today there was little left of the fire but heat pockets that required watching in case of a flare-up.

We just said goodbye to Charlotte, who was rushing to get home before night settled in. She hates driving in the dark.

"So is someone going to explain how you went from moving north to fix up an old motel, to hosting the

400

shootout at the fucking O.K. Corral?" Gwen asks, sitting down hard after clearing the plates from the table.

"Language," Matt mutters from the other end of the table and I have to bite back a chuckle.

"Hush," Leelo admonishes him before turning to her daughter, a look of disappointment on her face. "Honestly? I didn't do anything. I didn't invite it, I didn't cause it, and I didn't host it. I just showed up and landed in the middle of this mess."

I watch as Leelo's sharp tone hits home with her daughter. I don't think she's heard it much.

"I didn't mean—" she starts, but Leelo cuts her off with a sharp shake of the head.

"Maybe not, but it's a habit of yours. Jumping to conclusions that aren't usually in my favour. There were a few times, I'm not ashamed to admit, you were dead on in your negative assumptions, but that was a long time ago and it's not fair that you're still making me pay for those. Especially since that kind of accountability only seems to apply to me."

Gwen drops her head, shoves her chair back from the table, and beelines it out of the kitchen without a word.

"*Shit*," Leelo hisses, moving to go after her, but I catch her wrist.

"Give her a minute. I have a feeling that was brewing for a while." I reach up and wipe a tear from under her eye.

"I know, but I was harsh."

"Had to be said, Mom. After all these years, we all have to own up to our part in the dysfunctional mess our family has turned into."

Leelo's eyes go big and her mouth falls open in surprise at Matt's insight, and this time I chuckle out loud. Matt, a little sheepishly, joins in.

"Not just brawn, but brains on this one too," I tease him, earning me a punch in the shoulder and a muffled, "*Shut up.*"

"I should go check on her." She looks in the direction Gwen disappeared.

"Let me," I offer. "I think I might actually be able to help."

-

"I didn't even know your mother, never laid eyes on her before, and I was dead sure I had her all figured out."

Other than a slight stiffening of her back, Gwen doesn't show any response when I find her sitting at the end of the dock, beside my boat. I kick off my leather sandals and gingerly lower myself beside her, sticking my bare feet in the surprisingly chilly water.

"She was lying spreadeagled on a roof to keep the rain from damaging her motel, terrified to tears in the middle of a thunderstorm. But she didn't let go." I grin and shake my head at the not-so-long-ago event. "I believe I may have called her an irresponsible fool or some such thing. Whatever it was, it wasn't flattering. I tried so hard to try and find fault with her over the weeks that followed, but was drawn to her at the same time. Drove me nuts. Until I realized the reason I was so desperate to see her in a negative light was because I instinctively knew that this was a woman who would have the power to hurt me badly, if I let her. I'd been taking out my own insecurities on her."

402

I keep my eyes out on the water, even when I feel Gwen's gaze on me.

"Are you implying I'm insecure?"

I really have to work hard at not rolling my eyes, because this is a typical knee-jerk reaction from someone who *is* insecure and is doing their best to cover it up.

"No," I answer, patiently. "What I am saying is that perhaps it's easier for you to focus on your mother's possible shortcomings, than it is to risk getting hurt by her again. If you always assume the worst, you can never be disappointed, right?"

"She done some really stupid things," Gwen says softly.

"I'm sure she has. She's forty-six, I'd be worried if she hadn't. I've done my share, and I'm probably not done. You'll have plenty of opportunity to do your own stupid things, and don't think you won't," I tell her, nudging her shoulder with mine.

"Yeah, but like you said, getting on that roof in the middle of a thunderstorm, who does that?"

I chuckle, understanding where this girl is coming from, but also appreciating the other side of that particular coin.

"Actually," I try explaining. "Your mother on that roof? She wasn't being irresponsible. She wasn't up there just blindly defying the horrible odds and taking unnecessary risks. Your mother was up there hanging onto her dream, the only way she knew how, in that moment. It's easy to judge from the safety of the shore, if someone who is in the water, drowning, is taking all the right steps to prevent it. Try being the one in the water."

"Right," she confirms with a little nod.

"That's what your mom's been doing here these past months, just absorbing every damn hit that came her way. Every time she'd take it on the chin, shake it off, without barely even breaking stride." I tilt my face to her and catch her watching me intently. "Don't judge her for the things she's done wrong—see her for the great woman she is, not afraid to take risks, make mistakes, and brave enough to take full ownership of the life she's creating."

I'm a little worried when I see Gwen's eyes glisten with unshed tears. Going with instinct, I wrap my arm around her narrow shoulders and tuck her close; well aware I might be crossing into dangerous territory. Luckily, instead of twisting off my testicles, she snuggles closer.

"My dad's an asshole," she sniffs against my shoulder.

"So I gather."

"Mom is actually pretty great."

"No argument from me on that either."

"You may have a point," she says finally, after a long pause, and I wisely decide to refrain from editorial comment on that one. Good move, since right after that, she pushes my arm off and climbs to her feet. "If you breathe a word of any of this." I press my lips hard together to stop from chuckling when she waves her arms around. "To anyone," she adds, sticking a finger under my nose. "I know ways to end you."

I grin as I look over my shoulder and watch her saunter back up to the lodge, with more attitude than should fit that skinny body.

I like her.

She's more like her mom than she realizes.

404

Leelo

"Are there flights from Toronto to Wawa?" Gwen asks.

I look up from the website I'm now completely revamping.

"I think Sault Ste. Marie is the better bet, probably. I think if you keep an eye out, you might find some good deals. I can always pick you up, or Matt will."

"I don't really want to drive back tomorrow," she says, and I close my laptop, turning to face her.

"I don't really blame you," I admit. "It's a really long drive. It may not be a bad idea to fly next time, it might be worth the few hundred bucks."

"Mom?" She pulls out the chair next to me and sits down. "Are you ever going to come visit me in Toronto?"

This kid, she kills me, sitting there with her eyes cast down, her fingers fiddling with the edge of the table runner.

"Of course I will, why do you say that?" I assure her, covering her restless hands with one of mine.

"But there's so much work to be done here, and after that you'll have guests all the time. How are you ever going to get away?"

"Summers might be tricky, but winters shouldn't be a problem; the only thing that'll stay open is the restaurant and the motel units, and from what I hear, there's not

405

going to be a run on those during the winter months," I point out. "It's just a matter of organizing, Sweetie. Planning."

"Right," she responds pensively. "Maybe next year, when you and Matt have settled in a bit more, I can see what there is in my field a little further north. I'm thinking maybe Sudbury? Or Sault Ste. Marie?"

Throwing all caution to the wind, I grab both her hands and turn her to face me.

"Whatever you want to do, make sure you do it for you. Not me. Not your brother, or your father, but for you. If living in Toronto makes you happy, then that's where you should live and we will make it work. If you want to give Sudbury or the Soo a try, then by all means do. Heck, even if it turns out you want to head west and try the Rocky Mountains, do it—although, I should probably warn you that I might cry. My point is that you focus on what's best for you, because in the end that's all any of us can control."

I take a deep breath and quickly let go of her hands when she starts fidgeting, as I knew she would. My girl is not one for overt affection, but I'm not ashamed to sneak some in when I can. I watch as she silently gets up and walks away, I know she'll be thinking about what I said. Turning back to my computer, I flip up the screen, ready to work on my website some more when I feel two arms wrap around my neck.

"Love you, Mommy," my girl mumbles in my neck, barely giving me a chance to answer her back.

"Ditto, Gwenny. You make me so proud."

-

Roar did his fish fry tonight.

Insisted that since he ate Gwen's fancy stuff, gourmet food, the other day, he should be able to introduce her to the full Jackson's Point experience, and that includes a fish fry.

Well, Gwen wasn't too keen when she discovered it meant the fish would be caught fresh and cleaned on the spot, instead of bought from the frozen section in the grocery store.

Despite her initial misgivings, Gwen stepped up to the plate, like I knew she would, downing four entire fillets, feeding only little bits and pieces to Ace, who of course took up his usual spot under the table.

"We should go out on the boat when it gets dark tonight," I suggest when we've burned off the remains of dinner.

My comment draws a strange look with raised eyebrows from Roar, making me laugh. Since that night he and I went out on the lake under stars, all I have to do is mention the boat and he thinks I'm talking about sex. The tension has really been ramped up since we haven't touched each other, other than to kiss, since we were released from the hospital. A combination of our respective injuries and kids, who somehow both ended up staying at the lodge with us these past few days.

"I'm game," Matt readily agrees, jumps up, and starts walking down the dock, pulling Gwen along. "You know they've got the best stars up here?" he says to his sister, who just snorts.

"Same damn stars, Einstein," she laughs, giving him a little shove toward the water.

"Good idea, Sunshine," Roar rumbles in my ear as we follow the kids to the boat, his arm around my shoulder. No physical labour for either of us for a couple of days at least, but no one said we couldn't go out on a boat.

The kids have taken their respective seats on the bow benches, battling for a prime spot with Ace, who was not going to be left behind, and I carefully step down into the boat and sink into one of the captain's chairs, grateful for the added padding it offers.

With the engine at a relatively low throttle, Roar directs us north, and for a moment I think he's going to turn into the inlet he took me to before. Oh, he winks at me suggestively, but ultimately passes it by.

"Tease," I accuse him.

"Damn right," he admits freely, on a grin. "Just keeping the interest high until I can get you back there."

"I don't know exactly what you guys are talking about," Matt calls out from the front. "But whatever it is, I'm pretty sure we're not supposed to hear it."

"Oh God," Gwen blurts out, clearly disgusted, and I burst out laughing.

"Watch," Roar suddenly says, pointing at the sky ahead after we coast quietly for a while.

"Is that—" Matt starts, not finishing his sentence.

The rest of us just stare at the very faint, green and yellow light dancing along the horizon.

"Aurora Borealis," Gwen sighs.

"Northern Lights," Matt corrects.

"Same thing," I mediate, and Roar just chuckles.

THIRTY-FOUR

She's the beginning of every new day.

Roar

"Are you awake?"

I gently rock my hips against Leelo's ass, which has been teasing me for the past hour, since first sunlight came through the window.

"Mmmm."

"Been too long," I groan.

"The kids," she protests.

"Gwen is back in Toronto and Matt is back across the lake. It's just you and me, woman."

"How is it fair that I have to deal with unwanted hair and hot flashes, and you don't even have a hint of erectile dysfunction?" she complains, muttering with her face in the pillow.

"You don't like my morning wood?" I bury my face in her hair at the back of her neck, giving my hips a little extra wiggle.

"It's not that I don't like it," she says, turning her face, which now has half her hair plastered to it. I reach up and gently swipe it aside before kissing the corner of her mouth. "It's that I haven't shaved in over a week, and I'm pissed that you're ready to play when I'm not," she pouts, looking cute as fuck with her sleep flushed face.

I slip my hand between her belly and the mattress, inching slowly down until I feel the small curls at the apex of her thighs. Despite her protests, she spreads her legs slightly and I run my fingertips along the seam of her leg down to the warm heat of her, feeling the gentle abrasion of short hair.

"I don't care about your stubble," I mumble, my mouth slightly open as I drag it along the soft skin of her shoulder.

"Roar!" she scolds, blindly slapping at me with her free hand. The only thing she manages to hit is my ass, and I'm taking that as encouragement.

"Hush," I order, grabbing her hand when she goes for another pass and stretching it over her head against the headboard. "Hold on tight, Sunshine. We're gonna get this day started right."

Surprisingly she doesn't object any further when I coax her to her knees, and line up my angry red cock, teasing her slick folds.

"Tease," she groans, her face once again buried in the pillows, followed by a loudly hissed "*Yessss,*" when I bury myself to the hilt inside her soft heat.

"I won't last," I warn her, slipping a hand between her legs to play with her clit as my hips helplessly pound inside her. The bed starts rocking, hitting the headboard against the wall.

"Harder, honey," she pleads underneath me, one of her hands sliding over my fingers between her legs and pressing down.

"I go harder, we'll be knocking this wall down," I pant, ignoring the pain in my ribs.

"I need you *harder*."

This was more of an order than a plea, but works equally well because now my hips are pistoning furiously. Skin slapping against skin, headboard against wall, and something…

"*Fuuuck!*" I can't help yell when, without warning, I go off like the grand finale at the local Canada Day fireworks display.

"Don't stop," Leelo begs, and I have to power through a few more strokes, more involuntary muscle memory than coordinated effort, but I know she's right there when I feel the first pulse rippling over my cock.

"What was that sound?" she asks when we both can breathe normal again.

"Like something rolling around? I heard it to."

I swing my legs off the bed and duck my head down, reaching my hand as far as I can under the frame. I feel it wedged underneath the mattress up against the headboard; a smooth, cool cylindrical surface. I manage to get a grip, and pull it free.

"You tossed my jar under the bed?"

"What? No! Oh my God. I had that under my pillow when you gave it to me on my birthday. I was so tempted all day, but wanted to save it for bedtime. It must've slipped between the mattress and the wall."

Poor Leelo looks near tears and I quickly kiss her hard on the mouth.

"Relax. I'm teasing you. You've been a little busy. We both have. I forgot about it myself."

I reach for the jeans I tossed on the floor last night and fish out my wallet from the back pocket. From the billfold I pull a handful of new scraps, unscrew the top of the jar and drop them in.

"More?" she says, smiling at me.

"Every day I write down one lingering thought. Every day since the moment we first met, the prevailing thought has been about you."

Her hand comes out and strokes my beard, the smile still shining on her face.

"I love you," she offers, looking me in the eye.

"I know," I respond, taking my time to watch her happy flushed face on my pillow.

Finally, I lean closer and add, "Because I love you, too."

Leelo

"You ready for this, Sunshine?"

Even sitting on his lap, I have a hard time hearing Roar's voice over the engine noise, so I just give him a thumbs up.

Two days after Gwen left for Toronto, the building permits came through.

Bill had filled us in that the network Brian Dinker had set up with the backing of Northern Lights, and the help of Kline, Kline & McTavish, was impressive and had reached as deep as the municipal building and planning department. The law firm closed its doors the week after I found Henry Kline's dead body, and soon thereafter, Ian McTavish was arrested as well.

Heads rolled at the building and planning department and the moment that happened, all the permits for the Whitefish Motel upgrades and additions were miraculously approved within twenty-four hours.

Bill also mentioned that Wawa was not the only town along the Trans-Canada Highway impacted by the criminal dealings of Northern Lights Development. Other places had been subject to coercion, intimidation, and blackmail to get Edwyn Laramy—owner of Northern Lights and son of software mogul, Walden Laramy—first dibs on the real estate market.

We were just the only town where it had led to murder.

It had taken us a few days to order supplies, set up a schedule, and rent some equipment, but today we *break ground,* as I'm told is the appropriate term.

First thing on the agenda this morning is to tear down that blasted laundry shed.

"Hand on the gear, baby," Roar yells in my ear, covering my hand on the knob with his and shifting the gear forward. The large bucket, centered on the front of the bulldozer, jerks and bounces a little when the tracks start rolling, making this less than a smooth ride. It doesn't diminish the huge grin on my face.

I wave at Matt, who is sitting on the roof of the motel, filming it all on his phone.

"Hands on the wheel," Roar barks in my ear.

"Sorry!" I do as he asks, but I still feel like a kid on a carnival ride. "Can we go faster?"

I can't see or hear him, but I can feel his laughter shaking his body behind me.

"Not a race, Leelo."

The first crunch, when the teeth of the bucket hit the facade of the shed, is a sound I'll never forget. A symbolic demolition and levelling of the old to make room for a new and better me.

I don't even notice I'm crying until Roar shuts down the engine, when there's nothing but rubble left, and turns me on his lap.

"What's wrong?" he asks, concerned right away.

"Nothing's wrong. Not a single thing." I smile through my tears and throw my arms around his neck, while the small crowd that showed up—Charlotte, Bill, Patti, and even Travis—starts to clap.

-

"Are you going to read them?"

Roar is lying next to me in bed on his side. Elbow in the mattress, head propped up on his hand, watching me.

We've had a good day. No—a great day.

Charlotte brought a cake from a bakery in town to celebrate. Once Roar helped me down off the bulldozer, she hustled us all inside, where we stood around the old kitchen counter, eating cake from paper plates with our hands, because according to Charlotte, Bill had forgotten the forks. A fact he strongly denied. He did bring the napkins, however, which helped.

What also helped was the bottle of champagne that magically appeared from Matt's backpack, along with a stack of plastic cups.

It was the absolute best start to the day.

The next seven hours flew by, as the guys used the bulldozer to dig and level the beginnings of the foundation for the three cabins along the water's edge. I volunteered to haul every scrap of roofing, wood, and brick from the rubble pile we left, into the wheelbarrow and up the makeshift ramp to dump in the big container in the parking lot.

It was cathartic. By the end of the day, my muscles were sore and heavy but my heart felt light and free.

We barely managed to wolf down a few sandwiches for dinner before we got ready for bed.

That's where I am now, sitting cross-legged in the middle of the bed, playing with the lid of the glass jar for the past five minutes. Clearly, I'm driving Roar nuts.

"What if I'm reading them in the wrong order?" I'm not sure why I'm delaying this. Is it because I'm afraid I'll jinx the good thing we have going? Or maybe that something he wrote will hurt my feelings?

"It doesn't matter," he says, taking the jar from my hands. "But I'll put them in order for you if that makes you feel better."

"How could you possibly remember?" I question him, looking at the large number of scraps in the jar.

"I'll remember when I read them."

"Hand me the jar," I say, taking it back, and immediately unscrewing the lid and turning it upside down in the middle of the bed.

I only hesitate for a moment when I pick up the first paper, and read it out loud; *"Peaches & cream; every rich and succulent inch."*

"Easy," Roar says. "That was the first time I saw you naked. Well, your naked reflection in the mirror of your

415

bathroom. You had the door open a crack and had only covered your front."

"*In the blue of endless skies in her eyes, I see a raging storm.*"

"That's the day I hauled your ass off the roof. The first time I looked in those pretty eyes. You were pissed as hell that day."

I chuckle at the memory, before grabbing one more.

"*A careful touch has the power to wipe the battle from her eyes.*"

"A yes," he says, with a smile. "The first time we made love. You were so jumpy and I was nervous as fuck I'd make the wrong move."

"How is it possible that feels like years ago, when it really was only a few months?" I want to know.

"Dog years," he deadpans, earning him a slug on the arm with my fist. "Ouch. Keep going."

For the next two hours, I read out every scrap of paper, and he tells me the context for his beautiful words. By then, I'm in tears, which shouldn't be a surprise, I'm like a leaky faucet these days.

"You're a poet. I love them." I gently brush my hands over the pieces of paper littered around me. "Each one of them."

"I'm glad," Roar growls, shifting on the bed so he can drop his head in my lap and circle my waist with an arm. "Because I don't think I could stop writing them if I tried."

He lifts his closed hand in front of me, before turning it palm up and slowly opening his fingers, exposing one more piece of crumpled paper.

"Today's thought."

I pick up the scrap and carefully unfold it, silently reading what it says.

She's my fantasy, my fortune, my fate, and my future.

EPILOGUE

A wonderful life.

Leelo

"Mom! Toss me your hammer, mine slid off the roof."

I look over at Matt who is on his knees, nailing down flashing around the new chimney. Instead of tossing—since that would surely end in two hammers down below—I carefully make my way over to him, my hand on the head of the hammer, tucked in my awesome tool belt.

I've been cleaning crap from the eavesthroughs and the top of the downspouts, since yesterday's unexpected rain caused fucking Niagara Falls to run down the front of the restaurant.

Roar stopped me when I climbed out the bathroom window after my son, demanding I wear a harness. He's never liked me going up on the roof. Not since that first time he pulled me off last year. To be honest, I don't like it much myself, still don't like heights, but that's why I keep going up there. If this past year has taught me anything, it's that you have to keep challenging yourself. Keep pushing the boundaries of your comfort zone, every now and then, or you lose your flexibility.

It's amazing how beautiful things are when you occasionally risk a change of view.

Of course, I put on the damn harness and let myself be latched to my son, because despite the fact he'd rather ban me from the roof altogether, Roar pushes his own boundaries by letting me go up there. The harness is a small concession on my part, and besides, although I'd never admit this to Roar, it makes me feel a little more secure up there as well.

I can't believe how fast everything is coming together. We were lucky the winter wasn't too bad, and for the most part, we were able to continue with the work, focusing on the inside. That's how the beautiful fireplace was built, in place of where the old bar used to be.

That was Matt's idea, actually. He noticed early on, when the snow started falling, that there were several snowmobile trails running along the highway. Thought I could lure them in with a hot soup and a warm fire so I'd still have some income over the winter months.

Bright kid, my boy.

"Check it out, Mom," Matt says when I crouch down beside him.

I follow the direction his hand is pointing to a spot at the water's edge, well south of the dock, where the tree line runs much closer to the shore. A moose cow is drinking from the lake, her front legs slightly spread in the shallow water. Through her tall legs, I can just make out the much smaller shape of her calf.

"This is why I'll never regret moving up here," he says softly.

My boy has taken to the life up here like a fish to water. He works hard, he plays hard, and from the impressive collection of girls I saw coming in and out of his cottage over the winter, he parties hard too. I'd wanted to talk to him about that, but Roar shut me down. "He'll find his way, just like I did and you did." That shut me up in a hurry.

"Me neither, Bud. Me neither," I whisper back.

"Have you heard from Grandma?"

I wedge the phone between my shoulder and my ear as I try to finish cutting the bacon for the quiches.

"Last time I talked to her was at Christmas. She called to make sure the self-help book to firmer thighs she'd ordered me had arrived. Why?"

"Because she says she, and whatever husband she's on now, are moving to Toronto and she wants me to go apartment hunting with her." The sheer horror in Gwen's voice makes me chuckle.

"Better you than me, baby," I tease her.

"Mo-om! She's your mother."

"Oh believe me, I'm well aware, but I take no responsibility for her."

"That's not fair," Gwen whines.

"Really? Because not so long ago, I believe it might have been Christmas as well, didn't I hear you say to that cute young man you were with, that you refused to be held accountable for the behaviour of *your* mother?" I remind her, grinning.

"That was different. You were doing an impersonation of Tom Cruise in *Risky Business* while we were trying to eat breakfast!"

"It was a great impersonation, though," I defend myself, smiling at the memory. "I totally rocked Roar's flannel shirt, and before you say anything, it *so* covered all my bits."

"*Mom,*" she groans. "This is a crisis in the making. I'm thinking this may be a good time to look at that job opportunity I found in Sault Ste. Marie."

I walk over to the sink and wash my hands, when suddenly Roar's arms sneak around me from behind. I must've yelped out loud.

"Are you even listening, Mom?"

"Yes, Sweetie, I am. That was just Roar, uh, startling me," I say, frantically slapping at his large, groping hands that have worked their way under my shirt. "I heard. Grandma moving to Toronto, you're packing for the Soo. All I can say is; don't let Grandma chase you off, honey. If you want to stay in Toronto, it's not like it's not big enough for the two of you. Hey!" I blurt out when Roar snatches the phone away from my ear.

"Hey, Gwenny."

I still melt when I hear his deep rumble use that name on her. Since that little tête-à-tête those two had last year on the dock, there's been something special between them.

"Never met the woman, but from what I hear it's best to steer clear, so what do I hear about the Soo?"

I turn, lean my butt against the sink, fold my arms over my chest, and watch and listen as my man almost effortlessly calms my daughter down.

Ten minutes later he hangs up, and Gwen is undoubtedly calling Sault Ste. Marie real estate agents as we speak.

Roar

"Peter! Good to see you."

I smile at the older man coming toward me with a somewhat reluctant teenager in tow.

"Nice place, Doyle. Nice place." He looks over his shoulder at one of the new cabins.

"Thanks." I give his offered hand a firm shake. "You actually started this idea. Last year, when you stayed here? It got me thinking it wouldn't be a bad idea to expand a little. Give people an alternate option. A slight change of view, if you will."

"Well, I'm glad we get to christen the place," Peter says, his shoulders slumping a bit. "This might well be the last time we make the drive up here. The grandkids have other things to do with their summers and Margaret—" He pauses, looking over his shoulder at the cabin again. "She's not been well."

"Sorry to hear that," I tell him, clapping him lightly on the shoulder.

"You get to be our age, things start rattling right, left, and center," he chuckles. "All in the natural order. But I'm glad to see you and the colourful Ms. Talbot have joined forces in every way that counts."

I grin at the old man's chuckle.

"That we have."

-

The brief conversation follows me around all day, as we celebrate the official opening of the new and improved Whitefish Inn. The slight change in name was better suited to the new concept.

Leelo actually cried when Matt revealed the beautiful new signs he made for her. Not that crying is necessarily new, but these were pure and unadulterated happy tears, which got even me a little choked up.

The symbolism of this day does not escape me. There's a lot in our everyday mundane life that has a poignancy I didn't recognize before Leelo.

More depth, more nuance, a fuller experience.

Joie de vivre.

Something my Leelo definitely taught me.

"Can I ask you something?"

I flip a log on end and sit down next to Charlie, who is enjoying the bonfire at the water's edge. She looks up at me with a smile in her eyes.

"Of course you can, my boy."

"Do you regret that I never gave you grandchildren?"

Charlie twists in her seat and squints her eyes. "Where does that come from all of a sudden?"

I shrug. Hard to say when I started taking stock of my life. My guess is somewhere around the time I was lying in a gully, with a burning tree on my chest, wondering if I was taking my last breath. But my talk with Peter earlier brought it to the forefront.

"I just never really thought about the fact I'm going to leave this life one day with no legacy. Ouch!" Her hands may be arthritic now, but my mother's sharp smack on the back of my head holds as much bite now as it did when I was on the receiving end of a hell of a lot more of them.

"Didn't raise you for a fool, Riordan Doyle. You've been nothing but a blessing in my life and the life of others, and over the last year you've given me even more." Charlie's eyes seem to search for Leelo, who looks to be having a deep discussion of her own with Mrs. Zhao on the other side of the fire. "A wonderful woman I couldn't love more if she were my own daughter, and two fine young people I already consider my grandchildren. Don't for a minute think that just because you came into their lives a little later, you don't have a powerful impact," she says, grabbing my hand and pulling me closer. "I see the way Matt has found his confidence because of the trust you showed him. In the way Gwen knows what she deserves because she sees firsthand from you how a real man should love and respect a woman as his equal." Charlie cups my face in her hands, like she used to when I was a kid and she needed my focus. "My boy, look around, you're living your legacy."

-

"The North Star," Leelo says, pointing up at the sky.

Quiet has returned with the departure of the last of our guests, half an hour ago, but we weren't ready to call it a night yet. When Leelo suggested doing some stargazing from the water's edge, I willingly followed her out there.

The surface of the lake is smooth, the only ripples caused by our movement on the dock.

I lie down on my back and pull Leelo down with me, her head resting on my shoulder.

"It's a wonderful life," I mumble.

"I love Jimmy Stewart," she says and I turn my head to grin at her.

"I love you," I fire back and soak up the smile I get in response.

"You weren't talking about the movie, were you?"

I shake my head.

Leelo snuggles back into my side, her hand resting loosely on my stomach as we ride the gentle bobbing of the dock.

"Roar?"

"Mmmm."

"It *is* a wonderful life. The absolute best."

THE END

ACKNOWLEDGEMENTS

I am blessed with a contingent of awesome and loyal people who help me bring a book to the point of publication.

These are names you will find in most every single book I've released thus far, simply because they share a common love of the written word, and they are as loyal to me as I am to them.

Thank you to my editor Karen Hrdlicka, my Alpha reader Natalie Weston, my proofreader Joanne Thompson and my fantastic Betas: Deb, Debbie, Catherine, Nancy, Lena, Chris, Sam and Pam. These fabulous women are always ready at the drop of a hat to scrutinize my words and share their opinions. I adore each and every one of them.

Thank you to some very wonderful author friends I've been fortunate enough to make in this industry. Without their encouragement and support I'd be nowhere.

I have to thank Dana Hook, who is always and will ever be, my highlight. She is imperative to my mental health and looks after me like no other can.

I'm frankly not sure what I did before Natalie Weston became my PA. She keeps me organized and on track, which is something that is very hard to do! She is also one of my staunchest supporters.

To Ena Burnette and her team at Enticing Journey, as well as the countless amazing bloggers, thank you for sharing my books with the world. I am forever indebted to you.

My readers. I continue to be humbled by your love for my characters and your passion for my stories. You have no idea how important your encouragement is to my ability to write!

ABOUT THE AUTHOR

Freya Barker inspires with her stories about 'real' people, perhaps less than perfect, each struggling to find their own slice of happy. She is the author of the Cedar Tree Series and the Portland, ME, novels.

Freya currently has two complete series published, and is working on two new series; the Snapshot series, and Northern Lights. She continues to spin story after story with an endless supply of bruised and dented characters, vying for attention!

Stay in touch!

https://www.freyabarker.com
https://www.goodreads.com/FreyaBarker
https://www.facebook.com/FreyaBarkerWrites
https://twitter.com/freya_barker

or sign up for my newsletter:
http://bit.ly/2w7f1on

ALSO BY FREYA BARKER

NORTHERN LIGHTS Collection

A CHANGE IN TIDE

CEDAR TREE Series

Book #1
SLIM TO NONE

Book #2
HUNDRED TO ONE

Book #3
AGAINST ME

Book #4
CLEAN LINES

Book #5
UPPER HAND

Book #6
LIKE ARROWS

Book #7
HEAD START

PORTLAND, ME, Novels

Book #1
FROM DUST

Book #2
CRUEL WATER

Book #3
THROUGH FIRE

Book #4
STILL WATER

SNAPSHOT Novels

Book #1
SHUTTER SPEED

Book #2
FREEZE FRAME

Printed in Great Britain
by Amazon